"You're bleeding. Come with me."

She glanced down, saw a trail of blood down her right leg. "I'll be fine."

"*Ja*, you will," he said, "after I put a bandage on it."

"I don't need your help."

His eyes narrowed and he looked annoyed. He heaved a sigh. "Would you like me to pick you up and throw you over my shoulder?" he murmured for her ears alone.

"You wouldn't dare!"

"Wouldn't I?"

Face flushing, Charlie glanced around and saw that no one found it odd that she and Nate were having a conversation. The last thing she wanted to do was to cause a scene. She'd done enough impulsive things in her life that had given her parents undue worry. "Fine. Let's not make a big thing of it," she muttered, meeting his gaze.

To her relief, he simply nodded. He didn't look smug that he'd won their argument. In fact, she felt an odd little flutter in her chest when she saw the way he continued to eye her with concern.

Rebecca Kertz was first introduced to the Amish when her husband took a job with an Amish construction crew. She enjoyed watching the Amish foreman's children at play and swapping recipes with his wife. Rebecca resides in Delaware with her husband and dog. She has a strong faith in God and feels blessed to have family nearby. Besides writing, she enjoys reading, doing crafts and visiting Lancaster County.

Carrie Lighte lives in Massachusetts next door to a Mennonite farming family, and she frequently spots deer, foxes, fisher cats, coyotes and turkeys in her backyard. Having enjoyed traveling to several Amish communities in the eastern United States, she looks forward to visiting settlements in the western states and in Canada. When she's not reading, writing or researching, Carrie likes to hike, kayak, bake and play word games.

REBECCA KERTZ

Her Amish Christmas Gift

&

CARRIE LIGHTE

Her Amish Holiday Suitor

LOVE INSPIRED

INSPIRATIONAL ROMANCE

LOVE INSPIRED®
INSPIRATIONAL ROMANCE

Recycling programs
for this product may
not exist in your area.

ISBN-13: 978-1-335-22989-2

Her Amish Christmas Gift and Her Amish Holiday Suitor

Copyright © 2020 by Harlequin Books S.A.

Her Amish Christmas Gift
First published in 2018. This edition published in 2020.
Copyright © 2018 by Rebecca Kertz

Her Amish Holiday Suitor
First published in 2019. This edition published in 2020.
Copyright © 2019 by Carrie Lighte

This edition published by arrangement with Harlequin Books S.A.

For questions and comments about the quality of this book,
please contact us at CustomerService@Harlequin.com.

Harlequin Enterprises ULC
22 Adelaide St. West, 40th Floor
Toronto, Ontario M5H 4E3, Canada
www.Harlequin.com

Printed in U.S.A.

CONTENTS

HER AMISH CHRISTMAS GIFT

Rebecca Kertz

For my family…those I've known forever
and those I've been happy to meet recently.

And for my ancestors—
without you, I wouldn't be here.

If ye abide in me, and my words abide in you,
ye shall ask what ye will,
and it shall be done unto you.
—*John* 15:7

Chapter One

Charlotte Stoltzfus stood near home plate in the makeshift baseball diamond on Abram Peachy's back lawn with the bat inches away from her right shoulder.

"Come on, Charlie!" Joseph shouted. "You can do this, cousin. Keep your eye on the ball and bring Jed and me home."

Meeting his eyes across the distance, she gave a jerk of her head. She wiggled into her stance. And focused. She breathed deeply as she stared at the pitcher, her cousin Noah, and watched him swing back his arm to let the ball fly.

"Aren't you tired of playing with boys?" a male voice said behind her just as she swung her bat.

She growled as she missed. Heart beating wildly, she turned to glare at the man who'd spoken. "Nathaniel Peachy, mind your own business and stop trying to distract me." She was furious. Determined to ignore the one man who got her back up more than anyone on this earth, Charlie breathed to calm herself and got ready for the next pitch.

"Why would I distract you?" Nate said as she swung

the bat. She swung and missed again, then she gasped and glared at him.

"Go away," she snapped.

The way he arched an eyebrow made her bristle. She stiffened and became more determined not to let him rattle her. She'd hit the ball despite his presence.

"It's *oll recht*," Jedidiah called out to her. Her eldest cousin, he stood on third base and gazed at her with a smile of reassurance. "Keep your eye on the ball. You can do this."

I can do this. She was a decent player. Isn't that why they first asked her to join the game? *Ignore Nate Peachy. Ignore him. Ignore him.*

Noah watched for her cue. Charlie gave a little nod, and her cousin pitched the ball. She kept it in her sights and swung. The impact made a loud *crack* as wood met leather and sent it sailing over the head of her cousin Daniel near third base, past the stand of trees beyond the property. With a whoop of joy, Joseph ran from second to third as Jedidiah sprinted home. Charlie ran to first base and made it to second then to third, as Nate's younger brother Jacob came out of the bushes with ball in hand. She took a chance, followed Joseph and raced toward home. As the ball headed in her direction, she slid into home plate and grimaced as she felt the sting of a scraped knee.

"Are you *oll recht*?" a deep voice said. She glanced up and saw concern flicker in Nate Peachy's blue eyes. She started to get up and the man was there helping her. "Charlie," he murmured into her ear. "Are you hurt?"

She shook her head, not wanting him to know how

much her knee stung and her hip ached from the jolt against the ground.

"Great job, Charlie!" Jed hollered. She grinned at her teammates, who carried on as if she'd won the lottery. Then she looked over at Nate smugly.

"Yahoo!" Joseph yelled. "We won! You never let us down, cousin!"

She forced herself to grin at them with triumph.

Jacob Peachy grumbled good-naturedly as he threw the ball to Noah, who then grabbed the bat and markers they'd used for bases. Jacob met her gaze. "How did you learn to hit a ball like that?"

She shrugged. "From playing with my cousins." She'd been playing baseball with them for over a year. She could still recall the day Joseph had asked her to play and the thrill of her teammates' pleasure when she scored a run.

Jacob shook his head as he smiled. "I should have picked you for my team."

"Now you'll know better for next time." She paused. "If you get the chance," she added. He laughed, then headed to join his friends.

"Charlie." Nate came up from behind her and stood close, too close. "You're bleeding. Come with me."

She glanced down, saw a trail of blood down her right leg. "I'll be fine."

"Ja, you will," he said, "after I put a bandage on it."

"I don't need your help."

His eyes narrowed and he looked annoyed. He heaved a sigh. "Would you like me to pick you up and throw you over my shoulder?" he murmured for her ears alone.

"You wouldn't dare!"

"Wouldn't I?"

Face flushing, Charlie glanced around and saw that no one found it odd that she and Nate were having a conversation. The last thing she wanted to do was to cause a scene. She'd done enough impulsive things in her life that had given her parents undue worry. "Fine. Let's not make a big thing of it," she muttered, meeting his gaze.

To her relief, he simply nodded. He didn't look smug that he'd won their argument. In fact, she felt an odd little flutter in her chest when she saw the way he continued to eye her with concern. She followed him at a distance, not wanting to draw attention to the fact that he was leading her into the house. She glanced around and saw the rest of his family outside. She could catch the deacon's wife's attention, have her give her first aid, but she had a feeling that Nate would cause trouble for her if she did. Besides, what was one little bandage, right?

Nate went to the side door and held it open for her. Charlie drew a sharp breath. The man was good-looking; she'd give him that. But those gorgeous blue eyes in a face with fine features under a crop of dark hair weren't what made the man, and she wasn't sure she liked Nate in any way, shape or form. But she'd seen his compassion and tenderness when dealing with his younger sisters. She'd seen it whenever someone needed his help and he'd been right there to assist. And now, to her shock, he was concerned for her.

He wants to help me. Why should I allow it to bother me? Because she suspected that he disapproved of her, and she feared getting a lecture about acting like a proper young Amish woman.

She met his gaze as she climbed the steps. The way he stared at her gave her goose bumps.

"Afraid?" he asked softly.

"Of what?"

His expression filled with satisfaction. "Exactly. There is nothing to fear."

It was a clear autumn day with pleasant temperatures and sunshine. The house was silent, especially for Visiting Sunday. The warmer weather would soon be gone. Everyone preferred to enjoy these last days outdoors. As she glanced around the Peachy kitchen, Charlie raised a hand to tuck fine strands of hair under her prayer *kapp*. She became aware of Nate as never before.

He gestured toward a chair. "Sit," he ordered.

Annoyed, she lifted her chin.

"Please," he added softly.

She sat, willing to listen after he'd asked nicely.

He opened a kitchen cabinet and pulled out a tube of ointment and a box of bandages. He set them on the table close to her before he reached into a drawer for a clean tea towel. He ran the sink, wet the cloth and returned to her. "Where exactly did you hurt yourself?"

She reached for the wet towel. "I can clean it." But he ignored her and hunkered down to wipe up the trail of blood. She blushed. She was barefoot and her feet were dirty, as were her legs from playing ball and sliding across the yard into home plate.

Nate was gentle as he washed her leg. He wiped up what he could see then looked up at her. "Here," he said, his voice husky. "You can clean the rest."

Charlie nodded and waited until he turned away to raise her dress just enough to reveal her scraped, bleeding knee. As the cloth touched the wound, she hissed out with pain. Nate spun and locked gazes with her. He glanced down then scowled at her. "Charlie Stoltzfus, look what you've done to yourself."

She stiffened and looked away, unwilling to see the condemnation in his eyes. "I had a home run."

"*Ja*, you did," he said with a chuckle that had her shooting him a startled gaze. "*Gut* job, by the way."

She gaped at him. He wasn't scolding her; he was praising her. Stunned, she could only stare at him.

"You've dripped bloody water on the floor," he said gently. He reached and took the cloth from her then washed it under the faucet. "Are you hurt anywhere else?" he asked casually. She averted her glance, glad that he couldn't see the rising heat in her cheeks.

"I'm fine," she said too quickly.

He looked at her then, arched an eyebrow as he returned to her side with the washed cloth. "Charlie."

Her gaze pleaded with him. "I'm fine."

He observed her a long moment, his expression softening. "As long as you're sure."

She bobbed her head.

He towered over her, a tall man older by at least seven years. "Will you let me take care of your knee?" He regarded her kindly.

She drew a calming breath. *"Ja."*

"*Gut* girl."

She glared at him. "*Please*. I'm not a child."

He knelt and gently cleansed her knee and the lower half of her leg. He dried it with another clean cloth that she hadn't noticed he'd held. "What are you? All of sixteen?"

"I'll be nineteen in two weeks."

He seemed taken aback at her answer. She wasn't sure but she thought he'd murmured, "I had no idea." But he didn't look at her when he spoke. He was busy applying first-aid ointment before he covered her scrape with a bandage. "There you go," he said without expression. He reached for her arm and helped her to her feet.

"Danki," she murmured and quickly turned to leave, her arm tingling where he'd touched her. He didn't stop her from going. Charlie hurried outside to join her family for lunch. She didn't look back to see if Nate had left the house. She went right to the food table, grabbed a plate and helped herself. Spying her family at a table under a shade tree, she made her way over and sat down with a smile. If anyone wondered why it took so long for her to join them, they didn't mention it.

"*Gut* game, Charlie," Henry Yoder said as he set a plate in front of his wife then slid onto the bench next to her.

Charlie didn't say anything at first as she stared down at her plate. She should have been there to help the women. She'd been so focused on the game that she'd lost track of time. Now she felt guilty for not doing her share. She'd have to make sure she did most of the cleanup afterward.

"Charlie?"

She blinked and realized that her brother-in-law had spoken and she hadn't answered. "I'm sorry." She saw him eyeing her with concern. She managed a grin. "It was a *gut* game. Noah and Daniel aren't happy with me right now."

"*Ja*, but Joseph and I are."

She gave him a genuine smile. She really liked her sister Leah's husband. They'd been married a year, and her respect and liking of him had only grown. The fact that he made her sister ridiculously happy only heightened her feelings for him.

"You didn't hurt yourself when you fell, did you?"

She shook her head. "*Nay*, I'm fine. A little skinned knee is nothing when we got the win."

"Did you take care of it? Your knee?" her sister Leah asked with concern.

"All cleaned and bandaged." Fortunately, her family didn't question that she'd taken care of her injury. She looked down at her plate as she felt her face heat. She'd spent enough time in the Peachy house watching their youngest children that she knew where everything was kept.

She grew silent as Nate's tender first-aid ministration played on her mind. She caught sight of the man deep in conversation with his brother across the yard and felt a kick to her belly as his gaze brushed over her casually before he looked away.

"Do you think it's wrong of me to like playing baseball?" she asked no one in particular as she paused in her eating.

Her brother-in-law frowned. "*Nay*. Why?"

She shook her head. "It doesn't matter." Nathaniel Peachy didn't matter, she thought, but knew she was lying to herself to believe it.

Henry studied her a long moment, his expression softening. "You had fun, didn't you?"

She nodded.

"*Gut*, because we did, too, and we like having you on our team."

Charlie smiled. She started to eat, then froze when Nate slipped onto the far end of the bench at the next table. Why couldn't she get him out of her mind? The man was years older than she was, and she was more than a little fascinated by him. Which wasn't wise, she scolded herself. Not wise at all.

Nate studied Charlie and felt his stomach tighten. Charlie Stoltzfus had shown time and again to be a good ballplayer. Her focus couldn't be questioned. Every Sunday, whenever there was a game, the young men within their Amish community fought good-naturedly over which team would get Charlie.

He scowled. Good ballplayer or not, Charlie was too wild, too impulsive.

A lot like Emma.

A shaft of pain hit him hard, making his chest hurt with the memory of the girl he'd loved and lost. Emma had been wild and reckless, always searching for excitement. In the end, her wild behavior had led to her death.

Charlie Stoltzfus needed someone young but stable to keep her in check. Someone who could keep her safe and alive. Someone like… Nate glanced about the yard, searching for a prospective suitor for her, but he didn't find anyone suitable.

"Nate, aren't you going to eat?" his younger sister asked. Ruth Ann sat across the table from him.

He nodded as he flashed her a smile. "What are you having?"

"Roast beef and sides. And there are sandwiches if I'm still hungry."

"You love sandwiches." He recalled making them

for her when she was much younger after his mother had died. He experienced a moment's sadness for a young life cut short too soon until he thought of his stepmother. *Mam* was as different from Charlie Stoltzfus as night and day. She had made his father—his whole family—happy. She was pregnant again, due sometime in early January.

At his age, Nate never thought he'd have a baby brother or sister. In fact, he'd hoped that he'd be married with children of his own by now. But he hadn't found the right woman yet. Someone kind and loving who wanted the same things from life as he did. There was farm property down the road from his parents he'd been hankering after. Once he acquired the land, he'd be ready to find someone to marry. Someone older and mature. Someone unlike Charlie Stoltzfus.

Nate started to eat. He stilled with fork in hand as he glanced toward the table where Henry sat with his wife, Leah, and Charlie. Her sister Nell and her husband, James, were seated across from them.

"Aren't you hungry?" Ruth asked.

Desperate to ignore Charlie Stoltzfus, he nodded at his sister then ate the food off his fork. Unfortunately, he and Charlie faced each other, and he found himself unable to keep his eyes off her. She had beautiful features with a pert little nose and pretty pink lips. Her red-gold hair glistened brightly under the sun. Her eyes were a deep shade of vivid green. Her spring-green dress only heightened her coloring, highlighting her beauty.

He looked away. She was trouble, and he had to stop thinking about her.

"Charlie played a *gut* game today," his brother Jacob commented.

"She's got a lot of energy, that girl," his sister Mary Elizabeth said.

"She didn't help you with the food," Nate murmured and immediately regretted his comment.

Mam raised her eyebrows. "We had more than enough help. Take a look. Do you see a lack of women here? Charlie enjoys the game, but she would have come if we'd asked." Her speculative look made Nate squirm.

"I've never seen anyone hit the ball like she does," he said softly, sincerely, brushing the awkward moment aside. "She brought everyone on base home then slid into home plate, giving the team the win."

"*Ja*, I wish I could play like that," Ruth Ann said.

He blinked, but he didn't say a word. He waited for his father to comment, but the man only chuckled.

"You're much better off spending your time gardening," *Dat* said.

Nate breathed a sigh of relief. "*Ja*, gardening is a fine way to spend your time. Did you pick the last of the vegetables?"

"Plan to do it tomorrow," his sister said. "If there are any left. I haven't checked recently."

Ruth loved to garden so bringing up the subject was brilliant. He had to give his father credit. The man knew how to deal with his children in a way that was natural and loving without being overbearing.

Nate hoped that someday he could be the kind of father his *dat* was. And a leader like him. Some folks within his community thought that one day Nate would be asked to serve as deacon, preacher, or even bishop.

Nate closed his eyes. He hoped not. Being asked to serve as deacon would mean that his father had passed, for the position was lifelong. He didn't want to think of the day *Dat* was no longer with them. And he couldn't see himself as preacher or bishop. He could never live up to the title. Nate didn't feel good enough to be a church elder.

But he enjoyed farming. His father's farm wouldn't be his to inherit. The farm would go to his youngest brother, not the oldest son, as was the Amish way. Not that Nate minded. He would work for what he wanted. He had nearly enough money to bid on that other farm.

Charlie stood, immediately catching his attention.

He watched as she returned to the food table with her sisters Leah and Nell. They were chatting. Charlie laughed at something Nell said, and the change in her features was so startling that Nate was unable to look away. She was even more beautiful when she was happy. She'd always been a pretty little thing, but the way laughter changed her face stole his breath.

She was oblivious to his regard as she filled her dessert plate. He heard Leah chuckle and watched Charlie as she talked animatedly while gesturing with one hand, her movements nearly unseating the chocolate cake on her plate. The women kept up a steady conversation as they headed back to their table. Charlie giggled at something Leah said, but her good humor died quickly when she encountered his glance. Nell spoke and Charlie looked away, her smile restored. Awareness surged inside him. He recalled how he'd felt when he saw the blood on her leg. Anxiety. Anger. The strongest urge to protect her. He scowled. *I can't do this again.*

His chest tightened but he managed to eat his lunch before heading to the dessert table with Ruth Ann. He didn't know why, but he was ready for the day to end.

"*Soohns*, we'll be leaving for Indiana first thing in the morning," his father said as Nate returned to the table. "I'd hoped the two of you would stay home and take care of things here."

Nate nodded. He'd known about his father's plans to take the family to see his grandparents. "We'll take care of the animals and make hay."

Jacob smiled. "Won't take us long."

"We'll take turns cooking," he warned his brother.

His brother shrugged. "I can survive on sandwiches."

He laughed. "I think you'll get sick of sandwiches, but we'll see."

After he finished eating, Nate rose to throw away his paper plate. He turned and caught a glimpse of Charlie standing at her cousin's paddock, watching the horses at play. Her glorious red hair was like a beacon that called to him. Why couldn't he stop thinking about her?

He headed in her direction.

Charlie gazed at the horses and felt a rush of pleasure. What she wouldn't give to race like the wind on the back of a horse! She smiled. The chestnut mare pranced and chased her companions into a playful gallop. She'd give anything to feel the freedom of riding through the fields with the warmth of the sun against her skin and her hair unpinned without a head covering. She closed her eyes and enjoyed the cool breeze tempered by the afternoon sunshine.

This week she wouldn't be babysitting for the youngest Peachy children. The family was going out of town, which made her sigh. She loved spending time with them and missed them when she wasn't needed. She loved children. It was her biggest wish to take over the teaching position at the Happiness School when the current schoolteacher left. That would be in a month or so, when current schoolteacher Elizabeth Troyer and her family moved to Ohio.

I'd make a gut *teacher.* She had done well in school, and she knew how to break down problems and find fun ways to make children remember what they'd learned. And she was ready. Her birthday was next month and she'd be nineteen. Her opportunity for teaching would be gone if it didn't happen soon. She planned to approach the church elders this week about her filling the upcoming vacancy.

The sun slipped beneath a cloud, and she felt a sudden chill. She hugged herself with her arms. The sky was only partially cloudy. In a few moments the sun would resurface and warm her again.

"Charlie."

She stiffened, recognizing his voice. She faced him. "Nate." The shock of his appearance made her heart flutter. Ironically, she'd come here alone to seek refuge from the feelings he'd churned up inside her.

He leaned against the fence rail with only a few inches separating them. She became instantly aware of the heat his nearness generated. Something within her urged to flee from him; yet, she didn't move.

She straightened her spine and stared. "What do you want, Nate? What are you doing here?"

"How's your knee?" he asked, his eyes soft with concern.

She swallowed hard. "Fine. Your first aid helped." She bit her lip. *"Danki."*

He nodded with satisfaction. "You like to play ball."

Charlie drew away, putting several more inches between them. *"Ja,* so?"

A tiny smile hovered on his lips. "You play well."

"Then why were you trying to distract me?"

"My *bruder* was on the other team."

She gaped at him for several seconds then laughed. She watched as his mouth curved into a grin before he joined in her laughter.

It felt good to laugh, yet strange to laugh with him. The fact that she liked the feeling made her stop laughing. Suddenly tense, she quieted and leaned against the fence and returned to her study of the horses.

They stood silently for a few moments. "What do you hope for, Charlie?" he asked. "In your life."

She hesitated. "I like children. I'd like to teach."

Clearly surprised, Nate raised his eyebrows. "You want to teach at our Happiness School?"

"Ja," she whispered. "I know there are some members within our community who won't think I'm good enough—"

"I believe you'd be an excellent teacher."

"You do?"

"Ja, I do." His gaze seemed intense as he studied her.

"What is it?" she asked.

"You surprise me." He paused, looking thoughtful. "I can help you."

"Help me what?"

"Become a teacher. My father is deacon. I could speak with him."

"Nay!" she gasped. "You mustn't."

"Why not?"

"I don't want or deserve the job if I can't earn it on my own."

He shook his head as he watched her, as if he'd learned something new about her that stunned him.

"Charlie!"

She glanced back to see Ellie waving at her. "Time to head home. I've got to go," she told Nate. "I—ah—*danki* again for helping me today."

"You're *willkomm*."

"I'll see you next Sunday," she said.

Nate nodded without saying a word, and Charlie turned and hurried toward their buggy, where her family had gathered to leave.

Her heart hammered within her chest. Nate Peachy was a complex man, and she didn't understand him. With one breath, he'd told her she'd be a good teacher, but then in the next, he'd proven that he didn't believe it unless he stepped in to help. She sighed with sadness. If Nate felt this way, then there was every chance that no one would consider her seriously for the soon-to-be vacated teaching position. *Maybe I'm being foolish to try.*

When she was younger, her tendency to be impulsive frequently got her into trouble, but she was older and wiser now and she'd learned from her mistakes. She'd meant what she'd told Nate. If she couldn't get the job on her own, then she didn't want—or deserve—it.

Chapter Two

As his family left for Indiana, Nate watched the hired car that carried them until the vehicle disappeared from sight. He turned toward the house and saw his brother on the front porch, gazing after the car as if he, too, was affected by their departure.

Nate strode toward the house and climbed the porch steps. "Ready to make hay?"

"How about some breakfast first?" Jacob suggested.

"Didn't you eat earlier?"

"*Nay*, busy helping our sisters with their luggage."

He smiled with amusement. "You, too? I helped *Mam*, *Dat* and Harley with theirs."

The brothers headed inside for coffee and freshly baked muffins.

"I spoke with John King. His *dat* is lending us his hay mower for as long as we need it," Jacob said as he finished up his coffee a while later.

"It will make the job easier." He eyed his brother with approval. "Do we need to go get it?"

"*Nay*. John said he'd bring it by first thing. He should be here anytime now."

Amos King, John's father, was also his stepmother's *dat*. He was a good man with a kind heart.

Nate washed the breakfast dishes while Jacob put the remaining muffins back in the pantry. The sound of horse hooves drew them outside to discover John King's arrival with the mower.

After John left with his brother Joshua, Nate hitched his father's two black Belgian horses to his *dat*'s equipment for his brother to use. He would mow the front field with Amos's mower while Jacob started work at the back of the property.

It was a busy workday. By late afternoon they'd mowed just over a third of the hayfields. He and Jacob put away the mowers. They ate leftovers for dinner, before heading to the barn to make sure all of the animals were settled in for the night.

There was a definite new chill in the air when Nate arose the next morning. He dressed, made coffee and waited for his brother to rouse and join him. The kitchen filled with the rich scent of the perked brew as Jacob entered, looking sleepy-eyed with tousled hair.

"'Tis colder today. We'd best grab our woolen hats and jackets before we head out."

Jacob nodded as he turned from the stove with a mug of coffee. "Think we'll finish today?"

"We'll be pushing it. Didn't get much more than a third done yesterday."

His brother agreed. "We can do it."

Nate smiled. "We can try." The mowed hay would be left to dry in the fields before they baled it.

"Let's move," Jacob said as he set his mug in the sink.

Charlie drove down the road toward Whittier's Store. It was a chilly November morning, but she didn't mind. She wore her black bonnet and woolen cape with a heavy blanket across her lap. Her mother's list was on the seat beside her with the apple pie *Mam* had baked for Leah and Henry. She would stop first at Yoder's Country Crafts and Supplies, her sister Leah's shop, to deliver the pie before continuing on to grocery-shop.

The sunshine was bright across the surrounding farmland. A farmer cut hay in the fields ahead and she watched him as she steered her horse closer. The man maneuvered his horse-drawn mower down the length of the hayfield before turning to mow the uncut section.

Charlie smiled. She knew how to use a mower. With five daughters and no sons, her father had been glad of her help, once she'd convinced him that she could handle the job. *Dat* had objected the first time, until her repeated requests made him finally relent enough to show her how. She'd been pleased by his smile of approval after she'd mowed in neat, even rows across their field. After that he'd allowed her to relieve him while he'd completed other chores.

It had been a while since she'd mowed hay. Watching the farmer work made her smile and long for another chance on the back of a mower.

She returned her attention to the road. She had gone only a short distance when she heard someone bellow sharply in alarm. Startled, she drew up on the reins to stop her horse. Her heart went cold when she saw that the mower had tipped and the farmer lay on the ground. A second man raced toward the fallen farmer, and with a gasp, she recognized Nate Peachy. She pulled her vehicle off the road and secured her horse before she sprinted across the field to help.

She briefly locked gazes with Nate before she turned

her attention to the man on the ground—his brother Jacob. "Jake, are you hurt?" she rasped, out of breath.

"Charlie." Jacob met her gaze and smiled. "I'm fine." But when he tried to stand, he cried out with pain and fell back.

Nate's brow creased with worry. "Stay still. You are *not* fine."

Charlie hunkered beside the injured man and experienced the impact of Nate's startling blue gaze. She glanced away. "What hurts?" she and Nate asked simultaneously.

"My foot."

"Can you walk?" Nate asked.

"I don't know. I don't think so."

"My buggy is right there," Charlie said, gesturing. "Maybe we can lift him into it…" She bit her lip as Nate rose. He stared down at her thoughtfully until she stood. "I can bring it closer." She returned her attention to the man's brother. "Jake?"

"I can make it with help."

Her gaze met Nate's. "Where do you want me to park it?"

"Leave it," he said sharply. "Your vehicle is fine where it is." He narrowed his eyes. "Go back there and wait. I'll bring Jacob."

Unwilling to argue, Charlie stood by her buggy and waited. Jacob gave her a weak smile as the brothers approached. The young man was obviously in pain, and she worried about him. Nate bore the brunt of Jacob's weight as he half carried him with an arm securely around his brother's waist.

She wondered how to help, but knew instinctively that Nate would mutter something cutting if she tried.

Charlie watched silently as he lifted his brother into the back of the buggy.

"We should get him to the clinic."

Nate flashed her an irritated look. "*I'll* take him after I see to the horses and equipment. Drive around to the front of the *haus*," he ordered. "I'll meet you there."

His tone irritated her. She had to bite her tongue to keep from arguing with him. "I can take care of the horses and equipment for you."

"Nay," he snapped. "Absolutely not."

Charlie reeled back, offended. "I know how to handle farm equipment, Nathaniel Peachy. I've mowed hay for my *vadder.*"

"I don't want you touching *ours*, Charlotte Stoltzfus. If you want to help, then get my *bruder* back to the house. I'll meet you there."

"Fine," she agreed as she abruptly turned away. She didn't bother to look to see what Nate was doing as she climbed into the buggy and checked on Jacob. "How're you doing, Jake?"

"Foot hurts, but I'll live."

She frowned. "What happened?"

"I got distracted." He seemed embarrassed.

She flicked the leathers and the horse moved. "What distracted you?"

"I don't know. One minute I was mowing and the next I felt a sudden jerk on the reins. It threw me off balance."

"Do you see any blood?"

She heard Jacob take in a breath. *"Nay."*

She shot him a glance over her shoulder before she

returned her attention to the road. "Do you feel like you're bleeding?"

"My foot feels odd. I could be, I guess, but I can't tell for sure. I don't think so."

Charlie sighed with relief. "*Gut.* That's *gut.*" She could only hope that he wasn't. She knew what could happen if farm equipment tipped over. Injuries could be as mild as simple bumps and bruises to severe loss of limb or life.

It took ten minutes or more for her to drive to the Abram Peachy house. She pulled her vehicle onto the dirt drive and parked close to the barn just as Nate exited the building. At his approach, Charlie experienced a constriction in her chest.

"Hold on a minute, and I'll move him into our buggy," he told her as he drew near.

"Use mine. There's no need to move him." She hesitated. "You might aggravate his injury."

He sighed. "You're probably right."

It was clear that the last thing Nate wanted was for her to accompany them. "I'll wait for you here," she said quietly.

Something dark briefly crossed across his features. "The house is unlocked. You can warm up inside. Make yourself tea or something." He paused. "You know where everything is kept." And that bothered him, she realized.

Nate stepped back and waited for her to climb down. She watched as he got onto the seat she'd vacated before switching her attention to Jacob in the back. "You still *oll recht* in there, Jake?"

Jacob's face was whiter than it had been earlier, but he nodded.

"Don't worry. The doctor will fix you right up." She gave him a reassuring smile. "I'll see you when you get back."

"I don't know how long this will take," Nate said. "We could be gone awhile. Are you sure you don't want me to move him so you can have your buggy and leave?"

"*Nay*. There is no place I have to be." She stepped back and waited for them to leave.

Nate suddenly glanced down. "You've an apple pie in here." He speared her with his gaze as he lifted it for her to see.

She shrugged then approached to get it. "I was going to take it to Leah, but she doesn't know. I'll bring it in and you both can have a piece when you get back."

Nate handed her the pie through the open window along with her shopping list. "Pie smells *gut*." He gave her a twisted smile. "Did you make it?"

She stiffened. "*Nay, Mam* did." She knew instantly what he thought—that the pie wouldn't be edible if she'd made it. His look of disappointment surprised. "You should get going. Jacob doesn't look well at all."

Charlie watched until the vehicle was out of sight before she returned to the house with the apple pie. She debated whether or not to make tea, as Nate had suggested. But then she thought of the fields yet to be mowed and the forecast for rain for the next few days and she headed toward the barn instead. Without thought, she readied the smaller of the two mowers. It wouldn't take her long to finish the work that Jacob had started.

As she climbed onto the scat and urged the horses

forward, she thought of Nate. He'd be upset with her for doing what he'd considered a man's job. She drew in and released a sharp breath. The benefit of a job well-done was worth risking Nate's anger. Once he realized how efficient she was in cutting hay, he'd be glad to see that she'd mowed a substantial amount of ground.

The task went smoothly. Charlie enjoyed herself as she worked to finish the back section of Abram Peachy's farm. Time flew by and she realized that she'd been out longer than she'd expected. She stabled the horses and left the mower right where she'd found it.

There was no sign of her buggy in the yard as she headed back to the house. Her relief was short-lived as she became concerned about Jacob. The brothers had been gone a long while. Was Jacob that badly hurt?

Charlie put on the teakettle then set the table with the pie in the center. She made a fresh pot of coffee with the hope that the brothers would return soon enough to enjoy a hot cup. When she was done, she stepped outside. As the buggy pulled into the yard and parked near the house, she descended the porch steps.

"How is he?" she asked as Nate climbed out of the vehicle.

"He broke his foot," Nate told her. "There's a nice-size slice in it, too, which the doc stitched up." He reached in to lift Jacob into his arms. "He's been advised to stay off the foot for a while." His brother looked groggy as Nate carried him toward the house.

Charlie raced ahead to open the door. She made a sound of concern at Jacob's pallor.

"The doctor gave him a shot of pain medication," Nate explained as he carried Jacob inside.

"Do you need help?"

"I can manage." He shifted Jacob within his arms and brought him into the kitchen.

When she saw Nate looking for a place to set Jacob down, she rushed to pull out a chair. "Unless you want to take him into the great room."

"I'd like to sit here a bit," Jacob murmured sleepily. "Do I smell coffee? And what about that pie you promised us?"

She fretted as she studied him. "Jake, you don't look good. Wouldn't you rather lie down?"

"*Nay*. I will soon, though." Jacob frowned up at his older brother, who stepped back after setting him down. "I'll be of no help to you for a while, I'm afraid."

"I'll manage," Nate assured him.

Charlie felt her throat tighten as she went to the stove. "Nate, do you want coffee, too?" she asked easily, pretending that she wasn't upset by the morning's events.

"*Ja*, please." Nate took the chair next to his brother, as if he wanted to keep a close eye on him.

She could feel Nate's gaze as she poured two cups of hot coffee then set one before each man. "Apple pie, or do you want a sandwich first?"

Nate's study of her made her self-conscious. "Pie will do."

Her lips curved slightly as she nodded. Charlie cut two large slices of apple pie.

"Aren't you having any? Or do you have to leave?" Nate asked as she pushed a plate in his direction.

"I should go," she said, stung by the question. "But I won't until after I have some pie." He looked amused when she gave him a false smile.

It was quiet as they ate. Glad when Nate didn't

make a smart remark, Charlie glanced from her plate to Jacob, who slumped in his chair. She was about to express her worry to Nate then caught him studying his brother with a frown.

"Time to rest, *bruder*," Nate said gently. "Let's get you into the other room where you'll be more comfortable."

While they were absent, Charlie quickly cleaned up the kitchen. She covered the remainder of the pie with plastic wrap and left it on the counter for them to finish later. She washed the dishes but left the coffeepot on the stove in case Nate wanted another cup.

She felt his presence as Nate reentered the room and sensed him watching while she put away the last dish.

"He settled in?" she asked, turning to face him.

"*Ja*, he's already asleep."

"I'm going to head out. I need to pick up a few things at the store for my *mudder*."

He eyed her with consternation. "We've kept you a long time."

"'Tis fine. *Mam* doesn't expect me home yet. She'll think that I decided to spend the day with Leah."

"You had an unusual day today," he said.

She chuckled. "That's for sure."

He sobered. "It wasn't fair to ask you to stay."

"I didn't mind."

He seemed relieved. He followed her as she headed toward the door. "Charlie? May I ask you one more favor?"

She halted and faced him. "*Ja*, of course." He seemed to have difficulty choosing his words.

"What do you need, Nate?" By the look on his face,

she figured out what he wanted to ask. "Shall I come to stay with Jacob tomorrow while you cut hay?"

Nate released a sharp breath. "You wouldn't mind?"

She paused near the threshold. "Not at all."

Warmth entered his blue eyes. "Are you sure?"

Feigning annoyance, she tapped her foot and crossed her arms. "I'm absolutely sure, Nate."

"Danki." His expression became serious. "But I need you to promise that you won't tell anyone what happened," he said. "You know that our neighbors like to natter." His lips firmed. "Especially Alta Hershberger. If she or anyone finds out, word could get back to my *eldre*, and *Dat* will insist on cutting short their trip." He paused. "He's been waiting a long time to visit my grandparents. I don't want to ruin his plans."

"I understand," she murmured. "If anyone asks why I'm here, I'll tell them I'm cleaning house for you while you work in the fields."

"Doesn't your sister Ellie clean houses?"

"Ja, but I've spent enough time in your house helping your *mam* that it makes sense that I be the one to do it."

His expression was unreadable. "Appreciate it."

"I'd do the same for any neighbor," she assured him.

He accompanied her outside. "Drive safely, Charlie," he said sternly.

Annoyed, she nodded before she climbed into her buggy and drove away. She didn't mind coming back the next day. Nate would be busy and she wouldn't have to see or talk with him for long. She would be there for Jacob, the easygoing, much younger and friendlier Peachy brother.

Still, as she drove toward Whittier's Store to buy the

items on her mother's list, she couldn't help but think about Nate and wonder why she felt so drawn to the man. At times he treated her like a child, and she hated it. But then there were those other occasions when he studied her differently, as if he saw her as a woman, an attractive woman he found fascinating.

Charlie sighed as she stored the bought groceries onto the seat next to her. She was imagining things. Nate didn't find her attractive or pretty or anything good.

She would get through tomorrow then concentrate on getting hired on as the new teacher for their Happiness School. Better to focus on that than on her disturbing fascination with Nathaniel Peachy.

Chapter Three

Charlie stared at the cups and dishes that she'd left on the table after fixing Jacob and Nate breakfast then worked to clean up. Nate had left for the fields. She had given Jacob his pain medicine and he was in the great room, resting on the sofa.

Dishes cleaned and put away, she turned her attention to the time. Would Nate come in for lunch? He didn't say.

Nate had seemed relieved to see her that morning, but he'd said little except in appreciation of the food she'd prepared for him and Jacob.

With breakfast done, she found herself at loose ends. Now what? What should she do now?

Charlie grinned. She'd clean the house from top to bottom. The brothers' *mam* would be surprised to see a clean house when only her sons were in residence.

She'd hung up the wet tea towel she'd used to dry dishes when suddenly the back door slammed open. She gasped and spun to see a furious man. "Nate? What's wrong?"

"Charlie Stoltzfus," he snapped, "did you take out

the mower yesterday while Jacob and I were at the doctor?"

Charlie flushed guiltily and glanced away. "I wanted to help."

"And I told you to stay away from the equipment!" he burst out.

"I know how to mow hay!"

He approached, grabbed her roughly by the shoulders, but despite his intimidating height and expression, he didn't hurt her and she wasn't afraid. "You saw what happened to Jacob yesterday," he said. His eyes were like blue ice. "What if you'd been hurt while we were gone? Who would have been here to help you?" He released her and stepped back. He turned away. Tension tightened the muscles of his back, and he clenched his fists at his sides. He spun to face her. "People die in farm accidents, Charlie!"

Guilt made her flush. She felt a painful lump in her throat. "You're right," she said. "I'm sorry."

Nate held her gaze. He looked big and handsome— and extremely upset.

"I'm sorry I used the mower without your permission." She drew a sharp breath then released it. "I wanted to help. 'Tis supposed to rain soon and I knew you'd be missing a day's work with Jacob's accident yesterday. I thought if I finished what he'd started there would be less for you to worry about." She fought back tears. Charlie shifted uncomfortably when he just stared at her. "Say something," she said.

"You want to be *schuul*teacher," he said harshly. "You have to think before you act, Charlie. Your behavior frequently gets you into trouble. How can you teach our community children if you jump into situations without giving a thought to the consequences?"

She felt the blood leave her face. "You don't think I'd be a *gut* teacher."

He sighed and approached her. "You need to be more careful. To grow up." He placed his hands gently on her arms then soothed them down their length to take her hands. "I think you could be a fine teacher. You have a way with children. They listen to you and will gladly follow your lead." He released her abruptly, his expression hardening. "But you won't be teacher unless you can lead them by *gut* example. You have to stop jumping rashly into situations that can potentially be dangerous."

"I know how to mow," she insisted, stung. "And you refer to things I did as a child."

He shifted away and crossed the room. "Maybe you do know how to mow. It doesn't matter," he said sharply. "I told you to stay away from the mowers and you didn't. *Gut* intentions don't make it right." He leaned against the wall near the door. "And you acted like a child. A spoiled, disobedient child."

"You're not my *vadder*!" she yelled.

"Thank the Lord for that."

Blinking sleepily, Jacob appeared in the doorway, clutching the door frame as he wobbled on one foot. "What's going on?"

Nate studied his brother. "What are you doing up? If you fall, you'll do further damage to yourself."

"I thought I heard arguing." The younger man glanced from her to his brother and back.

Charlie blushed. "We were just…"

"Having a serious discussion," Nate said. His lips firmed. "She mowed hay yesterday while we were gone."

Jacob glanced at her with surprise. "You did?"

Charlie hesitated then inclined her head. "I know how to mow. I've done it for my *dat*."

Nate's brother grinned. "How much did you get done?"

"I finished the back acreage where you left off and a little more."

"Don't," Nate warned Jacob. "Don't encourage her. You know what can happen when an accident occurs with the mower. She could have been hurt or worse."

His expression sobering, Jacob gazed at her. "He's right."

She lifted her chin defiantly. "Maybe."

Nate stared at his brother. "Jake, you need to lie down before you fall."

To Charlie's surprise, Jacob agreed. She moved to help him into the other room, but Nate reached him first. As if he didn't trust her to help Jacob. Hurt, she stayed in the kitchen while the brothers disappeared into the other room. While she waited for Nate to return, she felt the strongest urge to flee. But she didn't. She might have made a huge mistake with the mower, but she was just trying to help. Charlie still thought he'd overacted, and she wouldn't run as if she'd done something wrong.

But she didn't want him to think her unreliable and immature. She wanted the teaching job and needed to show him that she was a dependable, no-nonsense young woman who would make the best teacher ever hired for their Happiness School. A wrong word from Nate or anyone else within the community would end her chances to teach. As much as it upset her to change, she understood she needed to be on her best behavior. Even if it killed her to change into someone other than herself.

* * *

After making sure Jacob was comfortable on the sofa, Nate returned to the kitchen. He paused in the doorway, his gaze immediately homing in on Charlie. She stared out the window over the sink. There was a defeated slump to her shoulders, and he could feel her dejection like pain in his belly. But as much as it hurt him to see her this way, he knew he was right to be hard on her.

He stepped into the room. "Charlie."

She spun as if taken by surprise. A look of vulnerability settled on her pretty features. He scowled. He didn't want to notice how lovely she was or to recall her misguided intentions to help. If she didn't rein in her tendency to jump into potentially dangerous situations, she could get seriously injured. Or die.

Her breath shuddered out. "Jacob *oll recht*?"

"*Ja*. He's asleep."

Her mouth softened into a slight smile. "The pain medication."

He nodded, unable to take his gaze off her. He'd been more than a little alarmed when he'd realized that she'd used the mower. If something had happened to her...

A memory came to him sharp and painful of another young girl who'd been reckless and wild like Charlie. He'd loved Emma with all of the love in a young boy's heart, but it hadn't been enough. Despite his repeated warnings, Emma had continued to take risks in her quest for excitement. She'd claimed that she loved him, but in the end, he wasn't enough to keep her happy. He'd warned her to avoid the young *Englishers* in town, but she hadn't listened.

Instead, she'd called him a spoilsport for ruining her fun. Then one night she'd slipped out of the house during her *rumspringa* to spend time with her new English friends. The teenage driver had crashed his car, the accident seriously wounding his passengers, three English girls, and killing Emma immediately.

Nate hadn't known of Emma's plans that night. Later in his grief, he'd realized that Emma would have hated being married to an Amish farmer. Never content to be a wife and a mother, she would have always craved—and gone looking for—excitement.

Charlie shifted uncomfortably under his gaze and he looked away. Charlie needed a husband, he thought. A man to ground her. Someone closer to her age with enough sense to help her reach her potential as a responsible wife and mother.

"Charlie—"

"I only wanted to help, Nathaniel," she said.

He stifled a smile at the use of his formal given name. She tended to use it whenever she was upset with him. "I know."

"But I didn't, did I? I made you worry and I didn't mean to."

He sighed. "Next time you need to listen when I tell you something."

"I guess that will depend on what you say," she said cheekily.

"Charlie," he warned.

"I'm not a child, and I can only be me."

"I need to get back to work," he said abruptly. He had to maintain his distance. He mustn't think of her as anything other than a child.

"Will you be back for lunch?"

He hesitated. "I'm not sure. If I am, most likely I'll be late. If the two of you get hungry, eat." He grabbed his hat from the table where he'd tossed it earlier. "I need to stay out and cut as much hay as possible before it rains."

An odd sound made him spin around. Charlie looked as if she was going to say something but she didn't.

Nate studied her face and had to stifle amusement at the aggrieved look in her green eyes. "Stay in the *haus*, Charlie. Jacob needs you."

She sniffed as if he'd found fault with her. "I'll keep an eye on him."

He didn't release her gaze. *"Gut."* Jamming his hat on his head, he opened the back door and took one last look to find her reaching for the broom. "Charlie."

She spun as if startled. *"Ja?"*

"Behave."

She glared at him. "Go mow your hay, *vadder*," she mocked.

Nate chuckled under his breath as he left, pulling the door shut behind him. He was overly conscious that Charlie was in his home, doing her best to help out in a bad situation. He didn't know what he would have done if she hadn't been there yesterday.

He gauged the sky, noting the gathering dark clouds in the far distance. The last thing he needed was for it to rain before he was done.

He couldn't dawdle. Time was passing too quickly, and he'd already spent too much of it at the house when he should have been in the fields. But after realizing what Charlie had done, he hadn't been able to stay away.

Nate scowled. Lately, Charlie was taking up way too many of his thoughts. She wanted to be a teacher. Maybe that was just what she needed—a job to keep her busy and that would make her take responsibility more seriously. His *mam* frequently sang Charlie's praises for the way she handled his younger siblings. *Mam* obviously felt Charlie responsible enough to watch her children while she did other things.

He had a ton of work to do, Nate reminded himself. He forced Charlie from his mind to focus on the task at hand.

Four hours later he was pleased to realize that he'd cut more acreage than expected. He hated to admit it, but Charlie's work in the back fields the previous morning had helped him. As he stabled his Belgian team, he felt the first of the rain. He closed the barn door then headed to the house, his thoughts immediately returning to Charlie and the lunch she'd promised him.

Nate was overwhelmed with a sudden chill as the rain began to fall in earnest, soaking him. As he reached the house, the door opened and Charlie stood, studying him with a worried look. "'Tis raining," she said, eyeing him carefully, noting his soaked clothes.

Nate nodded. "I know." Water dripped from his straw hat onto the porch decking. He tugged off his hat, and his hair underneath was sopping. The hat had done nothing to keep out the rain. She held out her hand for the hat then stepped back so he could enter the house. He followed her with his gaze. "You were worried."

She looked away, apparently unwilling to admit concern. "I made soup," she said.

He let it go. "Sounds *gut*." He shivered. "And hot." He smiled. "I need warming up."

"You should change into dry garments," she suggested.

He spun toward her. "Is that an order?"

"It would help." She blinked. "And it was just an idea."

He grinned, silently laughing at her. "'Tis a *gut* one." He started across the kitchen toward the hall to the stairs. He halted and faced her. "How's Jacob?"

"Seems *oll recht*. He's resting. In fact, he's been sleeping most of the morning. He woke up about an hour ago and I made him tea, but I think he's fallen asleep again."

"He needs his rest." He turned to leave.

"Nathaniel."

He spun back. *"Ja?"*

"Did you finish the mowing?"

"I did."

She looked relieved. "*Gut*. I'll check on Jacob then put the soup on the table."

"What kind of soup?" he asked, curious.

"Ham and lima bean."

His favorite. *Humph.* Was she aware? He studied her a moment. *Nay*, he decided, eyeing her with approval. So she could make soup. What else could she cook? He needed to know if he was to find her a husband. *After I help her to get the teaching position at our Happiness School.*

Jacob opened his eyes as Charlie entered the room. "How are you feeling?" she asked softly.

"Like someone slashed my foot with a sickle."

"I'm sorry," she said with genuine sympathy. "Is there anything I can do to help?"

"Nay." He gave her a small smile. "I'll live but *danki.*"

"Are you hungry? Nate's back." She'd been sick with relief when he'd walked, dripping wet, into the house. She'd fretted all morning, wondering if the mower had overturned and pinned him beneath metal.

"Nate's home?"

She shook off the mental image. *"Ja.* 'Tis raining. He's changing into dry clothes." She waited patiently as he sat up. "Can I help you into the kitchen?"

"Nay. I need to talk with him first," he said gruffly. "You go. We'll be there in a few minutes."

Not understanding why Jacob's comment stung her, Charlie returned to the kitchen. She set out bowls, napkins and silverware. She sliced the loaf of bread she'd found earlier in the pantry and cut up a block of cheddar in case they wanted a sandwich.

Nate entered alone moments later as she debated whether or not anything was missing from the table. She knew the exact second he entered the room.

"Did Jacob eat?" he asked.

"Nay. He'll join us, but said he wants to talk with you first." She watched Nate's brow furrow before he left to check on his brother.

He was gone a long time. Now that he was home, there was no need for her to stay. She would eat, then clean up before taking her leave.

Nate entered, his arm supporting Jacob. He helped him to the table and pulled out a chair. Charlie adjusted the seat opposite for Jake to use as a footrest.

"The soup smells *gut.*" Nate grabbed the chair next to his brother. "I'm starved. How about you, Jake?"

Looking pale, Jacob didn't answer.

Charlie frowned. "You don't like ham and bean soup, Jake?"

"I like it well enough. I don't feel much like eating."

"I can heat up a can of chicken soup. There's one in the pantry."

"Nay," Jacob said with a genuine smile. "I'll have a cup of the ham and bean."

Charlie ladled the soup into a large tureen and placed it in the center of the table. She held out her hand for Nate's bowl. His gaze locked on her as he gave it to her. The intensity of his look made her face heat. She hoped he'd believe it was from the hot soup rather than from her reaction to him. She set a filled bowl carefully before him then reached to fill a cup for Jacob. "Would you like bread, Jake?" she asked. "If your stomach is upset, it may help."

He looked surprised but nodded. Charlie passed him the bread plate and butter dish. Jacob reached for a slice and buttered it.

"Don't I get bread, too?" Nate teased.

She felt suddenly flustered until she realized that he was giving her a hard time simply because he could. A little imp inside made her cheeky. *"Ja.* Jacob, pass your *bruder* the bread plate, please."

Nate continued to watch her. Her stomach reacted when he gave her a slow smile. She looked away, filled her soup bowl then sat down across from Nate.

The men expressed appreciation for her cooking, and Charlie felt inordinately pleased by their praise. She ate her soup slowly, not wanting to rush and spill it. The brothers discussed the farmwork to be done once the rain stopped.

"I need to fix the leak in our storage building roof," Nate said.

"Can't you just bale it into rolls and cover them in plastic to leave outside?" Charlie asked. Many Amish farmers within her community stored hay that way.

Surprisingly, it was Jacob who looked at her as if she were an oddity.

Nate calmly explained why they chose to bale the hay into blocks instead. They would lay plastic over the top of the stack to protect them from the weather until they could move the hay inside. "'Tis easier to store. Hay wrapped too long in plastic can ferment. Feeding fermented hay to our animals can make them tipsy. *Dat* doesn't like to use fermented hay."

"My *vadder* has used rolled hay bales." She paused. "I have seen tipsy cows on occasion."

Nate regarded her patiently. "Many use rolled bales successfully, but my *vadder* isn't one of them."

The men finished eating. Charlie ate the last of her soup then stood to clear the table. Nate rose and helped Jacob into the other room. He returned within moments as she stacked dirty dishes on the counter near the sink. "You have plenty of soup left for another meal," she said as she ran hot water into a dish basin. When he didn't comment, she faced him. "Is something wrong?" She sighed with disappointment. "The soup didn't taste *gut*." Dismayed, she began to wash dishes.

"It was delicious," he assured her as he approached. To her shock, he pulled out a dish towel and started to dry the dishes.

"I'm glad you liked it." She grew silent. "You don't have to dry dishes."

"I want to. Like you, I don't mind helping others."

She didn't know how to respond. Was he mocking her? "Is that a subtle reminder of what I've done wrong?"

"Nay." He continued to work in silence.

She was conscious of him working beside her, the way his big hands handled the bowl carefully as he ran the towel over its surface. As he dried each one, Nate stacked them on the countertop near the cabinet where they'd be put away.

She needed to leave, she thought. Being this close to Nate made her uneasy.

"Now that you're here, I'll leave once I'm done here."

She felt him tense up. "Will you come back tomorrow?"

"You want me to?" she asked with surprise.

"I need someone to stay with Jacob," he said without warmth. "Tomorrow I'll be working with Jed."

Charlie closed her eyes briefly. When she opened them, it was to find Nate staring at her strangely with dish in hand. "I'll send one of my sisters if I can't make it. Either way, *Mam* needs to know."

"That's fine. But make sure she understands that no one else can know. My *dat* has waited a long time for this trip. If anyone accidentally lets the news slip when he calls to leave a message, he'll insist on coming home."

After the leftover food was put away and the kitchen cleaned, Charlie reached for her coat by the back door. "I'm heading out," she said.

"Danki." The intent focus of his blue eyes gave her goose bumps.

She lifted her coat only to feel it taken from her hands. Nate held it open for her so she could slide an arm into each sleeve. Then, to her shock, she felt his hands briefly settle on her shoulders before she'd pulled the garment closed. Pulse racing, she avoided his gaze. "Tell Jake I hope he feels better."

"I will." There was an odd huskiness to Nate's voice that she'd never heard before. He eyed her with an expression that made the back of her neck tingle as she met his gaze.

She cleared her throat. "I'll make sure someone is here for him tomorrow morning."

"Fine." He accompanied her to the door.

"What time?"

"Eight? Jed will be here at eight thirty."

She nodded. "Someone will be here before then."

"Be careful," he said, seemingly unmoved by the knowledge that she wouldn't be the one coming. "The roads can be slippery when wet."

Charlie didn't respond, although she could have argued that she'd driven in the rain hundreds of times without any problems. She donned her traveling bonnet before she dashed outside. She sensed that Nate was behind her. She spun to face him. "*Nay*, go back inside! You'll get wet again."

She didn't wait to see if he listened. She climbed inside her vehicle, picked up the leathers, then left without another look. Her thoughts were in turmoil as she steered the horse toward home. She'd ask Ellie if she could stay with Jacob. If Ellie wasn't available, she'd ask Meg or Nell.

Tomorrow she'd speak with the bishop about becoming teacher. She couldn't avoid it any longer. It was time to get her life in order. Her sudden desire wasn't because the thought of seeing Nate so soon again thoroughly unnerved her.

Or was it?

Charlie released a sharp breath, all too aware of Nate's negative view of her. She'd prove that she was the perfect woman for the teaching job, and that her students would benefit from her instruction. Not that it really mattered what Nate thought, unless it affected or hurt her chances in getting the position.

Chapter Four

Nate glanced at the time and grew worried. *Where is she?* He had to leave shortly and Charlie promised that she or her sister would be here by now. Had he been wrong to trust her to keep her word? He recalled everything she'd done for Jacob and knew that there must be a good reason no one had arrived.

He entered the great room, where Jacob sat in a chair with his injured foot propped up on a stool. "Charlie isn't here yet," he told his brother. "Will you be *oll recht* until she arrives?"

Jacob glanced up from his book. "Charlie's late?" he asked with concern.

"*Ja.* But it might not be Charlie who's staying with you today. She said that one of her sisters might come in her place."

Alarm settled on his brother's features. "Something must have happened."

Jacob's comment intensified his fear. "Jed will be here any minute." Nate prayed that Charlie arrived before Jed did. He swallowed hard. He prayed that Charlie was well and not lying hurt in a ditch somewhere.

There was a loud rap on the back door and then he heard Charlie's voice call out, *"Hallo?"*

"We're in here," he called back. He stifled the urge to run to her and waited instead for her to come to them.

She entered, looking lovely, flushed and out of breath. "I'm sorry I'm late. I didn't have the use of a vehicle this morning, so I walked."

Nate stared at her, aware of how pretty she was. "You walked?" he asked with disbelief.

Charlie nodded. *"Ja."*

"Isn't that three miles?" Jacob asked with appreciation.

Charlie shrugged. "More like four. Doesn't matter. I told you someone would be here, and so here I am. A little late, and I'm sorry about that."

Nate felt something inside him warm. "You're here now and that's what counts." He caught a glimpse through the window of a horse-drawn wagon pulling into the yard. "Jed's here." He met Charlie's gaze. "Are you sure you're okay?"

She nodded. "A little winded because I was in a hurry, but otherwise I'm fine."

Despite the fact that Jed waited, he hesitated. The sudden stark need to spend time with her startled him.

"Did you eat?" she asked. "Do you want me to fix you something before you go? A sandwich?"

"No need," he assured her. "I already made one." He held up a bag with a grin.

She smiled. "I'll see you later, then."

Jedidiah waited patiently for him as Nate left the house, crossed the yard and climbed onto the wagon seat next to him. *"Gut* morning," Jed greeted.

"'Tis a *gut* day," Nate responded. "Where are we headed today?"

"New Holland."

He raised an eyebrow. "That's quite some distance away."

"We're meeting a crew near Whittier's Store where a driver and car will be waiting for us."

Nate was relieved. He didn't want to be gone longer than necessary. If he kept her too long from her family, Charlie might not return. For Jacob, he assured himself.

Jed steered his buggy toward the road. "Is that Charlie I just saw in the window?"

"*Ja*, she's staying with Jacob today." He explained about his brother's injury and Charlie's arrival on the scene of the accident. Jed expressed concern, then understanding as he explained how he wanted to keep news of Jacob's injuries quiet. Happiness was a small community. If word got out, everyone would know and natter about it. Then someone was liable to say something to upset his father when he called to check in.

Jed grinned.

Nate scowled. "Why are you grinning?"

"Charlie helping out with Jake. She's growing up."

He sighed. Yes, he'd noticed. "She's been a big help."

Jed agreed quietly and quickly changed the subject as he drove toward Whittier's Store.

Nate relaxed, glad that the topic of Charlie had been dropped as they headed toward a job that would earn him the remainder of what he needed to finalize the purchase of his farm.

Charlie hadn't wanted to come, but none of her sisters were available and she'd promised that someone would be here to stay with Jacob. She watched Nate and Jed leave then went into the great room to check on her patient. "Do you want anything?" she asked. "Coffee? Something to eat?"

He shook his head. "*Nay*, but how about a game of Dutch Blitz?"

"Are you sure you want to play when you know that I can beat you?"

Jacob chuckled. "I'll take my chances. This isn't baseball."

She snickered. "Where are the cards?"

"In the cabinet to the left of the kitchen sink."

The morning went quickly as Charlie showed Jake just how well she could play by beating him at three games. But by the time lunchtime arrived, however, they'd won a total of five games each.

Charlie chose to clean the house after lunch. She started upstairs, dusting, sweeping floors and collecting dirty laundry. She had cleaned the bathroom when she heard thumping steps in the hallway outside the room. She was shocked to see Jacob on the landing. "What are you doing up here?"

The embarrassed look on his face told her all she needed to know. "Call out if you need help with the stairs."

With laundry basket under her left arm, she descended the stairs then went to put the wash on. She returned to the great room to check on Jacob when she realized that he hadn't come downstairs yet. She resisted the urge to check on him, knowing that she'd further embarrass him if she did. Heading into the kitchen, she decided to plan supper. She had no idea what time Nate would be home, but she didn't want him to worry about fixing a meal.

She put on the ingredients for beef stew, then debated whether or not to make biscuits to go with it. Charlie heard several loud thumps and a masculine yelp. Heart thundering in her chest, she raced to the stairs to find that Jacob had fallen down the steps.

"Are you hurt?"

"*Nay*, I'm *oll recht*," Jacob said but when he tried to stand, he gasped, turned white and couldn't get up.

"I'm taking you to the doctor." Eyeing him with concern, Charlie calculated the time it would take for her to drive Jacob herself. "Don't move. I'm going to get help."

Jacob nodded. "Trust me. I won't. It hurts too much when I do."

Charlie shut off the stove before she left the house. She ran toward the road and down the street until she reached the closest *Englisher*'s house. She knocked on the door and was relieved when a young woman answered. "I'm sorry to bother you, but may I use your phone? My friend hurt himself and I need to call Rick or Jeff Martin to take us to the doctor."

"I know Rick," the woman, who said her name was Molly, said. "Who needs medical attention?"

"Jacob Peachy."

She looked concerned. "I know the family. I'll call Rick and see if he or Jeff can come to the house. If not, I'll find someone who can. I'd take you myself but my baby is napping. If I can't find anyone else, I'll wake up my son."

Charlie smiled with relief. "Thank you. I should

get back to the *haus*. I don't want to leave him alone for long."

"Someone will be by soon," the woman promised.

She raced back to the house. Jacob still hadn't moved and she was both glad, yet worried, that he'd listened to her. Charlie sat down beside him on the floor and waited for help to arrive. "Someone will be coming soon," she assured him. "I want to write Nate a note. Did he leave a phone number where he can be reached?" Her cousin's wife, Sarah, would have it, but she couldn't leave Jacob.

"It's in the right top kitchen drawer."

She found it just where Jacob had told her it would be. Charlie grabbed the paper to bring with her. She'd call Nate's construction boss, using a phone at the clinic. In the event the man couldn't get word to Nate, she wrote a quick note to explain what had happened.

What was taking so long? she wondered with concern. What if Jacob had pulled out his stitches under his foot brace? She felt responsible. She should have never left him alone upstairs.

A loud pounding on the door announced the help's arrival. Charlie answered the door, glad to recognize Jeff Martin. Within minutes Jeff had placed Jacob in the backseat of his car.

Jeff got them to the emergency room within minutes. She and Jeff waited while Jacob was wheeled into a back room.

"He'll be okay," Jeff said reassuringly.

"I hope so." She gazed at him with worry. "It was my fault that he fell."

"I doubt that," the man said.

Nate. She needed to call him. She stood. "I have to find a phone to call Nate."

Jeff nudged her arm to gain her attention and handed her his cell phone.

She smiled her thanks then dialed the number, relieved when Nate's construction boss answered. She explained the situation to Mike but then learned, to her dismay, that Nate had left the job for the day. "Nate already left work. May I make another call?"

"Feel free. You don't have to ask."

Charlie dialed her sister's cell phone number. She explained to Ellie what happened and asked if she could somehow get in touch with Nate.

"I'll get a hold of him," Ellie promised.

"Danki," Charlie said and hung up. She fought the urge to cry as she gave Jeff back his phone. She had to stay strong for Jacob—and for Nate.

Nate was tired when he got home. The day had been long and the work heavy but he didn't regret it. He'd made the money he needed.

He saw the buggy in the yard and smiled. Charlie would have fixed something for dinner. She was generous like that, and since Jacob's accident, he wondered how he could have managed without her.

Jed pulled in close to the house, and Nate got out. "Let me know if Mike needs help again," he said.

"Will do." Jed eyed him with a half smile. "Say *hallo* to my cousin."

He didn't acknowledge his friend's teasing. "Will do."

After Jed left, Nate headed toward the house. The sound of buggy wheels caught his attention. He was surprised to see James Pierce, Charlie's brother-in-law, climb out of the vehicle seconds later.

"James," Nate greeted.

"Nate." James's somber expression caused Nate immediate concern.

"What's wrong?"

As James explained, Nate felt increasing alarm.

"Do you know which medical center they went to?"

"*Ja.* The emergency room at Lancaster General. Come with me and I'll take you to Drew." His friend Drew was the veterinarian who took over the practice after James left to join the Amish church and marry Charlie's sister Nell. James now took care of farm animals while Drew gave medical care for the animals brought into the clinic.

"Why are we going to see Drew?" Nate asked, confused.

"Drew's done for the day. He'll drive you to the hospital."

Nate understood. *"Danki."*

"Do you need anything inside the house?"

Nate started to shake his head then changed his mind. "I'll be just a minute." He entered the kitchen, saw a note lying on the table. Charlie had written it in a hurry but she'd let him know that they'd gone to the doctor after his brother's tumble down the stairs.

He saw a pot of beef stew on the stove and moved it into the refrigerator. Then, with pounding heart, he rushed to don clean garments before hurrying to rejoin James. Charlie's brother-in-law filled him in with what he'd learned as they headed toward the animal clinic. Drew was waiting for them when they arrived. Nate thanked James and Drew as he climbed into Drew's car. James promised to check in with him by phone later.

* * *

Charlie closed her eyes and leaned back in her chair in the waiting room. What was taking the doctor so long with news? How badly was Jacob hurt?

Her throat tightened. The day had begun well with Jake and her playing games. She should have put off cleaning house. Or stayed upstairs and waited for him. She could have helped him down the steps and prevented his fall. A tear leaked from her right eye to trail down her cheek. She sensed someone's presence above her and knew immediately that it was Nate. She opened her eyes.

Nate gazed down at her, his expression unreadable. "Charlie."

Wiping her eyes, she sprang to her feet as he stepped back. "The doctor hasn't come out to tell us anything." She saw that he'd changed out of his work clothes.

"What happened?" His voice was quiet as if prepared to hear the worst.

Charlie told in detail and looked away with a flush of guilt as she did. She felt the increasing tension in Nate, knew he blamed her as much as she blamed herself. She fought the strongest urge to leave. She needed to know how Jacob was and to face his brother's anger, which she deserved.

A man wearing a white lab coat exited from the treatment area and looked at her as he approached. She stood and gestured toward Nate, who had risen from his seat. "This is Nate Peachy. Jacob's brother."

The doctor nodded. "Despite the fall, your brother isn't as seriously hurt as he could have been. He tore open his stitches. I restitched him then put on a stronger and shorter cast. He has a few bumps and bruises, but nothing that won't heal in a couple of weeks. I'd like to see him again in a few days to make sure everything is healing as well as it should."

"Do I bring him back here?" Nate asked, his features full of concern.

"I'm on call today. It'd be better if you came to my office." He handed Nate a business card. "Don't let him walk on his injured foot until after I check him again."

"I'll make sure he doesn't," Charlie said.

Nate shot her an even look that made her stomach burn. Clearly, he'd had enough of her help with Jacob. He was angry with her and no longer wanted her help.

An orderly pushed Jacob out of the back room minutes after a nurse went over Jake's discharge papers with them. His eyes widened when he saw his brother. "Nate."

"Are you *oll recht*?"

"*Ja*, I'll live. I'm sorry."

"You have no reason to be sorry." Nate's refusal to look at Charlie confirmed her worst fears.

Determined not to cry, she preceded the brothers out of the building where Jeff Martin waited to take them home. "All set?" Jeff asked.

"*Ja*," Charlie said quietly. She leaned close to the kind *Englisher* and whispered, "Will you take me home first?"

Jeff studied her a long moment. "Of course." He shot a look at the brothers before returning his attention to her. "Would you like to ride up front?"

She managed a grateful smile. "I would," she whispered.

Chapter Five

Nate was silent as Jeff pulled his car into the Arlin Stoltzfus driveway.

"You're not coming home with us?" Jacob asked with disappointment.

Charlie gave him a small smile. "Nate will be with you. You don't need me."

"And I'll be home tomorrow, too," Nate said, drawing her glance. "We won't need you then, either."

Jacob frowned. "Don't you have to bale hay?"

"Not tomorrow."

"But I'll be fine with Charlie."

"I'm staying home," Nate said gruffly. "I'm sure Charlie has other things to do."

She hid her pain. "Thank you, Jeff. I don't know what we would've done without you."

"You're more than welcome, Charlie." The man regarded her warmly. "Rest up. You look exhausted."

She spun toward the house without looking back at either brother in the rear seat. She'd reached the bottom of the front porch steps when the door opened and Ellie flew down the stairs.

"How's Jacob?" she asked after a quick glance toward the car.

"He's doing better," Charlie said, "but the doctor wants to see him back in a couple of days to make sure." She couldn't resist one last look at the vehicle as Jeff drove past toward the road. The action brought Nate's side of the car into view. His eyes seared hers briefly through the window before she averted her gaze. Her chest hurt. Her heart ached, and she felt perilously close to tears.

"*Mam* fixed supper. You hungry?"

Charlie shook her head. "I'm tired. Do you think she'll be upset if I go to bed?"

Worry settled on her sister's brow as Ellie studied her. "What's wrong?"

"I'm fine. Just tired. 'Tis been a long day."

"I'll tell *Mam* you're resting upstairs."

It was still early evening. Charlie could only imagine what her mother would think after Ellie told her that she'd gone to bed.

She pulled back the bed covering and slid beneath the quilt with her clothes on. Her entire body ached, and her emotions were all over the place. She'd done the best she could under the circumstances, but it hadn't been good enough. She was the reason that Jacob had fallen, and it'd been clear that Nate blamed her.

After a good quiet cry, Charlie slipped into a restless sleep. It was dark outside when she woke and sensed a presence in her room. She wasn't afraid, for she knew instinctively that it was her mother. A flashlight clicked on, confirming her identity.

"*Mam*," she murmured.

"Are you ill?"

"Just tired," she admitted. "And my head hurts."

Mam brushed light fingers over Charlie's forehead. "Ellie said that Jacob fell down the steps."

Charlie inhaled sharply. "*Ja*, he did."

"And you got him to a doctor."

She nodded.

"What happened?"

She told her about the events leading up to Jacob's tumble down the stairs.

"Tough day," *Mam* murmured.

"Ja." She looked away, unwilling to let her *mam* see how much Nate's reaction to Jake's accident had hurt her.

"What time will you be going tomorrow?"

Charlie shuddered out a sigh. "I'm not going to the Peachys'. I'll be here if you need anything. I can do the laundry."

Her mother was silent a long moment. "You're not going," she said with a frown.

"Nate asked me not to come." She sniffed. "He's staying home with Jacob."

Mam stood. "He probably thought you needed a rest after the day you had today…and you *were* tired." She caressed Charlie's cheek. "Sleep well, *dochter.*"

She didn't really believe that was Nate's reason for telling her to stay home, but her mother's touch made her feel better. Charlie rolled over, closed her eyes and comforted by her *mam*'s love, she fell into a deep sleep.

The next morning she woke early and headed to the barn. She wanted to spend time with the animals, especially the horses. She loved horses. There was something calming about them.

Charlie fed the animals then put the cows and goats out to pasture. She then returned inside to brush the gelding her father had purchased recently. She found brushing Buddy's chestnut coat soothing. Immersed in the task, she didn't immediately detect a presence behind her.

"Charlie."

She spun, gasped. "Nathaniel! What are you doing here?"

"I need to speak with you." Dressed in a blue shirt and navy tri-blend pants with black suspenders, he looked good. Too good.

She sighed, trying not to notice his appearance and the way her heart leaped. Flushing with guilt, she went back to brushing Buddy. "I know what you came to say, and I'm sorry."

His tension radiated from behind her. "About what?"

Charlie faced him with brush in hand. "It was my fault Jacob got hurt."

He frowned. "Did you push him down the stairs?"

"Nay!" She blinked as she registered his surprised expression. "I should have stayed upstairs and waited to help him down."

"He wouldn't have allowed it."

She eyed him curiously. "Then why did you tell me to stay home?"

She watched with astonishment as Nate's features softened. "You were exhausted. I was worried about you. It was a bad day yesterday and I thought you might need some time to yourself."

Charlie studied him a long moment. "Maybe I do,"

she said, thinking of her plans to visit Bishop John. "Then why are you here?"

"To thank you and to ask for your help. I heard from my *dat*. My *grossmudder* is ill, and my family will be staying in Indiana for another week."

"You need someone to stay with Jacob."

Nate stared at her. "*Ja.* You."

"I don't know if that's a *gut* idea."

He nodded. "I understand."

"Why me?" she dared.

"Because you have done a great job with Jacob and with the *haus*."

She felt both pleased and annoyed. She'd rather hear that he missed her than he missed her cooking and cleaning…and brother-sitting services, but she supposed the fact that he trusted her enough to want her back meant something.

"Well?" he asked.

"Well what?"

He studied her with patience. "Will you come back tomorrow?"

"I don't think so," she admitted. She had a terrible night, thanks to Nathaniel Peachy. She wasn't going to rush and jump in to help out, even though she wanted nothing more than to do so. "But I know for a fact that Ellie will be available to come tomorrow." She bit her lip. "How is Jake?"

"He's in pain, but the medicine helps."

"I'm sorry." She blinked rapidly and looked away. Resuming the task at hand, she kept her gaze focused on the horse.

Suddenly, Nate stood next to her. Close. Too close. He reached up to still her hand with his warm fingers. "I hope you'll be the one to stay with Jacob…if you're free." Then he turned and left her. She sighed and wondered how she was going to stay away from the Peachy farm. It would be hard now that Nate had asked nicely for her return.

Charlie hugged herself with her arms. She shouldn't, but she cared for him a great deal. He'd called her a child. He regarded her as a girl helpful but troublesome. There was nothing she could do to make him see her differently, she realized with sadness. Nothing to convince him that she was a responsible young woman…who was falling in love with him.

Nate had risen early, taken care of the animals then returned to the house to make breakfast. Today he would spend the day with Jacob. He had to bale hay soon, but not yet. He'd been shaken by the news that Jacob had fallen down the steps. After they'd returned home, he'd debated whether or not he should call his parents. He changed his mind after receiving word late last night that his grandmother had become ill and his family would be gone another week. He didn't want to further worry his father. Jacob would recover, while he had no idea how bad his *grossmudder*'s condition was.

He'd lain awake last night, obsessing over Charlie. She'd looked crestfallen yesterday when he'd told her to stay home. It had occurred to him during the night that she might have misunderstood the reason. It wasn't that he didn't trust her with Jacob's well-being. On the contrary, she'd done a good job getting Jacob medical attention. No, his concern was for her. She'd given them so much of her time, and he figured she was ready for a break. Which was why he'd gone to see her first thing this morning to explain, in case she'd had the wrong idea. And she had.

After his return from the Stoltzfus residence, Nate parked his buggy in the barnyard and hurried inside the house to check on his brother. He was relieved to find Jacob asleep. He wrote him a note to stay put— just in case—before he headed out to the barn to let the horses, goats and cows into the pasture.

He watched the horses run in the fields and thought again of Charlie. If only she was older. If only she wasn't like Emma, then maybe…

The best thing for the both of them would be if Charlie sent one of her sisters to stay with Jacob.

He needed coffee. He returned to the house and put on a fresh pot then searched through the pantry for something to eat. *Charlie has been busy*, he thought with a pang as he spied a plate of muffins, a fresh loaf of bread and a pie plate with the remains of an apple pie. He pulled out the bread and then grabbed butter from the refrigerator.

The coffee finished perking, and he poured himself a cup and added a spoon of sugar with a splash of cream. He brought it to the table, then grabbed a piece of bread and buttered it. His hand stilled in midaction as something occurred to him. The church elders would be seeking a permanent teacher for their Happiness School. Elizabeth Troyer would be leaving soon. Which left the opening for Charlie.

Nate grinned as he picked up his coffee. "She can start next week," he murmured before he took a sip. His grin faded. It would be a wonderful opportunity for Charlie, but it would also mean that she wouldn't ever be back to help with Jacob. He exhaled sharply. He didn't know how he felt about that.

After Charlie's sister came tomorrow, Nate would head out to speak with the bishop about Charlie.

He was shocked to realize that he'd miss her. Given his past with Emma, he shouldn't feel this way, but somehow Charlie had gotten deeply under his skin.

Because she's good with Jacob, he reasoned. He'd miss her help, her cooking…and her smile. *Because of Jacob.* Something inside him suggested differently, but he buried the feeling.

"I appreciate you staying with Jake today, Ellie," Charlie said.

"I'm available. I don't mind." Ellie studied her thoughtfully. "What are you going to do?"

"I plan to talk with Bishop John about the *schuul*-teacher position."

Surprise flickered across Ellie's expression. "You want to teach *schuul*?"

Charlie frowned. "I thought you knew that. I'm sure I told you."

Her sister shook her head. "*Nay.* I would have remembered if you had." Ellie smiled. "*Gut* for you."

"I hope I get a chance to teach," she said, giving voice to her fears.

"Why do you say that? You'd be a great teacher."

She softened her expression and she smiled. "*Danki*, Ellie. I hope the church elders agree."

"What am I supposed to do once I get to the Peachys'?"

"Keep Jacob company, fix him and maybe Nate lunch. I made a grocery list for Nate, but I don't know if he's had a chance to shop. You can always call Nell and ask her to bring you a few things."

Her sisters Ellie and Nell were the only two in the family with cell phones, allowed by the church elders because of their lines of work with Nell as part of her husband's veterinary practice, and Ellie because she cleaned houses for a living.

"Don't worry, I'll take *gut* care of him."

It wasn't Jacob she was worried about. It was Nate. She smiled her thanks. Charlie brushed a hand down the length of her white apron that she tied over her purple tab dress. "How do I look?"

Ellie smiled. "Vanity, *schweschter*? I'm shocked."

"I'm not vain… I don't think." At least she hoped not since vanity was a sin. "I need a little confidence for when I meet with Bishop John. It won't be easy to convince him that I'm the best person to be teacher."

She accompanied Ellie until she reached her vehicle. She climbed into the family market wagon while her sister got into her pony cart. She then waved at Ellie before she drove in the opposite direction.

As she parked the wagon close to Bishop John Fisher's house, Charlie felt a wild nervous fluttering in her chest. She sat unmoving in the wagon for several minutes. Too much hinged on this meeting, she thought.

Would the bishop remind her of every misdeed of her youth? Would he tell her that she was out of luck since the elders had already found a replacement?

She drew a calming breath then climbed down from her vehicle, went to the side entrance and rapped on the wooden door. Within seconds the door opened, revealing Sally Hershberger Fisher, who looked surprised but delighted to see her.

"Charlie!" the woman welcomed with a smile. "Come in!"

"*Hallo*, Sally. 'Tis nice to see you." She glanced down at Sally's pregnant belly and flashed her a genuine smile of pleasure. "How are you feeling?"

Sally smiled. "I'm well." She stepped aside and gestured Charlie into the kitchen. "Wonderful, actually. I'm feeling great and…" Her hands cradling her stomach, she leaned close and whispered, "I'm so happy."

Charlie beamed at her. "I'm pleased for you."

"*Danki.*" Sally eyed her intently. "Would you like tea or coffee?"

She shook her head. "I need to talk with Bishop John. Is he available?"

"*Ja.* Let me tell him that you're here." Looking curious, but clearly unwilling to pry, Sally studied her for a long moment before she left the room. She was back within seconds. "He's happy to see you. Come with me."

Charlie started to follow then froze as her chest tightened and she suddenly found it difficult to breathe. As if sensing Charlie's hesitation, Sally stopped and faced her. She must have read something in Charlie's expression because she quickly returned to her side. "Is everything *oll recht*?"

"I…" Why was she so nervous? If she didn't get the job, what would it matter? *It would matter to me*, she realized. It was important and she wanted her chance. "Sally, I've come to talk with John about the teaching position. Do I even have a chance? I know I was impulsive and a bit reckless when I was younger, but I'm not the same person now," she said, hugging herself with her arms.

Sally's expression softened. "I think you'd be a wonderful teacher."

She blinked. "You do?"

The bishop's wife nodded. "Go in and talk with him. Let him know you're interested. The decision isn't John's alone. He may not be able to give you an answer right away, but you won't be considered if no one knows how much you want to teach."

Closing her eyes, Charlie exhaled sharply. "I do want to teach." She bit her lip. "A lot."

"Then tell him that," Sally urged as she led Charlie down the hall until they reached the room where John handled church district business.

"John, Charlie's here," Sally announced then left the two of them alone.

Charlie stood a moment, wondering how to start.

"Have a seat, Charlotte."

Her heart hammered as she nodded and sat down.

Chapter Six

Charlie wore her spring-green dress. Matt Troyer, her sister's brother-in-law, had told her once that the dress brightened the color of her eyes. It wasn't vanity that drove her to wear it, she assured herself. It was just that she needed the confidence in knowing that she looked her best when she saw Nate again. The man made her nervous, and her heart fluttered whenever he was near.

She brought a lemon pound cake that she'd baked especially for the brothers last evening. She got out of the vehicle then reached onto the seat to retrieve it. She straightened and started toward the Abram Peachy house only to realize that the door to the farmhouse was open. Nate Peachy stood on the threshold, watching her approach.

Charlie didn't smile as she walked toward the house. There was no warmth in Nate's expression and the tension between them was thick. She felt it in her tight throat and the painful butterflies that fluttered in her belly. "Nate," she greeted just before he stepped aside to allow her entry.

His lack of reply halted her in her tracks and made her face him. She arched an eyebrow.

"You came back," he said.

"Looks like it," she replied briskly. Was he unhappy that Ellie hadn't returned?

A sudden smile hovered on his lips, making him even more attractive to her. She tried not to feel flustered. "Where's Jake?"

His good humor disappeared. "In the other room." She started toward the great room and he grabbed her arm to stop her. "I made an arrangement so that there will be no need for him to go upstairs…"

She blushed. "I understand. That's *gut. Ja, gut.*"

Nate's gaze warmed. Shaken by his look, Charlie spun and headed in to see his brother.

Jacob was seated on the upholstered chair with his leg propped up.

He looked up at her with a smile when she approached him. She responded in kind, her mouth curving with happiness to see him looking much better and not in pain.

"Charlie! You're here!"

She grinned. "How else will I be able to trounce you in cards again?"

Jacob chuckled. His features changed as he glanced past her shoulder to his brother. "You baling hay today?"

Nate nodded. "Not to worry, though. It'll get done. I've got the Lapp *bruders* coming to help out."

She eyed him with horror. "My cousins are coming?" When he nodded, she exclaimed, "But what will I fix? There will be many mouths to feed!"

Jacob scowled. "Hey! Who will keep me company?"

"I will. Only we'll be in the kitchen instead of out here." Charlie looked at Nate. "What are you still doing here? Don't you have work to do?" She gasped, as if realizing just what she'd said.

Nate's astonishment quickly turned to amusement. "*Ja*, Charlie." He spun to leave.

"Wait!" she called. "Can you help me get Jacob into the kitchen so he won't have to sit out here alone?"

Nate stared at her a moment before he nodded. He left the room and headed toward the stairs but then returned moments later with a wheelchair. "This should help," he said.

"*Danki*," she murmured and then watched Nate help his brother into the chair.

When she reached for it, Nate waved her away. "I'll push him."

Didn't he trust her to push Jake into the other room? She hoped that wasn't the case, but she couldn't help feeling that it was.

As Nate moved Jacob into the kitchen, Charlie heard vehicles in the barnyard. She went to the window and was pleased to see five of her Lapp male cousins. Upon seeing her through the glass, Jed waved. She saw him murmur something to his brothers and suddenly all five turned to stare at her. Blushing, she pulled back, eager to get to work. First thing she'd do was make coffee. Then she'd think about what food to prepare for lunch. She'd have to decide what to fix for supper, but she had a feeling that by the end of the day her cousins would want to go home to eat with their wives.

Without thought, Charlie poured Jacob coffee, fixed it the way he liked it and set a bowl of cereal before him. Jacob looked at the coffee and his breakfast, then grinned. She realized that she hadn't asked what he wanted, but he was pleased. She smiled back, knowing instinctively that she'd given him exactly what he wanted. She'd learned a lot about Jacob in the past few days and found that she liked the young man a lot. Despite his injuries, he still managed to smile and show gratitude for whatever she did for him.

Charlie thought of Nate and turned away from the table. No need for Jacob to know that she'd had serious doubts about returning today because of his brother. And her feelings for Nate.

Her cousins had peeked in to say a quick hello. After they went outside, Charlie handed Nate a pair of gloves. "Don't need you getting hurt like your brother."

He looked startled by her concern but took the gloves before he left to join her cousins in the hayfields. It was quiet with the men gone and Jacob silently reading a book. Charlie stared about the kitchen, wondering what to make for lunch. She needed to go grocery shopping—something she could handle tomorrow—but that wouldn't help her decide what to cook now. Feeding three was no problem, but having to make a meal for eight? That was something else altogether. She tensed as she started toward the refrigerator and opened the door wide.

Jacob looked up from his book. "What's upsetting you?" he asked, watching her closely.

"I don't know what to make for lunch."

He smiled. "Charlie, this is my *bruder* and your cousins. Cake, pie and cookies would be enough."

She gasped. "For dessert maybe, but not for lunch." She shut the refrigerator door. "I'm going to check the freezer." She started toward the back room, worried that she couldn't pull off a meal to be proud of, even though lunch was still a few hours from now. Charlie gasped when Jacob grabbed her arm. He had risen from his chair to reach her. "Jacob! Be careful. I don't want you to fall and hurt yourself again."

"I'm fine. Steady as a rock. See? I'm holding on."

"What do you need?" She swallowed hard. If she caused Jacob to get hurt again—and if she messed up the meal, then she'd never live it down. And she'd feel terrible forever. And Nate would never forgive her.

"I need you to stop worrying," Jacob said. "You're amazing. You'll do fine."

She released a sharp breath. *"Danki."* She briefly closed her eyes. "I hope you're right."

"I'm always right," he said teasingly, which made her smile. He released her arm and lowered himself carefully into his chair. "Go look in the freezer, but I'm telling you desserts will be fine. If you want more, you can offer peanut butter and jam sandwiches. Nate and I love them."

She felt herself relax. "I'll see what I can do." She paused on the threshold between the kitchen and the back room. "What kind of cake?"

"Chocolate?"

She grinned. "I'll see if you have all the ingredients."

Jacob went back to his reading while she assembled what she considered a makeshift meal. She only hoped it would be enough food for five hungry farmworkers.

By the time the men returned to the house for lunch,

Charlie had soup simmering on the stove and a plate of peanut butter with jam sandwiches on the kitchen counter ready to be served. She'd found three types of jam in the refrigerator—strawberry, peach and boysenberry. The soup was a simple chicken noodle recipe that her mother had taught her to make. There had been just enough frozen leftover cooked chicken. The bread was homemade, and she'd made chocolate cake with fudge frosting that morning. And there was the lemon cake she'd brought with her. She stood, watching as the men filed in. Her cousin Noah grinned at her when he saw the chocolate cake. Everyone in the family knew Noah's preference for anything chocolate. She had no idea what Nate liked best, but she hoped he'd be satisfied with the meal she'd provided.

"Smells *gut* in here," her cousin Jedidiah said.

"Chicken soup?" his brother Isaac declared as he moved to look in the pot on the stove. He grinned as he faced the others. "*Ja*, chicken soup with lots of noodles!"

Her fraternal twin cousins, Jacob and Elijah, expressed their appreciation as they took a seat at the table. Since all of their hands were clean, Charlie knew the men must have washed up outside despite the cold weather.

She chanced a look toward Nate, who chatted with Jed as he took his seat at the long trestle table. Worried whether or not she'd done well in the kitchen, she filled soup dishes from the pot on the stove, then carefully set a bowl before each man. Then she grabbed the dish of sandwiches from the counter and set them in the middle of the table. She'd placed small plates at each setting earlier.

"Peanut butter and jam sandwiches?" Elijah asked. Tensing, Charlie nodded.

Her cousin beamed at her. "Yum."

She smiled and turned for the pitcher of iced tea. As she spun back, she caught Nate watching her with an odd expression. Feeling her face heat, she looked away, unwilling to let him know how much he affected her.

The men ate their soup and sandwiches while they discussed the work they'd accomplished. She gleaned from their conversation that the hay was pushed into rows, which would be swept up from the field later by the baler. She knew what the work entailed, although she'd never been allowed to bale hay. A worker would run the baler over the rows of cut hay then bales would come out the end and be placed onto a platform. Once the platform on the baler was full, the bales of hay would be moved into wagons that would transport them closer to the barn. When they were done baling, the men would move the hay bales into a storage building on the property.

Charlie didn't eat or sit. She stood at the counter, listening. Not wanting to appear nosy, she worked to put away the dishes she used and washed earlier. She felt out of sorts, as if she didn't belong, despite the fact that Nate had asked her to come and the others were her cousins.

"I'll oversee the baler," Nate said.

"Nay," Jed protested. "You already have one Peachy man down. We'll not be taking a chance that you'll get hurt, too." He paused. "You can steer it."

"You all have wives and children. I don't," Nate insisted.

"I can do it," Isaac said. "I have a wife but no children."

Charlie snorted. "Yet," she said with a snicker. The women of the family had recently learned that Isaac's wife, Ellen, was with child.

Isaac smiled sheepishly at his brothers, and Nate raised his eyebrows as he offered his congratulations.

"That's it, then. I'll work behind the baler."

"Nate, it takes more than one man to run the machine. We'll take turns."

Nate gazed at his friends. "Fine. We'll take turns, then, and be very careful."

The men stood after finishing their lunch that ended with the chocolate and lemon cakes for dessert. Charlie was pleased that no one turned a slice down. Jacob asked for a second piece. Noah enjoyed a huge piece and asked Charlie if another one could be packed up for him to take. She laughed and told him she'd have it ready and waiting for him.

"Great meal, Charlie," Jed said.

Her other cousins echoed his sentiment. Nate hadn't said anything as he stood.

"Nate," Jacob said, "would you mind helping me into the other room?"

"I'm sorry, Jake," Charlie said. "I should have realized you'd had enough of the kitchen."

"I enjoyed watching you work," he assured her as Nate brought the wheelchair close and helped his brother into it.

Charlie started to collect the dishes and stack them on the counter near the sink while Nate pushed Jacob into the other room. She ran water into the dish basin and added a squirt of dish soap, then turned off the spigot when the basin was full. She grabbed a sand-wich plate and was washing it when Nate reentered the kitchen. He didn't say anything, and her discomfort grew. She was afraid that he wasn't happy with what she'd made for lunch—or that she'd kept Jacob in the kitchen for too long.

She tried to ignore him and the lump in her throat as she continued to wash dishes before setting them in the drain rack. Sensing that Nate hadn't moved, she spun to face him. "*What?* Is there something you want to say?" She blinked rapidly as she eyed him defiantly. He studied her a moment before he nodded slowly. "I know it wasn't the best meal, but I used what I had available," she muttered.

He frowned as she glared at him. "It was a *gut* meal," he said quietly. But his expression didn't clear.

She scowled as she wondered whether she'd done something wrong.

Nate started to approach then halted. "Don't look at me that way. I was just thinking that you made an amazing meal with little in the cupboard. I should have bought groceries," he said huskily. "I'm sorry."

Charlie felt a jolt. He was apologizing? That was the last thing she'd expected from him. "You didn't mind peanut butter and jam sandwiches?"

His features smoothed out as he gave her a genuine smile. "I love peanut butter and jam sandwiches." A look of amusement entered his blue eyes. "I'm sure Jacob gave away that little secret."

She felt her lips curve in response. "He might have mentioned it, but I wasn't sure if sandwiches were enough for you. You've all been working hard."

"You also made us chicken noodle soup and cakes."

He chuckled. "I've never seen anyone enjoy chocolate cake more than Noah."

She grinned. "'Tis common knowledge in our family that he loves chocolate."

He gazed at her with tenderness for several seconds. "I need to get back to work."

His expression serious again, he headed toward the door.

"Be careful," she called.

He halted and faced her. There was something in his eyes she couldn't read, but it was a look that somehow terrified and excited her. "I will," he murmured before he left.

Charlie went to the window and watched through an opening in the sheer white curtains as Nate joined her cousins in the yard. She saw him laugh at something Elijah said. The sight of his grin and happy face made her reel with pleasure. She cared for Nate Peachy. Too much. Maybe it would be best if she asked one of her sisters to stay with Jacob tomorrow, provided that Jacob still needed someone to come.

After she'd fixed herself a sandwich, put away the leftover food and cleaned the kitchen, Charlie went to check on Jacob. She smiled when she saw him seated in the wheelchair by the window. His foot was propped up on the ever-present wooden chair and he was fast asleep. Jacob was a good man. *And so is his* bruder. Her heart thumped hard as she returned to the kitchen. She shouldn't be thinking about Nate. She was here for Jacob and she had to remember that.

She grabbed pencil and paper from the kitchen drawer then sat at the table to make a grocery list.

Nate and Jacob would need to shop for food now that their family wouldn't be home for another week.

There was no telling if Nate would want her to come again after he finished making hay. He'd be around for Jacob then and he'd no longer need her. Still, they would need food. She checked the refrigerator for basic items, then she wrote the low or missing items on the list. There wasn't much flour left, she thought. The least she could do before she left was to make a few loaves of bread for them to eat after she was gone. She closed her eyes as a wave of feeling washed over her. She'd miss Jacob. She'd miss Nate.

She rose from the chair and went to the kitchen window that overlooked the pasture and the farm fields beyond. She could make out the men working some distance away, knew that with her cousins' help, the hay-making would be completed sometime today. Charlie felt a little pang in her chest as she resumed her seat and forced herself to concentrate on what needed to be purchased. Laundry soap, she thought and wrote it down. "Vanilla and cocoa powder." One couldn't make a chocolate cake or brownies without them.

She lifted a hand to tuck a tiny strand of red hair under her prayer *kapp* as she tried to think what else they needed. It had been a busy morning and she felt less put together. Charlie reached up and removed her *kapp* and combed fingers over her hair before donning her head covering. List complete for now, she stood and walked around the kitchen suddenly feeling at a loss. She felt antsy. She needed to do something. She'd visit the horses in the barn but she didn't want to leave Jacob alone in case he needed her. If he was awake, she could tell him where she was going and be confident that he would stay put until her return.

"You *oll recht* up there?" Jed asked.

Nate flashed him an amused glance. "I'm fine. What's the matter? Getting tired of walking along beside the baler, Jed?"

"He can always trade places with me," Isaac said from where he steered the equipment.

"I'm fine," Isaac's older brother said with a scowl.

Laughing, Nate said, "Don't look fine to me." He looked across the property to where the other Lapp brothers were working another hay baler. "You can always switch with Elijah," he suggested, noting that Elijah was positioned on the baler like he was.

"You don't look fine, Nate," Isaac said. "You keep looking toward the *haus*. Something or someone there on your mind?"

"Jacob?"

"I was thinking that maybe you've been thinking about my cousin."

Nate froze. "Not likely. Jacob is the one who's hurt. Charlie is just here to help."

"I'm surprised you didn't ask Mae to come by."

Mae King was Nate's stepgrandmother. "The less people who know the better," Nate said. "Charlie was there when Jake had his accident. We worked out an arrangement for her to stay with him while I was working."

"And that's all?"

Nate's throat tightened. "*Ja*, that's all. What else would it be?"

Isaac flashed him a crafty look. "*Ja*, what else can it be?"

He noticed one of the Lapp twins, Jacob, driving the wagon of baled hay in their direction. "Wagon's full," Nate called, eager to end the conversation about Charlie. Did they see something in his expression that gave his thoughts away? He only wanted to help Charlie. There was nothing more to his friendship with her. Distracted, he started to climb down from the baler and slipped.

"You *oll recht*?" Isaac asked.

"Fine." But his heart beat rapidly as he recalled how easily someone could get hurt after a fall. His thoughts went again to Charlie. She'd been on his mind too often lately. But he got a chill as he envisioned her on the mower, the danger in which she'd placed herself. He scowled. Why couldn't he get her out of his thoughts? She wasn't his responsibility. After the way he'd failed Emma, he was the least one capable enough to help her.

"'Tis nice to see Charlie mothering Jacob," Isaac said, bringing up his cousin again.

Jed continued to walk beside the baler. "Apparently, she has some nurturing instincts."

Despite himself, Nate couldn't control a smile as he held up his gloved hands. "She made me wear these." He snorted. "To protect my hands."

Isaac laughed. "'Tis funny that she'd be thinking of safety when she is the one who frequently got hurt and into trouble."

"I haven't seen that side of her in a long time," he admitted.

"*Nay*, she's grown up." Isaac climbed down to walk

alongside the baler while Nate got up into the seat behind the horses and Jed hopped up to exchange places with his brother Elijah near the back of the machine.

"*Ja*, she is." Elijah stepped onto the wagon attached to Nate's hay baler, catching the block of hay as it came out. "Charlie will make someone a *gut* wife one day. Matt Troyer seems interested."

Nate's jaw tightened. "I didn't know they were friends."

"His brother is Nell's husband," Isaac pointed out. The baler started to move and Isaac followed alongside on foot. "Her birthday is soon. *Mam* will be hosting a surprise nineteenth birthday party for her the day before. You, Jacob and your family should come if Jake is feeling up to it." He mentioned a date.

"My family should be home by then. I'll talk with Jacob and let you know."

"No need," Isaac said. "There'll be plenty of food. Just come if you can, and be *willkomm*."

Nate clicked his tongue as he flicked the leathers to get his team of horses moving. As he drove, he found his mind wandering again to Charlie. *Nineteen years old. Not a girl, but a young woman.* He'd known it, of course, but somehow it seemed better for him to forget the age difference. Safer to think of her as a girl and not a woman. He tensed up at the memory of Isaac's teasing remarks. Yet, the image of her married to Matt with children of her own formed a knot in his belly. He forced it away, reminding himself of all the reasons that he shouldn't see Charlie as more than a girl…more than a friend.

Go to a surprise party for her? Why not? As long as Jacob was well enough. If not, they would stay home. It wasn't as if Charlie expected him to come. She didn't know about the party. If he attended, he could watch how she interacted with Matthew Troyer, to make sure he was someone who could make her happy…who could love and handle her, keeping her safe—and alive. The knot in his stomach intensified.

What could he give her for her birthday? He had a little time to think of something but still, he couldn't stop wondering about a gift.

The men grew silent as they worked. Nate was thoughtful as he drove down one row of cut hay then carefully maneuvered the baler onto the next row. What could he give Charlie that she would like? He recalled how she loved horses and the way she looked when he'd found her in the barn brushing the coat of a chestnut gelding.

A slow smile came to his lips as he had a germ of an idea. He could do it. He could make her something special that he was surc she'd enjoy.

"Christmas is almost here," Isaac commented. "I have no idea what to give everyone this year."

Elijah smirked. "You always give the right thing, *bruder*."

"What about you, Nate? Do you think you'll have another little *bruder* or sister by Christmas?"

Nate shook his head. "Not supposed to. Baby is due in January." Men usually didn't talk about women's business, but he didn't mind. The Lapp brothers were his friends, and they were willing to discuss most any topic.

Jedidiah chuckled. "Babies don't always come when they're supposed to."

"'Tis going to snow soon," Isaac mentioned, changing the subject.

"You don't want to talk about babies," Jed said with a chuckle.

"Not supposed to," Isaac grumbled.

"I hope it doesn't snow," Nate said, understanding that a new father-to-be might be nervous. "At least, not until my family's safely home again."

"We usually have snow before Christmas," Jed pointed out, and the others agreed.

Isaac grabbed a hay bale and tossed it behind him onto the flatbed of the wagon. "Perhaps we should think about cutting pine and holly before it does."

"Won't last if we cut too early," Jed said.

Conversation lagged after a while as they stayed busy to complete the work.

Two hours later the men finished making hay. The bales were carted to an area outside the storage barn where they were wrapped in plastic to protect them from the elements of the weather. Tomorrow morning he'd move the rest of them into the building on his own. Jed and Noah had already moved most of the bales inside, so the work should be easy.

"I appreciate your help today," he told his friends. "The job was done in half the time because of you."

"We didn't mind. 'Tis only one day," Jed said. He glanced toward the sky and noted the setting sun. "But I do need to get going. Sarah will have supper ready."

"Martha will, too," Elijah murmured.

The other brothers made the same comment about their wives.

The men walked toward the barnyard where their

vehicles were parked. "I'll come for the baler within the next couple of days," Jed said.

Nate nodded. "I'll be happy to bring it."

Jedidiah shook his head. "*Nay*, you've enough to worry about."

Minutes later the Lapp brothers left, and Nate headed toward the house. He wondered what Charlie was doing.

He pushed open the back door. No one was in the kitchen. *"Hallo?"* he called as he headed toward the great room. He entered to find Charlie and Jacob sitting close with only a small table between them. On the table surface sat a wooden board with six sides and slots with marbles. They hadn't heard him, as they were teasing each other while they played Aggravation. Hearing their shared laughter, Nate felt a kick to his gut. She was never that relaxed and carefree with him. But then, she and Jacob were close in age and it was only natural that they should like each other.

"Who's winning?" he asked loudly as he approached.

Charlie gasped and Jacob looked up with laughter. "I am," his brother said with a smug smile.

She returned her attention to Jacob. "Maybe this game, but I won the last five."

"Huh," Jacob muttered, and Nate chuckled, knowing that Charlie had spoken the truth.

He approached and stood over them. Charlie refused to meet his gaze, but he caught sight of a pulse fluttering at the base of her throat and wondered what she was thinking. "We're done making hay," he said.

She glanced up. "That's *gut*."

His lips twitched. "I wore the gloves you gave me

all afternoon." He remember how she'd had handed them to him this morning right before he'd left for the fields.

"You listen well." His reward was her crooked smile. "Sometimes," she teased.

"What's wrong with your hands?" Jacob asked.

"Not a thing, and apparently Charlie wanted to make sure they stay that way." Nate pulled up a chair and studied the board. He felt her tense up as he leaned closer. "You going to let Jake win?" he asked, focusing on her flushed face.

Jacob grinned. "*Ja*, she is."

Charlie suddenly stood. "I'm sorry. 'Tis late. I need to get home." She turned away and headed toward the kitchen.

"You intimidate her," Jacob said sharply.

He frowned. "*Nay*, I don't."

His brother bobbed his head. "*Ja*, you do."

"I don't mean to." Nate stood and left the room to go after her. He had many mixed feelings when it came to Charlie Stoltzfus, but the last thing he wanted to do was to scare her. When he entered the kitchen, she was putting away the last of the dishes.

"Charlie," he said gently.

She turned. "There is chicken corn chowder in the refrigerator," she replied briskly. "There should be enough for two meals. Tomorrow for breakfast, there are eggs and you can eat the biscuits I made today."

He watched her shift nervously about the room. "Charlie," he said softly, approaching to gently clasp her arm. "Tell me what's upsetting you."

She blinked as she jerked away. "Nothing. Why?"

Nate blew out a startled breath. "Are you afraid of me?"

"Nay," she said firmly. She eyed him with a level gaze that convinced him to believe her. His relief made him realize how happy he was that Jacob was wrong.

"Here's a grocery list." She handed it to him. "Just a few things that you could use." Her lips firmed. "You may want to consider buying meals that are easy to prepare." She bit her lip. "For when I'm not here."

He stiffened with his disappointment. "You're not coming tomorrow?"

Charlie wouldn't meet his gaze. "I have a few things to do."

"Christmas shopping?"

She shook her head. *"Nay."*

"I see." He knit his brow. "Will someone be here for Jacob?"

Her eyes briefly locked with his. "Probably Ellie again."

"I apologize if we've monopolized your time," he said gruffly.

She blinked. "You haven't. I came here to help because I wanted to."

He regarded her with tenderness. *"Danki."* He sharpened his gaze when she blushed and suddenly busied herself. She bustled about the room as if she needed to get all her work done. As if she didn't plan to return. He reached out to stop her frantic movement, his fingers surrounding her upper arm, turning her to face him. "Charlie. What is it? Why do I make you uncomfortable?"

Her green eyes bright, she shook her head. "You don't." Her smile lacked luster, and he was upset because she had to work hard to convince herself that it wasn't true. "I should get home."

He had made her uneasy. He nodded. "May I carry something for you?"

"*Nay*, I've only this plate," she said, referring to the dish she'd brought with the lemon pound cake.

He followed her outside and waited as she climbed into her pony cart. "I appreciate everything you've done for us," he told her, watching her closely.

"I would have done the same for anyone," she said quickly. Then with a flick of the reins, she left while Nate stood in the yard, staring after her, wondering why it bothered him so much that she'd gone.

Chapter Seven

The weather was usual for mid-November. The air was crisp and clean with a hint of the upcoming winter. The leaves that had changed to reds, oranges and golds were now gone. The evergreens were full and thick and ready for the upcoming Christmas season. Soon the holiday would be here with the bitter-cold temperatures.

Nate headed out to haul the hay bales inside. As he carried one in, he couldn't keep his thoughts from Charlie. She hadn't come to the house this morning. Ellie had come in her place, after Charlie had claimed she had something to do. Had she been telling the truth? Or had he overwhelmed her with his desire to make sure she stayed safe?

There was something about the young red-haired woman that tugged on his heartstrings. He couldn't get rid of the image of her lovely bright green eyes and pretty smile. She kept him on his toes. She had the ability to make those around her feel alive. Make him feel alive.

He stilled, his chest tight. It was wrong to think

about her this way. He needed to keep his goals in mind, to get on with his life, settle on the farm property he wanted to purchase and find a suitable wife. Someone he couldn't fail, a more mature woman ready to start a family with a new husband. A woman unlike Emma...*or Charlie.*

As he moved bales into the building, he thought about the surprise party in less than two weeks. His whole family was invited. Going to the party would be a good way to show their appreciation for everything Charlie had done for them. He'd attend, then step back, put distance between them. He needed to find a way to cease worrying, obsessing, about her. How else could he move on to marry and have a family?

The air no longer felt chilly as he perspired while he worked. As he came out of the storage structure for the umpteenth time, he decided there had to be an easier way to move the rest of the hay. The stack hadn't looked big before he'd started, but its appearance had been deceiving.

Nate went into the barn to look for something to make the job easier. Then he saw the wooden wagon that he and his siblings had used when they were children, the wagon his younger half-siblings now enjoyed. It was larger than an English red wagon; his father had made it for five young children to share.

Nate pulled the wagon outside and began to load it with hay bales from the stack. He was able to tote four bales in the wagon. In a short time he'd completed the work, satisfied that the hay would stay dry. As he put away the wagon, he debated whether or not he should grocery-shop. There was enough food for lunch, he decided. He could put off shopping until the afternoon.

While in the barn, he spied a pile of wood scraps in the back corner of an empty stall. He rummaged through the pile and found a block of wood that had been left over from a previous construction project. He examined the piece from all angles and decided it was just what he needed. It was perfect for carving into. Nate smiled. The smooth, hard surface would be the basis for what he had in mind for Charlie's birthday present. He retrieved his pocketknife and two pieces of sandpaper from a worktable then headed toward a bright corner of the barn where he sat down to work.

As the wood fell away in shavings, Nate grinned. The scent of wood and straw was thick in the air. He had a vision to create, and he found pleasure in the work as he brought it to life.

Would Charlie like his present? Why should he care whether or not she did? He had a feeling that she would, but he couldn't be certain.

Nate sighed as he continued to work his knife. Why did his every thought return to Charlie?

He focused on the task, trying to think of the young woman who continually slipped into his mind at the oddest moments. He was making her a birthday gift, he thought. Of course he'd be thinking of her.

He was surprised that he missed seeing her this morning. It shouldn't matter who came to sit with Jacob as long as he wasn't left alone.

Thoughts of Jacob reminded him that his brother had his follow-up appointment at noon. He hid the block and tools in a safe place before he headed to the house to wash up and change his clothes. He thanked God that he remembered the appointment before it was too late.

"Ellie, Jake has a noon doctor's appointment. We're going to head out now."

"I'll wait here until you come back," Charlie's sister said.

Nate smiled. "We shouldn't be too long."

"Jacob, your foot is healing," the doctor said. "The X-ray looks good. You should continue to stay off it as much as possible. It's still too early for the bone to knit."

"How long do I have to keep this boot on?" Jacob asked. His brother didn't like wearing it. He didn't see the need for it since he couldn't walk on it anyway.

"For a few weeks yet. I'd like you to come back in three weeks, when I'll take another X-ray." The man smiled. "You may walk with crutches but only if you're careful and only for very short periods of time."

Jacob looked pleased. "I'll be careful." As they left, he turned to Nate. "I'll have to wear this boot to Charlie's party," he said with a frown.

Nate opened the buggy door and helped his brother in. "You will, but it'll be fine. You can use the crutches as long as you don't overdo it."

"Why did I have to hear about the party from Ellie? Why didn't you tell me? She said that you knew."

"I'd planned to tell you. I've had a lot on my mind." He paused. "And I wanted to make sure you were up for it."

"I'll be fine."

"*Ja*, you will," Nate replied. "I'm sorry I didn't mention it sooner."

"Ellie said the whole family's been invited. Do you think *Mam* and *Dat* will want to go?"

"I'm sure they will." The thought of celebrating Charlie's birthday with her family and giving his present to her gave Nate pleasure.

"I need to get her a gift. I don't know how I'll get out to buy one," Jacob said morosely.

"We've got time." He paused. "I'll go shopping for you."

His brother brightened. *"Danki."*

"Any ideas on what to buy?"

Jacob thought for a moment. Suddenly his features warmed as he grinned. "A board game."

"Life on the Farm?" Charlie and Jacob had been immersed in the game when he'd come in the fields on more than one day. She'd played the game before but she didn't own it.

"She'd like that."

"Life on the Farm it is, then." Nate steered the horse toward home and passed a buggy along the way. He glanced over and froze.

"Is that Charlie?" Jacob asked.

"Looks like it."

"I wonder where she's going?"

"I have no idea. She didn't say what she'd be doing today." He frowned. She hadn't once glanced in their direction, which was odd because Charlie usually waved to everyone. Even him. Nate stifled the urge to go after her since Ellie was waiting for them at the house. He could drop Jacob off then look for Charlie. He couldn't shake the feeling that something was wrong.

Ellie had a meal waiting when they got to the house. Nate smiled his thanks as he helped his brother inside. He ate his peanut butter and jam sandwich then told

Ellie and Jacob that he was headed to the store. After retrieving money from his room, he came downstairs to find the two immersed in a card game. When he told them he was leaving, they acknowledged him with a small hand wave but didn't look up. He grinned. The two would be kept busy for hours.

Her heart wasn't in the task as Charlie meandered about the grocery store, finding the food items her mother wanted. She still hadn't heard about the teaching job. Her meeting with Bishop John the other day hadn't gone all that well. She'd tried not to dwell on it, but she couldn't help but worry.

John Fisher had listened quietly while she'd told him why she wanted to teach, while she tried to convince him that she was the right person for the job. Unfortunately, Bishop John hadn't given her much hope. He'd been candid to the point where it'd felt painful, reminding her about a teacher's duty to lead her students by good example. As if he wondered if she could be a responsible adult in the classroom.

Would she never escape her past? She'd been young when she'd gotten into scrapes, and it'd been a long time since she'd started to think before acting. The more she thought about her visit to see John, the worse she felt about her chances of being hired.

Tears stung her eyes and she blinked them away. All was not totally lost. *Yet*. The bishop hadn't denied her the job outright. In fact, he'd told her the decision would be made by the church elders. What upset her was that John hadn't offered to give her a recommendation.

Charlie took a jar of blackstrap molasses from the

store shelf and stared at it until the label blurred in her vision. She knew she'd be a great teacher, but she might never have the chance to show her community. She sniffed as she put the jar into her market basket then moved down the aisle.

"Charlie."

The deep, familiar voice startled her. "Nathaniel. I didn't expect to see you here."

He studied her intently. "Something's happened," he said. "What?"

"Nothing."

"'Tis not nothing." His voice was soft. "Tell me."

She blinked rapidly and wouldn't look at him. When his fingers touched her chin as he turned her gently to face him, she gasped.

"Charlie," he breathed.

She exhaled sharply. "I spoke with Bishop John about becoming teacher."

He nodded and waited for her to continue. Her skin warmed with his touch. "And what did he say?" he asked softly.

"That children needed to be led by a *gut* example," she said. "Then he reminded me about my bad behavior as a child and asked if I thought I could lead by *gut* example."

"And what did you tell him?"

"I told him I could." She scowled. "I'm not a child. I wish he'd see that. I know that students look up to their teacher. That if I'm teacher, they will look up to me. 'Tis a responsibility I'd take seriously."

Nate frowned. "Did he say that you wouldn't be considered?"

"Nay." She was shocked to realize that he was gen-

uinely upset for her. His nearness, his disappointment on her behalf, gave her tremendous comfort. "He said it was up to the elders to make the final decision."

His brow cleared. "Then have faith that you may still get the job."

Her head began to pound. "I don't think so. He didn't offer to put in a *gut* word for me."

"How can he? If he did it for you, he'd have to do it for all the other candidates." He eyed her compassionately. "You shouldn't take it to heart. He's right. Our church elders will make the final decision and they'll consider every single person who has shown an interest." He briefly caressed her cheek before he withdrew.

"Every single person?" She groaned.

"I'm sure no one wants to be our new *schuul*teacher more than you. And believe it or not, that will work in your favor."

Her mouth curved. "I can't know that for certain." She was surprised when he reached for her hand. She stifled a gasp of pleasure at the simple touch.

She didn't want to pull away. The warmth of his skin against hers gave her goose bumps. She liked him holding her hand. Probably too much.

His gaze remained tender as he rubbed his thumb lightly across her wrist. She became overwhelmed with feelings she shouldn't have, with wishing that Nate would see her as someone he found attractive. A woman, not a child. She sighed but managed to control her wayward thoughts. "What are you doing here?"

He arched an eyebrow as he held up a list. "Buying food. The same as you."

She looked away. "Ellie doing well at the *haus*?"

"*Ja*. When I left, she and Jacob were playing cards."

Charlie stifled her disappointment. Apparently, neither Nate nor Jake had missed her.

"Will you be coming tomorrow?" he asked quietly, his blue eyes focused on her.

"Do you want me to?"

"Jacob will want you to come." He tore his gaze away to search the store aisle. "And I want you to come." She saw him study his list then examine the food items on the shelf in front of him. "Jake likes the way you challenge him. He said it's no fun to win every game. Ellie can't beat him like you can."

She allowed her lips to curve. "You mean, I'm *gut* at games other than baseball?"

Would she be as good of a teacher as she was a game-player? Her smile fell. She thought she'd be good at teaching, but she might never get the chance to prove it.

Nate selected an item from the shelf. As if he'd sensed her dismay, he abruptly faced her. "Charlie, stop worrying." He gave her shoulder a quick, reassuring squeeze. "We are here to shop. Since we're both here at the same time, why don't we shop together?"

She shrugged. "Why not?"

It was fun food-shopping with Nate. The man teased her every time she pulled merchandise off the shelf. He asked her what she needed it for, and if she was certain the item was exactly what she wanted. He was so outrageous in his comments that eventually all she could do was grin at him and razz him back.

Nate was handsome. She'd never known anyone with his particular shade of blue eyes. Nate's seemed to change colors to every available vibrant shade of blue. Every time their gazes met her heart fluttered.

She was setting herself up for heartbreak. She knew it but she couldn't regret the way he made her feel—giddy and happy and more alive than ever before. She knew that he'd never think of her in that way, but she didn't care. As long as she had a legitimate excuse to spend time with him, she could enjoy his company without fear that he'd guess she had feelings for him.

They meandered about the store together, selecting the items and placing them in their market baskets. Charlie helped Nate find everything he needed and suggested a few other items that she'd forgotten to include on his list. He bought whatever she told him to, which pleased her.

Charlie was feeling better by the time the cashier had rung up their purchases and they headed out the door. "I'll stay with Jacob," she said once Nate and she were outside in the sun. "If you really want me to."

His blue eyes flashed briefly. "I do."

She felt warm and shivery as they headed toward the hitching post behind the building where they'd parked their buggies. She loaded her grocery bags in the back of her vehicle, then faced him. "I'll see you tomorrow."

Nate hesitated. It seemed as if he wanted to say more. "I'll tell Jake you'll be by in the morning," he finally said.

Disappointed, she climbed into her buggy, waved, then left for home, wishing she could have spent more time with him, wondering if he'd be around for her to see him tomorrow.

He watched as Charlie drove away before he climbed into his wagon. The sight of her tears earlier had ripped through him like fire. She was upset and he hated it. There was nothing he could do but he wished there was. She had forbidden him to talk with his deacon father about her desire to become teacher. But what if he spoke with someone else? He wouldn't be breaking his promise to her, and it might make a difference for her if he told John everything she'd been doing for him and Jacob. He knew Bishop John well. Would it really hurt for him to talk with the man?

He had to get back. Ellie waited for him. She was no doubt eager to go home.

Ellie sat alone at the kitchen table, sipping tea, when he carried in the groceries ten minutes later.

"Jacob's napping," she said when he entered the house.

"He *oll recht*?"

"*Ja*, he's fine. He was tired." She grinned. "Probably of winning every single game." Her expression filled with concern. "He was hurting but wouldn't take his pain medication. I gave him aspirin with a mug of sweetened hot milk."

Nate smiled. *"Danki."* He started to unbag groceries. "Ellie, when I'm done putting these away, I'd like to run one more errand. It won't take long. I know you've been here all day."

"'Tis fine, Nate. Go ahead. I've no jobs today. I don't mind staying longer." She stood and reached for the other two bags. "Go. I'll put these away for you."

He beamed at her. "I'll be back soon."

A short time afterward Nate knocked on the bishop's door. It was John himself who answered. "Sally and Nicholas are sleeping," his friend and church elder said quietly after they'd greeted each other. "Come in." He gestured toward the kitchen table. "Want coffee?"

"I wouldn't mind a cup." Nate smiled his thanks when John shoved the sugar bowl and pitcher of milk toward him after he handed him a filled mug.

"Is this a social visit? Or do you have something on your mind?"

"Something on my mind," he admitted. "Actually, someone. Charlie Stoltzfus."

The bishop narrowed his gaze. "What trouble has the girl gotten into now?"

Nate nearly choked as he tried to swallow his sip of coffee. "*Nay*, you've got it wrong. Charlie hasn't been in trouble for years." And he suddenly realized the truth. He'd been telling himself that she was young and reckless, but that was a long time ago. He sighed, hoping this would make up for the way he'd misjudged her. "I heard she's interested in the teaching position at our *schuul*. I thought it might help for you to know a few things about her."

John leaned forward, looking interested. "The church elders have already selected a replacement, but tell me anyway."

Nate explained about Jacob's accident and Charlie's help. "She'd make a fine teacher," he said sincerely. "I'm sorry that I came too late."

The bishop smiled as he leaned back in his chair. "I'm glad to hear how you feel about her. She needs someone like you in her life."

"She's just a friend," Nate insisted, stiffening.

John nodded. "Still, I'm glad you came to tell me. 'Tis always nice to hear *gut* things about a church member." He rose and refilled his coffee cup. "The church elders have already made their choice. Unfortunately, I can't say until after we make an offer."

"I see." He rose. "I appreciate your time, John."

"We've known each other a long time. Your *dat* has been deacon for years. We're friends. I always make time for my friends and fellow church members." John followed him to the door. "And Nate? I didn't say it was too late. I said that the elders have made their choice."

Nate brightened with hope. "Do you mean…?"

"The elders have made their choice," the bishop said with a smile. "You'll find out after she does."

Nate offered up a silent prayer that Charlie would get her wish. The bishop made him wonder. If she didn't get the position, then he'd have to find a way to cheer her up. His parents would be home soon, and there would no longer be a reason for Charlie to return…unless his *mam* still wanted her to mind Mae and Harley. He was going to miss seeing her every day. A fact he'd have to get used to if she did become teacher with little time for babysitting or anything else.

He would make arrangements to buy that farm tomorrow. No sense in waiting. He had a future to plan… without Charlie. His pleasure dimmed as he pulled into the barnyard. Ellie was inside, waiting to go home. He wished it was Charlie in the house, then he could find an excuse to keep her awhile longer. Suddenly, he wanted to spend as much time as he could with her… before time ran out and she was gone.

He greeted Ellie as he entered the house. "Jacob still sleeping?"

"*Ja*, I have a feeling he'll be up soon." She grabbed her traveling cape. "You be *oll recht* if I head home?"

"We'll be fine."

Ellie smiled. She was a pretty woman with blond hair and blue eyes, but she didn't catch his interest as much as her sister did with her red hair and bright green eyes. "I have to work, but Charlie should be back tomorrow." She studied him for several long seconds. "If she can't come, I can ask Nell."

Nate stiffened but managed to smile. "We should be able to manage on our own."

"It might be best if Charlie comes until your *eldre* come home." She put on her traveling bonnet.

He felt his chest tighten. "You're probably right."

"She needs a man, Nate. Someone like you. Any suggestions?"

"Are you talking about Jacob?"

She shrugged. "Maybe. Maybe not. You know my sister. Do you think she and Jake would be happy together?" Ellie left then, leaving Nate stewing over the suggestion that his brother could make Charlie happy.

Was she suggesting that Charlie and Jacob would be a good match?

His mind rebelled at the thought, but there were worse prospects for Charlie's affection than Jacob. His brother was a good, kind man, and Charlie might be happy with him.

But how could he accept her as his sister-in-law when he wanted her for himself?

He and Jacob enjoyed a leftover supper that Charlie had prepared the day before. Nate studied his brother as Charlie's prospective husband. Jacob and Charlie got along well. They laughed and teased one another while they played games.

Charlie had tensed whenever Nate pulled up a chair

to watch them play…until recently when he and she had enjoyed shopping together.

Nate sighed. He wanted to be the right man for Charlie but he wasn't. That night, as he stared at the ceiling, he considered every young man within their Amish community who could possibly be a good match for Charlie. One by one, he dismissed most of them as unsuitable. There were only two men who might be good enough for her—his brother Jacob and Matt Troyer, her brother-in-law's brother.

He hated the thought of her with either man.

He wanted to be the one who cared for her, teased her. He loved watching her eyes light up whenever she was happy.

Even if she married someone else, he'd get to see her on Sundays. It wasn't what he wanted, but it was something. Nate groaned and covered his eyes with his arm. He wanted to wed Charlie…but he was afraid. He felt the pain of knowing he'd failed in the past. He couldn't do it again. He couldn't fail Charlie as he'd failed Emma.

Chapter Eight

Saturday morning Charlie headed over to the Peachy farm, her thoughts on the day ahead. Something had happened between her and Nate in the store yesterday. A turning point in their relationship, a warm kind of friendship that she'd enjoyed, maybe too much. He'd seemed to like her company as they'd shopped. They'd laughed as they chose groceries and teased each other whenever one of them picked something off the shelf that they didn't need or want. He'd made her feel better about her meeting with the bishop, but whatever happened, she knew she'd get over it. Teaching wasn't the only thing she could do. She could take other work, perhaps working for Ellie cleaning houses.

The air had grown colder, reminding her that it was nearly Christmas. She needed to decide what to give everyone. She could make something for her sisters, but it was harder to think of a gift for their husbands. For her parents, she'd buy something special. Maybe she'd make *Mam* a new apron, then she'd purchase a toy for the dog her father loved so much that he'd brought it in from the barn to live in the house.

Once again her thoughts turned to Nate, as they did a lot lately. She'd like to give him something—and to Jacob, too. She'd spent time with both of them this month, and they'd become friends. It just felt right to give a gift to her friend. Except she wanted more with Nate, although she'd never tell him unless he told her first that he felt the same way.

She pulled up to the house and climbed out. Nate came out of the barn and waved to her.

"Charlie!" His smile made her heart sing. "I'm glad you came." His face changed, filling with concern as he drew closer. "How are you?"

"I'm fine. No matter what happens I'll be fine."

Her breath caught when his mouth widened into a grin. "That's the best way to think. Have you had breakfast?" he asked, startling her.

"*Nay*, I thought I'd fix us something." She held up a plate. "And *Mam* sent muffins."

"I'd like to make you eggs."

She eyed him with shock. "You want to cook for me?"

He nodded. "You've done so much for us. I'd like to do something for you."

"You don't have to do that." She swallowed against a tight throat.

"I want to." His words made her heart beat more rapidly. He placed his hand at the small of her back as they walked toward the house together.

She halted at the back door. "Nathaniel, are you sick?"

He frowned. "*Nay*. Why do you ask?"

"You're being nice to me. You want to *cook* for me."

He shrugged but amusement glimmered in his blue eyes. "I'm sorry I've been such an ogre."

"*Nay,* I didn't mean that." She bit her lip, conscious of his nearness and loving every moment. "'Tis just that you like to—"

"Tease you?"

"I was going to say 'taunt' but I guess you were only teasing."

Nate bobbed his head. "I like teasing you."

She tilted her head as she gazed up at him. "Why?"

"Because you rise to the bait so quickly."

Understanding made her laugh. "I do, don't I?"

"*Ja,* you do."

They exchanged grins.

The new warmth in their relationship made her happy. "Well, now that I know, it's going to be harder to get a rise out of me."

"Will it?" he said as he reached around her to open the door.

The kitchen was warm and bright as the sun shone through the windows—one over the sink and one next to the back entrance.

Nate gestured toward the kitchen table. "Have a seat."

Charlie studied him. "Why do you want to feed me?"

"I told you… I want to do something nice for you."

"Wouldn't it have been easier to buy me an ice cream?"

His dark eyes gleamed. "You like ice cream? Perhaps another day after the weather warms again." Then something in his gaze clouded, and Charlie understood. She would no longer be around him then. He and she would never eat ice cream or do anything else together after his parents came home.

Jacob used crutches as he entered the kitchen from the other room. "*Gut* morning, Charlie."

She smiled at him warmly. "How are you feeling?"

"Better," he said as he pulled out a chair and sat down. His brows rose as he watched his brother take eggs out of the refrigerator and place a pan on the stove. "You're making breakfast?"

She shrugged when she met Jacob's gaze. "Apparently, he wants to do something *nice* for me."

Jacob's eyes narrowed as he turned back to his brother. "You want to do something nice for Charlie?" he asked doubtfully.

Without deviating from the task, Nate nodded. "And you."

Jacob leaned close to her ear. "I wonder what's come over him?"

She laughed. "I asked if he was sick," she whispered. Nate spun to gaze at them through narrowed eyes. She grinned at him. "Your *bruder* is wondering what's come over you," she told him.

He stared at his brother. "I've cooked for you before."

"True, but not when there was a woman in the kitchen."

"*Mam* was near."

"That's different."

Nate scowled. "I want to do something nice for her. What's wrong with that?"

Charlie regarded him softly. "Nothing, Nathaniel. Nothing at all. In fact, I like it." She smirked. "I might expect it more often."

His gaze grew tender. "We'll see, little one."

She frowned. Was he reminding her of their age difference? As far as she was concerned, there was no difference.

"What do you have to do today, Nate?" Jacob asked.

"Just a few farm chores and there's work to be done inside."

Charlie jerked as she stared at him. "You don't need me to stay."

"*Ja*, I do," he assured her. "I need someone to keep an eye on this one. If not, he's liable to get into trouble."

She relaxed. "Can't get into trouble if we're playing Aggravation."

Jacob laughed. "You mean if I beat you at every game we play."

"You wish." Charlie sensed Nate's gaze on her. She saw a flicker of emotion that he quickly masked.

He set a plate of scrambled eggs, sausage and toast before her and Jacob. "Enjoy," he said huskily before he turned back to the stove. She watched as he washed up the utensils and pans he used and set them to drain.

"Aren't you joining us?" she asked as he started to dry and put everything away.

"No time," Nate said.

She didn't understand. Then why did he stop to fix her breakfast? Nathaniel Peachy was a confusing man. A kind and complex man, who was thoughtful and wonderful, and she liked him. But there were times she didn't understand him at all. She stood to help him.

"Sit," he ordered. "Eat before your food gets cold."

"Nate."

"You've got games to play and I have work to do."

She eyed him with concern. "Nate. Is something bothering you?"

His smile didn't quite reach his blue gaze. "I'm fine."

Charlie nodded and let him be. There was nothing

else she could do. She watched him leave the room and heard him go upstairs. If she knew what had upset him, maybe she could help.

Jacob was clearly enjoying the breakfast that Nate had made for him. He seemed oblivious to his brother's mood, and he had always impressed her as a man who was quick with his concern.

Moments later Nate entered the kitchen on his way out the door. "I thought I'd go to the store first. Anything either of you need?"

Charlie shook her head. "I'm fine." She experienced a sniggle of uneasiness when he didn't look at her. "Didn't you buy everything you needed yesterday?"

He met her gaze. "I wouldn't be going to the store if I had, would I?"

His sharp tone made her stomach burn as the brothers exchanged looks before Nate left. She watched him go with a disturbing feeling of loss. She shouldn't feel this way. It wasn't as if she had his affection to begin with.

Jacob reached for his coffee. "Aggravation, Dutch Blitz or Life on the Farm?" There was a twinkle and challenge in his blue eyes so like his brother's.

She managed to laugh. "Doesn't matter. You pick. I'll trounce you in whatever we play."

Nate climbed into his buggy, his heart aching. Charlie and Jacob got along well together. His brother was a good man, and while it would kill him to see them married and with children, he understood that Jacob would make Charlie a good husband. Not that he would shove Jake in Charlie's direction. He would step back and watch it happen…and deal with the pain of seeing it all take place.

He steered his horse toward the new general store just outside Happiness. The shop had a great hardware section and he needed a new doorknob for his sister's bedroom. On the way there, he passed the farm he wanted to purchase and decided to stop and speak with the owner to make an offer on the land. To his delight, the man accepted it. Pleased, Nate continued to the store, then shopped with heightened spirits. He easily found what he needed then meandered through the rest of the shop looking for something for Jacob to give Charlie for her birthday. He still had work to do on the horse he'd carved for her, but there was time yet to finish it up.

He looked for the game aisle and finally saw all of their Amish community favorites. The only game that Charlie didn't have was Life on the Farm. He grabbed the box and continued down the row. He wished he could think of another gift for Charlie, something special. What if she didn't like the hand-carved figure?

His thoughts grew dark as he completed his purchase. Why should it matter whether or not she liked his gift? It wasn't as if she'd ever belong to him. She'd find a suitor and marry someone else. He scowled. Jacob.

The air stayed chilly and he knew he'd have to think about Christmas sooner than expected. As he drove toward home, he forced his feelings for Charlie from his mind and made a mental list of the tasks that needed to be done today. He needed to paint the outside window he'd recently replaced but the temperature was too cold. He'd fix his sister's bedroom doorknob, then tackle the various other items that needed to be done inside. He didn't really want to work in the house. Watching Charlie and Jacob together made his gut wrench.

A half hour later, as Nate worked on replacing the door, Charlie exited his room with a basket of laundry. "What are you doing?" he snapped irritably.

She halted and stared at him. "The wash."

"You don't have to do mine."

He saw hurt flash in her pretty green eyes and felt mean. "I've been doing it for nearly a week, Nate," she said quietly. "I like washing clothes." She paused and her face turned pale. "You don't want me to touch your garments."

He closed his eyes and struggled to soften his tone. "You don't have to."

"I know," she said and started toward the stairs.

His thoughts in turmoil, he returned to the work, turned the screwdriver one last time to tighten it and cried out as his tool slipped with the end digging into his finger.

Charlie was suddenly beside him, her expression concerned, her laundry basket on the floor next to her. "What happened?"

"A bit of an accident. I'm fine."

She gazed down at the redness of his injury and grabbed his other hand. "Downstairs now."

The last thing he needed or wanted was to be this close to Charlie. *"Nay,"* he snapped. "I said I'm fine."

She jerked as if struck. "I see." She retrieved the laundry basket and started to descend the stairs, pausing on one to scold, "I wasn't expecting anything from you, Nathaniel Peachy. I would have offered to help anyone!"

Then she left him standing in the hallway, his heart aching, his chest hurting. He put the screwdriver away, then waited a moment to get his emotions under control. He heard the washer lid slam, realized that even while angry, she had put his dirty laundry in to wash. With a sigh of regret, Nate went down to check on Jacob. His brother was asleep. Apparently, Charlie's fit of temper, although justified, hadn't disturbed Jacob in the least.

Wound tighter than a metal coil, Nate drew in a calming breath then entered the kitchen. She barely looked at him as she prepared a meal on the stove. Feeling properly chastened, he left the house for the barn. Where he had things to do, he assured himself. Finishing Charlie's present was just one of them.

A light snow fell Sunday morning as Charlie and her family climbed into their buggy and headed toward church service. Her cousin Elijah and his wife, Martha, were hosting today. *Mam* and Ellie had fixed side dishes for the shared community meal after church. Before she'd left the Peachy house yesterday, she had made a bowl of macaroni salad for Nate and Jacob to bring. The macaroni salad had turned out well. Jacob had tasted it and proclaimed it delicious while threatening to eat every bit. Coming in from outside, Nate had gazed at the huge bowl then studied her with a thoughtful look that made her uncomfortable. Tension had hung in the air between them, bringing her to the verge of tears, but she managed not to cry. At his brother's urging, Nate had tasted it then given her a compliment. As his small praise raised her spirits, she'd realized that she was deeply affected by his moods.

Cradling a dried apple pie, Charlie stared out the window as her father drove the buggy. The scent of cinnamon and apples drifted to her nose, tempting her to take a taste, but she didn't. She couldn't eat even if she wanted to. She felt butterflies at the prospect of seeing Nate. Maybe later, after service, she'd feel well enough to eat.

She enjoyed church as she looked around Elijah and Martha's great room, happy to see her family and friends and neighbors. Across the room in the men's section sat Jacob and Nathaniel. Nate held his brother's arm as Jacob stood, propped up on his crutches. Jacob glanced over at her and smiled. Her lips curved before her gaze settled on his older brother. As if sensing her study, Nate locked gazes with her. She caught her breath as she nodded then turned away. Heart racing wildly, she joined in to sing another hymn from the *Ausbund.* And silently prayed to get what she wanted most. The teaching job and a life with Nate.

Bishop John Fisher spoke during the service, followed by Preacher Levi. When it was over, Charlie joined the women in bringing out the food for the shared meal. She heard talk of her cousins organizing a baseball team. Normally, Charlie would have been eager to join in. But not this day. If she wanted to be teacher and to earn others' respect, she needed to be responsible and act her age. When Isaac came looking for her to play, she politely declined with the excuse that she wasn't up to it today. The day was warmer than it had been yesterday. When she peeked through the window to see how the game was going, she saw the young men of the community wearing their long white shirts with their black Sunday best vests and pants. The last thing she should do was play baseball in her Sunday best dress and slide in the dirt to score a home run. Her mother would tolerate it, simply because she was a loving parent, but *Mam* wouldn't be happy if her good clothes got dirty or ripped.

She turned away from the sight and gasped. Nate Peachy stood behind her with a tense look on his handsome face. "What's wrong? Is it Jacob?"

The man shook his head. "Jacob's fine." He was silent as he moved toward the window and glanced outside. "Why aren't you playing baseball?"

Charlie gave him a twisted smile. "Not feeling up to it. Besides, I'm wearing my church clothes and *Mam* won't appreciate it if I play in them." And she knew he didn't approve.

He turned from the window to study her intently. A small smile curved his lips. "I suppose she wouldn't."

"Jacob must be disappointed that he can't play."

"I'm sure he is but he'll get back to it eventually."

As she joined him at the window, Charlie sighed, for she had a feeling that her baseball-playing days were over.

"Charlie—" His voice rumbled from beside her. There was something so private about standing so close to him.

She met his gaze. *"Ja?"*

He shook his head.

She frowned. "Your family will be home soon?"

"Ja. I got a message that my *grossmudder* is doing better. They'll be home this week."

"I see." She knew a sharp disappointment.

"I appreciate all you've done for us."

The gratitude in his gaze bothered her. "It wasn't any trouble."

"Charlie!" a familiar voice called from across the room.

"My sister's demanding my attention. I guess *Mam* and *Dat* are ready to leave." She forced a smile. "I'll see you tomorrow." *Unless you don't want me.* She started to walk away then stopped after Nate gently clasped her arm.

"Danki," he said softly with heartfelt thanks.

"Charlie!" Ellie called, waving her to come.

"I've got to go." She walked a few steps then halted to face him. Her face warmed at the look in his eyes. "I'll see you tomorrow." Then she flashed him a grin and left. Snow started to fall as her father steered their buggy home.

The next morning, bright and early after doing her chores, Charlie arrived at the Peachy residence. Yesterday's snow lay across the ground like a transparent white blanket. She entered the house, and Nate murmured a quick greeting to her before he left her alone to spend time with Jacob. She didn't mind. Jacob was good company and despite how frustrating it must be for him with the boot on his foot, he was pleasant and fun to be with. Which didn't mean she didn't long to spend time with Nate.

Nate didn't come in for lunch. She knew he was working in the barn so she made him a sandwich and poured him a cup of coffee, then headed out to give it to him while Jake tucked in for a nap.

She felt a burst of nervous excitement as she carried Nate's lunch across the yard. Yesterday he'd wanted her here.

It was dark inside the barn when she entered. Not wanting to frighten him, Charlie called out. "Nate! I've brought you something to eat!"

He popped his head up over one of the barn stalls. "Charlie. What are you doing here?"

His brow furrowed, he sounded annoyed.

An ache settled within her chest. "I brought you lunch. I know you're busy." She set the plate and cup on a table outside a stall several yards away. "I'll just leave it here." Her throat felt tight. She was just trying to do something nice for him. She spun to leave. "I'll see you later."

She had taken only a few steps when he was beside her. "Charlie." She looked up at him, saw tenderness in his expression. She blinked, sure it would be gone when she gazed at him again. To her astonishment, he reached out to cup her cheek. "You brought me lunch."

She nodded, aware of the way her skin tingled where he touched her. "I wasn't sure, but I thought you might be hungry."

He smiled as she stepped back, and she felt the loss of his warmth. "I am. *Danki*."

She hesitated. It was none of her business what he was doing, but she admitted to herself that she was curious. "Do you need any help?"

He frowned. "Where's Jacob?"

"Resting."

Nate shook his head. "I'm managing fine, Charlie. You should get back inside in case Jacob needs you."

She walked away, feeling as if she'd been scolded. Then anger lit a fire in her, and she spun. "You know something, Nathaniel Peachy? I don't know what to say or how to act around you! You can be wonderfully kind one minute then cold and unfeeling the next!"

Then she turned and hurried out, blinded by tears. So she'd told him off. So what? It wasn't as if she'd had a prayer that he'd want a relationship with her. Still, as she ran toward the house, she prayed that she would be proven wrong and that Nate would one day see her as someone he could love and marry. She sniffed. She shouldn't want that, but she couldn't help herself. Her heart wanted him, and she couldn't control it.

Nate returned to the house not long after she did. She was embarrassed by her early outburst. "You can head home," he said gruffly.

And so she left. She wondered if he'd want her back but she didn't ask, certain that he was angry enough to want her to stay away.

Her mother looked relieved to see her when she got home. *"Gut!"* she exclaimed. *"Endie* Katie has invited us for supper, and I was afraid you'd be late. She wants to pick holly and cut pine for Christmas after we eat."

Charlie frowned. "It's only three o'clock."

"She invited us for four thirty," *Mam* said.

"Plenty of time." Enough for her to put on clean clothes. "Is Ellie home?"

"Ja. She came home at noon."

She nodded. "I'm going upstairs and wash up a bit."

"How is Jacob?"

"Gut. He's doing much better."

"When are Abram and Charlotte due back?"

"Any day." Abram's wife, Charlotte King Peachy, had the same first name as hers, which was why everyone within the community called her Charlie since her family's move to Happiness, her father's boyhood home, years ago. She didn't mind the nickname; she was young then, and the name had seemed to fit.

They headed toward her aunt Katie's shortly after. She wondered why they were going so early, but then she recalled that the days were getting shorter, and she figured that her father didn't want to drive in the dark. Just last week he'd heard about a terrible buggy accident toward New Holland. It had been dark, and the family had put on their running lights; yet, a car had come up from behind them and hit them, forcing the vehicle off the road. Sometimes one had to go out in the dark, but still it made one think twice after hearing of such a terrible accident. All four Amish members had been hospitalized. They had survived but with serious injuries. Bishop John had mentioned them during church yesterday and asked everyone to remember them in their prayers. Charlie had. She'd thought about them this morning and asked the Lord to grant them a speedy recovery.

There were three other buggies in the Samuel Lapp barnyard when they arrived.

"Your cousins," her mother told her before she could ask.

Charlie smiled. She couldn't wait to see her cousins and their wives. She saw them at church service, but there was never enough time to do more than briefly chat with them. Ellie climbed out of the buggy first and grabbed the pie from her.

"I don't know about you, but I'm hungry," her sister said.

"I could eat." Charlie climbed out and reached for the pie. Ellie shook her head and told her she'd carry it in.

The door swung open as Charlie climbed the porch steps, reaching it first. "Charlie!" Her cousin Hannah grinned at her. She was the youngest member of the Lapp family and the only daughter in a family of eight children. "Come in!" The girl glanced over her shoulder. "Charlie's here!" she called.

Suddenly, she was being dragged into the great room, where she faced a mass of familiar faces. "Surprise!" everyone called. "Happy birthday!"

Charlie felt her jaw drop as shock rendered her speechless. Her married sisters, Nell, Meg and Leah, were there with their husbands. All of her cousins were present as well as the Zooks, the Troyers and the Kings. She experienced a jolt of pleasure when her gaze encountered Nate Peachy, who stood next to Jacob, steadying his brother on crutches. He smiled and mouthed "Happy birthday."

Behind the brothers was their family, who must have returned within the last hour. She suffered a heavy heart as she forced herself to smile brightly. There would be no more time with Jacob. *No more time with Nate.*

"Are you *oll recht*?" Nell asked. As if sensing something wrong, her eldest sister had approached silently from behind.

She nodded, still without speaking. Everyone was looking at her, and she was the center of attention, this time not because of trouble but for something good. Still, it wasn't happy she felt. It was sadness because of Nate. But she would force herself to be happy for her aunt and uncle and everyone who had come to celebrate her birthday.

"First time I've known Charlie to be speechless!" her cousin Isaac called out.

Everyone laughed. Charlie, face red, eyed her cousin. "Don't get used to it, Isaac!" she shot back, which made everyone roar with laughter. Even Nate Peachy laughed and looked amused.

"Food's ready," her aunt declared, and everyone dispersed.

Her father approached and studied her warmly. "Nineteen. My youngest *dochter* is nineteen. 'Tis hard to believe."

"Because I still act as I did when I was fourteen?"

He shook his head. "*Nay*, because you're a woman now and I want to keep my little girl."

"Ah, *Dat*." She became emotional.

Her father drew a sharp breath. "I'm not ready for you to marry."

Charlie jerked. "Who says I'll marry?"

"You will when the right man comes along," her mother said as she slipped her arm around her waist.

"I doubt anyone would be brave enough to take me on," Charlie said drily.

"By some of the looks you've been getting today, I can tell you you're mistaken." *Mam* nodded toward the corner of the room. "Jacob Peachy seems fond of you."

She smiled. "Jacob and I are *gut* friends." And it wasn't Jacob who had grabbed her interest; it was his older brother. An impossible situation.

"Charlie, come and eat," her cousin Hannah urged.

"I'm coming." Her mother released her and joined her father. Hannah grabbed her arm and tugged her toward the food table in the kitchen. Charlie glanced back and saw her parents' amusement with Hannah as they followed them into the other room.

They ate a delicious meal of Charlie's favorite foods—fried chicken, mashed potatoes, corn, coleslaw, fresh yeast rolls and fried apples. After filling their plates with food, everyone moved back to the great room to eat. Charlie stood off to the side, picking at her meal while watching everyone in the room. She'd been greatly moved that her aunt would host a birthday party for her, that everyone had come and seemed to be having a good time. *Nineteen.* She was nineteen years old, and she had yet to figure out what she would do with her life if she didn't manage the next step, which was to be teacher at their Happiness School. Today was for celebration, she reminded herself. Not for contemplating all the reasons that she wasn't going to get the job.

Someone approached from her left side—Matt Troyer, her brother-in-law James Pierce's half-brother. "Aren't you going to open your presents?" he asked with a grin.

Charlie shook her head as horror clutched her chest. She didn't want to open presents in front of everyone. "'Tis not my birthday until Wednesday," she reasoned.

Her gaze swept across the room, zooming in on Nate Peachy, the man who'd stolen her heart and made her breath catch. Matt hadn't moved. He watched her with a glimmer of admiration. She was flattered, but she didn't need his attention as other than a friend.

She turned her head to find Nate studying her. His expression was unreadable.

"Is there cake?" she asked Matt. "I love cake. Don't you?"

Charlie continued to feel Nate's gaze as she and Matt left the room for the kitchen, where cake, pies and a number of other desserts sat out on the counter.

Chapter Nine

Nate watched Charlie with Matt Troyer and endured a painful squeezing in his chest. Jacob, Matt… Who else noticed and appreciated Charlie Stoltzfus? He had no right to be upset—or to be jealous. She needed a man her own age, someone she could rely on, and it looked as if there were a number of potential beaus vying for her affection.

"Aren't you going to eat?" Jacob asked, eyeing Nate's plate. "You've barely touched your food."

He shrugged as he dug into his mashed potatoes with a fork. "Not hungry. You want to eat mine?"

"*Nay.* I have room enough for dessert." His brother grinned. "I want some of Charlie's birthday cake."

Nate caught his brother eyeing Charlie with a smile. "Doesn't it bother you?"

Jacob frowned. "What?"

"Seeing Charlie and Matt together."

He made a dismissive sound. "They are in-laws," Jacob said. "Besides, Charlie and I are just friends."

And heading toward something more, Nate thought with a grimace.

Hannah approached them with a look of displeasure. "Charlie won't open her gifts. She said it's not her birthday yet."

"Want me to talk with her?" Jacob offered.

"Would you?" The young teen looked up at him with a glimmer of hero worship.

Nate sighed. "Leave her be. I think she's uncomfortable with all of the attention." He sympathized with her. He wouldn't have been comfortable being the center of attention, either. Fortunately, he didn't have to worry about anyone throwing him a surprise birthday party. He was too old for one.

"I can still try if you want," Jacob said, although he seemed to understand and appreciate what Nate was telling him.

Hannah shook her head. "*Nay.* We'll let her open her gifts on her birthday." She paused. "At home."

Nate saw Charlie exit the kitchen with a small plate and a huge grin on her face. Matt said something to make her chuckle as she pushed a fork into a piece of frosted angel food cake. She lifted a bite of cake to her mouth and placed it daintily between her lips. He watched as she chewed and swallowed, then as she murmured something that made Matt laugh.

Unable to stop himself, Nate approached. "Is that angel food cake?" he asked with a gentle smile.

He saw Charlie stiffen as Matt answered, "*Ja*, with maple syrup whipped cream." He took a quick bite then finished, "Charlie's favorite cake."

Matt saw someone across the room and he excused himself to talk with Barbara Zook, Annie Lapp's younger sister.

Nate was surprised to see Charlie blush. Because

she was embarrassed over her enjoyment of cake? When she wouldn't look at him directly, he reached for her plate. "You'll share, won't you?"

Charlie's eyes shot daggers, and Nate chuckled. "I wouldn't steal your cake, Charlie." He eyed her with warmth. "Unless you wanted me to."

Her brows drew together in confusion. He gave in to the urge and swiped his finger to grab a dollop of whipped cream off her plate. He closed his eyes as he brought it up to his mouth and tasted. "Delicious."

"Don't," she warned him when he reached for more whipped cream.

He grinned at her. She stared at him in shock, then comprehension. "You're teasing me."

He nodded. "You said I couldn't get another rise out of you."

"You like it?"

"*Ja.* Who made it?"

"My sister Nell. She knows it's my favorite. It wouldn't be my birthday celebration without angel food cake with maple syrup whipped cream."

The two of them stood alone. Matt hadn't come back, and Nate was miffed with him. Clearly, he wasn't the right man for Charlie. He'd abandoned her for Barbara.

"You should get a piece," she told him, "before it's gone."

Nate saw Matt heading in their direction from across the room. "*Ja,* I suppose I should," he said politely as Matt joined them with a smile. He didn't feel any better with Matt's return.

There'd be no birthday cake for Nate. He'd lost what little appetite he'd had. *Happy birthday, Charlie.* She was a lovely woman. Not a girl—a woman, and he'd been making excuses about their age difference when he knew the real reason was Emma…and his past.

It was still light outside, but it wouldn't be for long. Needing some fresh air, Nate slipped out of the house to take a walk. When he returned inside, he accidentally overheard a conversation between Charlie and her sisters.

"Jacob's been paying you a lot of attention," Ellie said, teasing Charlie.

"So has Matt Troyer," Meg added with a smile.

"You have a number of handsome young men interested in you," Nell said.

Charlie waved them off. "Don't be ridiculous. They're my friends. They're not interested in me in that way."

Nate closed his eyes as he turned away. He had seen the way the men regarded Charlie. Did she really not see their interest? He scowled. She could have her pick of them whenever she wanted.

He slipped outside again. This time snow was falling as he escaped to the barn to seek solace in the silence of a familiar place. The sounds of the farm animals shifting around, the noises they made individually, soothed him. He didn't know how long he was there, but when he came outside it was past dusk and the snow was heavier. He spied someone standing near the fence, watching the horses that had yet to be brought in. *Charlie.*

Pulled in her direction, he approached, noting the slump of her slim shoulders. "Charlie," he murmured softly so as not to scare her. He slipped in to rest against the fence beside her. "Needed a few moments alone?" he asked when she didn't say anything.

She looked up at him with glistening green eyes and nodded. "It's a little overwhelming in there."

He stifled the strongest urge to pull her into his arms for comfort. He leaned against the fence rail and gazed ahead, waiting, hoping that she'd say something.

"What's wrong?" Nate asked.

"Nothing." How could she explain that she found her feelings for him confusing, terrifying yet somehow exciting?

"We're friends, aren't we?" he said gruffly. "You can tell me anything."

She glanced at him. "Are we friends, Nate? After today, I wasn't sure."

"Because my parents are back?"

"Nay!" she exclaimed, no longer able to keep silent. "I told you off."

"Oh, that." He seemed unconcerned.

She gaped at him. "It didn't bother you?"

He shrugged. "Why? Because you were honest with me?"

Charlie averted her gaze. She hadn't been honest about her true feelings for him.

"So, tell me. What did you decide? Jacob or Matt? Both are *gut* men—"

She stiffened and glared at him. "You didn't just dare to ask me that," she said tightly. She swung back to the view, her heart hammering in her chest, her muscles taut with anger. *Calm down*, she told herself. *Please, Lord, anger is a sin. Forgive me and help me to be a better person.*

A lengthy silence ensued. "I'm sorry," he said. "'Tis none of my business."

Closing her eyes, she drew in a cleansing breath, released it. "You're correct. 'Tis none of your business, but…" She forced herself to relax. "I shouldn't have snapped at you."

Their gazes locked. When Nate smiled, Charlie felt her fierce attraction for him from her head to her toes. Trembling, she faced ahead, lest Nate somehow read what was in her heart.

They stood side by side at the fence as darkness descended. Their moments became peaceful, and Charlie was able to relax and enjoy his company. The little bit of time she'd have left with him.

No one came looking for them, which was a miracle to Charlie, clearly provided by the Lord, perhaps for her birthday. A goose honked overhead, the lone bird soaring high on a quest to find its flock.

Snow fell quietly, landing on her black coat and on Nate's jacket and bare head. His warmth surrounded her. He stood at her side as if he, too, felt enjoyment in the moment.

"I'm glad your family is home safe. I guess I won't be seeing you, except on Sundays."

"Charlie…"

She met his gaze, surprised to see a strange look in his eyes. "I appreciate all you've done." He reached out.

Charlie stilled as he brushed his fingers across her brow before he tucked a stray lock of hair behind her ear. "I didn't mind," she said hoarsely.

"Nate? Are you out here?" Charlie immediately recognized the voice as his sister Ruth Ann's. "Jake's foot is bothering him, and *Mam* and *Dat* think we should head home."

"I'll be right there," he called back. He gave her a wry smile. "I guess 'tis time for us to go. They're all tired. I'm surprised that they wanted to come." His voice grew husky. "I'm glad they did."

She didn't say anything. She studied his handsome features, his lit blue eyes, his firm jaw and devastating smile, and she experienced a longing so sharp it stole her breath.

He didn't move; he simply gazed at her. "Happy birthday, Charlie."

She smiled. "My birthday isn't until Wednesday."

Nate touched her cheek then stepped back. "Close enough."

As he turned and headed toward the house, Charlie felt her heart soften and leave with him. She wanted more from him, and she had to accept that she'd never have the relationship she wanted. She didn't follow him. She stayed at the fence and watched two of her uncle's horses cavort in the snow. It was flurrying out when minutes later Nate exited the house with Jacob and his family.

Seeing her, Jacob hobbled his way on crutches toward her. "Happy birthday, Charlie," he said with a pained smile.

"Go home and rest, Jacob."

Charlotte Peachy, Nate's stepmother, broke from the group and approached. "Happy birthday, Charlie." Her smile was warm. "*Danki* for taking such good care of my sons."

She could only smile in response. The woman

placed a hand on her arm and gave it a squeeze before she rejoined her family.

She followed her to their buggy, where the man she loved waited. Nate helped his mother and brother get in and waited while the rest of his family was settled with his father in the front passenger seat before he faced Charlie. "Here. There's a gift in the house from my family, but this one is from me."

With trembling fingers, she took something wrapped up in a piece of linen, probably a pillowcase. "Nate…"

"Happy nineteenth birthday, Charlie," he whispered. Then he climbed into the buggy and within seconds he was driving with his family down the street toward home.

Charlie stood in the barnyard, watching as they left, clutching Nate's gift in her hands. It was true that she hadn't wanted to open the gifts until her birthday, but it was different with this one. This one was from Nate, and she had to open it now.

She moved into the barn, where no one would see her if they came looking. It would only take a moment to see what he'd given her, then she'd head into the house. She unwrapped Nate's gift and gasped with pleasure. It was a wooden carving of a horse. A perfect, smooth figure that looked alive and ready to prance if she set it on the ground. Emotional, she turned the figure, noting the detail and the tiny NP carved into the underside of one leg. NP. Nate Peachy. It was the best gift she'd ever been given. She loved horses, and Nate had noticed. She would cherish the little wooden horse forever, even after their paths went in different directions. She'd never forget that he'd taken the time to make something special for her birthday.

Charlie smiled with happiness even as tears filled her eyes and trailed down her cheeks. *Happy birthday to me.*

She hid the horse under the backseat in her family's buggy, ready to retrieve later when no one was around to see. Nate's gift would be for her eyes only. She would hold it, a precious thing, and recall the night he'd given it to her and all the times she'd enjoyed in his company.

The next morning while making coffee, Nate wondered if Charlie had opened his gift and if she'd liked it. He loved her. It was wrong but he couldn't help how he felt. The solution, he realized, was to keep his distance and move on with his life.

Chapter Ten

"Bishop John," Missy Stoltzfus greeted. "Come in. I'll make you a cup of coffee?" She stepped aside to allow the man to enter the house. "What brings you to see us this morning?"

"Your *dochter* Charlie. Is she in?" he said as he took a seat at the kitchen table.

"Is who in?" Charlie said as she entered the room. It was the day before she would turn nineteen, and the first day she had no reason to see Nate. She tensed as she saw their visitor. "Bishop John."

"Charlie, just the one I'm here to see."

She swallowed hard. *"Ja?"* Had he come to tell her about the new teacher?

"Since you expressed an interest in the position, I thought I should come and tell you that the church elders made their choice for our new *schuul*teacher."

She nodded as she sat down across the table from him with a lump in her throat. She watched her mother set a cup of coffee before the bishop, then nodded when her parent offered her a cup. "So who got the job?"

"I'm hoping you'll understand their choice." Bishop

John studied her thoughtfully. "I didn't know how much you wanted the position."

"I didn't make it clear?"

"I see that it's clear enough now how much you want to teach."

"Ja." She looked away as her throat thickened and she fought back tears. She didn't get the job. "Who's the new teacher? Barbara Zook?" Barbara Zook was her brother-in-law Peter's sister. She had recently returned to Happiness after a long period of absence spent out of state with her grandparents.

The bishop shook his head. "There were a number of young women considered."

Charlie waited patiently although everything inside her wanted to scream for him to hurry up and tell her, so that she could have a good cry in her room.

"Charlie, the church elders have decided that you should be teacher if you still want the job."

She blinked. Her mouth gaped open. She drew and released a sharp breath. "Me?"

He nodded, his eyes crinkling with good humor. *"Ja.* Do you still want the job?"

"Ja." She'd grabbed on to the opportunity since she couldn't have what she wanted most—Nate's love.

Bishop John grinned. "'Tis settled, then. You are now officially the new teacher for our Happiness *schuul."*

There was only one person she was eager to tell, because she knew he'd be pleased for her. Nate Peachy. Thinking of him made her rise abruptly. "I'm sorry, Bishop John, but I have to leave." She paused. "I'll come by your house later for details? When will I start?"

"The week before Christmas. Elizabeth Troyer will be moving with her family that Saturday and will be done teaching on Friday."

She bobbed her head with excitement. That was in just over a week. "I'll be there then before *schuul* starts at eight."

The man looked satisfied. *"Gut."*

"Mam," she said, turning toward her mother. "I need to run an errand." She grabbed her coat then headed toward the door. "Bishop John?"

The man looked at her.

"Danki. I won't let you or the church elders down."

He smiled. "I know you won't." He waved her toward the door. "You'd better go and tell whoever you have to tell."

Blushing, she nodded, put on her coat then ran out the door. Several minutes later she was on her way to the Peachy house. The day was clear, but the nip of winter was in the air. She tugged up on her coat to better protect her neck. She was almost there. She grinned, eager to see Nate and tell him her good news.

She parked in the yard, went to the back entrance and knocked before opening it. *"Hallo?"*

"Charlie!" Nate's stepmother came out from the laundry room. "'Tis nice to see you. Did you enjoy the party?"

She nodded. "It was truly a surprise," she said with a smile. She looked about, hoping for a sight of Nate, eager to tell him the good news.

Charlotte Peachy smiled at her with genuine affection. "I hear that you've been keeping Jacob company." She gestured toward a kitchen chair. "Tea?"

"*Nay*, but I appreciate the offer." She smiled. "And Jacob and Nate needed help. I was happy to give it."

"You kept the *haus* clean."

She shrugged. "Needed a way to keep busy while Nate worked and Jacob slept."

"I appreciate it. I didn't know what I'd find when we returned."

Charlie smiled. "It must be *gut* to be home."

"*Ja.* We had a lovely time, but I missed being here. I enjoyed meeting Abram's *eldre*, though. They are wonderful people. I knew they would be given that they'd raised my wonderful husband to be the fine man that he is."

"Is Nate around?" she asked, feeling uncomfortable for asking.

"*Nay.* He went grocery-shopping."

"I want to talk with him, but I can come back another time."

"Do you want to leave him a message?"

"*Nay.* But if Jacob's awake, I'd like to say a quick *hallo*."

Nate's stepmother beamed her approval. "He is. I'm sure he'll be glad to see you. He's talked about all the games you've played together while we were gone."

"I suppose he told you he won most of them."

To her surprise, Nate's *mam* shook her head. "Actually, he confessed that you beat him most of the time."

Charlie grinned. "An honest man. I like that." She hurried into the great room, where she found Jacob with a book open on his lap. "I just wanted to say *hallo* before I head home."

"You're leaving?" Jacob appeared disappointed.

"Your family's home. I didn't plan to stay."

"Play one game with me."

"*Nay*, you have siblings to play games with you now. I need to get home. There are chores to be done. I'll see you on Sunday."

"*Danki* for spending time with me," Jacob said warmly. "I'll have to sharpen my game skills before we play again."

"It was a hardship staying with you, Jake," she retorted mockingly, which made him grin.

She left then, disappointed and sad that her daily time spent with the two brothers was over. She climbed into her buggy and headed home. She had no idea where Nate had gone shopping, and she couldn't spend hours looking for him. She'd have to wait until Sunday to tell him her good news.

As she drove home, Charlie spied a market wagon coming from the opposite direction. She recognized Nate in the driver's seat. She brightened. She wouldn't have to wait until Sunday after all.

As his vehicle approached, Charlie lifted her hand and waved to gain his attention. She pulled off the road, pleased when Nate parked his wagon and got out.

"Charlie," he said as he crossed the street. His expression flickered with concern. "Has something happened?"

"I went to your *haus*, saw your family. You must be happy to have them home."

He nodded. There was no sign of welcome in his expression. As she gazed at him, she felt a prickle of unease. "You need something from me?" he asked.

She swallowed hard. She wouldn't tell him her news. It was obvious that he wasn't pleased to see her. "I wanted to thank you for the birthday gift. I love the horse."

"I'm glad you like it," he said without feeling. He

glanced back toward his wagon. "Anything else? I should get home. *Mam* is waiting for these groceries."

"*Nay*, you can go," she whispered as she held back tears. "I'll see you on Sunday."

"*Ja*, I'll see you then." Then he turned and crossed the street to his wagon, climbed in then left without another glance in her direction.

Hot tears escaped to dampen her face as she got into her buggy and continued home. Nate no longer needed her and didn't feel the need to be friendly toward her. She cried in earnest, her tears nearly blinding her as she drove home. How could he be so cruel?

She didn't understand this new, bewildering tension between them. Had her time with him during her birthday party been a dream? The laughter they'd shared while shopping together? Had she only imagined that he'd enjoyed her company? *And why did he go to the trouble of making me a special gift?*

Was it just something for him to do? She wiped away her tears so she could see. "A thank-you gift," she murmured, blinking rapidly. Nothing more. She shouldn't have hoped that it meant something more.

Nathaniel Peachy wanted to keep his distance from her, and she would accommodate him. She had a new job to look forward to. She'd be a good teacher and she'd enjoy her students while teaching them things they'd need for adulthood. And she would do her best to get over the heartache of her unrequited love for Nathaniel Peachy.

Nate clenched his jaw as he drove home. The image of Charlie's face when he'd fought to put distance between them would forever haunt him. He would miss seeing her every day, the light in her gorgeous green eyes when she was happy, the warm smile on her pretty pink lips when she was pleased. He had settled on his property recently, but having his own place meant nothing without a woman to share it with. This woman in particular, he realized. Charlie.

I love her. He could admit it to himself freely, but to no one else, most especially Charlie. The best thing he could do for her now was to nip their growing friendship in the bud.

If he hadn't known Emma, learned the truth of his failure and his inability to protect a loved one, he might have enjoyed a life with Charlie.

Tension clawed through him, causing his neck to tighten and his head to pound.

Jacob no longer needed her, but he did. Unlike him, she would get past the pain.

He was pleased that she liked his gift, but he couldn't show emotion. He couldn't allow her to see how special she was to him. If he did, his heart would crack open and spill the love he had for her inside.

He wanted her to be happy, and while he wanted to be the one to make her happy, to take care of her, protect her from the evils of the world, he knew better. Emma had taught him the truth about his failings.

Chapter Eleven

Charlie lay in bed and stared at the ceiling. She couldn't sleep, hadn't slept well in weeks. The excitement of securing the teaching position two weeks ago had been dimmed by the loss of her friendship with Nate. His lack of warmth when she'd encountered him on the road still bewildered her. His subsequent cool, unemotional behavior toward her ever since was like a harsh kick to her sensitive stomach, painful and making her gasp while unable to catch her breath.

She didn't understand him. She'd thought they'd stay friends after his family's return. She rubbed her aching temples with her fingers. Apparently, she'd been grossly mistaken about being Nathaniel Peachy's friend.

After tossing and turning as she tried to sleep, she finally gave up and got up. It was extremely early in the morning. The rest of her family would be in bed for hours yet. She felt anxious, antsy. Nate continued to weigh on her mind. She sought comfort with a visit to the horses, heading immediately to see her father's new gelding. As she stroked the animal's sleek neck, she felt the pinprick of tears. She still had the horse fig-ure that Nate had carved for her. She couldn't get rid of it. It was the only thing she had that he'd given to her freely. Tears stung her eyes and she gasped out a sob.

It was a bitter cold December morning but she didn't care. She wanted to ride despite the weather. Charlie haltered Buddy then led him outside through the rear barn door. After shutting the door behind her, she swung up onto the horse's bare back and kicked his sides. Buddy sprang forward, and she cried out as she felt herself fly. The wind whipped through her hair, tearing at her prayer *kapp*, but she didn't care. The cold felt good against her face as she urged the horse into a gallop toward the back section of her father's farm. There was snow on the ground, but Buddy ran sure-footed, and she cried out with joy. For the first time in weeks, she was able to find happiness in something that wasn't Nate.

The gelding Buddy was young, and she knew her father had paid good money for him. She'd ridden the family's horses before, but she'd been a child then. Now she was a woman who knew what she was doing, although her father might not be too pleased that she'd chosen Buddy to ride.

She hung tightly to the reins, laughing as she flew across farmland, her delight making her feel alive. Her prayer *kapp* loosened and she felt the pins give and her head covering fly off. Charlie reached to grab it, just as the gelding neared the road. She jerked on the reins the last minute to turn him back, and Buddy reared up, causing her to fall. She gasped with pain as she hit the ground. Filled with concern for her horse, she sat up, watching helplessly as Buddy ran off. She had to get him before he ran into the road and got hit by a car or worse. Her father would be angry with her when he found out. And once the elders learned of the incident, she'd lose the teaching position she'd wanted so desperately and then she'd have nothing.

Charlie closed her eyes. Maybe she hadn't changed at all. She struggled to her feet and looked down. Her stockings were torn but she wasn't hurt. But still she limped a little as she walked along the roadway while calling out for her runaway horse.

Nate drove his wagon along the road toward Adam Troyer's house. Adam had asked him to come early to help with a replacement window. It was barely dawn. Normally, they'd have tackled the work in the warmer weather, but the glass had been broken recently. And if the job wasn't done now, the cold winter weather would bluster inside the house, making it difficult to keep it heated.

Adam didn't expect him yet. It was too early, but Nate figured he'd take his time and head over. He had too much time on his hands—and too much on his mind—lately. And too many images of Charlie in his thoughts.

As if he'd conjured her from the air, he saw her. She was walking along the road that bordered the rear of her father's property. He scowled. Was she limping?

Nate parked his vehicle on the side of the road and rushed to her. "Charlie," he greeted with concern. "You hurt herself. What happened?"

He heard her groan with horror as she met his gaze. "I'm fine. I'm not hurt. And I'm not sure I want to tell you what happened."

Nate arched his eyebrow. "Tell me anyway."

"I took Buddy for a ride and fell off." Her glistening eyes met his. "He bolted, and I have to find him. He's my *dat*'s newest gelding, and my *vadder* is not going to be happy that I've lost him."

He frowned. "'Tis slippery out here. There's snow on the ground. You could have been seriously hurt." He glanced down. "You were limping. Come with me."

She shook her head. "No need. I feel fine. And I'm not limping now. See?" She started to walk across the field. "I just want to find Buddy."

"Charlie!" He hurried up to her. "Are you sure you're *oll recht*?"

She gave him an annoyed look. "I'm fine."

"Then I'll help you look for him." He felt the hard thump of his heart as she looked up at him with bright green eyes. He accompanied her as she went right and crossed a field.

"If I don't find Buddy, I'll not only be in trouble with *Dat* but with the church elders, too. I'll lose my chances at being hired as teacher," she whispered brokenly.

He halted and reached for her hand. The sadness in her expression made him want to take her in his arms to comfort her. "We'll find Buddy," he promised, "and no one will know."

She stared at him. "You won't tell?"

He gave her a soft smile. "Tell what?"

Charlie rewarded him with a trembly smile. *"Danki."*

"But no more bareback riding, *ja*?" He caressed the back of her hand. "No more taking risks?"

She bit her lip and nodded. "Why are you being so

nice? I didn't think you wanted to be my friend anymore."

Shocked, he released her hand. *"Charlie,"* he groaned. "'Tis not true."

"Except for Sunday, I haven't seen or talked with you in two weeks," she confessed. "And when we did see each other during church or Visiting Day, you avoided me. You barely acknowledged me. Like I didn't matter now that you no longer needed me for Jacob."

He closed his eyes for a long moment to control the yearning he felt for her. When he met her gaze, he shook his head. "'Tis not that, Charlie." He struggled to control his emotions. "I like you too much. 'Tis better that we don't get too close. The difference in our ages…"

"Pfft! You're the only one concerned with our age difference. I couldn't care less."

"Well, you should." He took off his hat and rubbed a hand across his forehead before he put it back on. "'Tis not only our ages. There are other reasons."

"What reasons?" There was an innocence in her features that made him want to forget about all the reasons why he shouldn't get involved with her. "Charlie…"

She narrowed her gaze. "There are no reasons. You just don't like me."

"That's not true."

"Not like I want you to," she breathed and he stilled. "Nate, if those reasons, whatever they are, weren't there, then what? Would we be friends?"

He lifted his hand to run a finger along her cheek to

her chin before he released her. "*Nay*. We'd have been more. I would have courted you and made you mine."

Joy burst inside her chest, making her heart speed up in response. Until he stepped back, and she saw his face. "Why can't we try? I like you, Nathaniel. More than any other man I know."

"Don't." He looked alarmed. "I'm not the right man for you."

Charlie saw something in his blue eyes that gave her courage. "I think you are."

He turned away, stared across the field. "Is that the way Buddy went?" he asked, changing the subject.

"Nate, I want to talk more about this. Us."

"There is no us," he said sharply.

She drew back. "You won't consider it?"

"*Nay*. Now is that the way Buddy went?"

"Go away. I'll look for him myself."

"I'm not leaving until we find your horse and you and the animal are safely back inside."

"Fine!" she said with a huff. "*Ja*, he went that way." She gestured in the direction.

"We'd better hurry, then."

As if they'd spent too much time talking. Her lips firmed. "We should split up and search in different directions," Charlie suggested. She wanted to be alone. He'd hurt her feelings and she needed time to herself.

"I'm not leaving you alone," he said firmly. "We'll look together. Two sets of eyes are better than one."

"'Tis a horse," she replied drily. "Can't miss a chestnut gelding if he's within eye distance."

"Better still that I come along in case you need help catching him once you find him."

"More like you're afraid I'll hop on his back and ride off again," she muttered.

He stopped and caught her arm. "You promised. No more riding bareback."

She arched an eyebrow. "Did I?"

He didn't respond. His brow knitted as he gazed beyond her. She followed the direction of his gaze and gasped as he said, "There he is!"

To her relief, when she approached, Buddy didn't bolt. Nate remained several yards away. That he was allowing her to do the work when she suspected that he wanted to help made her love him more. Pain settled in her chest as she reached for Buddy's reins. She turned and caught him studying her with tenderness in his expression, which he quickly hid. Her resolve firmed. Somehow, someway, she'd convince Nate that the two of them belonged together. She didn't care about his reasoning for them to stay apart. She'd seen the look in his eyes, heard the regret and conviction in his tone when he'd told her that under different circumstances he would have courted her.

Brightening, she approached him with a smile and Buddy in tow. "I'll ride him back," she said cheekily, trying to get a rise.

His features became fierce. *"Nay, you won't."*

"I won't race him," she sweetly assured him.

"Nay, you won't. Because you won't be riding him back."

"Who's going to stop me?" She made as if to climb on.

He grabbed her by the waist with a growl. "You have to ask?"

Tenderness made her soften toward him. "I'll be

fine, Nate. The only reason I fell was because I was trying to grab for my head covering."

"I'll be fine." She lovingly examined his features and saw genuine worry and fear. Charlie frowned.

"I can't let you ride back," he whispered emotionally. "I can't." He held out his hand. *"Please?"*

"You don't have to worry about me." But she gave him the leathers.

"As if I can breathe without worrying," he mumbled as he reached out to run a hand down Buddy's neck.

"Who will drive your buggy?" She knew she was pushing him but couldn't help herself. "You can't leave it here."

"You can," he said, surprising her. "I'll take Buddy and meet you behind the barn."

"And if my parents see you?"

He shrugged. "Buddy got away. I helped you look for him." His smile was grim. "'Tis the truth."

She nodded. They wouldn't actually be lying. She didn't want to think about how wrong it was not to confess to her parents what she'd done. Charlie knew she'd tell them eventually. How could she not? She believed in right and wrong, and she'd always confessed the truth, even when it got her into trouble.

He started across the field toward the house. "Charlie," he called as she started to get into his vehicle. "Be careful."

Irritated, she wrinkled her nose. "I'll not damage your precious buggy, Nathaniel."

He changed directions and approached until he was close. He stared down at her with an exasperated expression. "You don't know me very well if you think it's the buggy I care about, Charlie." Then he tugged on a strand of her hair and walked away.

Her throat had gone dry. He'd told her that he cared for her. Hadn't he? She watched him start back across the field.

"Nate?" she called. He turned. *"Danki,"* she said, her voice soft as she gazed at him with affection. She glimpsed what looked like tenderness in his expression before he blinked and turned away.

Charlie was overwhelmed with a sense of satisfaction as she climbed into Nate's vehicle. She studied the interior of the vehicle. It smelled like him. A woolen hat lay on the seat next to her. A toolbox lay on the floor on the passenger side.

He liked her. Despite trying to, he'd been unable to hide it. Now she just had to figure out a way to fully break down his defenses and prove to him that they would be good together.

She didn't believe it was about age. It was something else that held him back. She flicked the leathers and steered the horse back to the house, where he'd be waiting for her. Nate was twenty-six. There must have been a girl in the past, someone he must have once cared about. Charlie fought a twinge of jealousy. Was that the main reason why he didn't want to get involved with her? Because of a girl in his past? Did he still love her?

After putting on the battery blinker, she made a turn. His concern for her, the look in his eyes when they'd talked, had any jealousy melting away. He cared about her. A lot. She was sure of it. And he'd already captured her heart.

He stood waiting for her by the barn when she

pulled onto their dirt road. She left the vehicle close to the street. No sense raising her parents' awareness of Nate's presence and the reason he was here.

He didn't smile as she approached. She didn't care, as she suspected he was trying hard not to show any of his feelings. "Here in one piece, I see," he quipped.

She beamed at him. "I'm a capable driver—and rider," she added with a wink.

Nate laughed. "Come on. Let's put him in his stall."

She shot a look toward the house. "Why don't I take him? It might be better if you go before anyone sees you."

His good humor restored, he arched his eyebrow. "Ashamed of me?" he teased.

"Never," she said quietly, seriously.

The grin left his face as he handed her the leathers. "I'll leave. I promised to help Adam this morning."

"Danki," she murmured, her eyes locked with his. "I'll see you."

As he left, she followed him with her gaze and a deep-seated longing for him in her heart.

Chapter Twelve

Her first day at school had finally arrived. Elated, Charlie headed toward the Happiness schoolhouse on the edge of her aunt and uncle's property. It would be her first day as the new schoolteacher. She didn't feel as excited as she might have been. She missed Nate. Yes, she'd seen him on church Sunday, but that had been the only time, and he'd managed to avoid any time alone with her. She'd been hopeful of seeing him on Visiting Day, but the Abram Peachy family had been notably absent. At least to her.

How was she going to convince him that they belonged together if she never got to see or spend time with him?

The air was frigid. The wind whipped brutally through the morning against her legs as she climbed out of her buggy. As she let herself into the school, she found that someone had come earlier and thoughtfully fired up the woodstove. The classroom was warm and cozy. She ran back outside for the pine and holly she'd brought to decorate the classroom for Christmas. Her arms full, she struggled to get back inside. After setting the greenery on her desk, she took off her coat and hung it on the back of her chair. Then she spread pine and holly about the classroom, safely away from the heater.

Satisfied, Charlie took a good look at her surroundings, at the shelves flanking the front chalkboard, at the row of wooden desks, and the empty wall hooks just waiting for students' coats. She meandered about the room, recalling her days as a child. She'd loved school, and she hoped she could make every one of the children in her class love it, too.

Students talked and laughed as they filed into the school. She could feel their excitement with Christmas when they caught sight of the holiday greenery. One boy saw her in a corner and froze. Everyone grew quiet and stared at her.

"Hallo!" she greeted with a smile. "I'm Charlie Stoltzfus, your new teacher. As soon as you hang up your coats and get seated, we'll start."

"Did you bring us the holly and pine?" one little girl shyly asked.

"Ja." Charlie beamed at her. "I thought you'd enjoy a little holiday cheer."

"It looks nice!" another girl said.

"Ja," a young boy added. "'Tis nearly Christmas!"

The flurry of excitement over the holiday continued as she waited while the children hung up their coats then scrambled to their seats.

"Most of you already know me." She saw several heads bob. "But I think we should go around the room and say our names and a little about ourselves, don't you?"

She listened carefully to memorize names with the faces that she wasn't as familiar with, although she knew of most of her students' families.

"Josiah," she said to an older boy in the room after everyone had introduced themselves. "Has someone been assigned to hand out the readers?"

"I can do it," the boy offered.

"I'd appreciate that."

Charlie called on one of her younger students who was six years old. "Mary, can you tell me about the routine you had with Elizabeth?"

She listened carefully while the little girl spoke, smiling at her as she explained about their morning and afternoon schedule. Sensing movement behind her, she glanced back and caught two boys exchanging secretive looks. She understood then that she might have a challenge on her hands with the two students.

The first part of the morning went quickly as the children changed desks to form smaller groups with an older student helping the younger ones with their English lesson. Afterward, Charlie taught weights and measures during their arithmetic session, then called a brief time-out for recess. Despite the cold, the children wanted to be outside. They bundled up warmly and went into the fenced play yard.

She had pulled on her own coat and bonnet and she stood outside the door watching her students interact. The younger children gravitated to the two swing sets while the older boys played baseball in an area away from the swings. A gathering of girls stood chatting and laughing as they watched the swing set. She smiled as one of the older girls broke away to check on a younger sibling and push her on the swing. The cold didn't seem to bother any of them.

She was infused with a sense of well-being. She had

enjoyed the morning, and her experiences teaching so far had been wonderful and fulfilling.

Charlie rang the handheld school bell. "Time to come in!" She observed as the children stopped what they were doing to return to the classroom. "If you're cold, warm yourself by the fire," she invited as they hung up their coats.

She recognized the glint of mischief in one boy's expression as he turned from the coat hooks and whispered something to a fellow student, who flashed her an uneasy glance.

"Thomas," she said, addressing the boy with a smile. "I understand you're good with multiplication. Do you think you could help Peter and James with it this afternoon?"

He shrugged and kept his gaze averted. Charlie let it go for now, but she would bring it up again this afternoon and insist that Thomas and the other boy, Ethan, be somehow engaged with their fellow students.

"Time for penmanship," she announced with a smile.

Nate had come to see how Charlie was making out on her first day as teacher.

Doing well, no doubt. He shouldn't be here, but he found he couldn't stay away. It had been weeks since he'd been close enough to talk with her. Although he was the one at fault, he still missed her. He longed to see her red hair, the bright green of her eyes and the way her lips curved whenever she smiled.

The play yard was empty as he parked his buggy some distance away on the dirt road that led to a cottage used by a number of teachers in the past. He didn't want her to see him. He didn't want to interrupt her work. He just needed a quick look inside. He took position near a window and peeked inside. A sudden gust of frigid wind buffeted him, and he shivered and hugged himself with his arms.

Charlie stood in the front of the classroom with her students seated in rows of desks facing her. Confident and in control, she was talking and gesturing with her hands. He experienced warm pleasure as he watched her movements, her bright smile that told him a student must have answered her correctly. She was in her element, and he couldn't be happier for her.

A sharper wind gust caught him off guard, slamming him against the side of the building. The noise drew her attention, and he groaned when her eyes widened in his direction. She said something to her students and disappeared from sight until the schoolhouse door opened. The air stilled as, bundled up in bonnet and cape, she exited and gazed at him warily.

"Nathaniel," she said. "What are you doing here?"

"I wanted to see you working on your first day." He gazed at her with amazement and pride at how naturally she'd handled her students.

She frowned. "Why?"

He closed his eyes. "To make sure you were *oll recht*." And he desperately needed to see her. It had been too long since he had.

"Seriously?" She became tight-lipped. "I'm teaching school, Nate, not riding bareback." Her features changed with her dismay. "You decided that I couldn't handle the job so you came to see if I needed help."

"That's not true!" His voice was loud in the stillness. It was as if God had ceased the wind for them to have this conversation.

"Isn't it?" she mocked. "Go away, Nate. I don't want you here." Her tone suggested that she didn't need him anywhere or anytime.

"I'll leave," he said softly. As he turned, the wind picked up, blowing against his bare head. He hugged himself tighter as he moved toward his buggy. He halted then spun back. "Congratulations, Charlie. I know you're a great teacher."

She hadn't moved. Her features had softened with concern. "You're freezing, Nate. Come in out of the cold. You can warm up by the woodstove."

He debated whether to go or leave. He studied her expectant face and made his choice, then followed her inside.

"*Hallo*, Nate!" Several of the children chimed in to greet him.

He grinned at them, his face lighting up with pleasure. Charlie stared as more students called out to him. He was so good with children. Her heart gave a lurch and she felt a warm, fuzzy feeling inside.

"You come to join us?" one boy asked.

"Came inside to get warm. 'Tis freezing out. Just taking a moment by the woodstove." She saw how he noted all the rows of desks. "And I came to see Charlie."

"She your sweetheart?" an older boy asked with a smirk.

Charlie caught her breath as she waited for his answer.

He shot her a look as he took off his gloves and set them on the floor near the woodstove. "She could be, but right now she's a *gut* friend. A very *gut* one."

"You like her!" a little girl said.

"*Ja*, I do."

"Enough to come out in the cold to see her," the child added.

His lips curved. "Apparently." Charlie blushed as he caught and held her glance as if he was trying to send her a secret message. He had unbuttoned his coat to allow warmth to penetrate beneath. He rubbed his bare hands to warm them in the heat of the wood fire.

She swallowed hard as she became overwhelmed with confusion and love. His answers to the child's questions made her spirits rise. She turned to the class. "Children, let Nate get warm without all the questions. 'Tis time to get back to practicing your penmanship…"

Movement behind her caught her attention. She suffered extreme disappointment to see Nate buttoning his coat.

"I appreciate the use of your fire," he told her as he pulled on his gloves.

She eyed his bare head. "Why aren't you wearing a hat?"

"'Tis windy and I left it in the carriage."

"You should have worn a woolen cap," she murmured as she approached him.

"Ja, Mam," he teased with a twinkle in his blue eyes.

"You worry about me, but I can't worry about you?"

He sobered. "Charlie…"

Her pulse raced as she watched him. "What? What do you want from me?"

He broke eye contact. "I should go." After a smile for the children, he went to the door.

One of the students spoke up. "Nate?" When Nate looked at him in question, the boy said, *"Dat* said he saw you here early this morning. *Danki* for making it warm in here for us."

"You're *willkomm*."

Charlie shot him a glance. He wouldn't look at her. "You fired up the stove?"

Nate reluctantly met her gaze. "It was nothing."

Her heart melted. Oblivious to her students, she placed a hand on his arm as he opened the door. "It wasn't nothing to me," she whispered with gratitude and love.

Then he left, and Charlie understood that something was changing between them. His kindness, his appearance, meant something more than a neighbor watching out for the new teacher. What it meant exactly, she wasn't sure.

Midweek came quickly. Charlie stood in the doorway of the school building and waved goodbye to her students as they left for the day. All in all, she'd had a great week with the highlight being Nate's visit two days ago. At first, she was hurt that he'd come, believing that he didn't trust that she would do a good job, that she'd help. But then his conversation with the children, learning that he'd come to the school early to make sure the classroom had warmed to a comfortable level, made her see his visit differently.

Every morning since, when she'd arrived, the school was toasty warm, and she knew it was because of Nate. She held on to hope. That he cared enough about her to go out of his way to come early to the school and fire up the stove made her believe that he had feelings for her that were more than just friendship. And after all, he'd told the children that she could be his sweetheart.

She longed to see him, but except for a brief stop before school started when she wasn't here, he didn't visit.

She now slept better than she had in a long time because of Nate. She went back inside to prepare the building so that she could leave. She dampened the fire in the wood-stove, put away pencils and any clean sheets of paper left on her students' desks, then bundled up against the cold in her black winter coat and traveling bonnet.

As she locked the door behind her, Charlie noticed an increased nip to the air. The sky was cloudy, and it looked like snow. She should take the time to stop and see her sister Meg's father-in-law. If anyone could accurately forecast the weather, it was Horseshoe Joe. After a severe injury to his leg while falling off a ladder years ago, he forecast the weather by the intensity of his pain.

Deciding to forgo the visit, she drove home. She was exhilarated by her success in the classroom but physically tired. She'd help *Mam* in the kitchen to prepare supper, then she'd seek an early bed. Christmas was only days away, and she'd be seeing Nate again. In light of their last encounter, she was delighted at the prospect. Life couldn't get much better than this, she thought with a smile.

With her first week of school over, Charlie had a brief pause. Saturday morning Charlie, her sister Ellie and her mother worked in the kitchen to put the finishing touches on a meal. Nell, Leah and Meg were coming with their husbands. She was eager to see them, as she had much to tell them about her first week in school. After supper her family would head out to cut holly and pine boughs to decorate their houses for the upcoming holiday.

The morning had begun with snow flurries. With Horseshoe Joe, Peter's father and Meg's in-law, predicting a worsening of the weather, the family had decided to gather at midday instead of early evening.

Charlie grinned as Meg entered the house, her belly big with child. She gave her sister a hug then directed a smile at Peter. "Your *dat* still think there will be a heavy snow?"

"Ja," Meg answered with a smile at her husband. "And he's *gut* with his weather predictions."

Peter handed her a covered plate. "My dear Meg insisted we bring something," he said with a soft look toward his wife.

"'Tis your favorite dessert, husband. Are you complaining?" Her sister gazed at her husband with love.

"Never, wife. Never."

Charlie watched with longing in her heart for love like theirs—with Nate—as she followed them into the great room, where the rest of the family was gathered. Nell and James sat close together in one corner of the room. Leah and Henry had taken a seat on a wooden love seat nearby. Her father and mother stood, happily chatting with the four of them. The genuine care and affection between her parents was apparent without a word or a touch.

The meal was a huge success. The topic of the Peachys' trip came up, and Charlie froze as the men discussed what they'd learned from Abram. When Nate's name entered the conversation in passing, she felt her face warm. She rose and started to clear the table. Her mother and sisters joined her, and the leftovers were put away and the dishes done in no time.

"Ready for holly and pine gathering?" Henry said with a smile.

"I ate too much." Meg groaned as she cradled her belly. "I'll just sit right here."

Peter bent close to her. "But, dearest wife, the exercise will be *gut* for you and our child."

Meg gave in graciously, and the family started to trek across their farm to a nearby woods just down the road.

"There!" Leah cried. "There's a holly tree!"

"I see pine," Nell exclaimed.

The family went to work, cutting holly and pine enough for each home. Every person carried an armful as they headed back to the house. Snow had begun to fall by then. Peter looked at the sky with misgiving. He was worried about Meg and suggested that they should leave. When the snow began to fall in earnest, everyone agreed. After storing their Christmas greenery in the backs of their vehicles, they left.

Charlie's mother gazed out the window with concern. "I'm glad they left," she said. "It doesn't look like it will be stopping anytime soon." Their holly and pine had been brought into the great room. Charlie and her sister Ellie grabbed several branches of pine and laid them on every available safe surface, well away from the heater.

Charlie felt the loss of her married sisters' company. Two hours later she, too, was glad they'd left. It was a blizzard outside with heavy snowfall and the sudden fierce onset of wind, which blew in every direction. She could barely see outside.

There was only one weekday before Christmas, and that was Christmas Eve. Fortunately, they didn't have to worry about getting to school in the inclement weather. School wasn't scheduled to resume until after second Christmas, which was the day after Christmas and five days away. The increasing intensity of this snowstorm was frightening. The only need to venture outdoors was to take care of the animals that were safely in the barn.

Her mother and father relaxed in the great room. Ellie was upstairs in her bedroom. Charlie turned from the window and decided to work on her lesson plans in her room.

"Heading upstairs," she told them.

"Going to work on your lesson plans?" her mother asked.

"*Ja*, I brought some books home with me. I thought I'd go over them and come up with a lesson plan to make learning more fun."

"You enjoy teaching," her father said.

Charlie smiled. "I love working with children."

"Someday you'll have children of your own," he said.

She murmured an answer then left them. As she climbed the stairs to the second story, she thought of Nate and her desire to wed and have children with him. Once in her room, lesson plans were the last thing on her mind as she was consumed by thoughts of Nate. The thought that she might never have his love brought tears to her eyes and an increasing ache in her heart. She wasn't about to give up on him. She straightened and opened a schoolbook. Her gaze skimmed the page's contents, then she looked up with a sigh.

I would have courted you and made you mine. His words came back to her in a flash and her heart lightened. Their age difference meant nothing. His reasons, although she didn't know what they were, meant nothing. She would just have to talk with him to convince him.

She grinned. *"I need you, Nathaniel Peachy,"* she murmured. "I won't settle for less."

Chapter Thirteen

Sunday morning the snow stopped abruptly. The plows came through early afternoon, making it easier for her church community members to handle any necessary outside farm chores. Church had been canceled that morning, but her family had gathered to pray.

The sun cast a glow into her room, drawing Charlie to the window. She stared outside, noting the thick snow covering the yard. Her cousin Isaac had stopped by, not long after the roads had been plowed. He'd driven over in a sleigh to let them know that the roads were good and the church elders had decided that there should be school on Christmas Eve. School would be closed for Christmas and Second Christmas before resuming on Thursday, the next day.

The temperature dropped by the next morning, keeping a layer of packed snow on the streets. Word about school had traveled, thanks to her Lapp cousins. Elijah had arranged those for whom he'd crafted sleighs to transport students safely to the schoolhouse. Her cousin Isaac would be coming for her.

She dressed quickly in winter gear after she saw a sleigh pull into the yard. Isaac was bundled up with his heavy dark coat and a navy woolen hat. Charlie made sure every inch except her face was covered. "I'm leaving for *schuul*!" she called to her mother from the bottom of the stairs. "Isaac's here!"

Her mother appeared at the top. "Say *hallo* to him. Will he be bringing you home?"

She grinned. "One of my cousins will."

Her *mam* smiled. "Have a *gut* day, Charlie, and be careful. 'Tis icy out there."

"I will, *Mam*." Then she left by the back and shrank back against the cold wind that whipped inside, bringing an instant chill into the kitchen.

Head down, she ran toward the sleigh. She didn't look up but felt a presence and grabbed the hand that appeared in front of her. She gasped as he caught her by the waist and lifted her easily onto the seat. She tugged her coat against the cold as she waited for Isaac to climb onto the other side.

"Here," a deep, familiar voice that was not her cousin's said as he wrapped a blanket around her.

"Nate," she gasped. "I didn't expect you."

He gave her a wry smile. "Isaac said you needed a ride."

Blinking against the wind, she studied him. "And so you got unlucky?" Had he offered to take her or had he been roped in? If he'd wanted to see her, he could have come to see her sooner at school.

He stared at her. "Don't be silly—"

"I'm going to be late." She pulled the blanket around her more tightly.

Nate didn't immediately move. She refused to look at him, and he finally flicked the leathers. She didn't speak as he steered the horse-drawn sleigh toward the schoolhouse. She didn't know what to say, because she knew she'd overreacted. It was good to see him, and she'd been unable to tell if he felt the same way. Fearing the worst, she'd acted badly.

She knew she should apologize, but the wind made conversation difficult. With him so near, she was conscious of his every move. He had seen to her comfort and stirred up feelings she wanted to share with him but was afraid to.

Tears filled her eyes and the wind blew them across her skin, dampening her temples and her cheeks. The schoolyard loomed ahead, and Charlie realized that she probably wouldn't see him this afternoon. Nate parked the sleigh close to the school.

"Danki," she said and turned to flee.

He caught her arm. "Charlie."

She froze. She started to tremble as she met his gaze. "It was nice of you to come to bring me."

"I wanted to bring you. I *volunteered* to get you."

She blinked. "You did?"

"Ja." He leaned in close. "Don't move. I want to help you get down." There was warmth in his gaze but his tone brooked no argument.

Nate skirted the sleigh to get to Charlie's side. Then he followed her to the building and waited as she tried using the key to unlock the door. He noted that her fingers shook too much to insert the key. He gently took it from her and quickly unlocked the door. She looked half-frozen but she didn't complain.

"Danki," she murmured after he'd opened the door and gestured her in. "I know you have to go."

"I have a minute," he said as he went to build a fire in the woodstove. Shivering, Charlie hugged herself with her arms and watched him, but didn't say a word. Confident that the fire would take, he faced her. "It won't take long to get warm."

She blinked rapidly and that was when he noticed that her eyes seemed overly bright. He gave a sound of sympathy when he saw the frozen tear tracks on her cheeks. "You're always taking care of me," she whispered.

Nate gave her a tender smile. "I don't mind." It wasn't hard to give her help when she needed it. He surveyed the classroom, taking more time to note the large letters near the ceiling around the perimeter of the room, the room full of desks…the teacher's desk in the front right corner.

"What time do you normally start?" he asked. It had been a long time since he'd been in school, and he wasn't sure if the schedule had changed in the ensuing years.

"In about a half hour." She paused. "But I don't expect everyone to be on time this morning."

"I should go…" He felt a tightness in his chest. He didn't want to leave her, but there were children waiting for him. He watched as Charlie shifted closer to the stove and held out her hands to warm them. "I need to pick up your students. Will you be *oll recht* here alone?"

"I'll be fine," she assured him. She met his gaze, her green eyes glistening. "I appreciate the ride."

"It was my pleasure." In fact, if he hadn't been told to get her, he would have insisted. It had been too long since he'd spent any time with her.

Nate gazed at her a long moment as the wind rattled the windows and gusted against the sides of the building. "I'll see you later," he said as he turned toward the door.

"Nate!" she called and he stopped in his tracks. She approached. "Can we talk later?"

He shifted uncomfortably. As much as he wanted to spend time with her, he didn't think it was wise.

He must have taken too long to answer. "Never mind," she said.

The wind buffeted him as he climbed onto his sleigh. He took one last long look at the building and caught sight of Charlie in the window watching him. He stifled the feelings growing within his chest and headed toward the road. The house behind the school was vacant. The last teacher hadn't lived there during her time as schoolteacher. If the winter continued like this for the rest of the winter, it might be best if Charlie stayed at the cottage so that she wouldn't have to worry about the snow.

The cold bit into his cheeks and he reached up to pull his woolen hat over his ears. He didn't like the thought of her living alone even in the cottage, even though it wasn't far to her aunt and uncle's place. She would be alone.

She wanted to talk. He closed his eyes briefly before he got onto the sleigh. They probably should talk. But what would he say that wouldn't be a lie? If she asked, he couldn't tell her that he didn't care, because he did care for her. He loved her.

He had to remember Emma. If he didn't, he'd give in to his feelings for Charlie, and then he'd fail her, too.

Charlie watched as her students straggled in after they were dropped off by sleigh at school. Thanks to

Nate, the room was toasty and warm. The children murmured with relief as they took off their coats and hung them up. The children chatted happily. It didn't seem to bother them that they were in school the day before Christmas.

The school day ended quickly, and sleighs arrived to bring the children home. She smiled and waved as they left. She caught sight of Nate helping students onto his sleigh. She waited for him to acknowledge her but he never did. He left and she turned back inside to wait for her ride.

She was more than ready to go home. She didn't understand why the elders decided that there should have been school today, unless they knew something that she didn't. Like another blizzard was on its way. She pulled on her coat and put on her traveling bonnet while she waited. A half hour passed and then an hour. She became worried when no one came. She hadn't fed the fire since she was due to leave, and it was already getting cold inside. Where was Isaac?

Snow fell heavier than before. If she didn't get home soon, she'd be stuck in the schoolhouse. There was a little firewood left but not enough to keep her warm all night.

Then she remembered the teacher's cottage close by. Wasn't it heated with wood or propane? She didn't know. And besides, how would she get inside if she needed to? It wasn't as if someone had given her a key.

The howl of wind against the roof made her shiver. She searched for a key in her desk and panicked when she couldn't find one. Should she rebuild the fire? Venture outside to bring in more wood? Any wood there would be snow-covered and probably too wet to burn.

She hugged herself with her arms and tried not to cry. She had to think clearly, to decide what to do.

There was a loud pounding on the door. Relieved, she hurried to answer it. Her ride was finally here. She swung open the door and stared.

"Nate!" Relief and joy hit her hard. She felt suddenly safe, and although she was freezing, she felt a burst of warmth that sprang from her heart.

He brushed past her as he entered, his jacket and hat covered in snow. "You're still here," he said as if stunned. "Why are you still here?"

"No one came for me," she replied, her voice wobbly. She bit her lip. "You didn't know?"

"*Nay*, I just stopped to make sure everyone was gone. I never expected anyone to be here." She shivered, and Nate gazed at her with an intensity she found disconcerting. He made a sound of concern. "You're freezing." He started to unbutton his coat.

"*Nay*, I don't want to take your coat. You'll get sick." Charlie placed her fingers over his to stop him. "I'm fine." Now that he was there.

"Are you sure?" He continued to eye her worriedly.

She bobbed her head. "*Ja*, I'm sure." He stole her breath when he reached out and rubbed her arms with his gloved hands.

"I'll be right back," he said. He locked gazes with her. "I promise." Then he opened the door and disappeared into the white.

She grew colder after he left her. Fortunately, he was back within seconds with a dry quilt wrapped in plastic in his arms. "I had this under the seat." He tugged off the plastic before he unfolded the quilt and placed it around her shoulders until she was cocooned with warmth. His eyes held emotion as he studied her. "You've got your key?"

"Ja."

"Let's go, then." Placing his arm around her, he held her against him as they left the building. "'Tis bad out," he murmured close to her ear. "Keep your head down." She felt the heat of him as he steered her through the storm to his sleigh. After making sure she was still wrapped up in the quilt, he stepped up onto the side of the sleigh and set her gently onto the seat.

"You *oll recht*?" He observed her without moving.

"I'm fine." She blinked rapidly. *"Danki*, Nathaniel."

His tender concern brought her to the verge of tears. She desperately wanted this man in her life, and if she didn't figure a way to get him soon, she'd be destined to be unhappy forever.

Apparently reassured, Nate skirted the vehicle and climbed onto the driver's side. The wind continued to blow snow, hampering visibility, but Charlie wasn't worried. She was with Nate and she knew he wouldn't let anything bad happen to her.

No one had come to pick up Charlie. The knowledge upset him. He'd been assured by her cousins that one of them would be bringing her home. He would have come sooner if he'd known. Nate wasn't sure why he felt the need to stop at the school and double-check. He thanked the Lord that he had. Seeing Charlie teary-eyed, cold and scared had him yearning to take her in his arms and hold on tight.

As he steered the horse through the snow toward the Arlin Stoltzfus residence, he experienced the strongest desire to take her home where he could take care of her, ensure she was safe and warm. The wind, strong at first, died down, and the snow fell softly over the sleigh and the landscape. He shot her a glance. She sat, wrapped in a blanket, her eyes ahead. "Charlie." She looked at him. "You'll be home in a few minutes," he said.

She nodded. "*Danki*. I don't know what I would have done if you didn't come when you did."

The thought of what might have happened terrified him. He kept his gaze on the road as he fought his fear. "I should have come for you sooner, but I thought Isaac or Elijah had taken you home."

"But yet you stopped to make sure." Her voice was soft, almost affectionate.

He met her gaze briefly before returning his attention back to the road. "*Ja...*" He couldn't finish. How could he admit that he'd worried about her, that he always worried about her? She was constantly in his thoughts. She wasn't Emma, because she wasn't a child. His feelings for her were different than the ones he'd felt for Emma.

They were silent for the rest of the ride. Nate checked for oncoming traffic before he steered the sleigh onto the road on her father's property. He parked close to the porch steps, climbed down and ran around the vehicle before Charlie had a chance to move. She turned and he reached up and lifted her out, setting her down in front of him. Close, they gazed at each other for several long moments. He noticed the vivid green of her eyes, her cheeks pink from the wind and her perfectly formed mouth. His hand lifted on its own, touched her skin reddened from the cold.

"Nate..."

"You should get inside. You're freezing."

She inclined her head. "Come in for a minute for something hot to drink? You can have coffee, tea or hot chocolate."

He shouldn't. He should probably go, but he couldn't resist her. "A quick minute." The way her eyes brightened made his heart pump harder.

Her smile was soft as she lifted her gloved hand to stroke his cheek. "As much as you've rescued me, you probably think I need a keeper," she murmured.

His chest tightened. *"Ja,"* he whispered.

"Maybe I do. And I wouldn't mind one if it were you." She turned and hurried up the steps, her words leaving him shocked and standing still. She flashed a concerned look over her shoulder. "Nate? Aren't you coming?"

Stunned, he followed her up the stairs. He took off his woolen cap before entering the house.

"Mam! Dat!" she called out. "I'm home!"

"Praise the Lord," her mother said, her brow clearing as she exited the kitchen. "I was worried. 'Tis late—" She stopped. "Nathaniel! What a nice surprise."

"Nate gave me a ride. He's been transporting students all afternoon. I think he could use something to warm him." She smiled at him. "How about a mug of hot chocolate?"

"Sounds *gut*." He'd answered automatically. Charlie's words kept playing silently in his mind.

Before he gave it another thought, she grabbed his hat. "Take off your coat," she urged. He took off his coat, and she grabbed it and headed into the kitchen. He followed her, immediately feeling the warm coziness of the room. When her mother followed them in, he felt the kitchen fill with love.

Charlie opened the door then held out his coat to brush off the snow. When she was done, she hung it up then handed his hat to her *mam*.

Missy disappeared into a back room while Charlie retrieved milk from the refrigerator and a pot out of a kitchen cabinet. She poured a generous helping of milk into the pot, then turned on the stove. Nate watched her as she moved about the kitchen. He was comfortable in the Stoltzfus kitchen, comfortable with Charlie. He almost could imagine her living in another house, the small farmhouse he'd finally managed to purchase recently, cooking on his stove. *As his wife.*

Charlie added rich chocolate to a mug of milk. "Whipped cream?" He shook his head. With a smile, she set it down before him. "Here you go." She smiled at him. "Want some cookies? We have chocolate chip."

"*Ja*, that sounds *gut*." He couldn't keep his eyes off her. Surprisingly, the image of her in his life was crystal clear and not unwelcome.

She flashed him a pleased look before she put several cookies on a plate. He eyed the treats as she placed them on the table. "Help yourself." He could feel her gaze on him as he took two cookies. He glanced up.

She smiled at her mother as Missy entered the room. Missy handed something to her daughter. Charlie turned and extended a dry knit cap toward him. "This is *Dat*'s. He has plenty to lend. Nate, please take this. I'll give you back yours, but 'tis too wet for you again."

Nate accepted the woolen hat. "I'll return it," he promised.

She nodded then made herself a mug of hot chocolate and sat across from him.

He wanted desperately to continue the conversation they'd started outside. About her needing a keeper and her wanting it to be him. But it was neither the time nor the place for it. And it wasn't something he'd want to discuss in front of her mother.

"I'm glad you could stay for a while," she said softly.

"You are?"

"*Ja.* I…" She suddenly blushed and looked away. She stood abruptly, as if she was suddenly uncomfortable and couldn't sit still.

Charlie was pretty and smart, and she had a sense of humor. He loved looking at her. And he loved who she was. He wouldn't want to change her. He cared about her, felt the ever-present need to protect her. *To love her.*

He left shortly afterward with her father's hat on his head, a full belly and a warm heart. And with thoughts of Charlie.

He had to talk with her. He now understood that no matter how hard he tried he wasn't going to stop loving her. But their discussion would have to come later. At present, it would take all of his concentration to drive home as the increasing snowstorm became a blizzard that threatened his and his horse's safety.

Chapter Fourteen

Charlie worried about Nate as she watched him leave. It was a blizzard outside and he had a long way to get home. She was confident in his abilities to drive the sleigh, but she couldn't help but fear the storm. She loved him. Worrying and caring went hand in hand with love. She stood on the front porch until his sleigh disappeared from sight, which wasn't long given the whiteout conditions. She offered a silent prayer for his safety. Her mother would need help with the meal. She needed to keep busy or go crazy with thoughts of Nate in an accident.

"Is Ellie home?" she asked as she entered the kitchen. She looked forward to working in the kitchen with her mother and sister as they prepared supper together.

Mam nodded. "She heard the weather forecast and came home before noon."

Charlie thanked God. Her sister was safe and she needed to have faith that soon Nate would be safe, too. "I'll call her downstairs."

"That was nice of Nate to bring you home," *Mam*

commented while she put the water on to boil potatoes as Charlie reentered the room.

"Ja." She picked up a potato peeler and began to take the skin off a potato. "I'm not sure what I would have done if he hadn't stopped to make sure everyone had gone safely home."

"You were all alone?" Ellie asked sharply, having overheard the conversation as she entered.

"Ja, and I was getting cold. I didn't stoke up the fire since we were leaving and there's no school tomorrow. I thought Isaac or Elijah was coming to get me. Nate was upset to learn that I'd been left behind."

"Thank the Lord that he came back for you." Her mother pulled bread out of a cabinet and set it on a cutting board.

Charlie murmured her agreement. Nate had rescued her. *Again.* She was always happy to see him, but this afternoon her fear of being abandoned in a cold building had gotten the best of her. She'd wanted to rush into his arms and hug him hard. Feel his strength surround her. He always made her feel warm and protected.

She recalled the times she'd rebelled when someone—Nate—had wanted to help her or warned her to be careful. She'd once thought relying on help meant she couldn't be independent. But the more she learned about herself—and Nate, the more she considered things differently. She'd come to know about the man's character. His kindness and concern were an integral part of him. And she loved him for exactly who he was.

Before he'd left for home, she'd caught him studying her intently, and it wasn't dismissal she'd seen in his gaze. And not just concern for her well-being. There had also been affection and a hint of longing in his striking blue eyes.

Please, Lord, please bless a union between us. They needed to talk. And she'd recognized that he wanted to talk as much as she did.

With the blizzard currently roaring across the countryside, it could be days before she saw him again. Days she could be cooped up inside the house with him constantly on her mind.

There was nothing she could do about it, but hope and pray that the Lord would decide that Nate and she belonged together.

"Christmas is tomorrow," *Mam* commented as she kneaded dough for flat dumplings.

"I'm ready," Charlie said. "What if the snow doesn't let up?"

Ellie started to slice the bread. "We'll have to make do."

"The snow will make for a white Christmas." *Mam* flattened the dough with a rolling pin.

"I don't mind a little snow, but while I love spending the holiday with you, *Mam*, and Ellie—and *Dat*—I really want to see Nell and James, Meg and Peter, and Leah and Henry." *And Nate.* She really wanted to see and talk with Nate. She had a special gift to give him and she couldn't wait to see his reaction. It wasn't as nice as the horse he'd given her for her birthday, but she had put a lot of thought into her present for him. She hoped he liked it.

"Something smells *gut*," her father said with a smile as he entered the kitchen.

"Where were you?" Ellie asked.

"Upstairs changing into dry clothes. I fed the animals." He viewed the women in the kitchen with affection.

"We haven't started to cook yet," *Mam* teased.

"Then why do I smell cake?" *Dat* grinned. He looked at the kitchen worktable. "You're making dumplings…"

"*Ja*, I know it's unusual to have potatoes and dumplings at the meal."

He grinned. "You'll not hear any complaints from me. I love both."

Charlie looked from her father to her mother and back. This was what she wanted—a loving relationship and marriage like her parents had. And the only one she could see herself married to was Nathaniel Peachy. *Please, Lord, please let him love me.*

Nate couldn't get Charlie out of his mind. Ever since he'd found her nearly freezing in the schoolhouse, he'd been consumed with thoughts of her.

He wanted to see her, needed to spend time with her. The snow had finally tapered off, and everyone was waiting for the roads to be plowed again. If the streets weren't cleared soon, then he'd walk to the Arlin Stoltzfus farm. It wouldn't be a Christmas celebration without Charlie. And it was well past the time to tell her of his feelings. And to find out if she returned them.

He loved her. The realization had come over him slowly, and he almost hadn't recognized it until he found her alone and half-frozen in the school. Charlie wasn't Emma, and he was older and wiser now. If the Lord gave him a second chance, he wouldn't fail.

Charlie wasn't foolish. She was industrious, kind and loving. Yet she'd teased and taunted him until he'd seen only red. He saw some of the things she did as dangerous, but she wasn't a child and she could handle herself.

Warmth settled in his chest as he thought about the possibility of having a life with her. Nate smiled. He still had to fix up the farmhouse he'd bought before they could move in, but he was certain Charlie would be pleased to live there after he was done renovating it.

He imagined Charlie holding his baby, caring for him, loving him. He grinned. The image was as clear as his view of the snow outside.

In a few hours it would be Christmas. He was eager to give Charlie her gift. If her reaction to her birthday gift was any indication, then she would love what he'd made for her.

The roar of a truck engine and the scrape of metal against snow drew him to open the side door. A huge snowplow cut a huge swath over the snowy street. He grinned. He'd be spending Christmas with Charlie.

On Christmas Day, Nate waited until afternoon when his family had exchanged gifts and enjoyed a big breakfast. Eager to see Charlie, he told his parents he was going out. Bundled up in warm, dry clothing, he went outside to prepare the sleigh. With no real plan in mind, he drove away from the house and steered his horse toward Charlie's.

The snow shimmered under the sun, which brightened the landscape. He drove past a farm where horses had been released inside a fence. The wind had blown snow, leaving an uncovered section of the paddock. The animals frolicked about the enclosure as if overjoyed to have the freedom of outdoors after being cooped up inside their dark stalls.

Nate slowed the sleigh and watched them. He knew

instinctively that Charlie would love seeing them. Maybe he could convince her to take a ride with him and he could show her.

He turned onto the road leading to the Arlin Stoltzfus house. The horse-drawn sleigh glided along without a sound as he parked. He got out and tied up the horses on a fence post near the barn. His heart started to race as he went to the front door. His breath quickened, and he could see the vapor it emitted into the chilly air each time he exhaled. He rapped on the door and waited.

Suddenly, the door opened. Nate stared then smiled as he faced the woman he loved. He was encouraged when her green eyes widened with pleasure and her pretty pink lips curved into a wondrous smile. She wore a green dress that deepened the vibrant color of her eyes. She gazed at him without a word. He didn't worry, for she looked stunned but happy to see him.

"May I come in?" he asked with genuine amusement.

"*Ja! Ja*, of course!" She stepped back to allow him entry. "The roads are *gut*?"

"*Ja*." He continued to study her. His gaze caressed her features, enjoying what it saw.

She frowned. Clearly, she hadn't expected to see him until tomorrow, Second Christmas, the day for visiting. "Is everyone well? Your *mam*—is it the baby?"

"*Nay*, she's not due until after Christmas," he said. "She's fine."

Charlie released a sharp breath. "*Gut*, that's *gut*." She smiled and her eyes softened. "Although a Christmas baby would be truly blessed."

Watching her, picturing her in his mind again as his wife with a baby in her arms and a loving smile on her face, startled him. "*Ja*, it would," he agreed gruffly.

"Why are you here?" Her beautiful green eyes gazed at him warily.

"Would you like to take a ride? There's an English farm not far from here, and the farmer let out his horses."

She blinked rapidly as if suddenly overcome with emotion. "You want me to see horses with you?"

He inclined his head. "'Tis chilly outside so you will need a warm coat and hat if you come." He swallowed hard. "Do you want to?"

She bobbed her head. "*Ja*, that would be *wunderbor*." She turned. "Just let me get my coat."

"Charlie." Nate softened his expression as he approached her. He reached out to tenderly stroke her cheek. He heard her sharp intake of breath and quickly withdrew. "Don't forget your hat, too."

"Okay."

"Oh, and Charlie?" he called out, stopping her again. "Merry Christmas," he said softly.

Charlie grinned. "Merry Christmas, Nate." She was happy and excited as she invited him to follow her as she went to the kitchen to get her winter garments. He had come to visit her on Christmas Day, as if he couldn't wait one more day to spend time with her. And he wanted to take her to see the horses! He knew how much she loved the animals, and he wanted to share what he'd seen. Her parents were at the table when she and Nate entered the room.

"Nathaniel," her mother greeted. "'Tis nice to see you. Merry Christmas."

"Merry Christmas, Missy. Arlin." He gave each one a respectful nod.

"Did you have trouble with the roads?"

"*Nay*, Missy. The sleigh glides easily over the packed snow."

Arlin frowned as his daughter put on her coat. "Going out?"

"I've invited Charlie on a sleigh ride. There are some horses I think she'll enjoy seeing."

Missy smiled. "She loves horses. She'll enjoy them, I'm sure."

"*Ja*, I will," Charlie agreed. Her gaze settled on her father, who studied Nate thoughtfully. She hoped and prayed that *Dat* didn't say anything to embarrass her.

"You'd better dress warm, *dochter*," *Dat* instructed.

Nate grinned. "That's what I said."

Her father looked at him approvingly. "How are your *eldre*?"

"Doing well. We all are. Jacob is fully recovered from his accident with the mower."

The conversation was nice, but Charlie was eager to spend time with Nate. She grabbed her coat from a hook and suddenly it was taken out of her hands. Nate smiled down at her as he held it open for her. She tingled with pleasure as she placed an arm into each sleeve. She saw something shift in her *dat*'s expression as he watched Nate's courteous act. She swallowed hard as she wondered what her father was thinking.

"I'm ready," she said, stating the obvious.

"Will you be gone long?" her *dat* asked.

"About an hour at the most. 'Tis too cold for Charlie to spend more time outside."

Her father nodded.

"Don't forget to tie your bonnet strings," Nate said gently. Charlie frowned at him. She didn't like him being bossy while her parents looked on. But when she looked at her father and saw his approval, she relaxed and secured her bonnet.

"I'll make a pot of coffee for when you come back," her mother said.

"Sounds *gut*," Nate replied with a smile.

Charlie headed toward the front door, eager to be away from her parents' prying eyes. She extended her hand toward the doorknob but Nate reached over her shoulder to open the door for her.

She was all set to object until the brightness of the day calmed her. "'Tis so nice to see the sun." She wanted Nate's attention. Why fight it when she had exactly what she'd desired?

Nate was quiet as they reached his sleigh. When she glanced up, he was smiling down at her.

"What?" she whispered. "Why are you looking at me like that?" Although she loved seeing good humor in his eyes.

"I like seeing you happy."

Her breath caught. *You make me happy*, she longed to say but didn't. "I am happy," she said and his eyes flared. "'Tis nice to be outside without a blizzard."

Nate surrounded her waist with his hands and lifted her onto the seat. He quickly released her then climbed onto the other side. "Are you warm enough?"

Charlie watched his breath release as warm mist into the frigid air. She felt her insides melt as she gazed into his beautiful blue eyes. "I'm fine."

He reached for something under the sleigh seat. "I brought this just in case." He pulled out the quilt he'd wrapped her in when he'd picked her up from the school yesterday and handed it to her.

"'Tis dry." She smiled at him as she unfolded it. "I think we should share it," she said as she laid it across both of their laps.

He didn't move to grab the reins. He studied her silently, intently, for several long seconds with a look that made her toes curl and her heart skitter within her chest. "Ready to go, then?"

"I'm ready." He flicked the leathers and she grabbed the edge of her seat as the horse moved forward.

Snow sparkled on tree branches, house roofs and lawns. Charlie felt a sense of inner peace and well-being as she took in her surroundings. She only felt this way in Nate's company, she realized. Everything looked better and richer with Nate next to her.

It wasn't long before Nate pulled the sleigh to the side of the road and gestured toward the pasture. "There."

She looked and inhaled with wonder. "They're beautiful!"

The three horses within the paddock were all chestnut brown. They looked healthy and well cared for with their shiny coats and strong bodies. They pranced and ran in circles, chasing each other. Charlie laughed with delight. Nate was silent beside her, but his lips curved when she flashed him a grin. *"Danki."*

"Would you like get a closer look?" he asked with good humor.

Charlie studied the snowy ground and the pile made by the snowplow along the edge of the roadway. She didn't think it would be wise to stay parked there. And she didn't relish the thought of stepping knee-deep into icy snow.

"I can see well enough from here." She was happy

enough to enjoy the view from here, on the seat right next to Nate. They could stay a moment then move on if a car came.

He was silent. She turned to find him studying the scenery with a thoughtful look. As if sensing her regard, he met her gaze. "Your cheeks are pink," he commented huskily.

"Oh!" She held her gloved hands up to her face. "I must look silly."

"*Nay.* You look beautiful," he said with a serious look in his eyes. He took her hands from her face and replaced them with his gloved fingers. He cupped her cheeks as he gazed into her eyes and then stared at her mouth. "Are you feeling warmer?"

She bobbed her head.

"I don't remember seeing you speechless before," he said. He pulled off a glove and stroked her face with warm fingers. "Do I make you nervous?"

She held his gaze, shook her head. *"Nay,"* she whispered. "You make me feel other things."

His blue gaze sharpened. "Things?"

"Ja, gut things."

He released her but held her attention. "Charlie— what you said…"

"About?"

"Me…" He stopped, looked away, almost as if afraid of her reply. "Us."

"About you being my keeper?" she finished for him quietly as she regarded him with tenderness.

He locked gazes with her. *"Ja."*

"You don't want to be?" She softened her expression. "I'd like you to be."

"And who is a keeper to you?"

"He is someone, like you, who is there for me when I need him. Someone who wants to protect and care for me. Someone I'll love forever and who loves me back." She briefly closed her eyes. "A husband to me and father to my children." She swallowed as she gazed at him. She couldn't read him. "That's what a keeper means to me." There was emotion in his expression, but she couldn't get a read on it.

"And you," he began in a strangled voice, "want me?"

She smiled and reached up to grab his bare hand. "You're a *gut* man, Nathaniel Peachy. I've never met or known anyone better. I know I'm not the sort of person you envisioned for your sweetheart. I tend to be independent and I like to do things on my own… I'm impulsive and prone to getting into trouble."

He tugged on her hand to pull her against him. "You may be exactly what I need, Charlie Stoltzfus."

She beamed at him. *"Ja?"*

He cupped her face, then kissed her gently before placing her back in her seat. "Have you seen enough of the horses for today? Your *vadder* will be wondering where we are. I don't want to make him angry after our first outing."

"First?" she breathed.

"Ja, first," he said. "And there will be more." She saw something in his eyes that made her sigh with pleasure. "I'd like to court you, Charlie Stoltzfus, the proper way. Will you let me?"

She felt warmed by the sun and the man. *"Ja*, I'd very much like that."

He grinned at her as he ran fingers down her cheek briefly then let her go. *"Gut*. Let me take you home."

Chapter Fifteen

Second Christmas Day dawned bright and clear. Charlie had hidden her Christmas gift for Nate under her bed. Besides her sisters with their husbands, Nate and his family were coming for dinner, as were all of her Lapp relatives. Yesterday Nell, Meg and Leah had helped to make extra food. Ellie and she had worked hard to clean the house yesterday after Nate had brought her home from their ride.

The scent of pine filled the air. The snow that blanketed the lawn made for another glorious and blessed holiday. She still couldn't believe that Nate wanted to court her. It was her dream come true and her best Christmas gift ever.

The first of their visitors began to arrive at nine thirty. Aunt Katie and Uncle Samuel came with Daniel, Joseph and Hannah, their three children who lived with them. Charlie's married sisters were due to arrive shortly after them. Soon everyone was there but the Peachy family, and the house felt near to bursting at the seams with people intent on having a good time. One hour passed and then another. She went to the window several times. The morning had grown late and yet Nate and his family hadn't come.

Had he changed his mind about courting? Maybe he didn't want to let her down in front of her family and friends. She quickly dismissed the feeling. Nate loved her, she was sure. Something else must have happened to make them late. But what? Concern filled her as she recalled that Charlotte Peachy's baby was due in just a few short weeks. Had she gone into labor? What if something worse had happened? Like the family had suffered an accident while on their way over?

She had to go to him. She had to find out. Fear had her scurrying to find her mother and let her know of her plans. "I have to check," she said with tears in her eyes.

"You should let Elijah or Isaac take you."

"I don't want to ruin their plans."

"Charlie…"

"I'll be fine. The roads are fine."

"At least ask Isaac if you can use his sleigh."

She agreed and ran to see if he minded. When he argued about taking her, she didn't relent and finally her cousin gave in.

Her mother nodded. "Take your time. If Charlotte is in labor, they may need you to watch the little ones, but first you have to get there safely." She paused. "You need to see Nathaniel," she said astutely. "You care a great deal for him."

Charlie blushed. "Is it that obvious?"

"Only to your mother," *Mam* said. "And I know he cares for you, too."

"You think so?" she whispered, pleased, hoping that it was really true and she hadn't imagined the feelings between them.

"I do. Call it a mother's gift." She urged her toward the door. "Travel safely, *dochter*. If you need me for anything, send word and I'll come."

Charlie raced to Isaac's sleigh and headed toward the Abram Peachy residence. She'd driven her cousins' sleighs before, so she felt confident as she drove. When she arrived at the Abram Peachy farm, she saw two buggies parked side by side in the barnyard. She frowned as she parked the sleigh alongside the buggies and tied up the horses. She then climbed the porch steps and knocked. The door opened within seconds. "Jacob," she greeted. "Is everything *oll recht*? When you didn't come, I became worried."

"*Mam's* having the baby." He looked solemn as he stepped back and gestured her inside.

"How is she?"

"I don't know. Something's wrong, I think. Nate left to get the midwife."

"Is she in her room?"

He nodded.

"May I go up and see her? Maybe I can help."

He looked relieved. "*Ja*, if she'll let you. *Dat's* in the kitchen. She didn't want him in the room. I think 'tis because he becomes upset to see her in pain. Mary Elizabeth left earlier to spend the afternoon with Mark's family. Ruth and Harley went with her. Mae Ann left with Nate."

Charlie was trembling as she went up to the second floor and approached the couple's bedroom. She heard the woman cry out and rushed to help. She stood at the closed door a second before another cry prompted her to open it. "Charlotte?" she called out. "'Tis Charlie. May I come in?" There was another sharp cry then silence. She couldn't see around an interior wall to the bed. *"Charlotte?"*

When the woman didn't answer, Charlie went in. Nate's *mam* was on the bed, propped up on pillows. She looked pale and her eyes were closed.

Charlie approached slowly. "Hey, *Mam*," she said softly. "How can I help?"

Her eyes flickered open, and the woman offered her a weak smile. "Charlie."

"Ja, 'tis me." Encouraged, she approached. "I understand that Nate went for the midwife. I'd like to stay until she comes if you'll let me."

"Ja, please stay." She laid her hands on her abdomen as she shifted in the bed. "I'm afraid," Charlotte admitted. "The baby isn't due yet."

Charlie reached for her hand. "Two weeks either way is normal. This isn't your first baby. I'm sure he or she will be fine."

Charlotte grimaced as a contraction tightened her belly.

"Blow through your mouth," Charlie reminded her. "Little puffs. I'm sure you did that with Mae Ann and Harley, *ja*?"

Obeying immediately, Nate's mother blew in and out in short breaths. Charlie recognized when the pain left her as she quieted and briefly closed her eyes.

"Is the midwife here yet?" she asked weakly.

"Nay, not yet, but I'm sure she will be soon."

The woman relaxed as her pain eased. "I understand that you like being *schuul*teacher," she said.

"Ja, I do. I love working with children."

"I miss seeing you every day."

"I miss you," Charlie said.

"You're perfect for the job—until you marry and have children of your own."

Charlie's heart gave a lurch. "I would like children someday," she murmured. Had Nate informed his parents that they were seeing each other? She studied his stepmother and saw nothing in her expression that suggested the woman knew. She sighed as she realized that Nate wasn't ready for others to know.

"Nate thinks you're a wonderful teacher," Charlotte said.

Charlie blinked. "He does?"

"*Ja*. Do you know he spoke with the bishop about you?"

She stiffened, grew chilled. "He talked to the bishop?"

The woman shook her head. "I don't know what he said but it wasn't long afterward that you were offered the position."

"And you think Nate had something to do with it?"

His mother grimaced. Her body tightened with another contraction and she managed to gasp, "*Nay*. You got that on your own." She panted as previously instructed to get through the pain. Suddenly, she cried out. "Charlie, I can feel the baby coming!"

Charlie pushed aside her own upset as she looked for something to wrap the infant in. There was a small quilt on the dresser, and she reached for it. She held up the quilt. "I'm sorry, 'tis a beautiful blanket but we need it." She'd never delivered a baby before. But she could do it, she thought. She would deliver this baby, because she was the only one here and God must have wanted her to help. "Do you feel like pushing?" she asked, her heart racing wildly.

"Ja!" she cried out as Charlie laid the quilt across the bed in the best position to set the baby down after he was born.

A short time later a tiny angry cry filled the room as a new Peachy son was born. Charlie carefully lay the child on the quilt. The door burst open and the midwife entered, followed closely by Nate.

Nate took one look at her with the baby and his eyes widened.

"You should leave," the midwife said to Nate. "I'll call you when they're ready." The woman had come forward to inspect mother and baby.

After briefly meeting Nate's gaze, Charlie looked away. She felt betrayed. He hadn't told her the truth when he'd said he believed in her. It had been a lie. He hadn't trusted that she'd get the teaching job on her own and so he'd talked with the elders even though she'd asked him not to. Even after she'd explained why. A lump rose to her throat as she stood back and watched the midwife examine her patients.

"Are they well?" she asked anxiously.

The midwife, a woman by the name of Sarah Locke, smiled. "They're fine." She eyed Charlie intently. "You delivered her baby," she said.

Charlie nodded. "I had to use the quilt." She glanced toward the baby's mother, who now lovingly cradled her infant son. "I'm sorry."

Charlotte frowned. "Why?"

"I ruined it. I'll make you another quilt. Until then, I'll go to Leah's store and buy you a new one."

The new mother laughed. "I don't need another quilt, Charlie. You did *gut*. Stop second-guessing yourself." Her expression grew serious. "*Danki* for being there for me."

She nodded. "I'm glad I could help."

"Would you tell Abram to come up?"

"I'll head down now." Charlie stepped closer for another look at the baby. "Congratulations on your son."

"Danki." Charlotte Peachy was beaming. She looked pale and exhausted but gloriously happy.

She went downstairs to tell everyone the news. "Sarah said that you can go up now," she said as she grabbed her coat and put it on. She felt the intensity of Nate's gaze but wouldn't look at him. "I have to go."

He touched her arm. "Charlie."

"I have to go," she repeated in a strangled voice. The others had left the room and she could hear them climbing the steps to see the new addition to their family.

"Charlie, what's wrong?" He looked concerned and dumbfounded at her behavior.

"You didn't trust me," she whispered achingly. "You didn't listen and you didn't trust me."

Then she raced out the door to her sleigh and drove home. She understood now that he didn't love her the way she'd hoped. Her tears fell as she steered the sleigh over the snow-packed street. She brushed them away as she continued to cry. When she got home, she went up to her room. Someone knocked seconds later. When she didn't answer, the door opened and Ellie entered.

"Charlie, what happened? What's wrong? Did something happen to Charlotte?" She frowned as she sat on the side of Charlie's bed. "You've been crying."

"I'm fine." She forced a smile. "Charlotte just gave birth to a healthy son."

Ellie beamed. "That's wonderful."

"I delivered him."

Her sister's mouth dropped open. *"You* did?"

Tears filled her eyes as she nodded. "You don't believe I'm capable of it, do you?"

"*Nay*, 'tis not that!" Ellie reached out to rub Charlie's arm. "I just thought that a midwife would be there…or another woman in the *haus*."

"Nate left to get her, but the baby couldn't wait any longer."

"And you were there for her." Ellie grinned. "You are something, aren't you?"

She drew a sharp breath. "Am I?"

"I'm sure Nate was impressed." Her sister paused. "You love him." She lowered her brow. "*Ach nay*, something went wrong between the two of you."

Charlie shot her a look. "I—how did you know?"

"You're my sister. I know you. I've seen the way the two of you look when you're together. It was easy to see how you feel about him." She smiled. "And how he feels about you."

She rubbed a hand across her aching forehead. "Doesn't matter."

Ellie's brow furrowed. "What do you mean?"

"It means that Nate doesn't feel the same way about me as I do about him." The pain in her chest grew. "He doesn't trust that I can do anything successfully on my own."

"I doubt he feels that way now. Not after delivering his brother."

Charlie snorted. "Too late—and 'tis not the same. Do you know what I learned? Nate spoke to Bishop John about me…to help me get the teaching position."

"So? What is wrong with that?"

"After I specifically asked him not to!" she cried as she sat up. "I wanted to get the job on my own, Ellie. I know

I've made mistakes in the past, but I needed to know that the elders considered me the best person for the job. Apparently, they needed Nate to convince them of it."

With a murmur of sympathy, Ellie tugged her into her arms. "I don't believe that's how Nate feels. Honestly? I believe he loves you so much he couldn't help but interfere. He wants you to be happy."

"Then he should have listened to me."

"*Ja*, perhaps," Ellie said, surprising her. "But he is a man and he's in love, and men in love sometimes do dumb things."

"He believes I need a keeper."

Her sister's expression softened. "Perhaps you do. And Nate is perfect for you." Ellie smirked. "Did you need me to recommend him?"

"*Nay.*" Charlie experienced a lessening of her hurt and anger. She bit her lip. "How can I get past the fact that he lied to me? And he never actually said that he loves me."

"I think you're mistaken. I don't believe for a minute that Nate would lie to you. About your love for him—have you told him how you feel?"

She frowned. "*Nay*, how could I when I don't know if he really loves me? He said he wants to court me, but I don't know…"

To Charlie's shock, Ellie laughed. "*Ja*," she said, still chuckling, "the both of you are most definitely in love."

"Too late. I wasn't nice to him when I left."

"It will all work out in the end."

Regretting her behavior, Charlie closed her eyes. "I hope so." She offered a silent prayer that it would be so.

Chapter Sixteen

Nate stood in the corner of his parents' room and looked on as his father held his newborn son. *Dat* was seated on the edge of his wife's bed. His stepmother lay, resting, propped up by several pillows. There was tenderness in her expression and a smile of happiness on her lips as she watched her husband with their baby. His siblings were behind their father. Each one exclaimed over the perfection of the tiny life. Harley, the baby until Lucas was born, studied his brother with fascination. Ruth and Mae begged to hold Lucas and were told they'd each have a chance to hold him later.

As he quietly listened to everyone in the room, he found his thoughts going to Charlie and the abrupt way she'd left. She'd looked angry and hurt. What could he have done to upset her?

Charlie had delivered his baby brother! The fact still gave him pause. After his initial shock, he should have known not to be surprised. She was a capable, amazing young woman with spirit and gumption, which he loved and appreciated about her. Charlie Stoltzfus could do anything she set her mind to, he realized.

Hadn't she broken clear through his resistance to win his heart?

He loved her and wanted her as his wife with every breath he took. She'd literally changed his life for the better. In truth, he wished he could forget the courting stage and wed her tomorrow.

Everyone in the room exclaimed over the new baby. Nate managed a smile as he saw Mae Ann and then his little brother Harley lean in to give his new baby brother a soft kiss on his tiny forehead. At their father's suggestion, everyone left the room so that mother and son could sleep. Nate, the last to leave, turned to go.

"Nathaniel," his mother called. He halted and faced her. "Where's Charlie? I expected her to see me before she left."

"She seemed upset and in a hurry to leave," he said with concern. "She wouldn't talk or look at me when she came downstairs."

His *mam* frowned. "That's not right," she murmured. "The girl cares for you."

Nate shook his head. "I don't know if she does."

"She loves you. Of that, I have no doubt. Why do you think she came racing over here when we didn't show up for Second Christmas dinner? She was afraid something happened to you. She was worried."

"I..."

"You love her. I know you do. So why are you still home? Why haven't you gone after her?"

"You just had a baby," he began.

"And you want a life. Do you think I haven't noticed how you longed to spend time with her?"

"Maybe she changed her mind and decided I'm too old for her."

Mam laughed. "Absolutely not. That's not who

Charlie is. Do you know that she used to avoid coming here when she knew you'd be around?" She smiled. "She was nervous around you because she cared for you even then."

He arched an eyebrow. "The Charlie I know isn't afraid of anything."

She regarded him with a soft expression. "*Ja*, she is. You were so far out of her reach she thought she'd never have you."

"She needs a keeper."

His mother laughed. "*Ja*, she does."

"I'm not a *gut* one," he said with a frown. "Did *Dat* tell you about Emma?"

Her face softened. "*Ja*, he did. And we both feel the same. You did nothing wrong. Her death wasn't your fault. You were a boy and you tried everything you could to help her. God doesn't help those who don't help themselves. You didn't fail Emma and you won't fail Charlie."

Was it true? In his youth, had he wrongfully taken the blame for something he'd had no control over? "I love Charlie. I don't want her to change. I just want to be there for her every day in case she needs me." He paused. "For the rest of our lives."

"Then go!" She gestured toward the door. "I've always loved Charlie. I wouldn't mind having her as my *soohn*'s wife." She lay back against the pillows and closed her eyes. "Now go tell that woman of yours how much you love her."

Nate smiled. "*Ja, Mam.*"

Charlie lay in bed, fighting tears. The ache in her heart wouldn't go away. She loved Nate, but how could they have a life together if he didn't respect or trust her?

Her sister had left the room. It was later in the day, and Ellie must have made excuses for her and explained about the baby delivery, because no one had come upstairs to bother her. And for that she was thankful.

She still loved Nate and she always would. Why hadn't he listened? Why couldn't he have trusted her to become a teacher on her own? When he'd offered to talk with his father, the deacon, she'd said no. She didn't want him to interfere. But that he had anyway hurt beyond measure.

"Charlie!"

Charlie rose at her mother's call. *"Ja, Mam?"*

"You have a visitor!"

"Who is it?"

"Why don't you come down and see."

Heart racing as she thought of Nate, she got up off the bed and descended the stairs. To her shock, her visitor was Abram Peachy, Nate's father.

"Abram," she gasped. "I didn't expect to see you. Is Charlotte and your baby *oll recht*?"

"They are fine. We've chosen a name for him—Lucas."

"Lucas." She smiled. "I like it." She eyed him curiously. "If everyone's fine, then why have you come?"

"To thank you for what you did today. I don't know how my wife would have done it without you. You have been a blessing to our family, Charlie, and for a long time. 'Tis why I told the elders you'd be a *gut* teacher and they agreed."

Charlie gazed at him speechless. "*You* recommended me for the job?"

"*Ja.*" He eyed her with concern. "You seem surprised."

"I thought I got the job because of Nate. I found out that he spoke with Bishop John."

Abram looked surprised. "He did?"

"*Ja.* Charlotte told me."

His brow cleared. "Ah! That must have been after we'd already made our choice." He smiled. "We made the decision to offer you the job before we left for Indiana."

"Then I got the position on my own?"

"*Ja*, of course. Why would you think otherwise?"

She shrugged. "No reason." She grinned, happy that she'd been offered the teacher job based on her own merits. But that didn't excuse the fact that Nate thought she couldn't have.

"I should get home."

Charlie nodded. Everyone would be gathering at Amos King's for church on Sunday. "I'll see you at Amos and Mac's." She followed him to the door. Nate was coming up the steps as his father was leaving.

"*Dat,*" he said with surprise.

"Nate. Come to see Charlie, have you?" he said with a twinkle.

"If she will talk with me." His eyes shifted to lock gazes with her. "Charlie."

"I'll see you at home, *soohn,*" Abram said before he left.

She started to turn away as Nate rushed up the steps and into the house. He gently caught her arm. "Charlie."

She scowled at him. "What are you doing here, Nathaniel Peachy?"

He seemed taken aback by her hostility. And despite her anger with him, she loved him and hated to see his pain. "What do you want?" she asked with a sigh.

"I need to talk with you."

"I *don't* need to talk with you." She gave him her back.

"Charlie, I love you."

She stiffened, unwilling to believe she'd heard correctly. He touched her shoulder before his hand slid up to cup her nape. "Nathaniel."

"I mean it, Charlie. I thought to be patient and take things slowly, but I can't do it anymore. I had to tell you today. I love you and I want us to be together forever." She saw him swallow hard. "I want to marry you."

Charlie closed her eyes on a wave of pain. "You don't think I can do things on my own." His caressing fingers on her neck stilled.

"*Ja*, I do. I believe in you. I told you that."

"*Ja*, words were all they were, but I know the truth." She faced him defiantly. "You went to Bishop John. You talked about me! You didn't think I could win the teaching position on my own."

"*Ja*, I did. And, *ja*, I admit talking with him. You amaze me, Charlie. I went to see John so that I could tell him about everything you did for me and Jacob. I couldn't not tell him. I love you and I needed to tell someone how wonderful you are, and I couldn't talk about you with anyone else!"

She gazed at him with mouth agape. "You think I'm wonderful?"

His expression softened. "You are wonderful, Charlie. And amazing, and I want you for my wife."

"You want to be my keeper," she said as the pain and anger she'd been feeling began to subside.

"I want to be your definition of a keeper. I want to be your husband, the one who will love you until death parts us…the woman I want to have children with." He stopped and his face filled with worry. "That is if you still want children after what you did today."

"And what did I do?" she teased softly. She really did love this misguided man, and she would continue to love him for a lifetime.

"Deliver a baby—my *bruder*. You saw what mothers must endure to have children."

Charlie laughed. When he looked stung, she softened her laughter to an affectionate smile. "I know what women go through while giving birth. How can I not? Do you think I've never seen birthing before? I have. But I must confess that I haven't been the only one in the room before today. 'Tis worth it, you know… the pain of childbirth, for once you hold a baby in your arms, you understand. All good things come to those who understand. And, Nate? I understand that I'd like nothing more than to be your wife and give you children."

Nate gazed at her with rapture. "You're certain? That I'm the right man?"

"I'm absolutely, positively certain." She reached for his hand. "And Nathaniel? I don't want to hear any more about the difference in our ages. Age means nothing when there is love." She gave him a tender smile. "And I love you with all my heart." She blinked at him as her eyes suddenly filled with tears. "I thought you didn't believe in me."

"I did. I do." He reached out to run his hand up her arm. "I believe in you and I don't want you to change."

"Not even a little bit?" she joked.

He tugged her closer until she could feel the warmth in his gaze within the beat of her heart. "Not even a little bit."

"I think you might regret saying that."

Nate laughed. "Maybe." He took both of her hands.

Charlie's mother came out of a room and headed toward the stairs. She froze when she saw them. "Nate!"

"*Hallo*, Missy. I've come to talk with Charlie." He beamed down at the woman whose hands he held.

She smiled. "I see. And how is your new baby *bruder*?"

"Lucas is fine. He's healthy and *Mam* and *Dat* are extremely happy and pleased that Charlie was there to help him into the world."

"Will you be going to the Amos Kings' for church service?" her mother asked him.

"I'll be there."

"*Gut.*" She continued past them to ascend the stairs, pausing once on the steps to smile down at them. "'Tis *gut* to see you here, Nathaniel." Then she disappeared from sight as she reached the second floor.

"I think my *mudder* knows how we feel about each other."

"*Ja*, I think so, too," he said, raising their held hands. "She doesn't seem to mind." He hugged her briefly then released her. "I should go, but I'll see you tomorrow."

She smiled as she bobbed her head. "Be careful going home," she said softly.

She followed him outside onto the porch. The air

was brisk and Nate looked back, frowned and said, "Get back inside before you catch your death."

"*Ja*, Nathaniel."

Charlie watched the man she loved drive away. She looked forward to spending the future with him. His behavior in front of her mother made it clear that he was ready to announce their relationship to everyone. *He loves me.*

She sent up a silent prayer of thanks to the Lord for granting her heart's desire.

Two days after Second Christmas brought snow flurries that fluttered down to earth in glorious white wonder. As she stood at the window at home, she wondered when Nate would arrive. Because his family hadn't enjoyed the holiday due to the baby's birth, they were to celebrate it today.

She hadn't seen him yesterday. The short separation after his declaration of love seemed like forever. She missed him. Where was he? She'd expected him here by now.

Hugging herself, Charlie gazed out into the barnyard. Suddenly, she was surrounded by masculine arms and pulled back to rest against someone's chest. "You had better be Nathaniel Peachy or I won't be responsible for my actions."

He laughed, and the sound was so lighthearted and joyful that she tugged out of his arms to face him. "Merry do-over Christmas, Charlie."

She enjoyed looking at him. His blue eyes sparkled. He looked relaxed…and happy and more than content. "I thought you'd never get here," she breathed.

"I've been here awhile," he admitted.

She froze. "You have?" Why hadn't he come to see her sooner?

"I stopped to talk with the bishop."

Charlie scowled. "What for?"

"To ask permission to marry you."

"You did?" she whispered with wonder.

A smile continued to hover on his lips. There was tenderness in his expression and warmth and love in his blue gaze. "*Ja*, and the deacon…and then I cornered your father to ask for his blessing."

"You did?"

He chuckled as he reached out to tuck in a lock of stray hair. "I did."

"And did you get my *vadder*'s blessing?"

"*Ja*." He leaned in until they touched foreheads. "'Tis official. Everyone approves and so now you will have to marry me." His smile dimmed a little as he straightened. "We'll have to wait a year until the month of weddings. I know it will be the longest year of my life, but at least I'm allowed to court you openly."

"So in a year, I'll become your keeper. And you'll be mine," she said breathlessly. "My husband."

"I'll be forever yours." He handed her a wrapped package. "Merry Christmas, love. I'm sorry I couldn't give you this sooner." A smile hovered about his lips. "Open it."

With hands that shook, she unwrapped the package and gasped. "'Tis a wooden mare and her colt!"

He nodded. "*Ja*, do you like them?"

"I love them!" She reached out to touch his face. "They are as beautiful as the other horse you made me." She played with the ends of his hair. "How do you know me so well?"

He shrugged. She reached toward a table where she'd set Nate's gift earlier. "Merry Christmas," she whispered as she handed him a box. "'Tis not as nice as the one you gave me." Inside she'd placed the new scarf she'd bought for him and something she'd made for him on her own. Something silly that she hoped he'd nevertheless appreciate.

The wrapping came off, and Nate opened the cardboard flaps. He saw the scarf first and grinned at her.

"For when you are cold," she said. "I'm sorry I didn't make it for you. I haven't mastered the art of knitting yet, but I will." She watched as he lifted the scarf out of the box and put it around his neck. He looked at what was left inside the box and started to laugh. "Ingredients for peanut butter and jam sandwiches," he said with a twinkle of delight in his blue eyes.

"I made all three—the jam, the peanut butter and the bread."

He looked at her with such love in his eyes that she caught her breath. "You will make me the best wife and keeper."

"Do you think so?" She felt a warmth that brought tears of happiness to her eyes.

"*Ja*, I do." His expression darkened for a moment, and Charlie suffered a moment of fear. "There is something I have to tell you. If you change your mind about me, I'll understand."

She swallowed hard. "What is it?"

"Do you want to know why I've kept my distance from you? Why I'm insistent about keeping you safe?"

She nodded, but felt unsure.

He reached for her hands and held them. "I had a sweetheart when I was sixteen. Her name was Emma," he began. "She was a bit reckless and impulsive. She always seemed to crave excitement. I cared for her a great deal, and I thought she cared for me. Maybe she did and maybe she didn't. Either way, she didn't listen to me when I warned her against her English friends. One night she had slipped out of her house to go joy-riding with them. The car crashed and the four *Englishers* were seriously hurt. Emma was killed instantly."

"Nate," she breathed, watching him, her heart filled with compassion for a wounded young man who'd lost someone he'd loved.

He released one of her hands to caress her face. "The way I felt for her is nothing like I feel for you, Charlie. I was a boy. I didn't know what love was until my love for you."

She blinked rapidly. She tugged her hand free, lay her head on his chest and slipped her arms about him in a heartfelt hug.

"Charlie," he said and she pulled back. "That's not all."

Alarmed, she could only gaze at him. "I've had a hard time with Emma's death because I saw it happen. The accident. I was the first on the scene and knew immediately that she was dead."

"Oh, Nate…" She raised up on her toes to kiss his cheek, his chin, until she finally settled a sweet kiss against his mouth. "I'm sorry."

He blinked. "I felt I'd failed her, Charlie. For a long time, I was afraid I'd fail you, too."

"And now?" She waited with bated breath.

"I'm older and wiser. I realize that I'm not the same person I was back then, and you're most definitely not Emma. You're Charlie, the woman I love. The only woman I've ever truly loved."

Epilogue

Christmas Day, Two Years Later

A baby's cry had Nate running up the steps to the master bedroom in their farmhouse. He halted on the threshold and caught his breath. His wife lay in bed, cradling their new baby. She looked radiant as she smiled at the infant in her arms. He'd been waiting downstairs it seemed like forever. If he'd had his way, he would have stayed right beside her, but the midwife had insisted that no men were allowed in the room during the childbirth.

Charlie glanced over to see him in the doorway. "Nathaniel," she said as she reached out a hand toward him. "Come and meet your son."

With a rush of love, he hurried to her side. He swallowed against a suddenly tight throat. He didn't fight the tears that sprang to his eyes and trailed down his cheeks. "A son," he whispered.

"Congratulations, Nate." Missy Stoltzfus stood on the other side of the room, watching with a warm smile.

He beamed at her through his tears before turning back to his wife, the woman he adored above all others. He sensed that his mother-in-law and the midwife had left the room to give them privacy. "I love you, *Mam*," he said, referring to her new status.

She jerked with surprise, then her features softened with a bright smile. "I guess I'll have to get used to him calling me that." She beamed down at her son. "'Tis a special gift, becoming a mother."

"You're my special gift. My Christmas gift for always," he murmured since it was during the Christmas season two years ago that he'd won approval from the church elders and their parents to take Charlie to wife. No one seemed bothered by the fact that he was older than she was by seven years. And he wondered now why he'd allowed it to bother him in the first place. He reached out to stroke his infant son's cheek. "Merry Christmas, *soohn*."

"Our Christmas blessing," Charlie said with happiness and love for him and their newborn in her expression.

"What will we name him?"

"I was thinking of Zacharias."

"Or Zachary," he murmured, liking both.

"Or Ezekiel," she said. "We could call him Zeke."

"*Ja*. I like that name best." He bent and brushed a kiss against her forehead. "You don't regret giving up your teaching job?"

She shook her head. "How can I? I have you and now, as if God has decided that we don't have enough happiness, a child of our own. Nothing can compare to the life you've given me."

"Amen," he breathed as he leaned in to kiss her. "Merry Christmas, my love."

"Merry Christmas, husband," she said with tears glistening in her beautiful green eyes, eyes he would forever be lost in—and love.

* * * * *

HER AMISH
HOLIDAY SUITOR

Carrie Lighte

For the readers who have followed my
Amish Country Courtships series, with much gratitude
for your interest and best wishes for your lives.

For the Lord seeth not as man seeth;
for man looketh on the outward appearance,
but the Lord looketh on the heart.
—*1 Samuel* 16:7

Chapter One

❧

"You did *what*?" Nick Burkholder asked as he guided his horse along the dark, winding country roads of Willow Creek, Pennsylvania. It was the Sunday after Thanksgiving, and he and his brother were on their way to a singing at Frederick Stutzman's house. Their plan was to make a brief appearance and then leave to hang out with Nick's Amish friends from Elmsville at an eatery in Highland Springs.

"On Friday night I, uh, sort of started a fire in Jenny Nelson's cabin," seventeen-year-old Kevin repeated, referring to the vacation house of an *Englisch* acquaintance.

The redheaded brothers were known for kidding around, so Nick assumed Kevin was joking. "Oh, I get it. You mean you started a fire in their fireplace. You sounded so serious you had me going for a minute there. *Voll schpass.*"

"I wish it were very funny," Kevin replied, using the *Englisch* term for *voll schpass.* It seemed to Nick his brother had picked up more *Englisch* phrases and habits during the first six months of his *rumspringa* than Nick had learned during the entirety of his own five-year running around period.

Kevin's voice was somber as he continued. "I mean, *jah*, initially I was trying to start a fire in the fireplace, but one of the newspaper logs I rolled must have—"

"Kevin!" Nick cut him off. "You should know better than to use newspaper logs after all the warnings *Daed*'s given you!"

"I just thought—"

"*Neh*, that's just the problem. You didn't *think* at all," Nick retorted, ironically using the same words his father often used when lecturing *him*. He brought the buggy to a standstill at the side of the road and turned to face Kevin. "Please tell me no one was injured."

"*Neh*. But there was a little superficial damage to the walls and ceiling."

Kevin proceeded to tell Nick he must have been distracted by the other guests summoning him into the kitchen to eat, because he forgot to close the protective mesh screen on the fireplace. He reckoned when someone opened the door to the cabin it created a back draft, and ash from the dry newspaper logs was swept through the air, because the next thing anyone knew, a pair of window curtains caught fire. The flames quickly leaped to a dried floral wreath hanging on the wall nearby, and before Jenny could retrieve the extinguisher, the wood paneling and ceiling had been burned, too.

Nick's mind was reeling, and he could hardly focus on the additional details Kevin provided about the mishap. If only Nick had attended the party with him, the fire probably wouldn't have happened. But Nick's parents had requested Nick stay behind and help take inventory at the hardware store his father owned.

"You just went out on Wednesday night. You're too old to be gallivanting around at every opportunity," his mother had said in a tone that indicated she meant business. "Your *daed* needs your help organizing and stocking up on specialty products the *Englisch* buy for *Grischtdaag*. Friday evening is the only opportunity he has."

Nick couldn't refuse. At twenty-one, he'd stretched out his *rumspringa* longer than almost anyone in his church district, which was a point of contention between his parents and him. They strongly implied if he didn't decide to join the church soon, he'd have to move out on his own. While he wouldn't be shunned, it would be disgracing for the entire family if he lived apart from them but stayed in the Amish community without being baptized into the church.

The choice should have been an easy one, and deep down, Nick had already made up his mind. He loved God, he loved being Amish and he loved his community. By now he knew that although some aspects of *Englisch* life were appealing, he had no desire to "go *Englisch*" for good. But he was also keenly aware that as long as he didn't join the church, he wouldn't be permitted to marry an Amish woman. And although he had courted most of the eligible young women in Willow Creek, as well as several from the Elmsville district, he hadn't met anyone he considered compatible enough to marry. Apparently, the same wasn't true for how the women felt about him; when he inevitably broke up with them, the women often expressed deep disappointment. Worse, they cried as if there were no tomorrow, no matter how gentle or diplomatic he tried to be about ending their courtship.

To Nick it seemed the women he courted didn't really care whether they were compatible with him. It was as if they were more interested in being married than being in a marriage *relationship*. Granted, there was no mandate requiring Nick to get married once he joined the church, but it was generally expected. Once he was baptized, the pressure—especially from his mother— would really kick in. So, by prolonging his *rumspringa*, Nick was securing his bachelorhood just a little longer. Meanwhile, someone new might move to town. After all, a spouse was a gift from the Lord, and who could say when and how the Lord might give him that gift?

Kevin spoke again, jarring Nick from his thoughts. "Jenny said if I pay for the repairs, she'll hire a contractor and then she won't have to tell her folks about the fire. So, can you lend me the money? Since we're passing Jenny's house on the way to Highland Springs, I sort of promised her I'd let her know tonight."

"Are you *narrish*?" Nick asked, calling his brother *crazy*. "I cleaned out my savings to purchase Penny last spring."

Penny, named for the color of his coat, was the horse Nick bought from an Amish man who had acquired the animal at a harness racing track. It wasn't unusual for the Amish to purchase American standardbred horses, which were most commonly used for buggy pulling, and Penny was a particularly fine gelding. Only four years old, he was exceptionally fast and strong, although not quite up to competition speed. As such, he cost more than the four-thousand-dollar limit most of Willow Creek's Amish spent on a horse, but Nick had saved for years. When he took Penny out for a test run, he immediately knew the swift, powerful, high-spirited animal was exactly what he wanted.

The cost was another point of contention between him and his parents, who thought it was foolish to splurge when an older, less expensive standardbred would have served his transportation needs adequately for years to come. His parents thought the purchase was prideful, but Nick wasn't seeking admiration; it was the speed and agility the horse provided that drew Nick to him. True, Penny could only safely run so fast when he was hitched to the buggy, but Nick had made adjustments to streamline his buggy, too. Those adjustments had cost him every last cent he had, and he reiterated that he was in no position to help his brother financially.

"Oh." In the dim light, Nick saw Kevin's features droop as he lifted his hat and swiped at his forehead. "I guess I'm going to have to tell *Daed* then."

"That's not a *gut* idea. You know how concerned he's been about finances ever since Harper's Hardware opened across town. And you know how worried *Mamm* is about his blood pressure and stress levels."

Kevin shrugged. "I don't know what else to do."

Nick rubbed his forehead. He didn't know what else to do, either, but telling their father was the last thing he could allow. Not only was he concerned about adding to his parents' burdens, but somehow Nick knew he'd get blamed for introducing Kevin to a group of "wild *Englischers*"—even if they were all very respectable Christians and the fire was solely Kevin's fault. Undoubtedly, his father would be so angry about

Kevin's carelessness that he'd finally put his foot down about Nick's *rumspringa* coming to an end, too. Nick couldn't let that happen.

"Give me a minute. I'll think of something," he said.

Twenty-year-old Lucy Knepp dawdled in the kitchen, drying the last pot. Usually the Amish didn't eat a large supper on the Sabbath, but there were so many leftovers from Thanksgiving they had dirtied half a dozen pans reheating the food. Lucy's stepsisters, Mildred and Katura, stepped into the kitchen just as she was hanging up the dishcloth.

"There you are." Mildred sounded triumphant, as if it were unusual to find Lucy cleaning up after supper.

Actually, Lucy did the majority of the housework, cooking and baking for her family. Born eight weeks prematurely, she had suffered respiratory problems since birth, which prevented her from helping with yard work, gardening and cleaning the stable, so she tried to make up for it by taking on more chores inside their home.

"You must *kumme* with us to Frederick's *haus* for the singing. We're also going to plan our *Grischtdaag* caroling rehearsal schedule," Katura announced.

Lucy didn't want to go with them. For one thing, Frederick had passed several notes to her at previous singings, a sure sign he was preparing to ask to be her suitor. Even though she'd tactfully but distinctly ignored his pursuit, his interest hadn't waned. Frederick was a nice enough young man, but Lucy had no interest in being courted by him. She had no interest in being courted by *any* of the single men in Willow Creek, for that matter. By and large they seemed too rambunctious and unreliable for her to imagine ever becoming a wife to one of them.

Likewise, Lucy had long ago accepted that she wasn't the kind of vibrant, vivacious woman most Willow Creek boys would want to court. With the exception of Frederick, who probably liked her because she was the only eligible woman who was shorter than he was—not to mention that his rather aggressive mother was especially fond of Lucy. Lucy had overheard enough comments to understand the bachelors in Willow Creek considered her personality to be dull. She realized her physical appearance didn't appeal to the men her age, either. She had plain brown eyes and ordinary brown hair. Her only distinctive features were her glasses—which earned her the nickname "Bug Eyes" in school—and her petite size, which made it even easier for young men to overlook her.

"You go ahead without me," Lucy suggested to her stepsisters. "I'll stay and help Betty clean up." Lucy had never known her own mother, who had died in childbirth, but in the five years since Betty had become her stepmother, Lucy still couldn't bring herself to call Betty *"Mamm,"* and she was glad when Betty didn't insist.

"But everything is cleaned and put away already. And you know *Mamm* won't let us go unless you *kumme,* too."

She was right. Even though Mildred was eighteen and Katura was the same age as Lucy, Betty was likely to prohibit her daughters from going out unless Lucy went with them. Sunday evening singings were intended to be a time of fellowship and fun for young people, but Lucy noticed the majority of Willow Creek's singles only went to the singings so they'd have an excuse to get out of their houses. They'd make a brief showing at the host house, where they participated in a few songs, and then they'd pair up to take off for parties or wherever it was they went.

Half the time Lucy brought a book so she could slip away to a corner to read. She frequently returned home without either Mildred or Katura, who would sneak off before she realized they had ditched her. By that time, her father and Betty were usually asleep, and the next day Lucy never mentioned where her sisters had gone.

"But I was planning to work on an embroidery project," Lucy objected.

"Work isn't permitted on the Sabbath," Katura scolded, as if Lucy weren't always meticulous about following the rules of her district's *Ordnung*.

With all the patience she could muster, Lucy explained, "This isn't something I'm going to consign at Schrock's Shop. It's the tablecloth-and-napkin set for the charity auction at the Piney Hill Christmas festival."

Since embroidering was quiet, sedentary work and the project wasn't for her own financial profit, Lucy felt she could work on the project on the Sabbath in good conscience. Moreover, she *needed* to work on the project that evening.

Her deadline for completing it was December 21, when the linens would be displayed with other items in a silent auction to benefit the *Englisch* soup kitchen where she volunteered on Wednesday nights. Interested buyers would have two days to bid on the goods and Lucy and her family planned to attend the festival the evening of the twenty-third, when the highest bid was announced. Last year she'd been sick with pneumonia and wasn't able to participate in any fundraising events for the soup kitchen. This year the organization was so strapped it couldn't even afford to repair their commercial oven, and they were counting on Lucy's contribution to raise at least half the funds they needed.

"Can't you do that tomorrow? You're home all day."

Mildred's ignorance was insulting; Lucy may have been home all day, but when she wasn't keeping house her time was spent working on items she consigned at Schrock's Shop so she could contribute to their family's living expenses. As it was, Lucy could barely manage to fill the customers' specialty orders for Christmas. She'd have to keep all unnecessary distractions to a minimum if she was going to complete the auction project on time, too. Unfortunately, she realized her stepsisters would keep wheedling until she gave in, and that in itself would be a distraction.

"Okay," she agreed. "But you have to take care of unhitching the buggy and stabling the horse when we get home." The weather was turning cold and she couldn't afford to get sick.

"Sure. We wouldn't want you exerting yourself," Mildred said, and Lucy didn't know if she was being sarcastic or sincere.

"*Mamm!* We're leaving now," Katura called after the trio bundled into their winter cloaks and donned their gloves. Lucy never understood why Betty didn't tell her daughters it wasn't polite to shout in the house. "We'll be home before midnight."

Midnight? Lucy didn't even want to stay past nine, but when she opened her mouth to protest, she quickly closed it again. Arguing would cost her more time. Instead, she said, "I'll be right back."

She darted upstairs and grabbed her embroidery materials and carefully placed them in a canvas bag. She figured by midnight she could probably finish embroidering at least one of the napkins—provided she could find a secluded place where no one would interrupt her.

After a few minutes of silence, Nick said, "I'll talk to Jenny about the damage. Maybe there's a way I can make the repairs myself." Having worked with his uncle's carpentry crew for a year when his uncle was ill, Nick was a better craftsman than Kevin.

"But when?" Kevin questioned. "It's not a one-day job. You know we won't get any Saturdays off until after *Grischtdaag*." He went on to explain that Jenny's family was planning a Christmas Eve reunion in the cabin with her ailing grandfather, who was traveling all the way from Spokane, Washington, to celebrate the holiday with them.

"I'll have to work on it in the evenings then, won't I?" Nick didn't try to temper his irritation at his brother.

Kevin snorted. "The store is open late on weeknights until *Grischtdaag*, too. There's no way *Mamm* and *Daed* will let you get out of helping."

"Actually, there is. *You're* going to insist you can cover for me at the store."

Kevin's jaw dropped. "I already told them I want to go caroling this year. If I have to stay late at the store, I'll miss the rehearsals during the week."

"Well, unless the money drops from the sky or you

suddenly develop expert carpentry skills, you'll have to tell them you changed your mind," Nick advised, annoyed that Kevin still didn't comprehend the sacrifice he was making for him. "Besides, you're not interested in caroling. You just want to get out of working at night during the week."

Kevin didn't deny it. "So what excuse are you going to give *Mamm* and *Daed* for going out on weeknights?" he asked.

"Maybe I'll say *I'm* joining the carolers." Even as he suggested the idea, Nick knew it wasn't plausible. For as many singings as he'd been to, he hardly ever sang. He couldn't carry a tune and his parents knew it, but because singings were chaperoned, they didn't discourage him from attending. "Or maybe I'll tell them I'm courting someone."

"Who? You've already courted all the *meed* in Willow Creek," Kevin countered.

Courtships among the Amish were usually private matters and Nick definitely hadn't told Kevin about his romantic relationships. "How would you know?"

"Word gets around. Everyone says you're a real heartbreaker," Kevin replied flippantly. "You'd practically have to leave Lancaster County to find someone you haven't already courted."

Nick was suddenly inspired. "Hey, maybe someone has a cousin visiting Willow Creek for the Thanksgiving holiday. Let's stop at Frederick's *haus* and check it out. Then we can go talk to Jenny about the repairs."

But when they entered Frederick's home and Nick scanned the room, his hope flagged. The only out-of-towner present was Frederick's cousin, Mark. The usual young women from Willow Creek and the Elmsville district were encircling him, batting their lashes and fiddling with their *kapp* strings. Katura and Mildred Peachy, Lucy Knepp's stepsisters, appeared downright enraptured, and it occurred to Nick he hadn't ever courted either of them. But asking to walk out with Katura or Mildred was a risk he couldn't take. He'd heard how outspoken the sisters had been about wanting to get married at the slightest hint of interest from young men who weren't even their suitors yet. That was exactly the kind of pressure Nick wanted to prevent.

He nudged Kevin, muttering "Let's get out of here," but just then Frederick's mother noticed them and insisted they take off their coats and have some hot chocolate. They couldn't refuse since she was the hosting chaperone, so they gave her their coats and shuffled into the kitchen. After eating popcorn and downing their mugs of cocoa, Nick meandered to the back room to grab their jackets so they could head to Jenny's house.

He had to dig through a heap of coats and cloaks piled on the bed before he found theirs. He was about to exit the room when he caught a small movement out of the corner of his eye. It was Lucy Knepp sitting in a circle of faint lamplight, her head bowed. Was she praying? No, she was sewing.

That was typical. Ever since they were in school Lucy had distanced herself from the other scholars. At recess she always stayed inside and cleaned the whiteboards. It was generally accepted she was the teacher's pet, and the boys believed she spied on them from the window and tattled about their wrongdoings to the teacher. More than once Nick received a scolding for antics on the playground the teacher couldn't have known about unless Lucy had told her.

She probably had matured by now, but she was still one of the most boring women he'd ever met—either that, or she was a snob, because she made no attempt at even the most casual of conversations. But she was respected by virtually all the parents in Willow Creek, who admired her good manners and quiet thoughtfulness, as well as her dedication to serving the less fortunate *Englischers* in their community.

Because Lucy didn't look up from her fabric, Nick decided he'd pussyfoot it out of the room without greeting her, but suddenly an idea struck him. *She* could be his pretend girlfriend! The plan unfolded almost instantly in his mind's eye: Kevin could "accidentally" let it slip in front of their parents Nick was courting Lucy. Once they heard that, they'd let him go out whenever he wanted, no questions asked.

But how would he convince Lucy he wanted to be her suitor? They were as different as salt and pepper. She'd never believe he genuinely wanted to court her, and even if she did believe it, there was no way she'd accept his offer. The only time they'd really spoken to each other had been when Nick was courting her cousin Bridget. But after Bridget broke up with him three years ago, Lucy hardly looked in his direction. *I'll have to tell her the truth*, Nick concluded. Or some version of the truth. He'd have to present his situation in a way that appealed to her sense of charity and compassion.

"Eh-hem." When Nick cleared his throat, Lucy glanced up and the lenses in her glasses reflected the weak lamplight. How could she see to sew? "Hi, Lucy."

"Hello, Nick," she replied, and adjusted her glasses on her nose. She gestured to the coats he was tightly gripping. "Do you want me to turn the lamp up or did you find what you came in here to get?"

"Jah," he replied, stalling.

"Jah you want me to turn the lamp up or *jah* you found what you needed?" she asked. Was she smirking or smiling at him?

"I've got my coat, *jah*," he said, glad the light was low so she couldn't watch his face turn as red as his hair. Why was he so nervous? He'd proposed courtship over a dozen times before and he'd never felt like this. "I actually, er, came looking for you."

"For me?" She cocked her head.

"Jah. There's a favor I'd like to ask."

Lucy didn't know what to make of Nick's behavior, but there was definitely something fishy about it. It reminded her of his tomfoolery when they'd attended school together. As he shifted from foot to foot she sensed he was there to deliver a joke, and she wanted him to get it over with so she could return to her embroidery. The lighting was terrible and she'd already had to undo her stitching several times, but she didn't want to turn the lamp up, lest she be discovered by dauntless Frederick or his pushy mother, Mary.

"Okay, what's the favor?"

"It's going to sound…it's going to sound *lecherich*. But I wondered if you'd consider allowing me to court you. I mean, I don't really want to court you, I just don't know who else to ask. You see—"

"You're right, that does sound *lecherich*," she interrupted, appalled he'd point out how ridiculous it was for him to consider courting her and then have the gall to admit he was only asking her because he'd run out of other prospects. "And I don't want to be courted by you, either."

She dipped her head and squinted at her stitching, hoping he'd scram. Did he think she'd be so enamored of him she'd gleefully accept his half-hearted offer, the way so many other women in Willow Creek had? They all knew he'd never be serious about sustaining a romantic relationship, but that didn't stop them from saying yes.

Even Lucy's favorite cousin, Bridget, had fallen for him—and then he'd broken her heart by striking up a relationship with someone else before his courtship with Bridget was over. Lucy was smarter than that. She didn't care how charismatic or impishly handsome anyone considered him to be, she didn't need the affections of Nick Burkholder to make her feel special.

"Lucy, please listen," he pleaded.

She glared in his direction and snapped, "What?"

Nick delved into a story about his *Englisch* friends, the Nelson family, whose vacation cabin was damaged by a small fire while Mr. and Mrs. Nelson were away for the Thanksgiving holiday. The family was anticipating celebrating Christmas together there one last time with their dying grandfather, but the parents didn't know the interior was a wreck. Nick's friend didn't want to add to their distress by telling them about the damage since they were already distraught about the grandfather's health. The goal was to complete the repairs before Mrs. Nelson began decorating the cabin for their party.

"I'm pretty confident I can get it all spruced up in

time for their celebration, but I need a *gut* excuse to go out in the evenings to work on it. That's where a courtship with you figures in."

Lucy was skeptical. The whole story was probably a fabrication, and she wouldn't be surprised if Nick's friends were listening at the door to hear if she'd fall for it. "Why don't you just tell your *eldre* the real reason you need to go out? They're warmhearted people. They'd want to help."

Nick rambled, "Like I said, Mr. and Mrs. Nelson don't even know about the fire, so I've got to keep it a secret that I'm renovating the walls. And, I, uh, I probably shouldn't be telling you this but my *daed*'s health has suffered and he's been under quite a bit of financial strain ever since Harper's Hardware came to town. In order to compete with them, we have to keep our store open late until *Grischtdaag*. Even though my brother absolutely can handle the customers without me, since the Nelsons are *Englischers*, well, my *daed* would probably say our family's business takes top priority." Nick wiped his palms against his trousers, casting his gaze toward the floor as he admitted, "If I were courting someone, that would be a different story, because my *eldre* are sort of eager to see me…to see me settle down, as you might imagine."

Lucy *could* imagine. Two Sundays ago after church, Mildred had babbled about how she'd overheard Nick's mother complaining to Doris Plank that she was worried Nick would never join the church and get married. Hearing that, Katura had sulked all the way home because Nick had never asked to be *her* suitor.

"Please, Lucy?" Nick entreated, and she suddenly understood why her peers said yes to walking out with him. There was something irresistible about his earnest manner, his big blue eyes, and the way his nose and cheeks were speckled with freckles. "My friend's *groossdaadi* might not live long enough to return to Willow Creek, but if he does, he'll be devastated to find his boyhood cabin in tatters."

Lucy's resolve was beginning to waver. She wanted the Nelsons and their grandfather to have a merry Christmas, especially if it was going to be their last celebration together.

"Please?" he repeated.

At that moment Frederick walked in. "Aha, I found you! There's something I want to ask you, Lucy."

Clearly Lucy wasn't going to get anything done tonight. She stashed her embroidery hoop in the canvas tote at her side. Allowing Nick's question to hang in the air unanswered, she turned her attention to Frederick. "Go ahead and ask."

"It's, uh, it's sort of private. So, um, I can wait until you and Nick are done talking."

Lucy had a feeling she knew what Frederick was going to ask and she wished he'd leave her alone. She wished *everyone* would leave her alone and stop forcing their social agendas on her. Then it occurred to her if Frederick thought she was walking out with Nick, he wouldn't ask her to walk out with *him*. Furthermore, if her stepsisters and stepmother thought she was walking out with someone, they wouldn't pester her to join their pre-Christmas social events or the caroling rehearsals, either. She'd finally have time to finish her project.

She stood up and rummaged through the coats, simultaneously saying, "Well, Nick and I were about to head out together, so you might as well ask me now. Nick, would you mind giving Frederick and me a quick moment alone to chat?"

A look of utter surprise crossed Nick's face before it brightened with elation. "Sure," he said. "I'll wait for you in my buggy."

"Denki," she replied in a syrupy voice, tilting her chin upward for added effect. After Nick left, she asked Frederick, "What is it you want to ask me?"

He stammered, "Oh, er, I was wondering if you'll be caroling this year? In a few minutes we're going to start the meeting to plan our rehearsal schedule and I thought you'd want to make suggestions about meeting times since I know you volunteer during the week."

"Denki for the heads-up, Frederick. But as much as I might enjoy caroling, I have… I have other social engagements that will be taking up my time."

Frederick looked forlorn, but he nodded and said he understood. She almost felt sorry for him, but then his mother entered the room, turned up the lamp and uttered, "Oh *gut,* I see Frederick tracked you down, Lucy! We didn't know where you'd escaped to. I set a mug of cocoa for each of you near the love seat."

A mix of embarrassment and empathy washed over Lucy as she noticed Frederick cringing. She nearly told him she'd stay after all, but Frederick said, "Lucy's going home now. Nick Burkholder is taking her."

"Nick Burkholder?" Frederick's mother was obviously incredulous. There'd be no stopping the rumors from spreading now.

Lucy excused herself quickly, saying, *"Jah,* and he's waiting for me in his buggy, so I'd better get going. *Denki* for your hospitality, Mary. *Gut nacht,* Frederick."

Speechless, Frederick lifted his hand in a wave. He looked stunned, but not nearly as stunned as Mildred and Katura appeared when Lucy bade them goodbye and informed them Nick was giving her a ride home.

"Why? Are you sick?" Mildred asked. "Because if you are, you can take the buggy and Katura and I can get a ride home from someone else. Maybe Frederick's cousin will take us."

"*Neh*, I'm not sick. It's just… Nick and I are…" Lucy allowed the innuendo to hang in the air before concluding, "I'll—I'll see you at home."

Leaving them with their mouths hanging open, Lucy couldn't help but feel a bit smug—not because they were surprised Nick was taking her home, but because for once they really would have to unhitch the buggy and stable the horse by themselves.

Chapter Two

Nick could have jumped for joy when Lucy accepted his offer of courtship. Or of pretend courtship. Before exiting Frederick's house, he signaled Kevin to follow him to the porch.

"Listen, I found someone I can pretend I'm walking out with. The important thing is you can't tell anyone—and I mean *anyone*—that it's not an authentic courtship. If word gets out this is a farce, it will only be a matter of minutes until *Mamm* and *Daed* find out about the fire and then we'll both be in trouble. You got it?" Nick tapped his finger against Kevin's chest, emphasizing his point.

"I got it," he promised, before slyly remarking, "So who's the fortunate *maedel*? I didn't see anyone inside you haven't already courted. Are you going to give one of them a second chance?"

Nick didn't appreciate Kevin's attitude toward young women, and his response was immediate and gruff. "I've already told you it's no one's business what *meed* I've courted in the past. Besides, what makes you think they'd give *me* a second chance?"

"I've always heard you're a charmer, that's all. It was intended as a compliment."

Hearing the admiration in his brother's voice, Nick set him straight. "Courting a lot of *meed* isn't necessarily a *gut* thing, Kevin. Neither is superficial charm. It's the quality, not the quantity of relationships, that's important. Courtship is intended to be an opportunity to discover if you and a *maedel* are compatible for marriage, but regardless of how long your relationships last, you'd better treat any woman you court with respect."

"You sound just like *Daed*, you know that?"

"That's because *Daed*'s right." Nick warned, "You've got your whole *rumspringa* in front of you. Your running around period is a time for you to make decisions on your own. There's a lot of freedom in that, but there's a lot of responsibility, too. I'll help you clean up the mess you've made this time, but if you make another one, you're going to have to take care of it yourself, understand?"

"*Jah, jah,* I got it already. So you still haven't told me who you're going to pretend you're courting."

Nick lowered his voice. "Lucy Knepp."

"Lucy Knepp?" Kevin chortled. "No one will ever believe you're interested in her. She's such a wallflower! Haven't you noticed how pale she is? I don't think she ever goes outside in daytime except to attend church. She's such a goody-goody."

"Exactly. Which is why *Mamm* and *Daed* won't object if they think I'm going out with her during the week," Nick reasoned. "So here's what's going to happen now. While I'm bringing Lucy to her *haus*, you're going to walk to ours. *Mamm* and *Daed* will still be awake and when they ask where I am, you can let it slip I'm taking Lucy home. Plant the seed in their minds, okay?"

"But what about going to Highland Springs like we planned?"

Nick shrugged. "I already told Lucy I'd take her home. If you still want to go to Highland Springs, go ahead and go. Just make sure you ask whoever gives you a ride to swing by Jenny's *haus* first so you can tell her you can't afford the cost of repairs to the cabin." Before turning to leave, he tossed Kevin's jacket at him and added, "Her *eldre* probably will just contact *Daed* instead of getting the police involved."

That got Kevin's attention. "Wait! I'll do it. I'll walk home now."

"Gut," Nick said. "And remember, you can't let on to anyone—not even Lucy—that you know this is a sham."

"Is it a sham?" Kevin jibed as he shoved his arm through his coat sleeve. "Or could it be this is the opportunity you've been waiting for your entire *rumspringa*? To court Lucy Knepp?"

Nick elbowed his brother. "You should be thanking me, not mocking me, so knock it off."

Grumbling, Kevin began his long schlep home and Nick went to unhitch Penny. A few minutes later, Lucy appeared. Kevin was right—she was so fair her skin glowed in the moonlight, which also reflected off her glasses. It was a good thing she was carrying a bag; it served as an anchor to keep the stiff wind from carrying her away.

"Here, let me help you," Nick offered, indicating he'd assist Lucy into his open one-seat buggy.

"I can manage," she replied, using her free hand to pull herself into the carriage. But the step was too high or the bag too heavy because she faltered backward and Nick steadied her by her waist—he could practically encircle his hands around it—before giving her a clumsy boost up. She scooted to the far end of the front seat, clutching her bag to her chest as if it contained gold.

On the way Nick tried to drum up something to say, but he drew a blank. Recognizing he and Lucy had absolutely nothing in common except they were both Willow Creek Amish singles, he was relieved this charade would last only a week, or two at most.

Finally, he remarked, "I really appreciate your letting me say I'm courting you. Knowing how quickly the rumor mill spins, everyone probably saw us leave and they're already gossiping that we're getting married."

Ach! It was true their peers were probably expressing curiosity about their relationship, but why did Nick even bring up the notion of marriage? As if this experience weren't already awkward enough as it was.

Lucy giggled behind her hand. "That's not likely," she said, and Nick didn't know if she meant it wasn't likely their peers were already gossiping about them or it wasn't likely the two of them would ever get married. Of *course* the latter wasn't likely, but it was kind of haughty for her to snicker at the idea.

Lucy dropped her hand to her lap again, guarding her bag. "So when do you want to get started on the repairs?"

"As soon as possible," Nick replied, glad to switch subjects. "I can't start on Monday because I'll be returning from a trip to one of our suppliers out of town. So I'll probably buy the stuff I need and begin the prep work on Tuesday night."

"That's fine. I'll arrange to make an early supper for my family and you can pick me up any time after six. I'll wait on the porch so Mildred and Katura won't accost you with questions."

"What?" Nick panicked, his pulse galloping. He only wanted to *imply* he was courting Lucy; he hadn't intended to actually take her out. "What do you mean, pick you up? You do realize this is a *pretend* courtship, don't you?"

Lucy didn't know whether she was amused or annoyed by Nick's alarmed reaction. It was obvious he'd never consider dating her for real. Not that she wanted him to, but still, he didn't have to act so repulsed.

"Of course I realize this is a pretend courtship. But I'm not going to lie about going out with you and I'm not going to allow you to use my name to lie about it, either. If you tell your *eldre*—if you even *imply* to them—you're spending an evening out with me, then you've got to actually spend some part of the evening out with me."

Nick gulped audibly. "You want to *kumme* with me while I work on the cabin?"

Lucy couldn't do that. The sawdust would cause her allergies to act up. "*Neh*. You can drop me off at the library and then pick me up when you're finished. That way, if anyone asks where we went—which they shouldn't, but that won't necessarily stop them—I can truthfully say you took me for a ride and we stopped at the library."

Nick hesitantly conceded, adding, "I always knew you were a bookworm but I didn't realize you like to read quite that much. I'll be gone for a couple of hours each evening, you know."

Lucy was surprised Nick knew she liked to read—their paths hardly crossed since they had been scholars in the town's two-room schoolhouse. She'd chatted with him a few times when her cousin Bridget still lived in Willow Creek and was walking out with him, but that was almost three years ago. For some reason it annoyed Lucy that Nick called her a bookworm, the same term her stepmother used to describe her.

"It's true I like to read. Reading allows me to learn about new ideas and places. But that's not why I want you to drop me off at the library," she said. "I have a special embroidery project I need to finish by December 21 and the library is a quiet place to do that." Then, to make it clear she was as disinterested in being courted by him as he was in becoming her suitor, she said, "That's the only reason I agreed to this arrangement. Otherwise, Betty and my sisters would pressure me into attending all the upcoming *Grischtdaag* social events and I'd never finish my project on time."

"Oh, so that's why you were embroidering at the singing," Nick replied. "I just thought you were too stuck—"

Nick cut his sentence short but Lucy knew what he was going to say. He was going to call her stuck-up. She wasn't unaware some young men thought that about her, but she'd never been told it outright. Why the *meed* in Willow Creek thought Nick Burkholder was such a catch, she'd never know, but Lucy wasn't impressed by his manners.

Changing topics, she asked, "How long will it take to make the repairs?"

"I should be done in a week. Ten days, at most."

Lucy was actually hoping it would take longer than that, but she'd just have to make the most of her time away from the house. "And then what will we tell people?"

"What do you mean?"

"I'll agree to pretend we're walking out together until your repairs are finished, but not any longer than that. It would be nosy for someone to ask us why we've broken up, but in case they do, it's a *gut* idea to have a credible answer ready. After all, two weeks is an awfully short time for a courtship, even for you," she said, not mincing words.

Nick puffed loudly, as if exasperated. "I suppose we'll just say it didn't work out."

"Ha," Lucy uttered. "If you think that answer will satisfy my sisters' curiosity, you don't know how persistent they can be."

"Then what do you propose we say instead?"

Lucy was quiet. How would she know what to say? She'd never been in a real courtship, much less a phony one. "I guess we'll have to cross that bridge when we *kumme* to it."

"Yeah, all right." Nick urged his horse into a quicker trot, as if he couldn't wait to get to Lucy's house to drop her off.

She had often heard Mildred and Katura nattering on about Nick's expensive racehorse, and the animal was certainly living up to its reputation. Because it was an open-seat buggy, Lucy felt the wind biting at her cheeks as they cruised along the country roads, but she didn't mind. Despite the horse's speed, the carriage wasn't bouncing about. Lucy might not have had many conversations with men her age, but she'd read enough articles in *The Budget* to know Nick probably tinkered with the suspension of his buggy springs, which was a popular trend among Amish young people. In any case, she felt surprisingly invigorated by the quick trip home.

When they pulled up her lane, she noticed lamplight in the window. Her father would have been in bed since he worked the early shift the next day, but Betty was probably still awake. Because the step down from the carriage was higher than Lucy was used to and she had to hold on to her tote bag, she allowed Nick to assist her. Even though they were both wearing gloves, her hand warmed from the pressure of his fingers but the sensation was fleeting because he let go as soon as her feet touched the ground. Then he began walking with her to the door.

"Why are you following me?" she asked, afraid he'd want to be invited in. If Betty got one glimpse of how uncomfortable Lucy was around Nick, their cover would be blown.

"I'm not *following* you. I'm walking you to the door. You know, like I'd do if I were actually courting you," Nick explained.

Lucy's cheeks stung. Since she'd never been courted before she didn't know whether all suitors walked their girlfriends to their doors or if this was part of Nick's supposed charm.

When they reached her back porch, he loudly announced, "So I'll pick you up at six o'clock on Tuesday night, okay?"

She put her finger to her lips. "Shh! My stepmother might hear you."

Nick leaned in and whispered, "*Jah*, that's the general intention, right?" He was close enough she could smell a hint of mint chocolate cocoa on his breath and she quickly skittered up the stairs.

"*Gut nacht*," she said over her shoulder before turning the knob to the door.

Inside Betty was sipping tea at the table and reading *The Budget*. "Hi, Lucy. I thought I heard a buggy. Are the girls stabling the horse?"

"*Neh*, they're still at the singing," Lucy answered ambiguously, avoiding meeting Betty's eyes as she removed her gloves, unwrapped her cloak and hung it on a peg by the door. She bent to unlace her boots.

"Oh? Then who brought you home?"

"Nick Burkholder," Lucy reported in what she hoped was an offhanded manner.

"Nick Burkholder?" her stepmother marveled. "Why would he bring you home? Are you sick?"

Like mamm, *like* dechder. Lucy was miffed Betty made the same assumption Mildred made about why Nick would bring her home. Lifting her chin she said, "*Neh*, I'm not sick. I'm going upstairs to bed now. *Gut nacht*."

Lucy scurried down the hall before her stepmother could ask any more questions. The upstairs room she shared with her sisters stretched the entire length of their Cape-style home. Mildred and Katura's beds and dressers took up most of the open space, whereas Lucy's dresser and bed were tightly tucked in the back section of the room beneath the sloping roof. Because Lucy was so short, she never bumped her head on it and she liked the roof being so close to her bed. During storms, she could hear raindrops pattering the wood and she felt as if she were sleeping in an ark.

She turned on the gas lamp, sat on her bed and removed her embroidery hoop from the canvas bag. As she began unpicking her earlier mistakes, her hands trembled. She tried to tell herself it was because she'd dashed up the stairs too quickly, but she knew that wasn't it. She was breathless and quivering because Betty and her stepsisters had found it preposterous that Nick would bring her home. But what right did she have to be angry? They were correct: it was inconceivable he'd want to court her.

Yet, when she recalled his strong hands embracing her waist, the notion of a courtship didn't seem so terribly far-fetched. At least, not from her perspective. She tried to focus on restitching a delicate snowflake in the center of the napkin, but her mind kept wandering back to Nick, and after pricking her finger three times she finally gave up and went to bed.

Nick was relieved. He'd presented his proposal to Jenny, and because she'd known Nick for years, she agreed to allow him to make the repairs, provided he restored everything to its former condition by the twenty-first of December. That was her first day of winter break from the local community college and Jenny and her mother were planning to decorate the cabin together in preparation for their celebration. Based on Kevin's description of the situation, Nick assured her he didn't think it would take nearly that long, and Jenny promised she wouldn't tell anyone he was working on it.

Gripping the key to the cabin in his fist, Nick traveled to the little house in the woods, where he discovered that although the repairs were manageable, the damage was more extensive than he expected it would be. *Terrific. Now I'm going to be stuck with Lucy longer than I anticipated*, he groused.

She was already getting on his nerves, acting like he'd never read a book in his life, or as if he wanted to be invited into her house. She was so prim he couldn't imagine what they'd talk about when he was taxiing her back and forth on these so-called outings. It was a small comfort that he could count on Penny's speed to decrease their traveling time.

The entire situation was far more inconvenient and uncomfortable than Kevin knew, and Nick decided as soon as he returned home, he was going to give his brother grief—and make him fork over his paycheck for supplies, too. But when he entered the house, it was almost eleven o'clock and he was surprised to find his mother, not Kevin, sitting in the parlor.

"*Mamm?* What are you doing up?" he asked quietly.

"I'm waiting for you," she said, and rocked back and forth in her chair a few times before saying anything else. "Your brother told me where you've been."

Nick's pulse quickened—Kevin had decided to own up after all. On one hand, Nick was relieved he wouldn't have to cart Lucy back and forth to the library after all. On the other hand, he dreaded the lecture his mother was about to deliver. He straightened his posture and resigned himself to shouldering part of the blame for Kevin's carelessness in causing the fire.

"I'm surprised, but I'm glad he did."

"Well, he didn't want to, but I insisted. So don't get angry at him."

Nick was confused. Why would he be angry at Kevin for telling the truth about the fire? Before he could tell his mother he didn't understand, she said, "Don't worry. Other than telling your *daed*, I won't mention to anyone that you're courting Lucy Knepp."

Oh, right—I forgot I told Kevin to plant the seed in Mamm *and* Daed*'s minds. That's where Kevin told them I've been—at Lucy's* haus, *not at Jenny's.* Nick didn't know why but he wasn't as disappointed as he expected he'd be when he realized he'd still have to carry through with his arrangement with Lucy. Still, he was surprised his *mamm* was bringing up the topic. As often as she lectured Nick that it was time he put his running around years behind him, she rarely spoke openly about the *meed* he courted.

"Denki," he said. "I appreciate that—"

His mother butted in, "Lucy Knepp is a *wunderbaar maedel.*"

Good—his mother approved. This was going to be easier than he thought. *"Jah,* she is—"

Again, his mother cut him off. "So you'd better not be up to any shenanigans."

"Wh-what do you mean?" Nick sputtered. Had Kevin let something else about their plan slip?

"She's not like other *meed* you've courted. You'd better not be toying with her feelings, *suh.*"

Nick clenched his jaw. While it was true he'd courted many *meed* who were frequently distraught when he ended their relationships, he never set out to hurt anyone's feelings. He was offended his own mother would think that was ever his intention. "I wouldn't do that, *Mamm*. I wouldn't deliberately play around with any woman's emotions."

His mother must have caught the defensiveness in his voice because she said, "*Neh*, I don't suppose you would, Nick. I only mean I want you to be careful, okay? As I said, Lucy's not like other *meed* you've courted. She's…she's special."

She's special *all right. She's so special she thinks she's a cut above everyone else*, Nick thought. As uncomfortable as he was discussing this subject with his mother, he felt it was important to emphasize, "I've always considered *every* woman I've courted to be special."

"I believe you have, *suh*. But some women are more…they're more *earnest* than others. I don't think Lucy has had many suitors and I wouldn't want her to get her hopes up about a relationship with you if that's not a real possibility," his mother explained.

It seemed a struggle for her to find the right words, but Nick knew what she meant. She meant he'd ended every relationship he'd had so far, and she was assuming he'd end this one, too. As much as Nick resented the implication, he admitted there was an element of truth to it.

"Don't worry," he assured his mother. "I've made my intentions very clear to Lucy. But she's not quite as naive as you think. I got the feeling she was reluctant to walk out with me. We're not even really courting, it's more like we're spending time together. I'm sort of helping her with…with one of her charity endeavors for *Grischtdaag*. After that, we'll have to see what happens."

His mother looked perplexed, but she smiled and

said, "Well, for your sake, I hope it works out this time. Who knows, Lucy might be a *gut* influence on you."

That was exactly what Nick was hoping his parents would think about Lucy, but now that he heard his mother say the words, he was disgruntled. Who was to say *he* wouldn't be a good influence on *her*? Maybe he'd show her a thing or two about how to lighten up and be a little more social. Didn't anyone ever consider that?

Mildred and Katura were considerate enough not to turn on the lamp while they were getting ready for bed, but their voices woke Lucy anyway.

"I wish Mark didn't have to go back to Ohio tomorrow morning," Mildred whined. "One of the rare few likable guys who comes to Willow Creek leaves as soon as he gets here. It's not fair. I hope he visits Frederick again at *Grischtdaag*."

"Speaking of Frederick, didn't you tell me he was planning to ask to court Lucy tonight?"

"That's what Melinda Schrock told me she heard Frederick's mother saying to Jesse's *ant* in the store last week," Mildred said, and her words caused Lucy to remember what the book of James said about a little fire kindling a great matter.

"Do you think Frederick got a chance to ask to court Lucy before she left with Nick?" Katura questioned.

"Probably not. Otherwise, she would have stayed until the singing was over so Frederick could have given her a ride home. Or she would have asked him for a ride right then since she was sick."

"I suppose that's true." Katura yawned. "Can you believe she asked Nick for a ride instead? That's awfully forward."

"*Jah*, but Nick's so nice he probably agreed because he felt sorry for her."

Lucy considered coughing to let her stepsisters know she was awake and could hear them, but she felt too humiliated. Why didn't Mildred and Katura believe she hadn't left because she was ill? Couldn't they at least *entertain* the possibility Nick was interested in her?

As if answering Lucy's unspoken question, Katura said, "One thing's for sure. He'd never consider being her suitor. She's not his type. Nick only courts women who are outgoing and adventuresome. You know, women who are more like you and me."

Lucy heard Mildred gasp. "That's it!" she exclaimed. "Nick probably wanted to talk to Lucy about one of us!"

"Do you really think so?" Katura questioned, and Lucy discerned the hopeful catch in her voice.

"*Jah*. That's how *buwe* in Willow Creek sometimes determine if a *maedel* is interested in being courted. They talk to her friends or sisters. Or if they're really shy, they'll pass a note," Mildred explained knowingly.

"But Nick isn't shy at all."

"*Neh*, not usually. But maybe he likes one of us so much he's afraid we'll reject him. Maybe that's why it's taken him so long to propose courtship—he hasn't been able to work up the courage. So instead of asking us straight out, he's taking the safe approach."

Lucy would have been inflamed, but instead she pushed her quilt against her mouth to suppress a giggle. Her stepsisters might have lacked self-awareness, but they sure didn't lack self-esteem.

"*I* should get him. I'm the oldest," Katura demanded, as if she were competing for a prize.

"You can't claim him. He'll decide for himself which one of us he wants to court."

As her stepsisters bickered about who was more worthy to have Nick as her suitor, Lucy rolled to her side and curled the pillow over her ear to block them out. They may have been right to think Nick didn't want to court Lucy, but they were just as wrong to imagine he wanted to court either of them. Once again, she stifled a guffaw. She couldn't wait for her cousin Bridget to visit at Christmastime so they could share a laugh over the hilarious irony of it all.

Chapter Three

Lucy woke early on Monday morning, planning to make breakfast for her father before he left for work. Betty and her daughters weren't early risers, so Lucy cherished the time she had alone with her *daed*. It was one of the rare occasions when she could get a word in edgewise, but sometimes instead of conversing they ate in companionable silence, enjoying the familiarity of the pattern they'd established years before Betty and the girls moved in. But by the time Lucy dressed, brushed her long hair into a bun and washed her face, she heard the wheels of a car rolling down the lane.

The Amish weren't allowed to drive or own automobiles, but they were permitted to accept rides from *Englischers*. Lucy's father's colleague, Ray, routinely picked him up since their house was on the way to the woodworking production company where they were employed. Not one to take a neighbor's generosity for granted, Lucy's father regularly assisted Ray with significant house and yard projects such as roofing or installing fencing.

Marvin just as well could have taken the buggy

to work, but Lucy had an inkling he wanted to be sure there was transportation at home for her. For one thing, if she needed to deliver her goods to Schrock's Shop, her father didn't like her to walk, even though Main Street was barely a mile away. For another, Lucy knew he secretly wanted to ensure there was a way for someone to seek medical intervention quickly in the event she developed breathing problems. Two years ago she suffered an acute respiratory attack while she and Betty were at home without a buggy. Betty had had to run to the phone shanty to call for help, and she had wound up gasping so bad by the time the ambulance arrived that the paramedics thought *she* was the patient. The episode had shaken Lucy's father deeply, and after that he always left the buggy behind.

Touched by her father's thoughtfulness, Lucy never let him know that most days it was Mildred or Katura who used the buggy to travel the short distance to their jobs on Main Street, where they worked part-time. They were both cashiers at the mercantile, which was a grocery and goods store catering primarily to Willow Creek's Amish. Granted, the two young women spent the better part of their shift on their feet, but most Amish *meed* in their area walked farther than that to get to their jobs.

When the two of them weren't using the buggy, Betty was. She frequently journeyed to Elmsville to visit her ailing sister. But Lucy never cared; she was so glad to have some quiet time to herself she would have offered to carry her stepsisters to town on her back if it meant she didn't have to listen to their prattle.

That's a very judgmental thing for me to think, she reflected. *The Lord makes us all different. I don't like them criticizing me for keeping to myself so I shouldn't criticize them for being so chatty.*

Since she was awake and dressed anyway, Lucy decided she'd make breakfast for the other women. They loved buttermilk pancakes and sausage, and a hot breakfast would hit the spot before they set out in the chilly November air. She set four places at the table, and just after she ladled the last scoop of batter onto the iron griddle, Mildred and Katura appeared in the doorway.

"That smells *appenditlich*," Mildred gushed.

"But you shouldn't have gone to the trouble. Especially not after being sick last night," Katura protested, showing a rare concern for Lucy's health.

"It's not a bother and, as I told you, I wasn't ill," she insisted as Betty ambled into the room.

"Guder mariye," she greeted the three young women. "What a treat to have *pannekuche* and *wascht*. What's the special occasion? Did something happen last night you want to tell us about?"

Lucy was taken aback by how blatantly Betty hinted she wanted to know more about why Nick had brought her home. Despite the fact most Willow Creek Amish youth kept their courtships to themselves, it was clear to Lucy this was one more way in which her stepsisters and stepmother abided by a different set of customs than Lucy did. She could never figure out if the difference was a matter of their personalities or if it was because they were from the Elmsville district, which was governed by a slightly more lenient *Ordnung*.

"Jah, something *did* happen last night!" Mildred blurted out. "Nick Burkholder left the singing early to give Lucy a ride home. And we think we know why."

Even though Betty was already aware Nick had brought Lucy home, she raised an eyebrow and asked, "Why?"

"He wants to court either Mildred or me. Probably me," Katura said. Then she demanded, "Out with it, Lucy. Did he give you a message to give one of us?"

It was one thing for Katura and Mildred to whisper about their theories when they thought she was asleep, but Lucy was dumbfounded they'd suggest right to her face Nick had brought her home only to inquire about them. No wonder they'd been so solicitous about her making breakfast—they were trying to flatter her. Maybe they were each hoping she'd put in a good word for them with Nick.

"*Neh*, he didn't mention either of you at all," she said, sounding as complacent as she felt. She slid the final pancakes onto a platter. After placing the dish on the table, she sat down and asked, "Shall I say grace?"

No sooner had she finished thanking the Lord for their food and asking Him to bless their day than Mildred coaxed, "You probably don't want to make one of us feel bad, but we can't stand not knowing who Nick's interested in. Please tell us, Lucy."

Betty cleared her throat. "They're right, Lucy. It isn't fair of you to keep the girls on tenterhooks like this."

That was the last straw. "Okay, if you must know," Lucy began, and Mildred leaned forward while Katura froze with her fork midair. "It's *me* he's interested in spending time with. In fact, he's picking me up at six o'clock on Tuesday evening."

Katura lowered her utensil and Mildred slouched back against her chair again. Lucy almost felt sorry she'd crushed their hopes until Mildred waved her hand dismissively and said, "Okay then, don't tell us the truth. We'll find out eventually."

"But she *has* to tell us which one of us he wants to court," Katura contradicted. "What if she convinces him I'm not interested? Or that you're not interested? I don't want her speaking on my behalf, do you?"

"Lucy, you can't—" Mildred began to whine.

To Lucy's surprise, Betty broke in. "If Lucy says Nick is interested in her, I think that's nice, so stop pestering her. You two girls will have plenty of opportunities to socialize with all the *Grischtdaag* parties and events coming up anyway." She reached over and patted Lucy's hand and said, "Don't worry, I'll tell your *daed* about your new suitor. As long as you finish your household chores each day, I'm sure he won't mind if you walk out with Nick at night."

Lucy wanted to retort that she always finished her chores and half of her stepsisters' chores, too, but she was so grateful Betty had put an end to Mildred and Katura's needling she let the remark slide.

At least that part of the plan is accomplished, she thought. She couldn't help but wonder if Nick was having as much difficulty convincing his family they were courting as she'd had convincing hers.

It was easier for Nick to get out of working late on Tuesday than he expected. Apparently, his mother had told his father he was courting Lucy, and there were no objections when he asked if there was any way he could leave work at his usual time that week.

"No problem. Kevin and I can manage things here,"

his father said, clapping Nick on the shoulder. Apparently, he thought as highly of Lucy as Nick's mother did.

As Nick was leaving, Kevin smirked and whispered, "Have a *gut* time. And remember, this is temporary. Don't break Lucy's delicate little heart." Then he puckered his mouth and smacked his lips in an exaggerated kissing gesture.

"Don't start anything on fire," Nick retorted as he set his hat on his head and exited through the back door.

When he turned down the lane to Lucy's house, he spotted her standing on the porch, clutching a cloak around her chest. It wasn't *that* cold outside, but she was behaving as if it were ten degrees below zero. He hoped she wasn't going to complain about riding in an open-seat buggy in this weather.

He hopped down from the carriage while she crossed the yard in the light streaming from the house windows. "Hi, Lucy," he said, and reached to support her as she climbed into the buggy, but she kept her arms snug around her chest. *She acts as if we're still* kinner *in school and I have the cooties*, he thought.

"Hello, Nick," she said in a hushed tone. "Don't look toward the window because I think we have an audience. I'm hiding my embroidery materials beneath my cloak. I don't want Betty and my stepsisters to see, because they might realize we're not actually walking out together."

Nick chuckled. So she wasn't as standoffish as he'd thought. "It's already too dark for them to see this far. They'll never know. But here, let me help."

He cupped Lucy's elbow to propel her upward, but she was so light he nearly tossed her into the buggy and she flung her arms out for balance, upending her tote bag.

"My linen!" she wailed as she retrieved a rectangle of fabric white enough to see in the twilight. "I hope it didn't get dirty."

"Sorry about that," he apologized, feeling like a bull in a china shop. Usually his confidence wasn't so easily rattled.

They didn't say another word until they were nearly at the library and Nick asked, "What are you going to say if someone sees you in the library?"

"I'll probably say hello."

Nick looked at her sideways, but he couldn't discern from her profile if she was joking or if she was just too obtuse to know what he meant. "*Neh*, I mean what excuse are you going to give them for being there alone?"

"Why do I need an excuse to be at the library alone? It's not as if anyone other than our families know we're supposedly going out together tonight, right? Your family will be busy at the store and mine wouldn't dream of coming to the library. So if I meet anyone else from our district, I'll simply greet them as usual."

Nick was dubious. He knew how quickly rumors spread in Willow Creek, especially when *meed* like Katura and Mildred were involved. If they told their peers Nick and Lucy were walking out that night and then someone saw Lucy alone, it wouldn't take long before their farce would be discovered.

"Do you suppose you could keep a low profile anyway?" he requested.

"Unfortunately, a low profile is all I can keep." Lucy giggled. "Let's just say being five feet tall is something of a *shortcoming*."

Amused, Nick smiled. Most *meed* he courted were too self-conscious to laugh at what they considered physical imperfections. Not that Lucy's height was an imperfection—it was how the Lord had created her—but she was unusually short compared to most of the Amish in their district.

In the library parking lot he offered to help her down from the carriage, but she insisted she could manage on her own. Covertly glancing around, he noticed a group of *Englisch* preteen girls hanging out on the library steps—probably waiting for their parents—but he didn't see any Amish people or buggies. "I'll be back at eight thirty to pick you up," he said.

"The library doesn't close until nine so it's fine if you're running a few minutes late." When Lucy smiled Nick noticed that her straight, white teeth gleamed in the light cast by the streetlamp. He watched as she trod past the *Englischers* who gave her a once-over and then giggled behind their hands. Not even as tall as the shortest of the girls, Lucy held her head high and swung her canvas bag as she passed them. Whether she was oblivious to their presence or deliberately ignoring their ridicule, Nick couldn't guess. Lucy was more complicated than she seemed on the surface, a characteristic he found both intriguing and frustrating.

Nick directed his horse toward an *Englisch* lumberyard in Highland Springs. Ordinarily, he would have purchased his supplies from the local lumberyard, but the *Englisch* one was open late and he was relatively certain he wouldn't see anyone he knew there at this time of evening.

Since he'd already made Kevin purchase most of the supplies he'd need from their father's hardware store, Nick only needed to buy paneling. It was a challenge to secure the long pieces of wood in his courting buggy, and he frequently had to stop along the way to the cabin to reposition them.

As he journeyed, Nick thought about Kevin grumbling over how much the supplies cost. That should have been the least of his brother's concerns. It was as if the boy didn't fully appreciate how much trouble he would have been in if Jenny Nelson hadn't extended such grace. Nick asked the Lord to touch Kevin's conscience and to open his eyes to his careless behavior. *Please,* Gott, *help me to be a better example to him, too.*

When he arrived at the cabin, he flicked on the lights and began unloading the supplies. Preoccupied with trying to figure out where to begin deconstructing the wall, Nick didn't realize how late it was until a clock chimed eight times—or was it nine? He glanced at the mantel place clock. It was nine. The library was closed and Lucy would be waiting. Experience told him the only thing worse than breaking up with a woman was being late for one. She was going to be madder than a hornet.

He flung the last of the materials into a messy stack in the corner of the room, locked the cabin door and bounded across the lawn to his buggy. This was one of the many occasions when it was clear that buying Penny hadn't been an impractical choice; the animal trotted as quickly as Nick allowed and he arrived at the library within fifteen minutes.

As he approached the building he couldn't see Lucy and he worried she may have left without him. But how? From what he could tell, it wasn't likely she'd undertake a walk that far in daytime, much less in the dark. His heart shuddered. Had something befallen her? But when he scanned the entrance area again, he spotted her partially obscured by shrubbery on the side of the library steps. Her bag was at her side and she was sitting with her arms wrapped around her knees. *She's so thin she's probably chilled to the bone*, he thought.

Her head was tilted toward the sky and Nick wondered if she was praying. Maybe she was asking God to hasten Nick's arrival. He brought his buggy to a halt and jumped down. His movement seemed to startle her, and she rose and absentmindedly brushed off her skirt.

"I'm sorry, Lucy," he said. "I got so involved with my tasks I entirely lost track of time."

Still looking upward, she replied, "I understand how that can happen. I was so absorbed in my embroidery I almost got locked inside the library just now. The librarian found me in a corner chair in the basement and chased me out. Look, is that Mars?"

Astounded that Lucy wasn't angry, Nick's eyes followed the skyward direction of her pointed finger. "*Jah*, I think you're right."

"It's beautiful, isn't it?" she asked. "I'm usually not outside at this time of night so I hardly ever get to see the planets and the stars."

Nick saw them all the time, but he never stopped to appreciate them the way she apparently did. They stood side by side in silence observing the sky until a shiver passed over Lucy and she said, "We'd better get going. It's late."

Reluctantly, Nick nodded and reached for her bag.

He repeated his apology. "I really am sorry I wasn't here when I said I'd be here. It won't happen again."

This time he assisted her into the buggy more gingerly than he had the first time, and instead of handing her the wool blanket he kept in the buggy, he spread it across her lap and tucked it beneath her feet with care.

Lucy had the sensation she was floating. She tried to convince herself it was because she'd made so much progress on her stitching, but that wasn't the only reason. The truth was, she liked the idea of being courted, even if it was a false courtship. The experience of being outdoors at night beneath the stars was romantic in itself, and no man except her father had ever assisted her into and out of a buggy. She'd been missing out. If the attentiveness of a young man who wasn't even a real suitor made her feel this blissful, how might she feel if the man truly liked her? Maybe when her stint with Nick was completed, she should accept Frederick as a suitor after all. She still couldn't really picture it, but then she never imagined a buggy ride with Nick Burkholder could be so pleasant, either.

"You're home late," Mildred commented. She and Katura were lounging across their beds, but they hadn't yet turned off the lamp when Lucy entered the bedroom. "Where did you and Nick go?"

"Oh, we went…out," Lucy replied vaguely.

Katura tossed her long, loose hair over her shoulder, clearly pretending to be indifferent. "Could you turn down the lamp, please?" she asked. "Some of us have to go to work in the morning."

It was a barb that ordinarily would have gotten Lucy's goat. She worked just as hard as her stepsisters did to contribute to their family's expenses, and she dared say she worked harder on keeping house. Furthermore, since Betty regularly visited her sister in Elmsville, most of the meal preparation fell to Lucy, too. But tonight she shrugged off the comment and dimmed the light as requested.

The room was quiet and by the time she eased into her bed, Lucy thought her stepsisters had fallen asleep. But then Mildred urgently hissed, "Spill the beans already, Lucy. What did you and Nick do tonight?"

A delicious vibration fluttered down Lucy's spine as she said, "We went for a ride and we talked."

Katura snorted, belying her earlier indifference. "That doesn't sound like very much *schpass*. Or very romantic."

"We also looked at the scars in the sty," Lucy bashfully confided.

"The scars in the sty? Don't you mean the *stars in the sky*?" Katura shrieked. She and Mildred laughed uproariously and Lucy's face felt scalding hot. She couldn't account for the slip of her tongue, but now her stepsisters were going to think she was so smitten with Nick she couldn't speak straight. "I must be overly tired," she said by way of excuse, and quickly joined in with their laughter so they wouldn't know how abashed she was by her mistake.

After they quieted down, Mildred pried, "Did it seem like he wants to take you out again sometime?"

"*Jah*. We're getting together on Thursday night."

"That soon?" Katura sounded surprised. Then she added nonchalantly, "I suppose that's all right, as long as he's able to attend our caroling rehearsal on Friday night. We're going out for pizza afterward."

It irritated Lucy that Katura acted as if she were granting permission for Nick to court her, but she didn't want to say anything in her defense, lest she trip over her words again. So Lucy simply bade her stepsisters good-night and pulled her quilt up to her chin.

She slept so soundly she realized upon waking she had missed another opportunity to prepare her father breakfast. And by the time Lucy was dressed, Katura and Mildred had already left for work, too. It must have been all that fresh air the night before—she never slept this late. Now she was going to have to hurry to make up for lost time. She had to complete a Christmas tree skirt she was custom designing for a customer from Schrock's by this afternoon so she could drop it off at the shop on the way to the soup kitchen that evening.

In the kitchen she discovered a note from Betty indicating she'd be spending the day with her indisposed sister again. She requested that Lucy prepare supper and instructed Mildred and Katura to sweep the floors and beat the rugs when they returned home. Lucy tried not to think ungracious thoughts, but preparing supper took longer than beating the rugs and sweeping the floors, especially since those tasks would be shared between the two sisters. Lucy didn't usually mind doing housework—in fact, she preferred the house being neater and more organized than the others did—but today she desperately needed time to work on the tree skirt.

Once she'd chopped vegetables and cubed the meat for stew, she put them in a pot to simmer throughout the day. Then she began making bread. In between kneading the dough, punching it down and allowing it to rise again, she embroidered the final touches on the tree skirt. With its array of pine trees and cardinals, church bells and candy canes, the design was exactly what the customer wanted, although it was too flashy for Lucy's taste. She preferred the simplicity of white-on-white snowflakes or perhaps the accent of a sprig of holly here and there.

Like their linens and curtains, the Amish tended to keep their house decorations simple, too, but Lucy relished the Christmas holiday season when she could place candles on the windowsills and arrange evergreen boughs on the mantel. It didn't take much to make their home feel festive and Lucy couldn't wait to begin adorning it on Saturday. Perhaps this year Katura and Mildred would help her. *I'll probably have to bribe them with cocoa and cookies though.* Immediately she regretted her sour thought and she asked God to forgive her attitude.

Mildred once asked Lucy if she got bored "sitting around embroidering all day," but Lucy seldom did. Not only did she enjoy creating freehand designs, but she also used the time to pray. For example, as she worked on the Christmas tree skirt, she prayed that the family who ordered it would have a healthy, joyful, Christ-centered time of worship together.

Then her mind drifted to Nick. Reflecting on his willingness to help repair the cabin for Christmas, she realized she wouldn't have guessed he'd demonstrate such a selfless devotion to his *Englisch* friend. Thinking of him, she was tickled by a chill, and she rose to stoke the stove and check on the stew.

By the time her stepmother and sisters came home, it was four o'clock. Her father returned at four thirty.

He knew how important it was for Lucy to work at the soup kitchen, so he always made a point to return home by four thirty on Wednesdays, even if it meant he had to walk whenever his *Englisch* coworker was putting in overtime and couldn't give him a lift home. This was one of those days.

"*Denki* for walking home, *Daed*," she told him after she'd dropped the skirt off at Schrock's and they were on their way to the soup kitchen. She was perfectly capable of handling the buggy herself, but he insisted, so she let him. It was another cherished occasion when she could spend time with him alone.

"What you do at the soup kitchen is important," he said. "Just don't let yourself get too run-down. Now that you're…you're socializing more, you might not have as much energy as you usually do."

Lucy caught her father's profile in her peripheral vision. Although he used the term "socializing" instead of "courting," she felt guilty. Grinning broadly, he appeared so pleased. "I'm not actually…" she began, but then she realized she couldn't back out of her agreement with Nick. It meant so much to him—and to the Nelsons. "I'm not going to get too run-down, *Daed*."

"*Gut.* Because you deserve to enjoy yourself. And any young man—er, any young person who keeps company with such a smart, engaging *maedel* like you is very fortunate."

Lucy was touched by how careful her father was to avoid using Nick's name, as well as by his endearing sentiments. She knew few men in Willow Creek besides her father would consider her to be engaging, but she appreciated his opinion all the same.

At the church where the soup kitchen was located,

Dan Ebersole was retrieving folding chairs from the closet near the back door where Lucy entered the building. Having recently moved from an Amish settlement in Ohio to nearby Elmsville and being reserved by nature, Dan didn't have many friends, but he and Lucy had struck it off well together. "Your face is… It's kind of glowing," he faltered. "I mean, you look really happy tonight."

"I *am* really happy," she said. "It must be because *Grischtdaag* is my favorite holiday and it's getting closer." But as much as she loved Christmas, Lucy had never felt quite this cheerful about the holiday before. No, this kind of joy came from somewhere else.

On Thursday evening before starting off for Lucy's house, Nick asked his mother for another wool blanket to stow in his buggy.

"Is there a snowstorm on the horizon?" she asked with a lilt in her voice.

"*Neh*, I want it in case Lucy gets cold," he answered before he realized his mother was teasing him. His ears blazing, he hurried from the house.

As he directed Penny across town, he reasoned it was only common sense to bring an extra blanket for Lucy. She was so thin the wind probably went right through her, and he didn't want her to complain. Then he began to worry that Lucy, like his mother, might interpret the gesture as something other than his being considerate; she might interpret it as a sign of affection. He couldn't have that. This was a phony, short-term courtship, nothing more. So after Lucy was seated in the buggy, Nick handed her the spare folded blanket instead of arranging it for her as he'd done on Tuesday evening.

"The library again?" he asked tersely.

"*Jah*, please," she replied.

A long silence followed until he grew restless and finally thought to inquire about her project. Her voice was animated as she described the soup kitchen and how the organization needed to raise at least one thousand dollars in order to repair their commercial-sized oven and cover other expenses associated with their service.

"Lately the soup kitchen should be called a sandwich and cookie kitchen, since we aren't able to serve hot meals." Lucy sighed. "I feel so bad because this is the time of year when people need something to warm their bellies more than ever."

Nick had had no idea her embroidering project was for the soup kitchen's benefit; he had assumed she was making it to sell for a profit. At best, he'd imagined she'd use the proceeds to buy Christmas presents for her family, but he hadn't considered she was working this hard to give the money away to charity. "That's really generous of you, donating your time and skills to the soup kitchen like that," he said.

She dipped her head modestly. "It's no more generous than what you're doing—using your skills to help someone else have a merry *Grischtdaag*."

Nick felt a pinch of guilt. There was a world of difference between what he was doing and what she was doing, even if she wasn't aware of it. "It's not a big deal," he said.

"Oh, but it is." She twisted toward him. "I've heard how much you like to socialize, and at this time of year there are so many parties and events going on that you're forfeiting just to help your friend's family— *Englischers* at that."

So she was also aware of how much he liked to socialize. Was Nick's brother right about his reputation preceding him? Or did she get that idea from someone else, like her cousin Bridget, whom he had once courted? Nick wondered what else Lucy had heard about him—specifically, about his courtships.

"Speaking of parties," he said. "As you probably know, there's a get-together on Friday night after the caroling rehearsal. I planned to work on the cabin, but if you're going to the party, then…"

Lucy picked up his sentence where he left off. "Then we'd have to go together?"

"Neh!" he exclaimed. "I didn't mean that. I meant if you're going to the party then I can't tell people I'm with you on Friday night because obviously they'll see you alone at the party."

"Oh, right. Of course," Lucy said. Nick couldn't read her tone for certain, but he got the sense he had offended her.

"Unless you wanted to go to the party," he offered guiltily. "I mean, if that's the case I should probably go with you. For the sake of appearances."

Lucy sat up straighter and shook her head. *"Neh*, definitely not. I mean, I don't want to go to the party with or without you, so it's fine if you work on the cabin. You can pick me up at the usual time."

"But isn't the library closed on Friday evening?"

"Jah, but there's a little bookstore café that's open until nine thirty or ten down the street from the library. I could do my embroidery there."

"You really wouldn't mind?" Nick couldn't believe how flexible she was being. Was she doing that just for him? He felt torn between wishing she was and hoping she wasn't.

"I'd consider it a favor," she said. "Otherwise, Betty will insist I go to the party and that will set me back on my embroidery."

Oh, so that was why. Nick should have known. "*Denki*, that would be great," he replied. But if the idea was so agreeable to him, why did he feel so let down?

Chapter Four

After working on her project three evenings during the week, as well as on Saturday evening after she'd decorated their home for Christmas, Lucy began to relax a little about her deadline. It was only the fourth of December; she had until the twenty-first to finish. By the Sabbath, she was almost relieved to take a break. It was an "off Sunday," which meant instead of gathering for church, the Amish families in Willow Creek held worship services in their individual homes. Afterward, the family enjoyed a light dinner of cheese sandwiches and chicken soup, and then everyone either read or napped. Except for Lucy—she pulled out a pen and paper to write to her cousin.

Dear Bridget,
It's less than three more weeks until you visit and I can't wait to see you again! Be sure to bring your ice skates—the weather here is unseasonably cold and if it keeps up, we'll be able to skate on Wheeler's Pond.

Although Lucy often got winded when she exerted herself in the cold weather, she and Bridget both loved to skate. Lucy had better balance but Bridget was faster, so they helped each other navigate the home-made outdoor rink at the local pond, which was often crowded with both *Englisch* and Amish skaters and ice hockey players. It was rare for the pond to freeze over at Christmastime; usually they had to wait until January or February, so Lucy was delighted to think she and Bridget might be able to go skating the way they used to before her cousin moved away.

Chewing on the end of her pen, Lucy pondered whether she should tell Bridget about her arrangement with Nick, and if so, what she should say. What had begun as an opportunity to complete her project had turned into… Well, Lucy wasn't sure what it had turned into, but she wasn't as eager to share the details of the arrangement with Bridget as she was when she thought they'd share a good laugh over the irony of it.

Am I worried what she'd say if I told her Nick is nothing like I thought he was? Lucy wondered. Truth-fully, she had to admit that was part of her hesitation. Lucy knew Bridget had experienced Nick's duplicitous behavior firsthand and, out of protectiveness toward her cousin, Bridget would warn Lucy about his cunning ways. But Lucy didn't need a warning because she wasn't going to become involved in a romantic relationship with Nick. She was simply enjoying his company more than she expected she would.

Which was a good thing, considering Nick told her his project was going to take longer than expected— perhaps more than two weeks. It had something to do with the drywall or plasterboard behind the paneling, as she vaguely recalled. In any case, Lucy would probably finish the tablecloth and napkins before he finished the walls. If that happened, she'd put an end to their arrangement… Wouldn't she?

"Lucy!" Katura startled her. "Didn't you hear me?"

"She was daydreaming about *N-i-c-k*," Mildred teased, just like a schoolgirl.

Lucy hadn't heard them enter the room. "I'm sorry, I was thinking about Bridget. What did you say?" she asked.

"We've planned a caroling rehearsal for tonight at Melinda and Jesse Schrock's *haus*. I know you're not participating in the caroling, but we're only going to practice for half an hour and then we're going to break for games and snacks. Do you want to *kumme*?"

Even though Melinda and Jesse were already married, the couple frequently hosted groups of young single adults at their home and Melinda was nicknamed "Melinda Matchmaker," a title she reveled in.

"*Denki*, but I've been out a lot this week."

"There's no need to boast. A simple *neh* would suffice," Mildred said, rolling her eyes.

"I only meant I'm tired. I want to catch up on my letter writing."

Katura sat down across the table from Lucy and leaned forward. "Did you and Nick have an argument?" she whispered.

"*Neh*. I'm just tired and I don't want to go out. I want to go to bed early this evening."

Before she finished speaking, Lucy's father walked into the room. "Then that's exactly what you should do," he said, donning his coat before going to milk the cows for the evening. "It's too cold outside for Lucy.

But if you want to go out tonight, Mildred and Katura, I'll hitch the buggy for you."

While Lucy appreciated her father's concern, as well as his attempt to thwart her stepsisters' badgering, she didn't want his overprotectiveness about her health today to interfere with her plans to go out with Nick later in the week since the temperatures were forecasted to drop even further. Plus—she hated to admit it to herself—it occurred to her belatedly Nick might be at the rehearsal, too.

"It's not that cold, *Daed*," she said, changing her mind about attending the singing. "Actually, now that I think of it, I've been cooped up inside all day and I'd like to go."

Her father opened his mouth, but Lucy shot him a pleading look, knowing he wouldn't protest when she added, "Even if I'm not going to be one of the carolers, listening to the singing always puts me in a festive mood. You know how I love *Grischtdaag*."

"Take an extra blanket then," her father advised. Having gotten her way, Lucy leaped up to wrap her arms around his midsection. Sometimes she felt as manipulative as her stepsisters. "And don't stay out late."

"We won't," Lucy promised. "We'll be home before ten."

Mildred grumbled, "Ten? Speak for yourself!" But then when Marvin narrowed his eyes she quickly suggested. "I mean, if you want to get home by ten, I'm sure Nick will take you."

"I don't even know if he'll be there." The very possibility Nick might be present caused Lucy to flush, and she looked away as she gathered her writing materials and left the room to wash her face and put on a clean dress, just in case he was.

Nick recognized it was prideful to wish he had a better singing voice, but since he was stuck with the voice he had, he figured it was better not to sing at all. Which didn't mean he was going to miss the caroling rehearsal on Sunday night. Melinda and Jesse Schrock were hosting, which meant there was sure to be a boisterous party with lots of good food after the carolers practiced their songs.

But the party wasn't the main reason he wanted to attend. He wanted to go, firstly, because he loved to exercise Penny at every opportunity. The animal seemed to enjoy it as well, zooming along at a smooth, swift pace. Some horses you had to urge onward, but Penny was the opposite, and more often Nick had to keep her from breaking into a hard run.

Secondly, he hoped Jesse might have invited Hunter Schwartz and possibly Fletcher Chupp. Although both of the men were married, Jesse and Melinda often opened their home to both singles and married couples, claiming the bigger the party the better. Fletcher was a carpenter and Hunter restored furniture, and Nick needed input about his project from both of them. The paneling he had removed from the wall was high quality wood, and while he had managed to salvage about half of it, Nick wanted to ask Hunter about staining the new pieces so they matched the original color. He also hoped Fletcher would give him advice about the drywall behind the paneling, which was in considerably worse shape than the paneling itself.

"Aren't you afraid you'll see Lucy there?" Kevin

asked when Nick told him he was going to the rehearsal.

Afraid? No. It was more like he was…hopeful. In fact, the hope of seeing Lucy was one more reason Nick had decided to attend the gathering.

"She probably won't be there," he said nonchalantly. "But if she is, then she is."

"But you said those sisters of hers know you're supposedly courting her."

"So what?"

"So won't it seem strange that you didn't offer to take her to the singing?"

"*Neh.* Lots of couples are discreet about their relationships."

Kevin chuckled. "*Jah*, but you're not. Or even if you are, most of the time your peers seem to know if and who you're courting. If you show up separately from Lucy, her sisters are never going to believe you're her suitor."

Nick hadn't really thought of the fact Mildred and Katura would be there scrutinizing his presence, but Kevin was probably right. "I don't know. If Lucy's there, maybe I'll take her home afterward or something. That should put their suspicion to rest," he said. As he said it, he smiled, realizing it gave him the perfect excuse to be alone with Lucy again.

He couldn't describe how he felt about the past week except to admit it had been far more pleasant than he'd expected. He enjoyed being alone with Lucy. Talking to her. Picking her up and dropping her off. It had become a routine, and even though he saw her the previous night and had plans to pick her up on Monday evening, he found himself longing to see her again on Sunday, too.

But when he got to the Schrocks' house, there was no sign of her. Nor of Hunter or Fletcher. There was, however, a tall, curvaceous blonde woman Melinda introduced as her closest childhood friend, Eve, from Ohio.

"Eve is staying with us until the *Nei Yaahr*, isn't that right, Eve?" Melinda said.

Eve flashed her dimples, saying, "Unless Jesse gets tired of having two women gabbing in the *haus* all day and sends me home early."

If Eve is as gossipy as Melinda, I wouldn't blame him if he did, Nick thought, glancing at the door to see who just entered. The room was so crowded he couldn't get a good look over the heads of the people standing closest to him.

"I was telling Eve about Penny," Melinda continued. "Eve's *daed* trains horses for the *Englisch*, so she knows a lot about them."

"Not a lot. But I do like to help my *daed* break them in. The wilder the better, the bigger the challenge," Eve said. "Although from what Melinda tells me, they're probably not as fast as Penny."

"Nick, why don't you take Eve out for a ride?" Melinda suggested.

Ordinarily, Nick might have appreciated Melinda's obvious attempt to pair him with a newcomer to Willow Creek. That was what he'd been praying for, to meet someone new. And someone new who liked fast horses—Nick had never thought to pray for that quality in a woman, so he should have been ecstatic. Yet there was nothing about Eve that drew him in. If anything, her association with Melinda worked against her.

"I'll probably be leaving soon. I was only dropping in for your famous brownies," he said, hoping his flattery would appease Melinda. It didn't.

"Then take her now. We'll start singing soon, and Eve's voice is as wretched as yours is, so she doesn't mind if she misses the carols," Melinda countered.

Eve blinked rapidly, clearly mortified by Melinda's put-down. Either that or Eve was as consternated by Melinda's insistence Nick take Eve for a ride as he was. In an attempt to ease both of their discomfort, Nick joked, "Let's go, Eve. We don't have to put up with Melinda's insults."

He gestured toward the door, figuring the sooner he got the ride with Eve over, the sooner he could leave. He led the way, bypassing the other guests, who bunched together balancing cups of cider and paper plates of brownies and cookies in their hands.

"It's a beautiful night for a ride," Eve commented when they stepped out onto the porch.

Nick was about to reply when he noticed movement in the dark a few feet from the porch.

A moment later, Mildred and Katura came into view. Terrific, now what was he going to do?

"Uh, hello, Mildred. H-hi, Katura," he stuttered as they climbed the stairs.

They froze, staring at him. Then a voice from behind them said, "Keep moving, please, I'm freezing." Lucy was so short her stepsisters blocked her from view, but Nick recognized her voice the second she spoke and his pulse bounded through his veins.

Lucy was impatient. It was just like Mildred and Katura to dillydally on the porch in the wintry air instead of going into the house's warm interior. When they didn't move forward, she swerved around them, nearly bumping into a blonde woman she'd never seen before. Nick was standing next to her.

"Oh, hello, Nick," she said awkwardly.

Nick cleared his throat. "Er, hi, Lucy. Have you met Melinda's friend, Eve?" He gestured to the woman at his side. "She's visiting until the *Nei Yaahr.*"

Lucy forced a smile. Her stepsisters were uncharacteristically silent, but she could feel their eyes on her. "*Wilkom* to Willow Creek, Eve," she said nonchalantly.

"*Denki.* I'm glad to be here. Everyone in this district is so friendly," she said. "Nick's even agreed to take me out for a ride in his buggy, since neither of us has a *gut* singing voice."

Katura made a coughing sound and Lucy's eyes smarted. So that was it? Nick was courting Eve now and Lucy's arrangement with him had ended, just like that? He could have at least had the decency to tell her before tonight. Now she looked like a fool in front of her stepsisters. *I should have known anyone who would court a second woman before he'd broken up with Bridget wouldn't think twice about courting a second woman before he ended a fake relationship with me.*

"Eve's *daed* trains horses for the *Englisch,*" Nick explained. "So she's an expert. She wanted to see Penny."

Lucy's tone was as cool as glass. "Well, don't let us keep you." She began moving around Nick, but he reached out and grabbed her arm near the elbow.

"Do you want to *kumme* with us?" he asked.

Baffled, Lucy didn't know what to think. If Nick was interested in Eve, why would he want Lucy to ride with them? But if he wasn't interested in Eve, why was he taking her riding alone? Either way, there was one thing she knew for certain: she didn't want to be within five miles of Nick Burkholder at the moment.

"I most certainly don't," Lucy retorted. Then, realizing how snobbish she must have sounded to Eve, she said, "I'm so chilled I can hardly feel my toes. But you two have *schpass*."

Without waiting for Nick's response, she entered the house with her stepsisters close on her heels. The mudroom was empty, but she could hear the clamor of guests in the kitchen. Her mind and stomach were spinning as she bent to unlace her boots.

"I *knew* you had an argument!" Mildred exclaimed, sounding far too happy for Lucy's liking. "He's trying to make you jealous, isn't he?"

As humiliated as she was by Nick's behavior, Lucy wasn't going to further embarrass herself by telling Mildred and Katura about their fake courtship. Covertly wiping her cheeks before she stood upright, Lucy replied, "*Neh*. He's showing hospitality to a visitor to Willow Creek, that's all."

"That's baloney," Katura stated emphatically. "Whatever you argued with him about, Lucy, you should just forget it or you're going to lose him."

"*Lose* him?" Lucy repeated incredulously. "He's not a coin! He's not a prize!"

"You know what I mean. He could court anyone he chooses," Katura said as she pulled off her gloves and stuffed them into the hood of her cloak before hanging it over someone else's coat on the crowded wall of pegs. "Although I don't see why he'd court a visitor like Eve when he hasn't even asked to be *my* suitor yet. But then, I didn't understand why he was pursuing you, either."

Lucy was so outraged she could hardly see straight to open the door to the kitchen. Blindly she picked her way past the people milling about the snack table and clustered in the parlor. If there was one advantage to being so short it was that she could go unnoticed in times like these. Finally, securing the door of the vacant washroom, Lucy removed her glasses and leaned to splash water over her burning cheeks.

Straightening, she put her spectacles back on and peered into the mirror. She had to stand on her tiptoes to see the entirety of her facial reflection. Observing her mousy hair and unremarkable features, she knew she was no match for someone like Eve. The Amish didn't place an undue importance on physical appearances, but that didn't mean they had no sense of what was aesthetically pleasing. Lucy recognized there was nothing about her physical appearance *or* her personality that would have captured Nick's attention.

Why should I care? she asked herself. Their relationship wasn't real, so what did it matter if he was interested in Eve? *There is no* if. *He's definitely interested in her,* she thought. Or at least it appeared he was laying the groundwork for courting Eve. Nick no longer had a need for Lucy now that she had served her purpose. Here she thought she was one up on all the gullible young women—including her own cousin Bridget—who fawned over Nick and then were devastated when their courtships abruptly ended. Instead, Lucy was the most pathetic one of all, because their courtship was only pretend. But her hurt was very deep and very real.

She could hear singing in the next room. Lucy didn't want to join the others, but she couldn't ask Katura and Mildred to take her home already. She wasn't about to give them the satisfaction of knowing how much Nick had upset her. So, she contorted her mouth into a smile and joined the carolers, even though she didn't feel the least bit festive.

It took more time for Nick to untie Penny from the post and back the buggy out of the lane than it did for him to take Eve on a quick spin down the road and back. She chattered about the kinds of horses the *Englisch* brought to her father and some of the problems they encountered. Ordinarily, he would have been engrossed in the conversation, but his mind was preoccupied with Lucy. Nick was acutely aware of how bad it looked for him to take Eve for a ride while he was supposedly courting Lucy, and he hoped Lucy hadn't ended up telling her stepsisters their courtship was a sham. He couldn't wait to get back to speak to her alone.

He offered to drop Eve off at the door, but she said she'd keep him company while he hitched his horse to the post farther down the lane, closer to the stable. As they walked toward the house, she asked him something, but he was so antsy he didn't hear.

"What was that?" he asked when he realized she was waiting for a response.

"Melinda wasn't wrong. Sometimes I'm really off-key when I sing. But I didn't realize it was so noticeable to anyone else." Stalling on the porch, she added, "I really wish we didn't have to go back inside just yet."

"Well, if you want to stay outside, suit yourself, but I'm not going to hang out here," Nick said. The light from a nearby window illuminated Eve's crest-fallen expression. He'd seen that look a dozen times. He hadn't meant to hurt her feelings, but he felt it was important to be up-front about where he stood; he had no romantic interest in Eve whatsoever. Still, he shouldn't have been so boorish. So she wouldn't feel personally rejected, in a softer tone Nick apologized, "I'm sorry, but I think Melinda may have given you the wrong idea about me. I'm… I'm kind of courting someone else."

"You are?" Eve's eyebrows shot up. "I didn't know. *Melinda* didn't know and she knows everything that goes on in Willow Creek… So, who is it you're courting?"

Nick feared she was doubting him, so he confessed, "It's Lucy Knepp, the woman I introduced you to. But listen, please don't mention it to anyone. Especially not to Melinda." If Lucy *had* already told her stepsisters the courtship was just an act after she saw Nick with Eve, Nick didn't want Melinda adding to the confusion by spreading rumors to the contrary.

"I won't," Eve promised. Nick wasn't sure whether he could trust her or not, but he was heartened by the fact she seemed to demonstrate more tact than her friend Melinda. She added, "Lucy must be pretty steamed with you right now. I know I would be if my suitor took another *maedel* for a ride."

"Hey, it wasn't my idea to go for a ride!" Nick protested.

"*Neh*, it wasn't. But that doesn't mean you're not to blame," Eve chastised him as they entered the mud-room. "You should have refused to go. That way you would have saved both me and Lucy from being upset about a misunderstanding."

Nick realized she was right and he promptly offered an apology for upsetting her, which Eve readily accepted. "I only hope Lucy is as forgiving as you are," he said.

But when he sidled up to Lucy on the periphery of the parlor, she pretended not to see him. She kept on singing even though he was so close he could have counted her individual eyelashes if they hadn't been so numerous.

"Lucy," he whispered during the chorus of a popular carol. "Can I talk to you in private?"

She stopped singing long enough to shush him from the corner of her mouth.

"There's something I need to tell you."

This time she turned toward him, scowling. In a hushed tone, she reprimanded, "Be quiet. We're trying to practice."

"But you're not even going to go caroling with them," he insisted.

Still glaring, she shook her head like a schoolteacher disappointed in a student, but she finally relented. The two of them backed out of the room and passed through the kitchen into the mudroom.

"Okay, so what is it you want to discuss?" she asked, wrapping her arms around her chest. It was cold enough for them to see their breath as they talked, and Nick shivered.

"Did you tell Katura and Mildred our courtship isn't real?"

"You dragged me out here to ask me *that*?" Lucy's voice was rising. Nick had some nerve. "If you were so worried about them finding out you're not really my suitor, you should have been a little more discreet about taking Eve for a ride in your buggy. That's not the behavior of a man who is genuinely courting a woman."

"But I asked you to *kumme* with us."

"Only because I caught you!" Lucy heard the screech in her own voice.

"You didn't *catch* me. I wasn't doing anything wrong."

Lucy inhaled deeply. Nick was right; technically, he wasn't doing anything wrong. What was the matter with her, acting as if he'd actually betrayed her by courting—or at least flirting with—another woman? Rationally, so as to diminish the intensity of her outburst, Lucy reasoned, "You know that and I know that, but Katura and Mildred don't know that. To them, it appeared you were seeing Eve behind my back or you were trying to make me jealous. Either way, I looked like a fool."

Nick's face was etched with lines. "I'm sorry I put you in an awkward position like that."

Since he really did look repentant, Lucy sighed and said, "It's okay, Nick. I denied there was any conflict between us, but I'll just tell Katura and Mildred you broke up with me and I didn't want to admit it."

Nick's big eyes drooped. "You're putting an end to our arrangement?"

"Well, I assume you don't need me now that you have Eve."

"I don't *have* Eve! I only took her for a ride because you weren't here and I wanted to get out of the house. Besides, it was the only way to get Melinda off my back. She was the one who practically pushed Eve into my buggy!"

Lucy felt more relieved than she cared to admit. Just to be sure she understood, she clarified, "So you still need me to cover for you while you make repairs to the cabin?"

"*Jah*. And despite my stupidity tonight, I hope you're still willing to."

Lucy sighed again. She wasn't quite sure she believed Nick had taken Eve for a ride just to appease Melinda. For all Lucy knew, Nick had proposed courtship and Eve had turned down his offer while they were out riding around. It was possible he was only coming back to Lucy because, once again, he had no other option. But then she reasoned if Nick wanted to continue their charade, it would still give her a chance to finish her project, which was the reason she'd agreed to the arrangement in the first place. Besides, she'd given Nick her word. She supposed she couldn't desert him now, for the sake of the Nelsons' Christmas reunion. But Lucy realized from now on she was going to have to keep her feelings in check. She couldn't afford to experience the kind of emotional turmoil she had tonight. It was too distressing, and she didn't want her Christmas season ruined.

"I'm still willing," she agreed. "But only until I finish *my* project. After that, we're 'breaking up,' whether or not you're done with the repairs." Then, just in case Nick still had any mistaken notion Lucy was a pushover, she added, "And when we do supposedly break up, we're going to say I'm the one who ended our courtship."

"All right," Nick said, nodding. *"Denki."*

He was so amenable to Lucy's conditions she almost wanted to rescind them. Almost, but not quite. *Don't let his big blue eyes or earnest expression get to you*, she reminded herself. *Or you'll end up like every other* maedel *he ever courted: sad and alone.*

Chapter Five

"I'm surprised Lucy's *eldre* allow her to go out so often," Nick's mother said to Nick before he went to milk the cows at first light on Monday morning. "I didn't mind you walking out with her on weeknights last week, but your *daed* has been looking especially run-down and I think he needs more rest. I'd like him to *kumme* home earlier in the evenings this week. You'll have to cut back on how much time you spend with Lucy so you can help Kevin at the store."

"All right, but I did promise I'd take her to the soup kitchen. The *Englisch* one where she serves supper on Wednesday nights. Is that okay?"

At the mention of the soup kitchen, Nick's mother said, "That's *wunderbaar* you're so committed to going to the soup kitchen with Lucy. Didn't I say she'd be a *gut* influence on you?"

Nick ambled to the barn, feeling guilty for allowing his mother to think he was actually going to help Lucy serve at the soup kitchen, when in fact he needed to reserve at least one evening away from the store during the week to work on the cabin. While he was milking the family's two cows, he reflected on the previous evening. Given how miffed Lucy had been about the business with Eve, Nick didn't look forward to calling off their previously arranged meeting tonight. While she said she forgave him, Lucy nevertheless had refused a ride from him, claiming she'd promised to wrangle her stepsisters home early that evening.

Not that he minded taking a break from being her pretend suitor. It was true that initially his fake courtship with Lucy had been more harmonious than any of his actual courtships, but their spat last night left him on shaky ground with her. That kind of conflict and sense of uneasiness inevitably resulted in Nick ending his relationships before things really soured or anyone's feelings were hurt even more. But this time, he didn't have the option of calling it quits, not until he completed the cabin repairs, anyway. *I'll have to keep things as amicable between us as possible for a couple more weeks*, he thought. Perhaps a brief separation would help toward that end.

Meanwhile, Nick was still at a loss on how to proceed with the repairs and he made it a priority to speak with Hunter and Fletcher that week. Since Hunter owned a furniture restoration shop on Main Street, Nick figured during a lunch break he could talk to him about replicating the color of the stain and the best method of application. As a carpenter, Fletcher frequented the hardware store, so Nick had hopes of speaking to him, too.

After breakfast Nick prepared to jot a note to Lucy informing her he had to cancel their evening plans. He'd give the written message to her sisters at the mercantile so they could deliver it to Lucy that afternoon. He picked up a pen and stared at the blank sheet of paper, wondering how to word it. He would put the note in a sealed envelope, but that didn't guarantee her stepsisters wouldn't open it. He was probably wrong to suspect them of doing something like that, but he couldn't be too careful.

He hesitated with the pen angled an inch above the paper. Should he address her "dear Lucy?" Or just "Lucy"? He decided on just "Lucy," writing:

Lucy,
My father needs a break from the store a couple of evenings this week, so unfortunately I won't be able to follow through with our plans for to-night. But I'll see you Wednesday, when I'll pick you up to go to the soup kitchen.
Thank you for your understanding.

The note sounded dry to Nick so he added, "I look forward to being with you again," and hastily signed his name. It would have to do. As he sealed the enve-lope, a selfish thought crossed his mind: *Let's hope she isn't able to continue embroidering until then. I need her too much to allow her to end our courtship just yet.*

When Katura and Mildred returned home on Mon-day afternoon, Katura extended an envelope to Lucy. "It's from Nick."

"Denki." Lucy left the room so she could have some privacy, but her stepsisters followed her into the par-lor. Betty was there, too, rocking in a chair and sip-ping tea. She greeted her daughters and asked what the commotion was about.

"Nick gave us a note for Lucy. Isn't that odd? We thought you were going out with him tonight. Couldn't he have waited until then to talk to you?"

It was frightfully cold outdoors and a draft swirled through the room so Lucy took a seat near the wood-stove. "Maybe something came up," she said, tearing the envelope open. After reading it, she announced, "See? I was right. Nick has to work at the store tonight because his *daed* is under the weather."

"Really?" Katura eyed her suspiciously.

Lucy thrust the letter at her. "Read it for yourself if you don't believe me." She was getting sick of her stepsisters doubting her word.

"Oh, I believe you. It's Nick I doubt. He was awfully friendly with Eve last night, no matter what excuse you claimed he gave you for taking her on a ride. Has it occurred to you he's getting ready to break off your courtship so he can court her instead?"

Lucy wanted to deny the possibility, but she wasn't positive she could defend Nick. She was still having the same doubts about him Katura had expressed.

"I doubt that's it," Betty interjected, to Lucy's surprise. "I was speaking to Nick's mother last week at church and she told me how worried she's been about her husband's health. Anyway, this works out better. Now Lucy can join us at Doris Plank's home this evening."

Every year Doris held a Christmas card–making event in her home. It was a time of celebration, and the Amish women from the Willow Creek district brought food for a potluck supper. Lucy generally loved the occasion, but she'd rather progress with her embroidery project.

"Actually, I have work to catch up on for my table-cloth for the auction," she said. "I'll stay behind and make supper for *Daed* and me."

"I've already prepared beef Stroganoff. There's enough for us to take and I've set aside some for him to have, too," Betty argued. "You really ought to *kumme*."

"I would, but I'm concerned about meeting the deadline for the auc—"

"Lucy Knepp, sometimes I think you suffer from *hochmut*," Betty said, using the Amish word for pride. "If you would have had enough time to go out with Nick, you should have enough time to spend with the women from church. It's only one evening."

Lucy felt stung. *Hochmut?* That was the opposite of what she felt like most of the time. She didn't feel proud—she felt small. And not just physically small, either.

"All right," she agreed. Fighting tears, she rose and said, "I'm going to go finish my work in my room. I'll be down in time to go to the gathering at Doris's *haus*."

"As long as you're working tonight, I'm going to take off early," Kevin said to Nick after their father had left for the evening. "I haven't been out on a Monday in ages."

"It's hardly been a full week!" Nick exclaimed. "Besides, I'm not going to manage all the customers by myself."

"Why not? I handled the *Grischtdaag* shoppers with *Daed* all last week so you wouldn't have to."

Nick couldn't believe Kevin's unmitigated gall. "That's because I was out fixing *your* mess!"

"Really? How do I know you were working on the

cabin all that time? For all I know, you and Melinda's friend, Eve, spent most of last week walking out together while you were pretending to be working at the Nelsons' *haus*," Kevin suggested. "Don't deny it—I saw you leave with her last night. And I saw the look on Lucy's face when you came back in. You'll be fortunate if she doesn't blow your cover out of spite."

"You're really something, you know that, Kevin? You've got to stop gossiping—it's going to get you in a lot of trouble some day. Especially since you don't have a clue about what's going on."

"I know a scorned *maedel* when I see one. I'm beginning to think little Lucy Knepp has a crush on you. Are you sure she knows this phony arrangement is temporary?"

"*Jah,* but it's going to be a lot more temporary if you don't knock it off, because I'll quit working on Jenny's cabin in a heartbeat if you so much as think about abandoning your duties here this evening."

"All right, no need to get huffy," Kevin griped.

Despite his bluster, Nick was concerned. How many others had noticed he'd left the singing with Eve? His father's health was precarious—Nick couldn't let anything jeopardize the secrecy about the fire Kevin had started. He was beginning to wonder if he should have let Kevin suffer the consequences of his actions. But then, that would have meant their father would suffer, too. Nick had come this far; he couldn't allow that to happen now.

But how could he be sure Lucy was still as dedicated to protecting their shared secret as Nick was? After all, this was the same woman who'd been a notorious snitch when she was a child. But that was ages ago and Nick couldn't imagine Lucy exposing their secret, especially not out of spite. In order for her to be spiteful, she would have had to be romantically interested in Nick in the first place. And if he'd ever thought that was possible, their interaction the previous evening rid his mind utterly of such a notion.

Nick resigned himself to putting his worries aside and focusing on the steady stream of customers winding their way through the store's aisles. As it happened, Fletcher Chupp was among them so Nick was able to ask his questions about the drywall for his project.

After advising him, Fletcher remarked, "Sounds like you're doing some hefty renovating. I don't remember there being paneling in your *haus*."

Nick coughed, stalling. "*Neh*, there isn't. This is for a…a part-time job I've taken on after hours. Just don't mention it to anyone, all right? It's a long story, but it's sort of a *Grischtdaag* surprise."

"Mum's the word," Fletcher said. "I've been staying late on my job, too—so I can build a new chest of drawers for my wife. Although I wouldn't be surprised if she knows already. Women are intuitive like that. Nothing gets past them."

Thinking of Lucy's stepsisters and of Melinda Schrock, plus his own mother, Nick could only hope that wasn't true.

There were at least two dozen women at Doris Plank's house and Lucy was glad she went. After sharing their potluck entrées, the women got busy making cards. Sending and receiving homemade Christmas cards was a cherished Amish tradition in Willow Creek, and designing them was one of Lucy's favorite activities because it increased her anticipation of the upcoming holiday and allowed her to keep in touch with people she held dear.

"Look at that, you're so creative," Doris commented over Lucy's shoulder as she circled the tables serving cookies. Lucy had used construction paper, glue and a sprinkle of glitter to create two pairs of skates hanging side by side from hooks. Next to them was a window with a wreath in it, and snow was falling outside the panes. The card was for Bridget.

"Denki," Lucy said without looking up. "But I don't think it's really very creative. It's more like a habit. When you embroider as much scenery as I do for the *Englisch*, it becomes second nature."

"Jah, Betty told me you were decorating a beautiful tablecloth for the Piney Hill festival. And Melinda Schrock said you've been a busy beaver, filling specialty orders for customers at the shop. How do you do it all?"

Lucy was amazed such mundane details of her life were fodder for Melinda and Doris's conversations. "It's not so difficult," she said. "I get a lot done in the evenings when I—"

Too late she realized she was on the brink of giving her secret away. Not knowing how to explain, she bit into a cookie and then tried to change the subject, saying through a full mouth, "These are *appenditlich*. Did you make them, Doris?"

"Don't let Lucy fool you," Betty cut in. "She hasn't been working as much as she says. She's been going out with a certain suitor nearly every evening. If he hadn't been busy, she wouldn't be here tonight."

Lucy wanted to slink beneath the table. The worst

part of Betty's gossiping was that she was beaming, as if being courted by Nick Burkholder was Lucy's greatest achievement in life.

"A certain suitor?" Doris's ears seemed fine-tuned to the slightest mention of a courtship. "I had no idea you were walking out with someone. But if I had to venture a guess, I'd say it's Frederick Stutzman. Am I right?"

Lucy dabbed a cotton swab into a pool of glue and then applied it to her card. How could it be Doris had heard the minutest details of Lucy's life, yet didn't know Lucy had turned down Frederick's offer of courtship? Speechless, she shook her head in reply to Doris's question.

"If we guess, will you tell us?" Melinda Schrock taunted from the far end of the table where she was seated next to Eve.

"Oh, leave her alone," Eve scolded, to Lucy's surprise. "In my district in Ohio we don't talk about our courtships."

Iris Schwartz chimed in, "We don't usually discuss them publicly in Willow Creek, and we don't pressure others into discussing them, either. Doris, please pass that cookie platter this way."

Lucy appreciated their tactful scolding, but Doris and Melinda ignored their hints to drop the subject.

"That's okay, I already know who it is," Melinda said in a singsong voice. "It's someone named Dan Ebersole, isn't it? I've heard about a young man who's new to the area and he volunteers at the soup kitchen where Lucy serves. It's got to be him. There's no one else who's available."

Lucy was mortified. All she needed was for Melinda to start a rumor that Dan was Lucy's suitor. She liked him as a friend, of course, but as his friend Lucy didn't want Dan to think Lucy had started the rumor. For a split second, she considered telling everyone at the table it was Nick, not Dan, who was her suitor. Somewhat surprised Betty didn't volunteer that information herself, Lucy glanced at her stepmother, who caught her eye and winked at her.

"There's no one else available to do what?" Mildred asked as she pranced into the room carrying another tray of cookies.

"To court Lucy. She's got her first suitor and she won't tell us who it is," Doris announced. Lucy was mortified she emphasized the fact this was Lucy's first suitor—especially because he wasn't actually her suitor at all. Did all of the women in Willow Creek know she'd never been courted?

"Oh, that's easy," Mildred said, and Lucy wished she could reach across the room and clap her hand over Mildred's mouth. "It's Nick Burkholder."

"Ha!" Melinda sneered. "If he turned down the chance to court Eve, he wouldn't court Lucy."

"Melinda!" Eve exclaimed. "What kind of thing is that to say? He probably has no interest in me *because* he's courting Lucy."

Lucy didn't know what was more humiliating: Melinda's proclamation Lucy was less desirable for courtship than Eve was, or Eve's condescending denial. She wanted to flee the room, but the heaviness in her stomach kept her anchored to her chair.

Eve's admonishment, coupled with the other women's silence, must have shamed Melinda into recognizing how offensive her remark was. "I didn't mean it the way it came out. I just meant Nick is so outgoing and so is Eve, and Lucy, well, you're as quiet as a church mouse."

Lucy wanted to tell Melinda what animal *she* was as loud as, but instead she silently prayed for grace.

"Sometimes opposites attract," Betty stated. Her face was blotchy, as if she were the one who'd been insulted, not Lucy.

"That's very true. In some ways, John and I are as different as night and day. For example, he used to love *kaffi* but I only liked tea," Doris said. "Yet while we were courting, he drank tea just to please me. It was so romantic."

As Doris continued to blather on about trivial differences between her and her husband, Lucy fought back tears. She wished she could sneak away to the washroom, but if she did, she'd draw more attention to how uncomfortable she felt. So she continued to work on her card for Bridget. *I'll be so glad when she gets here*, she thought. Bridget would understand how Lucy felt.

Knowing that Betty, Katura and Mildred wouldn't leave the party until everyone else did, Lucy tried to make the most of the evening. After finishing her cards, she went into the kitchen for a glass of water. She was turning from the sink when Eve walked in. Lucy briefly nodded and started toward the hall, but Eve stopped her.

"Lucy, I'm so sorry I let it slip that Nick's your suitor," she said quietly. "I didn't mean to, but I was so appalled at Melinda's remarks it just came out."

"It's all right," Lucy replied. "Mildred was the one who told everyone first."

"Well, for the record, I honestly wasn't all that interested in being courted by Nick. I mean, I *am* interested in having a suitor and Nick seems like a nice person. But I mainly went for a ride with him to keep Melinda from embarrassing both of us even more than she'd already done by pushing us together."

Lucy eyed Eve skeptically. Was she telling the truth?

"Melinda is my best friend from childhood and I love her dearly. She grew up without a *mamm* or any female influences in her life when she was a young *maedel*, so she lacks some of the...the sensitivity or *gut* manners other *meed* have. But sometimes I can't believe she hasn't matured more," Eve explained. Then she added, "Just so you know, Nick wasn't happy about taking me for a ride, either. He was so concerned about what you'd think he couldn't wait to get back."

Even though Lucy knew the reason Nick couldn't wait to get back was because he wanted to be sure she hadn't told her stepsisters they weren't actually courting, she was glad to hear he wasn't really interested in Eve. Lucy regretted not taking him at his word when he made the same claim himself.

Eve chewed on her lip before continuing, "I understand why you'd be upset with me, but please don't be upset with Nick. It's not my place to say, but he really cares about you. I knew it from the look in his eyes when he saw you near the porch and invited you to *kumme* with us. I should have told him right then and there I didn't want to go for a ride. I should have stepped aside and let you go with him alone. But I selfishly didn't want to face Melinda's interrogation if I returned to the *haus* without Nick, and I'm sorry about that."

Eve could tell Nick cared about Lucy? Nick might have cared about her as a friend, and he definitely cared about preserving their arrangement, but it was a bit of a stretch for Lucy to believe he cared about her romantically, the way Eve was implying. "*Denki* for telling me all of that. But there's no need to apologize. I assure you, nothing you did affected my...my relationship with Nick."

Eve clasped her hands together against her chest. "That's *wunderbaar* to hear because he seemed very worried about it. Not that I blame him—you're so talented and pretty. It probably took a lot for him to ask to court you in the first place. Men can be insecure like that sometimes. At least, that's why I tell myself I've only ever had one suitor."

Lucy was surprised by Eve's compliment, which seemed genuine even though she'd never before been called *pretty* by anyone other than her father, as well as by Eve's admission she'd only had one suitor. Lucy would have thought someone as gregarious and becoming as Eve would have had men lining up to court her—to marry her, in fact.

Lucy touched Eve's arm. "Those men in Ohio can't be too smart to pass you by," she said. But inwardly, Lucy was glad the men in Willow Creek—and Nick, in particular—had passed Eve by, too.

Nick rubbed his hands against his legs as he headed to Lucy's house on Wednesday night. As frigid as the air was, his palms were sweaty from the apprehension of seeing her again. But when she approached his buggy, she was all smiles. He eagerly offered assistance into the carriage, which she accepted since she was carrying a big plastic container she indicated held Christmas cookies.

"I, uh…it's really cold. You might need this," he stuttered, unfolding yet another blanket to add to the two she was already securing around her lap. As he bent down to arrange it around her feet, he clunked his head against hers and dropped back against the seat.

"Ouch!" he exclaimed. "Sorry, sorry. Are you okay?"

Lucy laughed, rubbing her head. "Fortunately, I think my bonnet absorbed the force of the blow."

He was glad she was so forgiving, but once again his size and ungainliness made him feel like an ox around her, both physically and verbally. Lucy, on the other hand, was extraordinarily chatty that evening. All the way there, she talked about how much she loved the month of December at the soup kitchen. She said during the holiday season several local *Englisch* companies donated an abundance of delicious treats and items such as toys, toothbrushes and wool socks for the people who came there to eat.

"I wish I could knit. Then I could make socks, too," she lamented.

"You don't knit? But you're embroidering an entire tablecloth," he said.

She giggled. "Knitting and embroidery are nothing alike. Sadly, I can't knit or crochet. I ought to make a resolution to learn because they're both much more useful skills than embroidering is."

"But your linens bring in an income. And you're using your talent to raise funds for the soup kitchen. How can you say embroidery isn't useful?" Nick marveled.

Lucy cocked her head thoughtfully. "I suppose it is. It's just… I don't know. Haven't you ever wished you had a skill that you don't have?"

Nick nodded. "*Jah.* I wish I could sing better," he admitted. "My voice is *baremlich.* Sometimes during church worship, I mouth the words. I'm thinking about what they mean and I'm trying to praise the Lord in thought, but I'm not singing aloud. I wouldn't inflict noise like that on everyone else."

Even though he was serious, Lucy laughed. "*Kumme* now, it can't be that bad. Besides, you're singing to the Lord. What business is it of anyone else's how *Gott* made your voice to sound?"

She was right, and Nick momentarily regretted having shared this shortcoming with her, knowing it made him seem vain. But then Lucy added, "For what it's worth, I think your speaking voice is pleasant. It's very masculine and comforting. Not too loud or overbearing, the way some men's voices can be."

Nick was sure he was blushing. "*Denki,*" he replied, relieved his voice didn't crack when he said it.

As they pulled up to the parking lot in front of the church where the soup kitchen was located, Nick spotted a young man on the sidewalk beneath the lights. Lucy simultaneously yanked the blankets over her head and dropped to her hands and knees on the floor of the buggy, causing Nick to halt the carriage.

"What's wrong?" he asked.

"That's Dan Ebersole. Usually my *daed* brings me here. Dan can't see me arriving with you. He'll think we're actually courting."

Nick was confused. He lifted the blankets enough

to peek at Lucy and asked, "Isn't that what we want people to think?"

Peeping up at him, Lucy said, "*Jah*, I guess you're right." Then she stood and brushed off her skirt. "Sorry. I've heard a lot of...of far-fetched gossip lately, and I suppose I panicked when I saw one of my peers. But since you and I will be ending our arrangement in a couple weeks anyway, I'd prefer that as few people as possible know we're supposedly courting. Too many already know about it, which means they'll all find out when we 'break up,' too. It's going to be awkward enough as it is to be the subject of that kind of gossip among our peers. The soup kitchen is the one public place I go where none of my peers go. Except for Dan, I mean. So I'd prefer it if he didn't find out about either our courtship or our breakup, if that makes sense. So would you mind dropping me off here? And can you pick me up a little later, say eight fifteen, so no one sees you?"

Nick agreed, "Of course. Hold on a minute and I'll help you down."

But Lucy insisted she could manage, and she was out of the buggy and down the walkway in a flash. Nick watched as she caught up with Dan, who turned and grinned and then carried the container of cookies for her.

At the cabin while he used the technique Hunter advised to apply stain to the new pieces of paneling, Nick thought about Lucy's reaction to seeing Dan. Rather, to Dan possibly seeing her. Her explanation about why she wanted to limit the number of people who knew about their pretend courtship made sense, but Nick couldn't help but wonder if Lucy was interested in being courted by Dan. Maybe that was really why she didn't want Dan to see her with him. The thought shouldn't have bothered Nick, but he was so distracted he spilled stain on the floor and then spent the remaining time cleaning it up.

Afterward he was relieved that when he picked up Lucy Dan was nowhere in sight.

"Was your evening productive?" Lucy asked as they got underway.

"Actually, I spent more time fixing my own mess than I did cleaning up Kevin's," Nick said.

"Kevin was helping you?" Lucy asked, startling Nick. He hadn't intended to mention his brother. His mind was really not where it should be tonight.

"*Neh.* But he borrowed my tool kit and I couldn't find anything I was looking for in it. Kevin's not the most organized person in the world." It wasn't a lie— Kevin *had* borrowed his tool kit and returned it in disarray, but that wasn't the mess Nick had been referring to.

Lucy clicked her tongue sympathetically. "That sounds like what Mildred does when she borrows something from my sewing basket."

Relieved, Nick asked, "How was your evening?"

"It was *wunderbaar.* Because of the cold weather, we had twice as many people *kumme* in as usual, so the place was jammed. Since the oven's broken, we couldn't prepare warm meals, but we put on a spread of picnic foods like potato salad and burgers and hot dogs, which the men made on the grills everyone brought."

"Ah, I get it. Instead of a '*Grischtdaag* in July' event, you had a 'July at *Grischtdaag*' supper."

Lucy clapped her gloved hands. "Oh, very clever! We should have thought to call it that."

Nick grinned, pleased she found his idea clever. Lucy was chipper as she described the scene at the soup kitchen, and her mirth buoyed Nick's mood, as well.

"There was a high school choir there singing *Grischtdaag* songs while everyone ate, and afterward we got to distribute some of the donated items. That was the best part. I don't know why *Gott* allows me to be in a position to witness joy like that, but I'm so grateful He does."

Moved by her sentiment, Nick stole a sideways glance at Lucy. She was glowing, her face directed toward the sky. He felt like he was the one who got to witness pure joy.

"Look!" she suddenly demanded. "Is that snow?"

Sure enough, white flakes dotted the night sky. They were so light they floated instead of fell, but they were undeniably snowflakes.

"I do believe it is," he replied.

"It's snowing!" Lucy yelled, pushing the blankets aside. She stood and flung her arms in the air. "It's snowing!"

"Hey, you're going to fall," Nick cautioned, attempting to slow the horse at the same time he reached to steady Lucy.

"*Neh*, I'm not. Don't slow down, please," she pleaded. "Go faster. Faster!"

"You're *narrish*!" he declared, but he honored her request to increase their speed, keeping one hand against the small of her back in support.

She rode like that for a good two miles, her arms

outstretched, her face tipped toward the sky. Her outer winter bonnet slipped from her head and dangled by its ribbons down her back. She removed her glasses, saying they were too wet to see through, and that's when Nick noticed what a gentle profile she had, with her delicately pointed nose and sharp cheekbones.

Finally, as they approached the bend toward her house, he said, "I think you should sit down now, Lucy. I don't want you to fall when we round the next corner."

"All right," she agreed readily, dropping to the seat. She was so close to him that if he had moved his knee an inch, it would have touched hers, but surprisingly she made no attempt to move away. Beneath a streetlamp, Nick could see her cheeks glistened with snow and the bun in her hair was coming loose.

"We, ah, better stop here so you can pull yourself together," he suggested.

"Ach, do I look that bad?" Lucy asked, although she giggled as if she hardly cared.

Actually, she didn't look bad at all. She looked, well, she looked *free*. She looked the way Nick felt whenever Penny ran this fast—as if everything was exciting and anything was possible. "*Neh*, but your hair is coming down, here," Nick said, gently lifting a strand. His hand trembled. "And I don't know where your prayer *kapp* is, but your bonnet is hanging down your back. I wouldn't want anyone to think…"

Modesty kept him from saying what he feared others might think, but Lucy seemed to catch on right away. "*Neh*, of course not," she said. When she lifted her hand to fix her hair, it bumped his hand, which made him realize he was still holding the silky lock between his fingers.

After fixing her bun and looking around in vain for her prayer *kapp*, Lucy donned her bonnet and tied it beneath her chin. They continued in silence to her house, where Nick bounced down to help her from the carriage, extending his hand. Her small fingers disappeared within his larger ones, but instead of stepping down, she lingered there until his eyes met hers.

"*Denki*, Nick. That was exhilarating."

Exhilarated was exactly what Nick felt when he looked at Lucy. He swallowed and said, "Anytime."

Chapter Six

Lucy was so jubilant after her Wednesday night buggy ride with Nick she didn't even object when Betty said she ought to accompany her, Katura and Mildred on a trip to visit their relatives in Elmsville for supper on Thursday evening. Although she was slightly behind where she wanted to be with her special embroidery project, Lucy figured on Friday night she and Nick would be able to stay out later so she could catch up then.

On Friday morning, she journeyed into town with her stepsisters to drop off an order at Schrock's Shop. Joseph Schrock, who managed the family-run business, was delighted to see her.

"Your linens are flying off the shelf, Lucy," he said. "One customer wanted to buy all of your Christmas place mats. I limited her to a set of six because I didn't want to disappoint other customers, but I promised I'd ask if you could make an extra twelve for them by next Thursday, the fifteenth. They're having a special family gathering this *Grischtdaag* and they want enough place mats for eighteen people. If you're not able to make them by then, they'd like to know so they'll have time to *kumme* up with something else to adorn their table."

Lucy hesitated. The place mats' intricate poinsettia pattern was more time-consuming than some of her simpler designs. She wasn't sure she could fulfill that request, plus keep up with her other orders and finish the tablecloth for the auction, as well. "I hesitate to commit to that," she said. "My hands are full with other things I need to do before *Grischtdaag*."

Lucy was unaware Melinda had sidled up to her until she butted in. "It's probably difficult to keep up with work when you've got so many...shall we say, *social commitments*." Because Melinda was married to Joseph's nephew, Jesse, she worked at the shop, and Lucy silently asked the Lord to prevent her from saying anything more about her courtship with Nick. It was bad enough most of the women in Willow Creek knew; Lucy didn't want the men knowing, too. It would only make things more awkward when her arrangement with Nick ended.

"Social commitments?" Joseph repeated blankly.

Concerned Melinda was about to go into detail, Lucy quickly offered, "I'll do my best to embroider another twelve place mats by Thursday, Joseph. I'll deliver them that afternoon, sometime after four o'clock."

He grinned. "*Denki*, Lucy. I knew you weren't the type to put pleasure before work."

Joseph shot a pointed look at Melinda.

Lucy understood he intended his remark as a compliment, but it rubbed her the wrong way. Didn't people think she liked to have any fun at all? After paying

Lucy, Joseph walked away quickly to serve a customer in the candle and soaps aisle.

Apparently, Melinda was supposed to be working the cash register, and she sauntered to the other side of the checkout counter and said, "I heard Wheeler's Pond is frozen over. If this cold snap keeps up, some of us are going skating tomorrow night. You and Nick should *kumme*. Unless you're too busy sewing. Or unless he can't make it for some reason."

Lucy felt more like Melinda was challenging her than inviting her to join their peers for skating. It was as if Melinda doubted Lucy and Nick were a couple. They weren't, of course, but Lucy was provoked all the same. "I'd really like that," she said. "I'm going to the hardware store next, so I'll see what Nick thinks of the idea. Usually he likes to keep me all to himself, but maybe tomorrow evening we'll squeeze in a little social time with the rest of you."

When Melinda's lower lip jutted out in a pout, Lucy felt victorious. But, after exiting the shop, she paused on the front stoop and clasped her hands together to keep them from shaking. It was true she'd intended to go to the hardware store next, but not to talk to Nick. Not specifically, anyway. She planned to purchase a toolbox for her father's wood-carving tools for Christmas. Now how was she going to break it to Nick she'd just committed them to showing up for skating on Saturday evening? Lucy considered not telling him at all, but she couldn't put it past Melinda to check up on her by questioning Nick. He deserved fair warning.

Lucy was only halfway through the entrance when she spotted Nick chatting with an *Englisch* customer, who held his rapt attention. Noticing the way Nick's strong hands gestured as he spoke, Lucy was reminded of how safe she had felt when he'd steadied her in the buggy the other night. A shiver wiggled down her spine, just as it had done from his touch that night. She heard Nick wish the customer success with his renovation, and then he turned in Lucy's direction. A wide smile broke across his freckled cheeks.

"Hi, Lucy," he said, ambling in her direction. "How are you today?"

"I'm fine, *denki*. I'm here to purchase a case or a toolbox. For wood-carving tools. Chisels. Knives. That kind of thing." Lucy was so nervous she could hardly communicate, but Nick didn't seem to notice.

"So you've taken up wood carving in addition to embroidery?" he joked.

"*Neh*, it's not for me. It's a present for my *daed* for *Grischtdaag*. But if you see him, don't tell him," she replied solemnly.

"I can keep a secret," Nick promised, winking at her. Her knees went weak then, and again when he touched the small of her back and ushered her down an aisle. "We keep our toolboxes over here. What kind are you looking for?"

"The best kind," she said, flustered by his nearness.

Nick threw his head back and laughed. "Well, that's *gut* because we don't stock the worst kind." His laughter put Lucy at ease and she chuckled, too. Then he questioned whether she wanted a wood or plastic toolbox.

"I guess I don't know what I'm looking for."

As Nick began to show Lucy the different types of boxes, she had a difficult time focusing on his descriptions. She felt heady from watching his hands pulling open the little drawers, from his masculine, musky scent, and from the clean, smooth skin of his jaw. She had to tell him about the skating at Wheeler's Pond now, before she lost her nerve.

"So, what do you think?" He paused, waiting for her response.

"I'll take whatever you recommend," she said. "I trust your advice."

Nick smiled and removed the wooden box from the shelf. "Then you'll definitely want this one. It's a little more expensive, but the feature that allows you to tilt the knife compartment for easier access is worth it," he said, and began to walk down the aisle, but Lucy grabbed him by the crook of his arm.

"I told Melinda we'd go skating at Wheeler's Pond tomorrow night." Her words were both quiet and rushed.

"You what?" Nick asked, leaning closer. He smelled so good. Too good. She released his arm.

"I told Melinda we'd go skating at Wheeler's Pond on Saturday," Lucy repeated. "I'm sorry. She was badgering me and I just—well, I don't know what came over me. We can make up an excuse not to go, but I had to tell you now so we can get our story straight in case she pops in here and interrogates you about it."

She held her breath, waiting for his response.

Nick couldn't take his eyes off Lucy. The color rising to her cheeks reminded him of how she had looked on Wednesday night after her madcap performance in his buggy. He wanted to say he'd love to go skating with her, but he wasn't sure she actually wanted to go to the pond herself. She was only telling him so they could come up with an excuse not to go, right? Nick didn't feel confident enough to ask her outright.

"I suppose after I'm done working on the cabin and if you're satisfied with your progress embroidering, we could stop by the pond," he suggested. "For the sake of appearances, that is."

Lucy let her breath out. "Are you sure you don't mind?"

"*Neh*, not at all. I enjoy skating. Haven't done it in years but I wouldn't mind taking a spin around the rink."

"Oh, Nick, that's *wunderbaar*," Lucy whispered. "For appearances, I mean."

Nick felt deflated. He shifted the large toolbox in his arms and asked, "So do you really need one of these, or was that just a pretense to *kumme* talk to me in private?"

"I really need one," she said in a normal voice again.

He led her back to the cash register, where Kevin had taken over ringing up the sales. "Lucy gets the carpenter's discount," Nick told his brother.

"Oh, she's building a *haus*, is she?" Kevin asked her.

Nick glared at his brother. Before turning his attention to another customer, Nick said, "If it's okay with you, I'll pick you up half an hour earlier tonight, Lucy. Kevin likes to assist the customers without my help. It makes him feel like he's in charge."

Kevin opened his mouth, and then closed it and grunted.

"I'll look forward to that, Nick," Lucy said sweetly. If she was surprised Nick was being so obvious about their supposed courtship in front of Kevin, she didn't let on.

The rest of the morning flew by, and soon Nick's mother stopped in with lunch for the four of them to eat in the back room. Nick noticed his father picking at his food; ordinarily, he had a hearty appetite. "We've got things covered at the shop today, *Daed*," he said. "You could go home with *Mamm* after lunch if you want."

Kevin still must have been peeved about Nick's earlier remark because he said, "*Jah*, Nick is so confident in my abilities, he's leaving half an hour early to take Lucy out tonight."

If Kevin was hoping to get Nick in hot water, his plan backfired. "I'm confident in your abilities to handle the store alone, too, Kevin, so I think I will go home after lunch," their father said. Then he turned to Nick. "Lucy's a *wunderbaar maedel*. You can leave even earlier if you'd like to."

"*Denki*, but that's not necessary," Nick said. Then, taking advantage of the opportunity, he added, "But I would like to get out of work a little earlier tomorrow afternoon so I can spend more time with her. She, uh, has some special things I'm helping her accomplish before *Grischtdaag*, and then in the evening we're going skating on Wheeler's Pond."

"Is Lucy up for that?" his mother asked. "She's in such frail health."

The potato he'd been chewing felt like it was lodged in Nick's throat. He coughed and thumped his fist against his chest. "What do you mean, she's in frail health?"

His mother swallowed before she answered. "Lucy's prone to pneumonia. Last year she had such a bad case of it she wound up hospitalized for nearly a week. It's a result of being born so early and having all those respiratory problems. You'd better be sure she stays bundled up, *suh*. Skating might be fine for half an hour or so, but don't overdo it."

Nick shook his head in disbelief. He never knew Lucy suffered from any kind of illness. After watching her stunt in the buggy on Wednesday night, he thought she was one of the toughest girls he'd ever courted. Why had she agreed to go skating if she was prone to pneumonia? "I didn't know she was in poor health. She never told me," he admitted.

"Ach!" his mother patted her lips with a napkin. "Listen to me. What a tale-teller I am. She probably didn't mention it because it's been such a struggle for her, but her *daed* says she prefers to keep it to herself and to act as if she's fine. He worries about her, though. So don't you give him extra cause for concern."

"I won't, *Mamm*," Nick promised.

For the rest of the afternoon he experienced a growing mix of concern and anger. He didn't want Lucy to get sick, yet he resented it that she'd put him in a position of jeopardizing her health. That wasn't fair. There was no way he was going skating with her now, no matter what Melinda deduced from their absence.

Later, when Lucy climbed into the buggy Nick placed a fourth blanket on her lap before signaling Penny to walk on.

"What's this for?" she asked. "I can barely move."

"You didn't tell me you were sick," he said accusingly. "That wasn't fair."

"What are you talking about? I'm not sick."

He pulled the buggy off the road. "You're prone to pneumonia," he accused.

Lucy stiffened. "I see some *bobblemoul* has been filling your ears with gossip."

Bristling to hear Lucy unwittingly refer to his mother as a blabbermouth, Nick replied, "It's not gossip if it's true."

"*Neh*, it's not slander if it's true, but it's still gossip," Lucy argued. "Either way, I don't see how it's any of your business."

"None of my business? I wouldn't have taken you out in this frigid weather if I had known about your health condition. You should have told me rather than to put me in this position."

Lucy slapped her hands against her lap. "I'm an adult. I don't need to get permission from you to go outside during the winter."

"Maybe not, but did you ever think what would have happened if you'd gotten pneumonia?"

"*Jah*, I would have suffered from it. Me. Not you. I would've been the one in the hospital."

Nick raised his voice. "Don't act like that, Lucy. Don't deny it wouldn't have had an effect on me, too. I would have known I was responsible."

"What are you talking about? You're not responsible for me. *I'm* responsible for me. And so is the Lord. I don't understand why you're being like this all of a sudden. If you want to put an end to our arrangement for some other reason, just tell me. You don't need to create some pitiful excuse."

Nick was so frustrated he took off his hat and smacked it against his fist. "I'm not creating an excuse. Your health is a perfectly valid reason to call off our deal. I don't see why you can't understand that."

"Okay," Lucy said, moving toward the edge of the

seat. "Deal's off." She jumped down before Nick could stop her and began walking in the direction of her house.

"Lucy! *Kumme* back here," he called. "You're being *lecherich*!"

Lucy turned and shouted, "I'm not your responsibility anymore, Nick. Not that I ever was. So leave me alone."

If Nick wasn't mistaken, she was crying. In all of the times he'd broken off a relationship, he had never felt as miserable as he did now when making Lucy Knepp cry. And his courtship with her wasn't even real. He couldn't let it end like this. Within a few paces, he'd caught up to her and a few paces after that, he'd gained enough ground to turn around and face her as she approached, holding his arms out to prevent her passage.

"Knock it off, Nick," Lucy shouted, tears streaming down her face. "I want to get by."

"And I want to take you home. *Kumme* on, Lucy. Be reasonable."

Even in her outrage, Lucy could see the sense in what he was saying. For one thing, it was bitterly cold. For another, if her father found out she'd walked home in that kind of weather, he'd be furious—not at Lucy, but at Nick. That wouldn't be fair.

"Fine." She turned and headed back toward the buggy. When he offered his hand, she pushed it away.

Nick took his seat next to her and picked up the reins, but before moving onward, he said, "I don't understand it, Lucy. Why is my caring about you such an awful thing?" His voice was quivering and Lucy felt a pang of guilt. She knew she was overreacting. Rather, she was reacting to a heartache that had plagued her for years, not one Nick had caused that evening.

"I don't expect you to understand," she said, wiping her rough woolen mitten across her cheeks.

"But I want to. Can't you explain it to me?"

Nick's voice was so forlorn Lucy let her defenses drop. "I've always been treated like this, my entire life. *Lucy's too weak, too fragile, too small, she can't go outside or run around or have any fun because she'll get sick. She'll stop breathing. She'll wind up in the hospital.* My whole life, Nick. And then, the one little taste of utter abandon I ever experienced—charging through the dark with a frosty wind whisking against my face, feeling totally invigorated and alive—you want to take that away from me, too."

She was crying so hard her words were barely intelligible, but Nick didn't interrupt or attempt to quiet her. When she finally settled down and could speak normally again, she sniffed and asked, "May I use your handkerchief, please?"

"Sorry, I don't have one," Nick said. "But here, you can use my scarf. I don't mind."

The offer to use Nick's scarf to dry her eyes and blow her nose was so ridiculous and sweet all at once it caused Lucy to chuckle. "*Neh,* that's okay," she said, removing her mittens to dab her eyes with her bare fingers.

"I really am sorry," he repeated.

Lucy was embarrassed. "That's all right. I've stopped blubbering. I don't need a handkerchief after all."

"*Neh,* I mean I'm sorry I treated you in a way that

made you feel…the way you feel. I didn't mean to. I was concerned. I care about you and I wouldn't want anything to happen to you. I especially wouldn't want to play a role in hurting you."

Lucy was overwhelmed by his words. No man had ever said anything like that to her before, even in friendship. "It's not your fault," she said. "And I do appreciate that you care. But I'm not as fragile as you think I am."

"Fragile? You? I don't think you're fragile at all, even if you are prone to pneumonia," Nick scoffed. "I think you're one of the most resilient women I've ever known."

Lucy was overwhelmed again. If this kept up, she was going to fall hard for Nick Burkholder. Maybe she already had. "Then let's continue our arrangement. We both have work left to do."

"Okay, but you have to promise me something," Nick said, peering at her. In the dark she could only make out the whites of his eyes but his voice was heavy. "Promise you'll tell me if all this running around gets to be too much for you. And if you even think there's a chance you're catching a cold, you have to—"

"I'll tell you," Lucy promised somberly. Then, in a lighter tone she said, "So in that vein, I'm getting cold now. Can we keep going, please?"

Nick released the buggy's parking brake and clicked for Penny to move on. They'd traveled a few hundred yards when he shook his head. It seemed he was thinking aloud as he said, "So when we were *kinner* in school…all those times you stayed inside and cleaned the whiteboards… That was because you weren't allowed to go outside?"

"That's right," Lucy said with a sigh. "I used to watch the rest of you from the window and daydream about what it would be like to be out there running around or playing hide-and-seek."

"No wonder you were always tattling on us. You must have been pretty envious."

Lucy was indignant. "I never tattled on anyone!" she said. "Not once, ever. Especially not on you. I loved watching your antics even if—sometimes *especially if*—you misbehaved. If I'd told on you, the teacher would have made you quit climbing trees or hiding lunch boxes or whatever other mischief you were causing. I would have been bored out of my skull just watching the girls playing jacks."

"Really?" Nick asked, and Lucy vehemently assured him she was telling the truth.

"I didn't even tell when you nicknamed me Bug Eyes."

"Did I do that?" Nick asked. "I honestly don't remember."

"Well, I sure do."

"Wow, I'm sorry. No wonder my nickname was Naughty Nick."

Lucy giggled. "I'd rather be known as Naughty Nick than Lovely Lucy. That was a hard title to live up to. But it was better than Bug Eyes." She affectionately nudged Nick's arm with hers.

He shook his head again. "Like I said, I honestly don't remember doing that. But in my defense, I really did love insects. So Bug Eyes might have been a compliment."

"*Jah*, nice try!" Lucy laughed. "It doesn't matter. I forgave you long ago. I wasn't really so lovely myself, and I had a lot of things I needed to be forgiven for, too. I still do."

Nick turned slightly in his seat. "For what it's worth, I'd never call you Bug Eyes now. Your eyes are beautiful, like a doe's," he said. Then he worried aloud, "That isn't an offensive wildlife association is it?"

"Not at all," Lucy murmured. It was lovely. Who would have thought it would take Naughty Nick to help her feel as if she truly was Lovely Lucy?

The fumes from the wood stain must have been getting to Nick, because early Saturday evening he felt woozy. He only had about thirty minutes before he was supposed to leave Jenny's cabin and pick Lucy up. He wished he could call it quits early, but there was too much to be done and time was closing in.

When he finally reached the café, he spied Lucy waiting outside the entrance. While he appreciated she was standing there so he'd know he didn't need to hitch the horse across the lot and come inside to get her, he had lingering concerns about her being outside in such unseasonably cold weather.

"Are you sure you're ready for this?" he asked shortly before they reached the road leading to the pond.

"*Jah*. I love to skate."

"*Neh*, I mean, to, you know, pretend." Nick didn't want to say the words aloud again. He and Lucy had vaguely agreed they'd put on enough of a show to convince any naysayers they were courting, but they wouldn't be so obvious it would appear they were flaunting their courtship—which in their community would have been a dead giveaway they weren't really a couple. But Nick hadn't discussed the specifics with Lucy because she said if they orchestrated their behavior too much, they wouldn't come across as natural. With any other woman, Nick would have executed his role with ease, but with Lucy, he wasn't quite sure what to expect. Or what she expected of him.

Arriving at the rink together might have been a convincing indication they were courting were it not for the fact the Amish were scattered throughout Willow Creek's countryside, so many of the youth traveled together.

Eve spotted them right away. "Hi, Lucy. Hi, Nick," she greeted them, causing Melinda to glance up from where she wobbled across the ice, her ankles bending inward.

Nick and Lucy waved to both of them. They sat closely next to each other on one of the logs arranged like benches near the edge of the pond so they could lace their skates. Then they tentatively made their way across the frozen earth to the homemade rink.

Lucy stepped onto the ice first and within a few strokes she was gliding so gracefully it seemed as if she was born wearing skates. She had perfect balance. In choppier movements, Nick skated briskly up to her and said, "You're really *gut* at this. You have no fear."

"That's because I don't have far to fall," Lucy joked. "And because I've been skating since I was pretty young."

Nick laughed. "How is it you had to stay inside during recess but you were allowed to go ice skating?"

"It wasn't really that I was *allowed*," Lucy admitted.

"It was that my *daed* didn't know about it. I'd use the skates Bridget had outgrown and the two of us would sneak off to the pond together. By the time my *daed* found out, I was a teenager and by then I was capable enough to convince him if I took it easy I could skate without losing my breath."

"Aha. That explains why you're kind of slow. Graceful, but slow," he taunted, and she whipped her scarf at him. He caught one end of it and asked, "Do you want a tow? Are you up for a little speed?"

"If you think you're strong enough to pull me, go ahead," she dared. He took off, pulling her in fast circles around the pond. She was shrieking and laughing, and he was laughing, too. Whoever else was on the rink, Nick didn't know; he only had eyes for Lucy.

"Okay, okay, I need a rest," she finally called, and he abruptly brought himself to a stop, holding out his arms to stop her, too. She glided right toward him, coming to a gentle stop beneath his chin. It was as if she fit perfectly there, and he dropped his arms to embrace her before she backed away. Although accidental, the public display of affection was more than most Amish youth demonstrated in public.

"How about some hot chocolate?" she suggested, gesturing across the lawn to where a bonfire was roaring.

"*Jah*, let's." They changed out of their skates and then Nick carried both pairs as they walked side by side to the bonfire. Lucy poured hot chocolate from one of the jugs someone had brought for the occasion and moved as close as she could to the fire.

Nick stood next to her, warmed through and through. The flames reflected off the front of her lenses, but from the side, he could see the corner of her eyes creased from her smile.

Suddenly, a deep voice questioned, "Lucy, is that you?" It was Dan, the young man from the soup kitchen. Despite Lucy's wish that Dan not discover their courtship, Nick found himself hoping the young man had seen them skating together. Or was it enough for Dan to see Nick and Lucy standing together like this in order to assume they were courting?

When Lucy grinned and replied, "Hi, Dan. I'm so glad to see you," Nick felt a stab of jealousy because she really did seem glad. "This is Nick."

That was all she said by way of introduction and Nick felt let down. Then someone nearby broke into song. Soon, everyone around the fire was singing Christmas carols, including Dan, whose singing voice was a rich baritone. Nick tried to recall what Lucy said about his own voice, but he couldn't. When she glanced his way and winked at him, he had to force himself to smile in return.

All the way home, Lucy raved about what a fun evening it was. "By the way, that little hug on the ice rink was a nice touch," she said. "I think we fooled everyone, don't you?"

Whether they fooled everyone or no one at all, Nick didn't care; he was consumed by the wish for their courtship to be as real as they were pretending it was.

Chapter Seven

"There was a skating party last night?" Mildred asked on the way home from church on Sunday. "Why didn't anyone tell us? Why didn't *you* tell us, Lucy?"

"You've always said you dislike being outdoors in the cold," Lucy explained, referencing the reason her stepsisters gave for needing to take the buggy instead of walking to their jobs. "Besides, you don't have skates."

"You should have let us know anyway. We could have hung out by the bonfire," Katura quibbled. "We haven't had any *schpass* all weekend. Not unless you consider helping our adolescent cousins bake four batches of sugar cookies for their school *Grischtdaag* pageant to be fun. Which I definitely do not."

Having met Mildred and Katura's cousins, Lucy couldn't argue. The young girls were notoriously messy, noisy and ill behaved. Lucy was glad her arrangement with Nick had spared her from spending late Saturday afternoon with them.

"At least there's a singing tonight," Mildred consoled Katura. To Lucy she said, "Are you and Nick going to that together, too?"

Lucy actually planned to stay home. It wasn't as if Nick could work on the repairs on the Sabbath. Besides, he'd mentioned his *ant* and *onkel* from Elmsville might be visiting their family after church and staying through supper, possibly overnight. "*Neh*, not this time. I think Nick has other plans."

Betty turned to face the three girls in the back seat. To Lucy she said, "It's wise of you to take a little break from Nick. Absence makes the heart grow fonder. And this way, you can go to the singing in the same buggy as Katura and Mildred."

"But I wasn't planning to go at all. I'm not in the caroling group," Lucy protested. She resented it when Betty pressured her to chaperone her stepsisters.

"That doesn't matter," Mildred insisted. "It's just like a regular Sunday singing, but we'll be singing carols to prepare for caroling. Everyone's invited."

"Maybe she's too tired," Lucy's father interjected from the front seat. "The Sabbath is meant to be a day of rest."

"If Lucy's that tired, she should limit her outings this week, too," Betty suggested. Lucy couldn't believe at her age her stepmother was still trying to control her activities, but she figured Betty was so used to doing it for her daughters she automatically did it for Lucy, too.

"I'm not too tired," Lucy argued. She didn't want anything standing in the way of her plans to be with Nick this week. "I'll go with Katura and Mildred."

The evening singing was held at the same place church had been held that morning—Doris and John Plank's house. After Jonas, Doris's stepson, led the three women to the large gathering room where the youth were hanging out, Doris approached and pulled

Lucy aside. She cupped her hands around Lucy's ear and whispered, "Nick is already here. He's over there, by Melinda."

Lucy's eyes darted to the far edge of the room. Melinda had literally backed Nick into a corner and, from the look on his face, he wasn't enjoying their discussion.

"I thought Nick wasn't going to be here, you little sneak," Katura jeered when she noticed Lucy staring. "No wonder you didn't put up your usual fight about coming with us."

Lucy didn't have the energy to insist she hadn't expected to see Nick that night. When Melinda suddenly moved away from Nick to make a beeline for Jonas, Lucy joined Nick in the corner.

"Lucy, hi!" He was smiling, but there was a tempestuous look in his otherwise bright blue eyes.

"Hi, Nick. I didn't expect to see you here tonight."

"I didn't expect to be here tonight, but I'm babysitting."

Lucy giggled. "I'm unofficially chaperoning, too. I thought Katura and Mildred were the only people who needed looking after. I didn't realize Kevin did, too."

"He doesn't—wait, I take that back. He does, but that's not why I'm here. I've been assigned to keep an eye on my cousins who are spending the night with us. But I've already lost track of them."

As Nick surveyed the room, grimacing, Lucy questioned, "Are you okay? I saw Melinda speaking to you and you seemed upset or something."

Instead of answering, Nick motioned toward the hall with his chin. "*Kumme* with me, okay?" Lucy followed as he led her from the room.

"What's wrong?" she asked again, and Nick explained how someone at church reportedly told Melinda he'd spotted Nick on the road to the Nelsons' cabin the previous afternoon. "It was around the time I supposedly would have been helping you accomplish some special *Grischtdaag* tasks you needed to do. Which I was, sort of, by bringing you to a quiet place so you could embroider, but, you know… Anyway, Melinda's nosiness has me concerned. I'm afraid somehow she's going to put two and two together. You and I are so close to completing our projects. I don't want her to spoil everything right at the very end."

Lucy saw red and she clenched her fists. "So what if some busybody spotted you alone in your buggy when you supposedly were spending time with me?" she fumed. "For all they know, you dropped me off at the mall so I could do some *Grischtdaag* shopping while you… I don't know, while you did shopping of your own. I'm not saying you should lie about it, of course, but that's just the point. There are infinite possibilities, none of which are anyone else's business. So why should you have to explain yourself to Melinda or anyone else?"

His eyes still stormy, Nick shook his head. "Melinda said she doesn't believe we're really a couple. And I think she's determined to prove it, Luce."

Nick had never called her Luce before and, despite her apprehension, Lucy was pleased by the familiarity of the nickname. "But she saw us together last night at the rink."

"Apparently, she wasn't convinced."

"Why does it matter to her anyway?" Lucy wondered aloud. "Is it because she's upset you turned Eve down?"

"It could be…" Nick hesitated. "Or maybe it's because, well, there was a time when Melinda and Jesse were courting and they broke up for a while. During that period, I walked out with Melinda. I quickly realized I didn't want to be her suitor, which she wasn't too happy about. Ever since then, I've kind of had the feeling she's been trying to get back at me."

Lucy stared at him, simultaneously trying to reconcile her annoyance at Melinda with her disappointment in Nick. Didn't he have any discretion at all, to court Melinda Schrock? For the first time, she understood how Katura felt that Nick never asked *her* out—Lucy felt the same way. She wondered what Melinda had that Lucy didn't have—except a talent for gossiping.

Shaking her head, Lucy realized that was beside the point at the moment. All that really mattered was how desperately the soup kitchen needed funds. Lucy was so close to finishing the tablecloth and napkins. If she and Nick ended their pretense now, she wouldn't be able to help raise funds, which would be like taking away hot meals from homeless people. And if Nick couldn't finish his repairs, he'd be denying the Nelsons the opportunity to enjoy one last family celebration in a place they held dear.

"I've got a plan," she said, trembling. What she was about to suggest was the most brazen idea she'd ever expressed, but Lucy refused to allow anything to stand in the way of accomplishing what she and Nick had dedicated themselves to doing.

Nick couldn't guess how Lucy thought she could remedy the situation, but he was willing to try anything. He couldn't bear the thought of his father finding out about Kevin's fire—or about Nick's involvement in the cleanup efforts. He shuddered to think how his father's health might suffer, at Christmastime no less. But Nick doubted there was any convincing Melinda, for once and for all, that he and Lucy were truly a couple.

"What is it?" he asked.

Lucy bit her lip. *Does she even have a plan?* Nick wondered. She looked downward as she wrung her hands, speaking so quietly he could hardly hear her. "We'll stay out here talking until Melinda walks by. She'll see we're spending time alone together. She'll see how close we're standing."

"She saw that last night, too, but it didn't convince her." Nick was losing hope.

"*Jah*, but tonight when she walks by, you're going to…" Lucy waved her hand about her lips.

He couldn't hear what she said, and he didn't understand what she was supposed to be miming. "I'm going to what?" he asked.

Averting her eyes, she pulled on the strings of her prayer *kapp*. "You're going to kiss me."

Nick's legs felt rubbery and he couldn't speak.

"Suddenly, I mean. As if we don't think anyone is watching and you're stealing a kiss," she explained, her cheeks flaming. Her ears were, too.

Her abashment was endearing but it was also contagious. Nick had never been so nervous in his life. Not even with his first kiss. "Okay," he said, and placed his hand on Lucy's shoulder.

Flinching, she huffed, "What are you doing?"

"I'm… I'm getting ready," he hemmed and hawed. "It—it will look more natural if I have my hand on your shoulder. You know, like I'm sort of leading up to kissing you." Upon saying the words "kissing you," Nick's mouth went dry.

"Oh, okay." Lucy allowed him to put his hand on her shoulder again. He could feel the angular bone of her clavicle beneath his thumb. "Should I take my glasses off?"

"*Neh*, that won't look spontaneous enough."

"Right," she whispered, nodding. "Let me know when Melinda comes by."

Because he could easily see over Lucy's head, Nick had a clear view through the entryway into the gathering room. They didn't have to wait long until someone clapped his hands to get everyone's attention, a signal the singing would soon commence. Nick figured it was a matter of seconds before Melinda came out looking for them.

"It won't be long now," he said as his stomach jittered. From beneath lowered eyelids, he peeked at Lucy, whose face was level with his chest, to behold her fine bone structure. Someone who was meeting her for the first time might have mistaken her for a much younger teen, but once you spoke with Lucy, you could never again see her as anything other than a bright, self-possessed and skillful woman. *How did I miss so many qualities in her?* Nick mused. A shadow crossed the door, and Nick immediately used his knuckle to tilt Lucy's chin toward him. He bent forward, his mouth hovering over hers.

"Sorry, false alarm. It was Doris," he said when he realized his mistake. His lips nearly touched hers with each syllable he pronounced.

Lucy smiled. "It might have been just as effective to have Doris see us as to have Melinda see us," she said, just as Melinda stepped into the hall.

Nick didn't have time to warn Lucy before he brushed his lips against hers. Their skin barely made contact long enough for him to feel the plush softness of her mouth before she drew back. He felt like a thousand hummingbirds were darting through his veins as his gaze lingered on her. In that moment, he couldn't have cared less about whether Melinda had seen them or not. It wouldn't have mattered if Lucy and Nick's entire plan failed and Melinda exposed their charade that very evening. Kissing Lucy was worth ten times the amount of trouble Nick would get into if his parents ever found out about the cabin.

When Melinda cleared her throat loudly, Nick turned his attention to her. She had thrust her hands on her hips. "There you two are," she said. Her voice registered annoyance, indicating she had indeed witnessed the kiss. "We're about to start singing and Dan said he heard about our group from you, Lucy, so I thought you two might want to share a songbook."

Nick had been so intent on watching Melinda's reaction to the kiss he completely missed noticing Dan, who was shifting from foot to foot behind her. "Hi, Lucy. Nick," he said awkwardly.

Appearing flustered, Lucy pivoted toward Dan and Melinda and gushed, "Dan, I'm so glad you could *kumme*. Let's go into the other room. After the singing Nick and I will introduce you to everyone."

Nick's elation was quickly replaced by a crush of disappointment. His legs felt wooden as he followed Lucy and Dan into the gathering room. After they took seats in chairs arranged around the periphery of the room, Nick kept ruminating on the fact that Lucy had invited Dan to the singing. When? At the soup kitchen? Or had she told him about it today at church? For a fleeting second, Nick's imagination ran away with him, and he wondered if Lucy had actually proposed the kiss to make *Dan* jealous.

No, that couldn't be. Lucy hadn't even been aware that Nick thought Melinda was on the verge of figuring out their secret until he told Lucy that evening. The kiss *had* to be Lucy's spontaneous plot to throw Melinda off, not a planned one for Dan's benefit. *I've got to get a grip*, Nick thought. But no sooner had he put one worry to rest than another one popped up in its place: Was Lucy only biding her time with Nick until they'd completed their respective Christmas projects? Was it her hope that after Christmas Dan would offer to be her suitor?

As the others lifted their voices around him, Nick decided he couldn't let that happen. No, he had to extend the length of the project at the cabin. He wasn't ready to let Lucy go just yet.

Although Mildred and Katura dropped off almost as soon as their heads hit their pillows on Sunday night, Lucy couldn't sleep, so she gathered her embroidery materials and crept downstairs. She still had to finish two more place mats for the special order Joseph Schrock had requested. She turned on a lamp and snuggled beneath a quilt, but she couldn't focus on embroidering. All she could think about was the kiss she'd shared with Nick. Never in a million years would she have imagined herself suggesting such a thing, but now she was so glad she had. As momentary as their kiss had been, it was the most powerful physical sensation she'd ever experienced and a shudder racked her body as she thought about Nick's thick, full lips skimming her own, her shoulder warm beneath the weight of his palm.

Of course, the kiss wasn't real. It was just for effect. No matter how many times she reminded herself of that, Lucy couldn't squelch the sensation of pure bliss at the memory. She would rather share one fake kiss with Nick than a thousand real kisses with…well, with anyone else.

How she wished their time together wasn't coming to an end. She felt like the fictional Cinderella character she'd read about in books from the *Englisch* library; at the stroke of midnight, her dream would vanish. Unless… She allowed herself to wonder if Nick would ever consider courting her for real.

But that thought was preposterous. Nick had been tolerant about her physical shortcomings, but that's because he stood to benefit from their arrangement. Lucy knew she wasn't "marriage material," as the saying went. Men wanted robust women; they wanted women who could bear half a dozen healthy children. At the very least, they wanted wives who weren't too feeble to go outdoors to beat a rug or sweep the porch. Besides, she and Nick were polar opposites, so it was useless to allow herself to hope Nick was interested in her romantically, wasn't it? She wished she had someone to confide in about the situation. If only she could write to Bridget for advice. But in a way, Lucy already knew what Bridget's advice would be: she'd tell her to steer clear of Nick. To save herself a world of heartache.

Any heartache is worth how elated I feel right now, Lucy thought before she finally dozed off, wishing she could slumber straight through until Wednesday night, when Nick would take her to the soup kitchen again.

But she woke the next morning to a draft of cool air followed by a loud click and then her father's footsteps tapping down the porch stairs. She wished she hadn't missed preparing breakfast for him once again. She sat up and blinked, realizing she should rise before Betty entered the room. Too late.

"Why did you sleep on the sofa, Lucy? Are you ill?" Betty asked.

Why did everyone always assume she was sick? "*Neh.* I felt like I couldn't sleep last night so I came down here to embroider for a while. I don't remember what happened after that, but the next thing I knew, it was morning." Actually, Lucy did recall thinking about Nick, but those thoughts felt more like a dream than something she'd willed herself to consider. They were too private to mention to Betty, anyway. "I'll put the *kaffi* on," Lucy volunteered.

To her surprise, Betty insisted she'd do it instead while Lucy gingerly gathered her embroidery and combed her hair. Betty served the hot beverage at the table along with eggs and bacon, but Lucy could hardly eat.

"Are you sure you're not coming down with something?" Betty asked.

This time Lucy snapped, "*Neh.* Why does everyone always assume I'm sick?"

Betty looked taken aback, and Lucy regretted her tone immediately. Her stepmother probably was worried, just as Nick expressed he'd been. "I'm sorry," Lucy apologized. "I know you're concerned about my health. But I'm not sick."

"Yet you still can't eat?" A smile played on Betty's lips as she blew on her coffee. "That happened to me, too, when your *daed* first began courting me. I couldn't eat, I couldn't sleep. Lovesickness is all it is."

Inwardly, Lucy groaned. She almost felt bad that Betty was so hopeful about her courtship with Nick, knowing the disappointment her stepmother would experience when they broke up in another week or so. "It's more likely I ate too many brownies last night, not that I'm lovesick."

"Oh, but she *is* lovesick!" Mildred chanted from the doorway. She was still dressed in her bedclothes. "She and Nick were hiding in the hallway kissing last night."

"Mildred!" Betty scolded, genuinely angry. "That's none of your business and it's inappropriate to talk about."

"It was even less appropriate for her to do it in public view." Katura was suddenly in the room. She slunk into a chair and poured herself a cup of coffee.

"It doesn't sound as if she was in public view," Betty said as she rose to get eggs for her daughters. Lucy was amazed her stepmother was standing up for her, but at the same time she wanted to cringe. Lucy and Nick hadn't wanted everyone to know about the kiss—just Melinda. But they should have known she'd tell everyone else, too. It had been embarrassing enough that Dan had witnessed the kiss firsthand without everyone else being given a secondhand account.

Betty continued to scold her daughters. "Do I need to remind you of what the Bible says about envy?"

"Envy? Pah!" Katura muttered, loud enough so Lucy could hear but not so loud that Betty turned from the stove. "That courtship isn't going to last. With Nick, it never does. Mark my words, within a month, he'll have moved on to someone else."

To Lucy, it almost sounded like wishful thinking on

Katura's part. But her stepsister was right; before the month was up, Lucy's arrangement with Nick would be over. *I'm not looking forward to bearing the humiliation of listening to Katura gloat.* But even worse, Lucy would have to bear the pain of ending her courtship. Right then and there, she decided until that day came, she was going to make the most of her time with Nick while she had it.

Nick could hardly wait to take Lucy to the soup kitchen. It felt like forever since he'd seen her. Since he'd kissed her. If only someone else needed convincing they were really a couple... He shook his head. Was he really that pathetic he'd daydream about excuses to steal another fake kiss from Lucy instead of being brave enough to ask if she'd ever allow him an authentic one? The answer, sadly, was yes. His courtship—and his kiss—with Lucy might have been contrived, but they were better than nothing. Which was exactly what he'd be left with if Lucy turned down his proposal to become her suitor for real.

"I heard you were really putting on a show with Lucy at the singing last night," Kevin remarked on Monday as they stacked bags of deicing material in a bin by the door before the store opened. Supposedly, snow was on its way, and their customers would need to treat their driveways and sidewalks.

Regardless of the public nature of his kiss with Lucy, Nick resented his brother's intrusive remark so he ignored it entirely.

"It can't be easy, pretending to like her. I just want you to know how much I appreciate what you're doing for me," Kevin added in a rare display of gratitude.

"It's not a problem. I like spending time with Lucy," Nick said, suddenly defensive. "She's…she's different than most women I've courted."

"You can say that again," Kevin said.

Now Nick was even more irked. "What exactly does that mean anyway?"

"Well, Lucy's sort of plain. She'd kind of, you know, dull."

"That just goes to show how little you know her," Nick said. "And how little you know about the other women I've courted. All that external facade, the animated conversations, the flirty gestures, the exaggerated giggling—*that* gets boring pretty quickly." Nick was articulating feelings he hadn't fully realized he had.

Kevin cocked his head. "All right, fess up. Are you and Lucy really a couple now or what?"

"Of course not. What makes you say that?"

"From the way you're talking about her. And from what Melinda described—"

"Melinda has big mouth and so do you, so you'd better shut it before you stick your foot in it."

"Okay, okay," Kevin said, holding his hands up. "How long until you're done with the cabin anyway?"

If Nick wanted to, he could finish up in about three more nights. But he didn't want to. "I've got a little sanding left to do. A couple more pieces of paneling to get right before I hang them. And of course there's the cleanup. I accidentally scuffed up the floor in a few places when I was moving furniture around, so I'll want to buff that, too."

"I know how to do those things. I could take over and you could tend the store at night."

Nick panicked. It was true; Kevin could handle those tasks on his own. "*Neh*, I started the project, I'll finish it."

"Because you want to spend more time with Lucy?"

"Because I don't trust you to get the job done."

But Kevin was right. Nick did want to spend more time with Lucy. As he sped to her house, an idea struck him: he'd help her serve at the soup kitchen. That way, his project would be extended one more evening and he'd get to spend additional time with her. More to the point, she wouldn't be spending time alone with Dan. Nick couldn't wait to propose the idea to her. Since Dan had witnessed them "kissing," as well as at the rink, Lucy couldn't argue there was a need to hide their courtship from him any longer.

"Oh, if you can spare the time that would be *wunderbaar*," she said when Nick presented his idea. "We're shorthanded because people have so many other commitments at this time of year. We need a few men to help set up the folding tables beforehand and carry the heavier trays during the meal. Then there's bussing the tables afterward. Dan does a lot of that, but he can't handle it all on his own. Although he sure tries. He's one of the hardest workers there, which is saying a lot since everyone is so dedicated."

At the mention of Dan's name, Nick's mouth soured. Lucy always seemed to praise him, and Nick was desperate to find out if she was interested in him romantically. "He seemed really glad to see you the other night," he hinted.

"*Jah*, well, since he's new in the next district I've been trying to get him to attend a singing. He's kind of shy. Or I guess you'd call him socially reserved, like me. Which is probably why we work so well together. Anyway, I was glad to see him at the Planks' last night. I think meeting a few people at the rink on Saturday helped him feel more comfortable about attending a singing, too. You wouldn't know this because you're so outgoing, but for us introverted types, well, let's just say social events aren't usually high on our list of things we love to do."

Her response did nothing to quell Nick's envy. To hear her talk about them, Lucy and Dan were perfectly compatible: both hard workers, both quiet. Dan was probably smart like Lucy was, too, and clearly he was charitable. Nick almost wished he hadn't offered to help serve on Wednesday night, because he didn't know if he could stand to witness the rapport between Lucy and Dan as they worked.

But when they arrived at the soup kitchen, there was no time for wallowing. The *Englischers* greeted him with gratitude and huge smiles. Then the place was bustling. Nick could hardly set up additional chairs and clear the tables fast enough to keep the crowd comfortable and content.

And Lucy... Well, Lucy was a force to be reckoned with. Nick knew she was industrious, but he hadn't realized quite how much energy such a small person could generate. She prepared sandwiches, served food, poured beverages and wiped up spills, yet he noticed she always had time to stop and chat with the diners, smiling all the while. Watching her, Nick smiled, too. And as a local church choir sang Christmas carols in the background, he found himself humming along. *At least I can hum in tune to the music*, he thought, chuckling at his own expense.

When most of the diners had left and Lucy was carrying a tray of glasses across the room, Nick noticed it was tipping precariously to her left. He hurried across the room to assist her, but Dan beat him to it. Nick noticed Dan's hands dwarfed Lucy's as he up righted the tray before taking it from her.

"*Denki*, Dan," she said. "That was close."

Yeah, too close, Nick thought begrudgingly. He didn't want envy gnawing at his gut, but he felt outdone. Dan was truly a generous and compassionate guy, serving others regularly, whereas Nick was just pretending to help a family in need. Of course, Lucy didn't know that and Nick intended to make sure she never found out. Otherwise, he wouldn't stand a chance against Dan for Lucy's affections.

Realizing he had to maximize his time with her, on the way home Nick finally worked up the courage to say to Lucy, "I'd like to pick you up early on Friday night, if that's okay. I thought maybe we could get a pizza or something before I drop you off at the café."

"Oh, sure," Lucy agreed breezily. Nick's self-esteem momentarily soared until she added, "I understand why you want to get an earlier start on your project. I do, too. We've been keeping some awfully late hours, haven't we? But there's no need for us to go out for supper. I'll pack something we can eat along the way."

That wasn't at all what Nick had in mind, but he was too embarrassed to tell Lucy he wanted to take her out to supper for the pleasure of taking her out to supper, so he just agreed with her idea. Next time, he'd be more forthright. *If there is a next time*, he thought, all too aware their arrangement was one day closer to drawing to an end.

the English embroidered table mats, for some reason the woman was upset. But when Sandra Nelson arrived...

Chapter Eight

Even though the temperature was in the high twenties, Lucy waited on the porch for Mildred and Katura to return from working at the mercantile on Thursday. When their buggy pulled up the lane, she dashed across the lawn so as soon as they disembarked she could take the reins and head back to town. That afternoon she'd finished embroidering the last of the place mats she'd promised to deliver to Schrock's before the shop closed. To her delight, the customer who had ordered them was eagerly awaiting Lucy's arrival.

"Lucy Knepp, I'd like to introduce you to Sandra Nelson," Joseph said.

"Oh, they're exquisite, just as I knew they would be!" the woman exclaimed after Lucy spread the place mats on the counter for her to examine. "I can't tell you how much this means to me. We're having a special Christmas celebration this year at our family's cabin for my father who's visiting us from Washington State. I'm probably going overboard with the preparations, but I want to create as festive a setting as I can. These are going to look lovely."

Lucy had been so intent on showing the customer the finished product she hadn't paid attention to the woman's last name. But when Sandra Nelson described her family's upcoming celebration, Lucy caught her breath. *This is the same Nelson family whose cabin Nick is working on!* she realized, utterly thrilled. *I can't wait to tell him about this happenstance!*

"Here you go, Mrs. Nelson," Melinda said from behind Lucy. She set two large red cinnamon-scented candles on the counter. "I guess we did have a couple of these in the back room after all."

"Oh, thank you, Melinda," Sandra replied. Carefully stacking the place mats, she said, "Everything is falling into place beautifully. Look at what Lucy just brought me, too."

Melinda barely glanced at Lucy's handiwork. "Did you say you're having a party at the cabin? That must mean it's all fixed up now."

"All fixed up? Hardly! I've collected most of the embellishments, but I haven't begun to decorate. In fact, I haven't even given the place a thorough cleaning yet. Because of my work schedule, that won't happen until next week. But I'm not worried about it, not at all," Sandra quipped, chuckling nervously.

Melinda began to clarify her question, saying, "*Neh*, I wasn't asking if you'd decorated yet, I meant has the cabin been—"

Aware Melinda must have heard about the fire and, mortified that she was about to let the cat out of the bag, Lucy had to act quickly. Since she couldn't think of any other way to butt in, she began coughing violently into the crook of her elbow. It was a phony cough at first, but the more she coughed the more she legitimately had to cough, and soon she was gasping. Mrs. Nelson patted her back as Joseph directed Melinda to bring Lucy a cup of water.

After catching her breath, Lucy said, "I'm sorry about that. Don't worry, I'm not contagious. I have asthma, that's all. I never know what's going to set it off." Lucy wasn't lying—the scented candles may have exacerbated her breathing difficulty. "I think I'll go see if Melinda has that glass of water. I'm so pleased I got to meet you and I hope you have a joyful celebration."

"We will," Sandra said. "Thanks in part to you, Lucy."

When she located Melinda in the back room, Lucy did her best to trap her there until she was sure Mrs. Nelson had left the shop.

"Denki," Lucy said, slowly sipping her third cup. "I don't know quite what triggered that coughing attack, but I feel much better now."

"The cold weather is probably too much for your delicate constitution," Melinda commented. "I heard it's going to snow tomorrow night, so if you were planning to go out, you might want to think twice. You don't want to catch a cold."

Aware her peers planned to socialize after rehearsing carols, Lucy was antagonized by Melinda's remark. She and Nick wouldn't have wanted to attend the party anyway, but it was insulting that Melinda was clearly trying to stop her. "I don't think the weather has anything to do with it. Nick always brings extra blankets to keep me toasty warm. If I am coming down with something, it's more likely I caught it from… I don't know, from sitting too close to someone who had a cold at church. Or something like that."

Lucy's thinly veiled reference to kissing Nick didn't escape Melinda's notice. Her eyes narrowed and she screwed her mouth into a frown, but for once she was speechless. Satisfied, Lucy followed her back into the main gallery, where she was happy to discover Sandra Nelson had left. *As long as she doesn't* kumme *back before* Grischtdaag, *my secret with Nick is safe*, Lucy thought.

Then she decided if Melinda was right about Friday's forecast, sandwiches wouldn't suffice for supper; Lucy would prepare a hot meal to take in thermal containers. So the next day she prepared *yumasetta* with rolls and "stained glass window" cookies—a favorite Christmas treat made from chocolate, walnuts and marshmallows—for dessert. It would be too awkward eating as they traveled, but Lucy figured she could give Nick his share to take with him to the cabin. Or, preferably, he could spare a few minutes to eat with her in the buggy before dropping her off for the evening.

"You're going on a picnic?" Mildred asked when she saw Lucy packing a basket. "In December?"

"Wow, I never knew Nick was so cheap," Katura added. "It's a *gut* thing he never asked to be my suitor. I wouldn't have abided by someone who couldn't even treat me to supper."

"It's not because he's cheap," Lucy said protectively. "It's because he has to work on the—" She stopped herself just in time. This wasn't the first instance when her temper had caused her to speak rashly. She ducked into the pantry hoping to change the subject. "Do we have any paper napkins?" she asked.

"Second shelf," Katura answered. "Nick has to work on what?"

Lucy feigned innocence. "Hmm?"

"You started to say Nick had to work on something tonight. I thought the two of you were going out."

"We are," Lucy insisted. "But we want to eat on the way because we're, uh… We're going to be on the road for a while to get to where…where we want to go—and before you ask me, I'm not going to tell you where that is. I deserve some privacy, you know."

Now Lucy's father emerged from the mudroom. Lucy hadn't heard him come in. "At the risk of invading that privacy, what do you mean you're going to be on the road for a while? It's only flurrying out there now, but it might keep up."

"*Jah*, but horses can maneuver much better in the snow than cars can."

"Exactly. That's why I don't want you on the road with the cars."

Entering the room, Betty asked, "Do you think it's too slick for the girls to go out tonight?"

Katura, Mildred and Lucy simultaneously voiced their protests until Marvin grumpily conceded. Lucy planted a kiss on his cheek. "*Denki* for thinking about our safety, *Daed*, but we won't take any unnecessary risks and we're in the Lord's care."

Marvin hugged his daughter and replied, "Nick had *better* not take any unnecessary risks with you or he'll have to answer to me." Then he shuffled into the parlor to read while Betty began setting the table so they could eat the meal Lucy had prepared.

"Nick won't take any risks?" Betty shook her head.

"That would be a first. Unless you've already tamed him, Lucy."

Lucy was indignant. "He's not a wild horse!"

"*Neh*, but you're so sensible I figured maybe some of it rubbed off on him."

Although Lucy suspected her stepmother was giving her a compliment, once again she felt like she was being called boring. But, since she'd gotten her way about going out, she shrugged it off and went to change her cape and apron. She was so eager for Nick to arrive she waited outside so she could see his horse coming up the lane.

Nick whistled as he sped toward Lucy's house on Friday evening, again grateful for how swiftly Penny cantered, despite the light coating of snow on the roads. After leaving work, Nick had made a quick stop at the *Englisch* candy shop, where he bought a box of Christmas candy for Lucy. Since she'd prepared their supper, the least he wanted to do was get her something special for dessert.

He selected an assortment of the kinds of treats they used to receive after their childhood Christmas pageants at school, including peppermint bark, Christmas tree nougats, peanut brittle, chocolate-covered orange slices and ribbon candy. The school performances traditionally included singing hymns and carols—even then Nick only mouthed the words—and reciting the Bible Nativity story from memory. Afterward, each child always received a small but treasured box of candy from their teacher and the school board.

As Nick recalled, Lucy usually had the longest passage of Scripture to recite and he even remembered one year his parents remarked what a clear voice she'd used; they were surprised someone so small could project so well. That same year, he'd witnessed two of his older friends snatch Lucy's box of candy when she set it down on the landing near the entrance of the school so she could dash back inside to retrieve her scarf. Nick had been certain he'd be accused of taking it, since he was nearby when it happened, but he had hesitated to squeal on his friends. Upon returning, Lucy's expression had wilted when she discovered her box missing, but apparently she never said a word about it to anyone. Or if she did, Nick never found out.

I hope she still likes peppermint bark, he thought as he spied her loitering on the porch. He halted the buggy quickly and jumped out to help her with the cumbersome basket she was carrying. Since romantic relationships were supposedly private, it wasn't a custom for young suitors to go inside the houses of the women they were courting, but Nick wished Lucy didn't always wait outside for him. It made him wonder if she didn't want her father to see her in Nick's company. Everyone knew Marvin Knepp was as upright and respected a man as could be, and Nick hoped he approved of Nick courting his daughter.

What am I thinking? I'm not *courting Lucy!* Nick reminded himself as he aided her into the buggy. Once they were situated, she began telling him about how she'd run into Sandra Nelson in Schrock's Shop.

"Can you believe it?" Lucy exclaimed. "Isn't that odd that we're both indirectly involved with helping the Nelsons have a happy *Grischtdaag* celebration? Of course, I got paid for my efforts, whereas you're doing yours out of true generosity."

Even though he was wearing gloves, Nick reflexively wiped his palms against his lap. "You didn't, uh, say anything to her, did you? I mean, let on you knew I was making the repairs?"

Lucy turned toward him, crinkling her forehead. "Of course not. Why would I do that? But it's a *gut* thing I was there because Melinda Schrock started questioning Mrs. Nelson about whether the cabin would be ready in time. I didn't realize Melinda knew there'd been a fire. Although I guess that shouldn't surprise me."

Nick's pulse drummed like hoofbeats in his ears. "So Melinda mentioned the fire to Mrs. Nelson?"

"She started to, but don't worry. I cut her off." Lucy giggled. "I suddenly developed a terrific coughing fit. Melinda had to get me a cup of water, and I cornered her in the back room until Mrs. Nelson left the shop."

Nick's shoulders relaxed, but only a little. He wasn't merely worried about Mrs. Nelson finding out about the fire—he was worried Lucy would learn the fire was Kevin's fault. Melinda hadn't been at the party that night, but by now word had probably gotten around that there'd been a fire. Granted, as long as Kevin kept his mouth shut, none of the Amish would know Nick was the one making the repairs, but Nick couldn't allow Lucy to find out that he hadn't been entirely forthcoming with her in the first place. What would she think of him if she knew he wasn't really as helpful or as generous as she thought he was?

"Melinda didn't say anything else?" he questioned.

"*Neh*, I didn't even let her finish her sentence, so Mrs. Nelson's none the wiser." Lucy gave his arm a nudge. "Why are you being such a nervous Nellie?"

Nick released a big sigh. "I don't know. I guess I wonder how Melinda found out about the fire, that's all."

"Who knows? I don't think much gets past her," Lucy said.

"*Jah*, that's why it was perfect when we were kissing at the Planks' *haus*. I mean, it was perfect Melinda was the one who saw us. It wasn't perfect that we were kissing. I mean, there wasn't anything wrong with our kiss, just—" The fact he'd even referenced their kissing aloud made Nick so flustered he couldn't recover enough to complete his thought.

Fortunately, Lucy was gracious enough to say, "It's okay, I know what you meant. Our plan worked perfectly, and I think Melinda finally accepts it that we're courting."

Even if we're not, Nick thought, but he bit the inside of his cheek. He didn't want to make a bigger fool of himself than he already had.

"Do you want to take a few minutes to eat here in the buggy?" Lucy asked when they pulled into the parking lot by the café. "I probably shouldn't bring food inside. Besides, it's so pretty with the snow. I always think the first snowfall is the prettiest."

"That would be *wunderbaar*," Nick agreed. His stomach was rumbling. Or were those very loud butterflies?

"I hope you like *yumasetta* because—" Lucy stopped midsentence and pointed at the darkened building. "Look. The lights are out. It can't be closed. It's Friday night."

Nick squinted. It was definitely dark inside the café. He climbed down to read the sign posted in the window. When he returned he explained, "The café is closed because they're having a staff *Grischtdaag* party off-site."

"Oh, *neh*," Lucy protested. Then she suggested, "I suppose I could sit in the fast-food restaurant down the road. I think they'll let me stay for a few hours if I buy something, won't they?"

Nick was skeptical about the shabby little restaurant. He didn't want to take the chance someone there might harass Lucy. "I could take you to the bookstore on the border of Highland Springs," he suggested.

"That's miles away. You'll lose any time you may have saved by picking me up early."

Nick rubbed his chin. His face felt chapped from the raw wind. Lucy was sniffling from the cold, too. "If you're willing you could *kumme* to the cabin with me. I've cleaned up the sawdust and I only have some very light sanding to do. It's warm inside and we can have supper there. That is, unless you'll find the noise too distracting."

The noise? That was the least of Lucy's distractions. Nick's earlier reference to their kissing had made it nearly impossible for Lucy to speak coherently all the way here, and it was still flitting through her mind. She had to keep focused.

"That sounds like a *gut* plan. This way, you can work as late as you need to because you won't have to worry about the café closing at ten." Lucy's stomach was twirling circles. Somehow eating at the cabin with Nick felt much closer to being courted than eating in the buggy. But she reminded herself it was a far cry from him actually taking her out for supper, as Katura had indirectly pointed out.

"Great. Just one more dilemma," Nick said. "I can either keep Penny to an even trot, in which case, we might be cold by the time we get there because it will take longer. Or, I can push her to a run, in which case we'll get there faster but we'll definitely be colder along the way from the breeze. Which do you prefer?"

"Do you really have to ask?"

Grinning, Nick pushed his hat farther down on his head and lifted the reins. And then they were sailing, their momentum matching the elation of Lucy's mood. With the snow falling around them the scenery was so pristine and romantic Lucy felt like she was dreaming. Only this was better, because she wasn't.

At the house Nick switched on the lights. "I don't like to turn up their heat when I'm here, but I'm happy to build a fire."

"Great," Lucy said. "While you're doing that, I'll get our supper ready. How about if we eat here on the floor in front of the fireplace? I'm chilly."

"It will be like a picnic," Nick agreed.

He made the room cozy warm in no time and then removed two oversize pillows from the sofa for Lucy and him to sit on. She asked him to say grace and when he was finished, she served him a heaping plate of *yumasetta*. Whatever awkwardness she had felt earlier dissipated as she dug into the hot meal. She was finishing her second helping of the meaty casserole and her third roll when Nick laughed.

"What's so funny?" she asked.

"For someone so petite, you sure can pack it in!" he guffawed.

Lucy blushed. She'd been called *short* before and she'd been called a *shrimp*. Once someone even referred to her as a *runt*. But somehow having a man call her petite felt… Well, it made her feel more feminine. It made her feel womanly instead of girlish.

"I haven't even gotten started on dessert yet," she admitted.

"Ach! Dessert! I'll be right back." Nick dashed out the door without his coat and returned clutching a large gold box tied with a satiny red bow. "For you."

Eagerly Lucy untied the ribbon and lifted the lid to find peanut brittle and gumdrops, ribbon candy and peppermint bark. "These are all my favorites," she said, suddenly self-conscious that he'd given her a gift. "We always used to get a little box of these after our school *Grischtdaag* pageants."

"That's why I got them," Nick admitted without the slightest hesitation. "To remind you of when we were young."

Lucy laughed. "Most people would say we're still young." She extended the box to Nick so he could take a piece, but a shadow crossed his face and he shook his head, refusing the candy.

"I was there the night Noah and Nathan Miller took yours when you went back into the schoolhouse to collect your belongings."

Lucy didn't know what he was talking about. Then it occurred to her, something she had to dig into the hazy recess of her memory to recall. "Oh, those poor *buwe*," she lamented.

"Poor *buwe*? They stole from you."

"*Jah*, but they ended up getting tummy aches and missing *Grischtdaag* dinner. Or so their *mamm* told me when she brought them over to apologize a few days later."

"That's justice well deserved," Nick said. "But I should talk. I got off scot-free. I saw what they did, and I didn't stop them or speak up."

"They were older than you and they were your friends. Stopping them or tattling would have been a difficult thing for a young *bu* to do."

"I imagine the way they acted was difficult for *you*," Nick lamented.

He looked so guilt-stricken Lucy felt bad for him. Shrugging, she said, "It was only candy. Besides, this more than makes up for it—look how many pieces are in here!"

Nick laughed, but Lucy was being genuine. She offered the box to him again, but he shook his head a second time. "Those are for you. You don't need to share. Besides, I'm so full if I eat another bite I won't be able to move and I've got work to do."

"You go ahead and get started, and I'll clean this up," Lucy said, motioning to their dishes. When she was finished, she asked if he'd prefer her to work in another room. She didn't want to crowd him.

"I think you should stay here where it's warm. Unless the noise bothers you."

Touched by how thoughtful he was about her comfort, Lucy snuggled onto one end of the sofa beneath a bright light. The cabin's electric lights shone brighter than the gaslamps in her home, affording her more precision as she embroidered. Even so, Lucy probably accomplished only half as much as she normally might have. She kept stopping to steal glances at Nick as he worked.

His hands were so capable and strong. She noticed he was something of a perfectionist, sanding a board and then eyeing the edge before sanding it a little more. He used the same meticulous approach when hanging the boards, too. She'd always known he was an energetic person, but until she observed him working, she hadn't realized how patient he was. Watching him work was so mesmerizing she kept losing track of her stitching.

"What's wrong?" he asked at one point, a couple hours later. "You're frowning."

"Am I? I was just thinking about how... I don't know, how I've misjudged you. Or I did in the past. I thought you were this impulsive, careless *bu*, but come to find out, you're actually quite thoughtful and particular and dedicated. I was really wrong. I suppose that's why the Lord doesn't want us to judge one another."

Nick experienced a rush of pleasure and an equal amount of guilt over Lucy's comments. On one hand, he was pleased by her compliments. On the other, he didn't truly live up to her revised version of him, either. After all, he hadn't been forthright about the reason behind the renovation.

"You probably judged me pretty accurately," he said. "Just ask my *eldre* what I was like as a *kind*."

Setting aside her embroidery, Lucy said, "Well, maybe in the past, when we were *kinner*, but not now. Not anymore." Standing, she stretched and she reminded him of a cat. A kitten. Then she walked over to his side and studied the wall as if looking at a sunset. "Your work is beautiful. How did you ever get the colors to match like that?"

Nick's throat felt as if he'd swallowed a handful of pebbles. He was coming unhinged by her praise and her presence. "I had help. Hunter Schwartz gave me some hints."

"You told him about the project?"

"*Neh*, I just asked him a few general questions about staining. I haven't told anyone about the project. You're the only one who knows," he said.

"Except for the Nelson *bu*," she reminded him.

Nick looked askance at her. "The Nelson *bu*?"

"*Jah, schnickelfritz*, the Nelson *bu*. You know, your friend whose family owns this cabin." She angled her head up toward him, a saucy grin on her face. He knew he ought to correct her assumption, to tell her his friend was a female named Jenny, but somehow, all he could think about was removing her glasses and kissing her eyebrows, which rose in perfect arcs right above her lenses.

Suddenly afraid she could tell what he was thinking, he said, "You've seen my work, now can I see yours?"

The palest pink tinged her face. "Sure, if you really want to."

She walked to the sofa and held up her embroidery hoop. Fastened within it was a linen napkin on which she'd embroidered an intricate snowflake pattern of white on white, with a hint of gold thread here and there. It reminded him exactly of how the snow looked falling in the moonlight outside the window.

He whistled. "Whoa. Someone's going to bid a lot for a set of those."

She bit her lip skeptically. "I hope so. I like it, but I'm afraid the *Englischers* won't. Most of them tend to prefer more colorful patterns. But I chose this one because…well, because I think it's beautiful in a surprising way. I mean it has a quiet kind of beauty, if you have eyes to see it."

"I know exactly what you mean," Nick said. And he did know, because what Lucy just said described exactly how he felt about her beauty. It was quietly winsome and true, not flashy or bold. He licked his lips, but as much as he wanted to, he couldn't kiss her. Not without asking to be her suitor for real, first. And he couldn't do that unless he was sure she felt the same way about him as he did about her. Never before had the possibility of rejection scared him so much. When he asked to court women in the past, he always leaped in, feet first, instead of weighing the consequences. *Am I becoming more mature or just overly cautious?*

Lucy sighed and said, "Well, either way, it's too late now."

"What's too late?"

"It's too late to change my pattern. I have to turn it in on Thursday. That's only six days away. But thanks to our arrangement, I'll meet the deadline. It looks as if you're going to finish on time, too."

The thought filled Nick with dread. He actually didn't want to finish yet. *"Jah,"* he said reluctantly. "Unless something goes wrong." The truth was, if he worked all afternoon on Saturday, he'd be done by evening. He didn't tell Lucy that, though. "Speaking of finishing, I think I've had it for the night, what about you? The fire is nearly out."

"Jah, my eyes are going to cross if I work on this any longer."

"I heard there's a gathering after the singing. Would

you like to stop by? Maybe we ought to reinforce the idea we're a couple."

Lucy pulled her head back and looked at him wide-eyed. Uh-oh, did she think he meant they ought to convince their peers by kissing each other again? "I mean, they'll see us together again."

"Oh, okay," she said hesitantly. "I suppose that would be all right."

She didn't seem enthusiastic about the offer, but now that he'd proposed it, Nick didn't know how to take it back. He suggested she remain inside until he loaded his things into the buggy and then he'd return to double-check that there were no live embers in the fireplace. But when he stepped outside, everything was dusted in a fine, fluffy powder and he had an idea.

"It snowed enough to sled down the hill in the back at least once," he told her. "If you think Penny is fast, you're going to love this!"

Lucy didn't question how he knew about the hill—she probably assumed he'd been sledding with his *Englisch* friend there before, but she did ask, "Do the Nelsons have a sled we can use?"

Nick hadn't thought of that, but he didn't let it stop him. "*Neh*, but we can use the lids to their garbage cans. Kevin and I used to do that all the time when we were *kinner*."

Lucy laughed. "Okay, if you go first."

Nick retrieved the two round metal tops to the garbage cans and flicked on the floodlight over the back deck. It illuminated a steep hill that disappeared into the darkness below. They made their way to the backyard, where Nick solemnly advised Lucy, "When you get to the bottom of the hill, if the sled—I mean the garbage can cover—doesn't stop, you need to roll off it. Otherwise you'll keep going right into the woods. There's a little ditch at the very end of the slope, but after that, it's all trees. I don't want you crashing into one."

"This sounds risky."

"That's what makes it so thrilling," Nick teased, "Don't be a chicken, Luce."

"Who's a chicken?" she bantered. "Not me. I'll go first if you want me to."

Nick had no doubt she would have, but he wanted to be sure he was at the bottom of the hill when she came down in case he needed to help stop her. "No way, I'm going first. I already called it! Now give me a push."

He plunked himself down on the lid, crossed his legs into a pretzel shape and scooted himself toward the edge of the hill. Lucy placed her hands on his shoulders and pushed for all she was worth, running a few feet behind him until he picked up steam and was sailing through the dark. The snow was so scant he figured most of his speed was gained from sliding over old, wet leaves, but it hardly mattered—he was cruising. Within seconds he'd reached the end of the decline and since he was traveling too fast to stop, he rolled off the garbage can lid just in time. The metal lid continued its trajectory without him, rattling against the rocks in the gully at the base of the hill.

"Are you all right?" Lucy called.

"*Jah.* But I'm not so sure about the lid," he yelled back. "Maybe you shouldn't do this after all."

"Just try to stop me!" she taunted, and then all was quiet until he saw her flying over the crest of the hill. She squawked, "Ahh!"

Nick could tell she was too light to steer the lid in a forward motion; it was spinning around and around as she zoomed down the hill, completely out of control. "Roll!" he yelled as she approached the end. "Roll off, now!"

But she had gained too much momentum. She was tearing right toward the gully! Nick jumped in her path and his lower legs suffered most of the blow as she barreled into him. For someone so thin, she packed a punch, and he flipped over her head and landed on his side as she continued traveling—slowly but unstoppably—smack into the gully.

"Lucy!" he yelled even before he was upright. He'd never forgive himself if she was hurt. "Lucy! Lucy, answer me! Are you all right?"

Suddenly, he saw her head pop up in the ditch. "I'm fine. Are you okay?"

He didn't know if his knees were weak from relief or from being knocked into by her, but he fell onto his backside in the snow. "*Jah*, I am now," he uttered weakly.

"*Gut!*" she exclaimed. "Because I never did anything like that before, but I want to do it again!"

They managed to get in three more turns apiece until there was no discernible snow left to sled on. As they slowly hiked back up the hill together a final time, Lucy's breathing was heavy so Nick slowed his pace.

"That was such *schpass*," she gushed deliriously. "I didn't know I had it in me to do something like that!"

"Really?" Nick was surprised. "I never had any doubt," he said.

Chapter Nine

When Lucy awoke in the early hours of Saturday morning shivering with cold, she figured she had never completely warmed up after sledding with Nick. She rose and donned a pair of wool socks, added another quilt to her bed and then drifted back to sleep. But when she woke again at sunrise and had a coughing fit that rivaled the performance she'd put on for Mrs. Nelson, she knew she wasn't just cold. She was sick.

She intended to hide her condition from Betty and her father, but they noticed the moment she finally walked into the kitchen sometime later, while everyone else was eating breakfast.

"What happened to you?" Mildred asked. "You look *baremlich*."

"I just overslept," Lucy began to say, but she interrupted herself coughing.

Her father immediately rose from his chair and placed his hand on her forehead. He'd been the one checking her for fever since she was a child, and the weight of his hand on her head was so familiar it was comforting even if she was sick.

"You're running a fever. You need to go back to bed."

"Here, let me feel her," Betty said, and took a turn placing her hand over Lucy's forehead. "Ach, he's right. You are a little warm. I'll make some tea and bring it to you upstairs. Katura, go fill the hot water bottle for Lucy. Mildred, please see to it she has enough pillows. She should keep her head elevated so she doesn't cough."

Lucy wanted to argue, but she acknowledged another hour of sleep would do her good. After that she'd be refreshed and ready to get to work on her weekend chores and then her embroidery orders. Climbing the stairs, she felt like she had lead in her socks. Mildred helped put a fresh case on a second pillow while Lucy removed a third quilt from the shelf in the closet.

Then Katura entered the room. "Have you seen the hot water bottle?" she asked.

Lucy gestured toward the chest of drawers. "It's in there, I think." She eased herself into bed as Katura pulled a drawer open.

"Look at this!" she exclaimed, and pulled out the box of candy from Nick that Lucy had hidden there. Katura lifted the lid and looked inside. "No wonder you're sick. How long have you had this? It's half gone."

"That's mine," Lucy said, and Katura dropped it back into the drawer.

"I know it's yours. I wasn't going to take it, but you don't have to be so selfish." She flounced out of the room without locating the hot water bottle.

Lucy hadn't meant Katura couldn't have any candy; she'd responded only like that because she was surprised her stepsister had opened her private gift from

Nick without asking first. "I didn't mean to offend Katura," she mumbled. Her lips and throat were dry and she felt teary. "You can both have some if you want."

"Denki." Mildred didn't hesitate to retrieve the box from the drawer. Even though it wasn't yet nine o'clock in the morning, she helped herself to a big piece of peanut brittle. "Yum, this is the expensive stuff. Did you get it from Nick?"

Lucy nodded, smiling at the memory. She felt so sick she didn't mind if Mildred ate the rest of the candy, but Lucy was going to save the box as a cherished memento.

"I can't wait until I have a suitor who brings me gifts like this," Mildred said in between bites, and Lucy smiled. Nick might not have been her suitor, but that didn't mean the gift wasn't thoughtful all the same. Uncharacteristically empathetic, Mildred said, "Don't pay any attention to Katura. Her nose is bent out of shape because Frederick Stutzman gave Fern Slagel a ride home from the caroling practice last night."

"Really? Fredrick and Fern?" Lucy was glad to know he was pursuing another courtship. Or that his mother was pursuing it for him. "But why would Katura be upset about that?"

Mildred rummaged through the box for another piece of peanut brittle. "She's developed a little crush on Frederick, but don't let on like you know. That's why she's so upset about Nick being your suitor. First you turned down Frederick and now Nick is courting you. She feels like she should be courting someone first, since she's older than you are."

"Only by three months," Lucy said drowsily, and

she wondered if she was dreaming. Because Katura made no attempt to hide her interest in Nick, it was surreal to discover she was interested in Frederick. Aloud Lucy muttered, "There's nothing to be envious of. Nick isn't really courting me."

"What?" Mildred's ears perked up, but Lucy was too tired to fix her mistake.

And then Betty must have walked in with a cup of tea. Lucy couldn't lift her eyelids to look, but she could faintly smell the honey-lemon tea—which actually contained no tea, just honey, lemon and hot water— Betty served whenever someone had a cold.

"I think she dozed," Mildred told her mother. "But she's definitely feverish. She was just talking gibberish about Nick."

"Is that candy you're eating? At this hour?" Lucy heard Betty ask Mildred. That was the last thing she remembered before falling asleep.

Even though he had told his father he wanted to spend the afternoon with Lucy on Saturday, Nick worked at the hardware store until closing time because he decided he'd rather stall his project than to forfeit an excuse to go out with Lucy the following week. So when she didn't come to the porch a few minutes after six thirty, their agreed-upon time, Nick decided to take the opportunity to greet Betty and Marvin. He climbed the steps and had lifted his hand to knock on the door when Katura emerged.

"Hello, Nick," she said warmly. "It's *gut* to see you, but Lucy's been sick all day, so she can't go out with you."

Nick's heart tripped, missing a beat. "She's been sick? How sick?"

Katura rolled her eyes. "It's probably just a case of the sniffles, but with Lucy, everyone babies her if she so much as sneezes. Anyway, where were the two of you going? There's a party after caroling practice, you know."

Nick had to think fast. Since he hadn't worked on the repairs that afternoon at all, he and Lucy had planned to spend a few hours at the cabin and then stop by the party after the rehearsal by way of putting in an appearance. Now that Lucy couldn't come with him, Nick figured he should briefly drop in on the carolers first and then go to the cabin. That way, even if his parents found out Lucy was sick, Nick could legitimately tell them he'd gone to the gathering instead of going out with her.

"*Jah*, I know. Since Lucy can't *kumme* out with me, I might drop by to listen to the carolers practice for a little while," he said.

"*Gut*, will you take me there, then?" Katura asked. "Since you're already here and all."

Nick stalled, trying to think of an excuse for not taking Katura without seeming rude. "I don't know how long I'll stay. If I leave before the rehearsal is over, you won't have a ride home."

"That's all right. By then Mildred will have arrived and she can bring me home. She's not ready to go to the singing just yet, but I'd like to get there early. I need all the practice I can get." Without waiting for Nick to agree to give her a ride, she added, "I'll go let her know I'm leaving now and I'll be right out."

Nick turned and waited in his buggy. He jiggled his knee, wondering what kind of illness Lucy had. If only he'd been able to talk to her for a few minutes…

"Can you help me up?" Katura asked when she arrived with a platter wrapped in tinfoil. "It's hard to balance this."

Instead of taking her hand, Nick reached for the platter. "You'll have an easier time if I take this for you." He placed the dish on the seat between them. "So, did Lucy ask you to give me a message or anything?" he inquired. He thought it was odd she didn't at least meet him at the door herself. If she was really that sick it must have struck quickly.

"She didn't say anything at all. Of course, she was sound asleep, so she couldn't have. Lucy's *daed* is the one who told me to tell you she couldn't go out tonight. But don't worry, he's just overly protective of her. I'm sure he doesn't blame you that she's ill."

Nick hadn't been worried until Katura mentioned that. It *was* kind of his fault—he was the one who'd suggested sledding. Nick swallowed, silently praying Lucy would recover after a bit of rest.

"Would you tell her I'm sorry she's under the weather?" Nick asked.

"I will if she's awake when I get home," Katura agreed. "You know what a little mouse she is. She always scurries off to a corner and hardly talks to anyone. And even if the only thing she does all day is sew, she's in bed by the time the clock strikes nine. Now that she's sick, she'll probably be even more lethargic."

"That doesn't sound like the Lucy I know at all," Nick said, annoyed her stepsister was casting her in such a poor light. "She might be small but she's a ball of energy. And when she's quiet it's because unlike some people, she waits until she has something to say before she opens her mouth."

He hadn't directly been making a comparison between Lucy and Katura, but to young women like Katura. However, she was insulted, apparently, by his insinuation, because she folded her arms across her chest and didn't say another word until they arrived at their destination.

"You can go ahead in while I hitch the horse," Nick suggested. The last thing he needed was for someone to start a rumor because they arrived together.

Katura stuck out her lower lip as Nick handed her the platter, and then she stamped across the yard toward the big barn where tonight's singing was being held. Now that he was here, Nick realized how hungry he was. He didn't want to sing, but he could at least grab some food before going to Jenny's house.

To his surprise, when he crossed the threshold he noticed several *Englisch* young people mingling with the Amish. Nick made his way to the snack table where Kevin was stacking cookies onto a plate. "What's going on? Why are the *Englisch* here?" he asked his brother.

"Our carolers invited some of the *Englisch* churches' singles' groups to go with them this year. They've been rehearsing separately, but since they'll be singing together all week in public when they begin making their caroling rounds tomorrow evening, they wanted to squeeze in a practice session tonight."

"*Jah*, well, don't forget what happened the last time you were around the *Englisch*," Nick warned. He recognized a few of the *Englisch* youth and he was surprised they were here. They didn't seem like the type who'd be interested in singing. Maybe Nick was misjudging them, but he was going to have to keep an eye on Kevin.

"Nick, try one of these." Katura interrupted his thoughts, elbowing Nick in the side and holding out a gingerbread cookie. Kevin took the opportunity to leave, presumably before Nick could lecture him any further.

"It's *appenditlich*," he mumbled after biting into it. It was actually too crunchy for his taste, but Nick didn't want to stay on Katura's bad side, especially since he was relying on her to pass his message along to Lucy.

"Hi there, stranger," a female said, tapping him on the shoulder. Nick twisted around to see Jenny Nelson.

"Hi, Jenny," he replied awkwardly, unnerved by the possibility she might mention the cabin repairs in front of Katura. After introducing the two women, Nick said, "I didn't know you like to sing, Jenny."

"I don't, but I just missed you at the hardware store today. Kevin told me I might find you here tonight. Since I really needed to talk to you about—"

"I don't sing, either," Nick cut her off. "And it sounds like they're about to start, so why don't we go outside to talk? Excuse us, Katura."

Katura's eyebrows were raised. "Of course, you two go chat in private," she remarked pointedly, causing Nick to worry about what she might be assuming.

Outside he said to Jenny, "Sorry for interrupting you like that, but no one knows about the cabin repairs. I didn't want Katura finding out."

"Don't worry, I wasn't going to say anything explicit. I've kept it a guarded secret, too. But I wanted to hear about your progress. My mother's been considering taking Monday afternoon off work to get a head start on cleaning the cabin."

Nick panicked. "Monday? I thought I had until Wednesday or even Thursday!"

"There's no chance you can complete the work early?"

"*Neh*. That would mean I'd have to finish it tonight since I can't work on the Sabbath." Even if Nick worked until midnight as fast as he could, he still wouldn't be able to finish the project. What's more, he wasn't prepared to call off his arrangement with Lucy yet.

Jenny frowned. "I'd hoped if you had enough time to come here, it meant maybe you were further along with the project."

"I can understand why you'd think that," Nick admitted. "But even if I had skipped the party, there's no way I could have finished everything at the cabin tonight. I'll do as much as I can though. Maybe I can finish by Tuesday. And just so you know, I only stopped by here to grab something to eat. I'm on my way to your cabin now."

"Okay, I'll do my best to keep my mother from coming over early. She has a million things to do in preparation for Christmas anyway, so if she takes the afternoon off I'll suggest she goes shopping or something."

"*Denki*," Nick said. "If you stop by the hardware store on Tuesday, I can update you on my progress then."

Jenny agreed, and then Nick said he had to get going. She replied, "Since you're going past my house, can I have a ride home? My friends are going to be here all night. And I've never ridden in a buggy in the winter before."

Nick couldn't say no after Jenny had been so patient about his progress on the cabin. "Sure," he agreed.

Jenny dashed inside to let her friends know she had a ride home. "All set?" Nick asked when she hoisted herself into the seat next to him.

"Yeah. They were in the middle of a song so I didn't want to interrupt them, but your friend Katura said she'd pass along the message for me."

Terrific, that's all I need—Katura starting a rumor about Jenny and me. But Nick had more pressing concerns on his mind. Namely, he was worried about Lucy. After Nick dropped Jenny at the end of her driveway, he continued to the cabin. He'd worked by himself there every night except Friday, but suddenly the place seemed to echo with emptiness because Lucy wasn't there. A month ago, Nick could have gone for an entire year without so much as waving hello to her; now, he missed her after spending even a single day apart. The longing felt nearly unbearable, so as Nick worked, he again prayed for Lucy's healing, adding, *And Lord, please give me patience until I can see her again.*

Lucy's head was swimming as she slowly made her way downstairs. Even before she reached the kitchen, she could smell something cooking and she felt guilty she'd slept so long; she had planned to make shepherd's pie for lunch, but Betty must have made something else instead.

When Betty saw Lucy, she set down a pot and came to Lucy's side. "How are you feeling?" she asked. Lucy saw the concern in her eyes. Betty wasn't her mother, but she had undeniable maternal instincts toward Lucy.

"A little groggy but much better. Sorry I overslept,"

she said. Katura and Mildred were clearing the table. "I was planning to make shepherd's pie, but it looks like you've already eaten lunch."

"Lunch?" Betty's forehead wrinkled. "We're cleaning up after breakfast."

"You are? But you just ate breakfast. What time is it?"

"It's eight o'clock in the morning. Sunday morning. You slept right through lunch and supper yesterday. Through the night, too," Mildred announced.

"Really?" Lucy was utterly discombobulated.

"It's true," Betty said, lifting her hand to Lucy's forehead. "Your fever is gone but you're very pale. Go sit in the parlor, and I'll fix you a cup of tea. Katura, please check to see if the fire needs more logs."

While Katura stoked the fire in the woodstove, Lucy took a seat next to it. *If I slept all through Saturday, what happened when Nick showed up yesterday evening?* she wondered. Katura seemed to read her mind.

"Don't worry, last night when Nick showed up I told him you were sick and couldn't go out. But he was kind enough to give me a ride to caroling practice. Penny is every bit as fast as I've heard she is."

Lucy was immediately ruffled. Did Nick take as much pleasure in demonstrating to Katura how fast Penny could run as when he'd shown Lucy? She brooded over why he had taken Katura to the rehearsal anyway. He had work to do on the cabin, so why was he at the practice? Then Lucy realized that since she'd been sick, Nick probably didn't have an excuse to get out of going to the rehearsal. She was dismayed to realize her illness had probably hindered his work.

Katura blathered on, "Of course, I had to ride home with Mildred since Nick left early with an *Englischer*. She was a blonde woman, but what was her name?" Katura tapped her chin as if trying to remember. "Ah, right, it was Jenny. Jenny Nelson. She was one of the *Englisch* carolers who came to the rehearsal, but she said she didn't like to sing. She'd *kumme* there looking for Nick. The two of them took off together after about ten minutes."

Lucy felt queasy. *Jenny* Nelson? Nick's friend whose family owned the cabin was a woman? Lucy had assumed his friend was a man, an assumption Nick allowed her to believe by not correcting her when she referred to him as the Nelson boy. Come to think of it, Nick hadn't ever told her his friend's name, had he? Why would he have concealed the fact his friend was a female? Lucy could think of only one reason. Suddenly, she felt like her lungs were made of cement and each breath she took required enormous effort.

Nick couldn't possibly be romantically interested in Jenny. Although Nick hadn't been baptized yet and technically could date an *Englischer*, Lucy had no doubt he was true to his faith. He was true to the Amish. But was he true to Lucy? *Did he set me up from the beginning?* she speculated. *Or am I letting my imagination run away with me because I feel so crummy?*

Lucy struggled to contain her qualms. Her trembling hands didn't go unnoticed when Betty brought her another cup of lemon tea.

"Steady now, or you'll spill it." Lucy's stepmother hovered over her, clucking her tongue. "It's a *gut* thing it's an off Sunday—you need more rest today."

Lucy swallowed a sip of the hot liquid before protesting. "I feel much better now, and by evening, I'll have even more energy. All that sleep really helped." She felt desperate to see Nick so she could address the situation between him and Jenny.

"I'm glad you're feeling better, but you still need to stay in today. No visitors," Betty said authoritatively, which annoyed Lucy. She wasn't a child.

When her father came in from outdoors carrying wood in his arms, Lucy told him how much better she felt, assuming he'd side with her about going out with Nick that evening. Instead, he deliberately arranged a log in the fire and said, "You're an adult, Lucy, so I'm not going to stop you from going out. But I think you should exercise common sense and do what's right for your health. I also think anyone who truly cares about you would be willing to wait another day or two until you're more rested before taking you out in the cold."

Her father's reference to Nick wasn't lost on Lucy, and since she didn't want him to think poorly of Nick, she begrudgingly agreed she'd stay in and wouldn't receive visitors. Besides, it was the Sabbath so it wasn't as if Nick could work on the cabin anyway. Even though she was desperate to see him for her own sake, Lucy was relieved her absence wouldn't set him back on the cabin repairs. Still, she harbored hope he'd stop by the house. That way, maybe she could settle her qualms by asking him about Jenny Nelson.

But the hours ticked by and there was no sign of Nick. While he wasn't obligated to check on her, Lucy was surprised he didn't, especially since the other night he'd claimed how concerned he was about her health. She tried to convince herself he didn't want to bother her while she was recovering, but her thoughts kept circling back to Jenny Nelson. Why hadn't he mentioned his friendship with her if indeed there was nothing to hide?

Fidgety all day, Lucy was too listless to work on embroidering her final napkin for the auction and by the time Katura and Mildred left for rehearsal, Lucy was grumpier than ever. It just figured the one time she actually wouldn't mind chaperoning them, Lucy was forbidden to go.

While Lucy silently stewed in the corner of the parlor, Betty brought her a piece of mail. "This came for you yesterday," she said. "I forgot all about it."

The return address indicated it was from Bridget so Lucy retreated to her room to read it. She carefully unsealed the gold envelope to reveal a homemade Christmas card. On the front Bridget had designed a simple star sparkling with glitter. Above it were the words, "All is bright," in big print. Beneath the star she'd inscribed the King James Version of John 8:12: "Then spake Jesus again unto them, saying, I am the light of the world: he that followeth me shall not walk in darkness, but shall have the light of life."

The note inside was short but sweet:

Dear Lucy,
Thank you for your beautiful card. I won't forget my skates and I'll also pack an extra pair of leggings to cushion me when I inevitably fall on my backside!
Even though I'll see you in a week, I have to tell you something that can't wait that long, something I can only confide in you about...

I have a suitor. His name is Joshua and he's a mason. I've never met anyone like him. He's dependable and trustworthy, not to mention good-natured and strong. One look from him and I forget my own name. I think I'm in love.

I can't wait to see you!
Love from your cousin,
Bridget

Sliding the card back into its envelope, Lucy suddenly understood how Katura felt—or at least, how Mildred said Katura felt—because Lucy had a suitor and Katura didn't. Even though Lucy loved Bridget like a sister, she had to admit she was envious. Lucy wanted good things for her cousin, but she wanted them for herself, too. *I want to be able to claim* I'm *in love and I want it to be real*, she lamented. She was tired of playing at a courtship and she was disheartened to realize Nick wasn't as "dependable and trustworthy" as Bridget claimed her Joshua was.

The worst part was, Lucy couldn't even confront Nick about his relationship with Jenny because Lucy was housebound. She was sick. Fragile. Weak. If Lucy was so frail she couldn't go out on a Sunday evening like everyone else her age, how had she fooled herself into thinking she might have been on her way to falling in love? How had she dared hope someone might fall in love with her, might wish to marry her?

It serves me right, she thought. *I tried so hard to convince others Nick and I were courting I almost wound up believing it myself.*

If there was one good thing about being ill it was that she had no energy left over to do anything else, including cry. So, instead, Lucy layered her bed with as many quilts as she could gather and dropped into a deep sleep.

Nick had a list of reasons for being agitated. Not only had he missed seeing Lucy on Saturday night, but he had stayed awake until two o'clock waiting for Kevin to return home. Nick met him at the door demanding to know why he was out so late. In response, Kevin lipped off, saying he didn't need a lecture from Nick.

"Better from me than from *Daed*," Nick had retorted. After all he'd sacrificed to repair the cabin—including indirectly putting Lucy's health at risk—his brother didn't seem to care one whit. Nick was beginning to wonder if he should have just allowed Kevin to suffer the consequences of his actions.

Then, on Sunday afternoon, Nick had intended to take a ride to visit Lucy, but his aunt and uncle and their family stayed later than they expected and once again Nick was corralled into entertaining his younger cousins. It was seven o'clock before Nick could finally break away. He wasn't sure what to do—stop at Lucy's or go to the singing in hopes of seeing her there. He was concerned if he stopped at her house and Lucy was still ill Katura would rope him into giving her a ride again. Ultimately, he decided he'd go to the singing first and find out if Lucy was feeling better. If not, he'd pay her a visit at home.

When he arrived, he didn't see her near the snack table, nor did he find her in the parlor. Aware she had a penchant for withdrawing to a quiet place, he looked but didn't find her in the bedroom where the coats were piled, either. Nick would have to ask one of her stepsisters where she was. When he spied Katura whispering into Melinda's ear, he circumvented the pair and located Mildred in the kitchen instead.

"*Jah*, she feels a lot better, but her *daed* strongly suggested she stay in," Mildred said. She'd just finished eating a cupcake and was licking frosting from her fingers.

"Okay. I'll pay her a visit at home, then," Nick replied, starting for the door.

"Uh, I wouldn't do that if I were you."

Nick did a double take. Was Lucy angry he hadn't checked in on her health? "Why not?"

"Her *daed* said something to the effect of anyone who really cared about her would give her time to get better. I'm pretty sure he was talking about you."

"Oh." Nick pulled his ear. He supposed that made sense. But how long would he have to wait? Then he was struck with an idea. "Could you give her a note from me?"

"Sure," Mildred agreed. Then she tittered, "I've never delivered a *liebesbrief* before."

Nick was too distracted trying to find a pen and piece of paper to reply to Mildred's remark. He found a felt-tipped pen someone had left near a list of the songs they were practicing, but all he had to write on was a napkin. Since there was no way to keep his comments private he kept them short.

Dear Lucy,
I'm sorry you've been ill. I hope it's all right if I call on you tomorrow night at six. Maybe if you're feeling better I can take you out for supper?
Nick

The ink was bleeding into the napkin, distorting his already messy penmanship, but it would have to do. He folded it in half. "Please don't lose this," Nick urged Mildred.

"I won't use it," she answered, having misheard him over the singing, which had begun in the next room. Then she added, "I won't read it, either."

Nick didn't care one way or another if she did, as long as she delivered it to Lucy. Since there was no longer any reason to stay at the singing, he headed for home as fast as Penny could take him. All he wanted was to go to sleep and wake up one day closer to seeing Lucy again.

Chapter Ten

*N*ick wants to take me out for supper? Lucy could only imagine it was because he felt guilty about Katura catching him sneaking off with Jenny. Lucy would go with him, but only to tell him she was ending their arrangement. She decided since she was finishing the last of the linen napkins anyway it would be better if she didn't prolong the inevitable by continuing to walk out with Nick even one more day. She was going to confront him about Jenny, too. Not that Lucy needed an explanation at this point, but she was curious. Also, she wanted to watch him squirm when he discovered Lucy knew about his relationship with an *Englischer*.

As eager as she was to end her arrangement with Nick, Lucy dreaded telling her stepsisters and Betty she was no longer being courted by him. It would only be a matter of time before Melinda Schrock found out, too, and she'd humiliate Lucy with her smug I-told-you-so comments. It wasn't as if Lucy would be in poor company; plenty of young women had been ditched by Nick. In this case, at least Lucy had the satisfaction of being the one who was doing the ditching. Besides,

Bridget was coming soon. She'd console Lucy. *Either that, or she'll tell me I shouldn't have been so foolish in the first place since I knew what Nick did to her.*

"Are you sure you're up to going out tonight?" Betty fretted. Lucy was glad her father was working late so he wasn't home to add to the anxiety.

"*Jah.* I'm only going out for supper. I shouldn't be gone for more than an hour or two."

"I hope not," her stepmother said. "Your father and I have been lenient about you going out on weeknights because… Well, I'm beginning to have second thoughts about our decision."

Out of respect for her father and Betty, Lucy carefully considered their advice and concerns, but that didn't mean Lucy needed their permission to go out at night. Once again, she resented Betty treating her like a child. Worse, Lucy suspected her stepmother had been close to saying they'd been lenient about allowing Lucy to go out during the week because they figured it was so rare for her to be courted they'd better take advantage of it while the taking was good. Even if their assessment was right, it was hurtful.

"I know the limitations of my health," Lucy retorted with needles in her voice. She rebelled by waiting on the porch for fifteen minutes before Nick was scheduled to arrive. By the time his buggy circled the bend, her nose was so cold she couldn't feel it.

"Lucy!" Nick exclaimed when he saw her. "You shouldn't have waited outside for me. You're shivering."

"I'm aware," she said, her voice even frostier than her face.

Nick tipped his head curiously. "Here, let me help you up."

"I can manage," Lucy said, pushing his hand away. Since she hadn't bothered to bring her embroidery, she used both hands to pull herself into the buggy. She allowed Nick to arrange the blanket around her, but even that irritated her. It was as if he were tucking a baby into its cradle.

They were barely down the lane when Nick said, "It's so *gut* to see you again. I was worried when I heard you were sick."

"I was hardly sick," Lucy scoffed. "I barely even had a cold. I just needed rest."

"Still, I thought maybe you'd gotten ill from playing around in the snow like we did."

"*Neh*. It wasn't your fault, if that's what you're worried about."

Nick pulled his spine up straight. "I wasn't concerned because I felt guilty. I mean I did feel guilty, but my primary concern was for you, Lucy."

Lucy wouldn't give an inch. "Well, you can see I'm fine now," she snapped.

Nick slowed the horse and turned to look at her. "I can see you're not sick, but you're definitely not fine. You're upset about something. What is it?"

Beneath the streetlamp Lucy noticed Nick's bushy eyebrows furrowed with puzzlement. It took all of her willpower to resist telling him to never mind, it didn't matter. But it did. "I think you know what it is."

Nick tipped his head to the side, completely baffled. "Was it because I didn't *kumme* to see you yesterday?" he asked. "I wanted to. But Mildred warned me your *daed* said you needed rest. I didn't want to upset anyone."

Lucy hadn't realized he'd wanted to see her on Sunday. That was sweet of him, but it didn't change the fact he'd left the singing with an *Englischer* on Saturday evening, the same *Englischer* he'd been pretending was a male friend. Sure Nick wanted to see Lucy on Sunday; he probably needed to secure their arrangement. He needed to make sure her illness wouldn't interfere with his Monday night plans to restore Jenny's cabin.

"You don't have an obligation to check on me when I'm sick," she said. "You're not my doctor."

"I know that, Lucy!" Nick barked, his eyes flashing. "But I do care about you. I thought you understood that."

"And *I* thought you were being honest with me," she shot back.

"Honest with you? I *am* being honest with you. I honestly don't know what I've done to offend you."

Lucy perceived he was genuinely perplexed, and suddenly she wondered if she'd made a mistaken assumption about his relationship with Jenny. After all, even if he didn't correct Lucy when she referred to his Nelson family friend as a male, he had never explicitly told her his friend was a male. And maybe Katura had misinterpreted the situation with him leaving the party. It wouldn't have been the first time her stepsister had spread a false rumor.

Still uncertain she should let him off the hook, Lucy pressed, "Are you sure there's nothing about our arrangement you haven't told me that you want to?"

Nick slouched and covered his face with his hands

before letting them drop to his lap. "Okay. There is something I haven't been honest about. Something I didn't tell you because I was afraid of how you'd react," he said, and as he turned to face her, Lucy inhaled deeply, bracing herself for the truth.

Nick hesitated, knowing what he was about to say would change the course of their relationship. It might even put an immediate end to their arrangement. But in this moment, he didn't care about finishing the cabin repairs or even about his father's reaction to the situation. All he cared about was that Lucy knew how he felt about her. The urgency to share his innermost feelings with Lucy threatened to consume him if he didn't tell her now.

"I… Over the course of this arrangement…of getting to know you…" Nick's throat was scorching. He had to stop stammering and just say the words. "I've developed feelings for you, Lucy. Romantic feelings."

Lucy's eyes widened noticeably behind her lenses, but she remained silent. With his heart pummeling his ribs, Nick bumbled onward. "I haven't known what to make of them. Haven't known whether they were authentic or whether I got caught up in pretending to walk out with you. But the more I've gotten to know you, the more I've realized my feelings are real and I'd like our courtship to be real, too. If you feel the same way, that is."

He scrutinized Lucy's face, but her expression was impassive. Penny snorted and flicked her tail. Lucy was clearly dumbfounded, but whether that was because his admission pleased her or disturbed her he couldn't tell. Was she trying to think of a way to let him down gently? When she remained silent, Nick's hope wilted.

Just when he thought he couldn't endure her lack of response another instant, she cleared her throat. "So you're not romantically interested in someone else?"

Now Nick was nonplussed. "What? No, of course not. Who would I be—? No, there's no one else I'm interested in. Only you, Luce."

There was no mistaking the flush of pleasure blossoming across Lucy's face. "I feel the same way about you, Nick."

He all but shouted *"Wunderbaar!"* and enveloped her in a tight bear hug before giving her a big kiss on the cheek. She instantly pulled back and exclaimed, "Oh!" But then she nodded and leaned toward him again, so this time he kissed her slowly and sweetly, warming her lips with his.

"Does that mean you'll have me as your suitor?" he asked. "For real?"

"For real," she replied. Their third kiss was long and firm, unequivocally sealing their new arrangement.

After they sat back against their seats again, Nick asked, "So, uh, may I take you to supper now?"

"Please."

"Please may I take you to supper now?"

"Neh, I mean, please do," Lucy said with a giggle.

"Oh, right." Nick blushed. He'd never felt so fazed by a woman's kisses before. "Where would you like to go?"

"It doesn't matter as long as it's warm," Lucy replied, rubbing her palms together.

Nick slid closer to her and embraced her shoulders. She fit so snugly beneath his arm it felt as if they'd always traveled this way. "Hang on, we'll be there in no time," he said, and Penny took off as quickly as Nick allowed.

They went to Hank's Hideout, a popular pizza place for Amish and *Englisch* young people alike. Nick was disappointed when they didn't see anyone there they knew. He'd never really made a public spectacle of his courtships before, but with Lucy, he wanted people to know about it now that it was real.

"Everyone will probably stop here after caroling tonight," she said. Then she asked him about his progress on the cabin.

"I'm almost done," he said. "I've got to make a few finishing touches, clean up my supplies and air out the place so it looks as *gut* as new. How much do you have to finish on your project?"

"I'm almost done, too. I didn't even bring my supplies with me tonight. After we eat I can help you clean up at the cabin if you want."

Nick shook his head vehemently. He'd gotten enough done on Saturday evening after dropping Jenny off that he was confident he could tie up the loose ends in no time. "I can do that tomorrow night. Tonight, how about if we just enjoy being together since it's our first official night of walking out?"

"I'd like that. Besides, I told Betty I wouldn't be out for more than a couple hours. She's worried I'll get run-down again," Lucy admitted. "I just hope you don't catch whatever I had."

It was worth it, he thought. Fortunately, the server brought them their food right then, which Nick hoped kept Lucy from noticing his ears were burning.

"I see your illness didn't affect your appetite," he teased when she reached for her fourth piece of pizza.

"Hey! I didn't eat anything all day on Saturday and hardly anything yesterday, either. I'm making up for lost time."

That's what Nick felt like he was doing: making up for lost time. All those years of courting weren't a waste, but they didn't compare to being Lucy's suitor. Usually he felt pressured to spend more time than he wanted to with the women he was courting, but with Lucy, he felt he couldn't spend *enough* time with her. He was already looking forward to seeing Lucy again on Wednesday, when he would accompany her to the soup kitchen.

"Are you sure you don't want to go somewhere else this evening?" he pleaded after paying the bill.

"I do, but I'd better keep my word to Betty," she said. "Let's take the long way, though, so we can see the lights in town."

Lucy's countenance was as luminous as the landscape as they traveled toward her home. The *Englisch* residents of Willow Creek decorated their homes and yards with bright lights, and the Amish placed candles in their windows and simple wreaths on their doors. The effect was mesmerizing, and the only thing that could have made it more festive was if it had been snowing again.

Nick noticed a lamp on at Lucy's home and he saw a shadow pass by the window, but he didn't care who might be peeking out; after helping Lucy down from the buggy, he held her gloved fingers in his hands. "One more kiss?" he asked.

"Please," she said. This time he knew it was meant

as an agreement, not a scolding, and he drew her to him. She stood on her tiptoes and he bent his head toward hers.

After they separated, he squeezed her hands before releasing them, too dazed to say anything as he watched her disappear into the house.

Four. Nick had kissed her four times tonight! *And every one of those kisses was as real as...as the lips on my face!* As she sprawled across her bed that evening remembering the sensation, Lucy lightly traced her mouth with her finger, nearly dizzy with giddiness. When she had set out with him that evening, she never could have envisioned the evening ending the way it did. Although she didn't know how to account for Nick not telling her his Nelson friend was a female, it no longer mattered. Lucy was relieved she hadn't accused him of being romantically involved with Jenny Nelson—not only would she have made a fool of herself, but Nick never would have wanted to court her.

Nick Burkholder is my suitor, she mused, nearly bursting with the desire to confide this development in another person. But who could she tell that didn't already think they were a couple? Lucy was hesitant to write to Bridget, knowing how Nick had acted toward her cousin in the past. *But he's changed,* she thought. Surely, Bridget would understand that? Lucy wasn't positive. She decided it would be better to tell her cousin in person, so instead of writing a letter, Lucy used a piece of stationery to doodle Nick's name beside hers as she daydreamed about their next kiss. *It can't* kumme *quickly enough*, she thought just before sleep overtook her.

The next evening, Lucy hummed Christmas carols as she slid a cookie sheet from the oven. This was her third batch, some she'd take to the soup kitchen and the rest would be for their family's celebration.

"Am I allowed to have one of these?" her father asked, reaching for one.

"*Neh!*" Lucy yipped. "They're hot. You'll burn your tongue. I've set aside a plate of them for you here, *Daed.*"

Her father accepted the dish as Betty came into the room. "You shouldn't be eating those," she said. "You know what the doctor said about your blood sugar."

Marvin hung his head like a scolded puppy. "You worry too much about my health."

"Now you know how I feel when you and Betty worry about me, *Daed,*" Lucy teased.

"I *don't* worry," Betty protested. "But I am vigilant. There's a difference."

"It's all the same to me if it means I can't have a cookie," Marvin grumbled, wrapping his arms around his wife's waist and kissing her on the cheek. Maybe it was because she was in love herself, but Lucy enjoyed witnessing this display of their affection.

"Oh, all right, you big *bobbel,*" Betty relented. "You can have a cookie. But just remember, I comment about your health because I care. And that goes for you, too, Lucy."

"I know it does—and I know *Daed* only comments because he cares, too," Lucy admitted, suddenly seeing their concern in a new light. "*Daed,* when you're finished eating those, will you please bring in the pine boughs?"

Her father had cut down evergreen branches from

the trees near the back of their property so Lucy could make two wreaths—one for their door and one for the door in the church hallway leading to the soup kitchen. She savored the natural pine scent—one of the few fragrances that didn't cause her to cough or catch her breath—as she and her father twisted the branches into a circle and then tied them around a wire. Then Lucy affixed pine cones around the periphery of the wreath and fastened a crimson bow at the top. Her father declared their creation perfect, which was the same way Lucy felt about the evening itself.

She was cleaning up the materials when Mildred returned from caroling, her cheeks rosy.

"Where's Katura?" Lucy asked.

"She's riding home with…someone else," Mildred answered evasively, probably embarrassed to mention it in front of Lucy's father.

Lucy raised her eyebrows and mouthed, *Frederick?* to which Mildred nodded vigorously. A smile broke out over Lucy's face. It was easy to be happy for someone else when she was this happy herself, and she offered to serve everyone eggnog.

"That would be lovely," Betty agreed, looking pleased. Lucy always thought her stepmother placed too much emphasis on courtship, as if having a suitor was an accomplishment instead of a relationship. But now she realized Betty was as delighted that Katura had a suitor as she'd been that Lucy had one. And it wasn't necessarily because Betty was afraid the young women might never be courted, nor was it because Betty herself valued courtship so highly. It was because Betty was happy that her daughters—including Lucy—were happy.

The foursome chatted and ate and laughed until almost ten o'clock. Everyone was so jovial Lucy would have been reluctant to turn in for the night if it wasn't that she couldn't wait for Wednesday to arrive. Not only would she see Nick again, but the soup kitchen was hosting one big, final festive supper before Christmas. Lucy lay awake in bed anticipating the celebration long after Mildred's breathing vibrated in the steady rhythm of a snore. A few minutes before midnight, Katura crept into the room.

Lucy was quiet as her stepsister prepared to go to sleep, and when she heard Katura's bed creak as she positioned herself beneath her quilt, Lucy whispered, "Did you have a *gut* evening, Katura?"

She could see the faint outline of Katura's head pop up from her pillow, and then she tiptoed over to Lucy's bedside and knelt down so their faces were even. "*Jah.* Frederick gave me a ride home. He asked if he could court me and I said *jah*!"

"Oh, Katura, that's *wunderbaar*!" Lucy sat up and squeezed Katura's hand. "I'm really happy for you."

"*Denki*, but I don't know how you can be, Lucy. I've been wretched to you and I'm so sorry for the mean things I said." There was a pause before Katura continued, "I'm afraid I was jealous because you're younger than I am and you had a suitor first."

Recalling how she'd begrudged Bridget a suitor when Lucy didn't have one herself, she said, "I understand. I've experienced my share of jealousy, too. Though I have to say, I had no idea you were interested in Frederick."

"At first I wasn't. Or actually, I was but I didn't think he'd ever want to court me because I'm half a head taller than he is. I think that's why I was so envious of you. You're fortunate you're so short—you never have to consider whether you're too tall for a man to be confident enough to walk out with you."

"Ha!" Lucy sputtered. "I've never considered myself fortunate to be this short, but I accept that this is how *Gott* created me. Besides, I don't think height really matters to a man of character. Obviously, it doesn't matter to Frederick."

"*Neh*, it doesn't. Although I think he had to stand on tiptoes to kiss me," Katura said, giggling. In true fashion, she divulged more intimate details about her romantic relationship than Lucy would have shared. She added, "There's only one thing I'm worried about…"

"What's that?"

"His *mamm*. She's kind of, well, pushy. I'm pretty sure she's going to announce it to everyone that Frederick is courting me."

Lucy intended no offense when she said, "I'm surprised you mind if everyone knows."

"I don't," Katura said. "I just want the pleasure of announcing it myself."

Lucy laughed and Katura joined her until Mildred complained, "Would the two of you kindly stop discussing your courtships in front of me? My dreams are probably the only place I'll ever have a suitor, so I'd like to go back to sleep now, if that's okay with you."

"I doubt that's true, Mildred," Lucy replied. "But we'll be quiet now." She wanted to get to sleep as much as Mildred did so she'd be that much closer to seeing Nick.

But the next afternoon when she returned from work, Mildred presented Lucy a note Nick had brought to her at the mercantile. This time it wasn't a napkin; it was a folded piece of paper he had taped shut.

> Dear Luce, *(funny how that nickname had grown on her)*
> I am so sorry—*Lucy held her breath in trepidation; she knew yesterday was too good to be true*—but I can't bring you to the soup kitchen tonight. I'll explain everything later. I still want to come and help serve, but I know you need to arrive early to set up, so it's better if your father takes you.
> But I'd like to take you home. Let's go back the long way, okay?
> Nick

Lucy remembered to exhale again. For a terrible moment, she thought Nick was going to call off their courtship. While she was disappointed he couldn't bring her to the soup kitchen, his reference to taking the long way home made her skin tingle. It was proof he wanted to be with her alone after their work at the soup kitchen was finished. What had she been so worried about?

Lucy's father said he was glad for the opportunity to spend time alone with her, but he asked if she'd mind if they stopped at the *Englisch* pottery shop on the way. "I'm picking up a gift I special ordered for Betty," he whispered. "The shop closes at five so I won't have time after I drop you off. I'll dash in and *kumme* right back out."

Tickled by her father's delight in buying a gift for his wife, Lucy thought, *I suppose it took being in love myself to appreciate it in others*, as she waited in the buggy. Cars and buggies streamed in and out of the parking lot in front of the small cluster of *Englisch* specialty shops. Lucy was trying to imagine what kinds of gifts the drivers intended to purchase when she spotted an Amish man with red curls sticking out from beneath his hat hitching his horse to the post. How many young redheaded Amish men were there in Willow Creek? Lucy only knew two: Nick and Kevin. *I must just have Nick on my mind*, she thought, giggling to herself. But when the man turned sideways, Lucy recognized it was definitely him. Why was Nick there instead of transporting her to the soup kitchen? Lucy's pulse ricocheted in her ears until she figured perhaps he had a special gift to pick up for his *mamm*. *Or maybe even for me*, she dared presume.

Her momentary calm was shattered an instant later when he strode not toward the store, but toward a car, where a young *Englisch* woman with long blond hair got out. Katura said Jenny Nelson was blond; who else could it be? Standing face-to-face the pair appeared to speak briefly before Nick took Jenny's hand. What Jenny did next sickened Lucy: she threw her arms around Nick in a big, delighted hug.

Her stomach cramping with revulsion, Lucy couldn't bear to watch any longer. She buried her face in her hands as her thoughts spiraled and her breath came in tight, short puffs. So she'd been right all along. Nick *was* engaged in a romantic relationship with Jenny Nelson. He must have sensed Lucy was on the brink of confronting him on Monday night. That's why he'd kissed her; he felt he had to pull out all the stops to distract Lucy from pressing the matter and exposing his secret romance with an *Englischer*. She never felt so used and betrayed in her life, and at that moment the very act of breathing in and out was more laborious than when she'd been hospitalized with pneumonia.

"Are you all right?" her father asked when he boarded the buggy. By then she was no longer gasping. Dropping her hands from her eyes, she looked up; Nick's buggy was still there, but the *Englisch* car was gone. Wherever they went and whether they went together or alone, Lucy didn't care as they were out of her sight and out of her life.

Nick was relieved. Having completed the final touches on the repairs and cleaned up the cabin on Tuesday night, he had just handed the key over to Jenny and he was home free. From now on, he could dedicate every evening he went out to actually being with Lucy. Whistling, he entered the china shop, which was located between the pottery shop and the cutlery store. His frequent sensation of being a bull in a china shop around Lucy had given him an idea about what to get her for Christmas, which was why, when Jenny checked in with him at the hardware store on Tuesday, he'd asked her to meet him at this particular location today.

He searched the mirrored shelves in the store until at last he found exactly what he wanted: a white teacup and saucer decorated with a delicate, thin line of gold around the rims. The china was every bit as understatedly elegant as Lucy was to him. Assuring Nick the piece was sturdier than it looked, the clerk boxed it up in a nest of packing material. Nick stowed it beneath the seat of his buggy and then made haste to the soup kitchen.

When he arrived, Lucy hardly looked up from where she was arranging cookies on platters. At first Nick assumed she didn't see him, but when he said hello, she mumbled hello back and retreated to the kitchen without making eye contact. Was she miffed he hadn't picked her up? Nick didn't know, but he decided to follow her to find out.

Just as he reached the kitchen door she emerged carrying a wreath, and Dan followed close behind with a stepladder. Nick stood motionless, watching from a distance as Dan climbed the stepladder and pounded a nail into the wall above the door frame. Then Lucy handed him the wreath, which he hung. Clearly she thought it was crooked, because she motioned for him to step down so she could climb up and adjust it. She had to stand on tiptoe, and when the bow was precisely aligned, Lucy began to wobble. Dan lunged forward dramatically, swooped her into his arms and set her upright on the floor.

Seething, Nick dug his fingernails into his palms. He'd witnessed Lucy's rock-solid balance as she stood in his buggy at full speed, and he'd watched her glide on one foot across the rink at Wheeler's Pond without wavering. Her fall from the stepladder was contrived, undoubtedly to capture Dan's attention. Maybe that was why she was so indifferent to Nick's presence; maybe she liked Dan. But then why had she allowed Nick to kiss her only two days ago? Why had she agreed to accept him as her suitor? Nick recalled suddenly that Dan had seen Nick and Lucy's fake kiss at the singing. Nick remembered he had suspected Lucy was trying to make Dan jealous way back then. His mind was racing. Maybe accepting Nick as her suitor for real allowed Lucy to continue her ploy to win Dan over. Perhaps she felt that once her phony courtship with Nick ended, she wouldn't have any leverage to make Dan more interested in her.

Livid, Nick stalked across the room and cupped Lucy's elbow. "I need to speak with you, now," he said, escorting her down the hallway before she had a chance to protest. He directed her to an empty room that must have been used as a nursery because there were animals painted on the walls and three cribs lined up in the far corner. Nick could practically feel steam escaping his nostrils as he fumed, "Just what is going on, Lucy?"

She yanked her arm free of his grasp and shoved her hands on her hips. "You tell me!"

Once again, Nick didn't know what she was talking about and it infuriated him. Instead of addressing any potential wrongdoing on his part, he said, "From what I can tell, you're flirting with Dan. Which is entirely your business, but if he's the one you're interested in, you should have had the decency to turn down my offer of courtship!"

"You want to talk about decency?" Lucy challenged, her voice rising. "Then tell me why *you* lied about being interested in Jenny Nelson! And don't deny it. I saw you holding her hand and hugging her in the parking lot at Buckland Corner today."

How dare Lucy imply he was romantically involved with Jenny, especially after Nick had demonstrated in no uncertain terms how he felt about Lucy! Did she still really have that low of an opinion of him?

"I can't believe you'd think I'm interested in her, but you don't have any idea what you're talking about. And quite frankly it disgusts me that you'd think I'd do anything so revolting as kiss one woman while I'm secretly courting another." Nick nearly choked on the words. "If you weren't so judgmental, you'd realize things aren't always as they seem to be, Lucy."

"*Neh?* Because what it *seems* like to me is you went to great lengths to keep it a secret that your Nelson friend was a woman. For all I know, you fabricated the entire situation with her cabin so you could use me as a cover for seeing her!"

"That's *lecherich* and you know it." Frustrated by Lucy's reasoning, Nick pounded a fist into his open palm as he snarled, "You saw me making the repairs yourself!"

Momentarily quiet, Lucy blinked repeatedly. It seemed she was backing down, but then she said, "Okay, Nick. I could be wrong. If you can look me in the eye and tell me you honestly were solely repairing the Nelsons' cabin out of the goodness of your heart… If you can tell me you simply wanted to give them a joyful *Grischtdaag* and that's all there is to it, I'll believe you. I'll apologize for ever doubting whether you've been completely truthful with me."

Nick swallowed, his head thrumming. He couldn't confirm what Lucy wanted him to confirm because it wasn't entirely true. But neither could he explain because then she'd be angry he hadn't been honest with her from the beginning. When his silence lengthened, Lucy threw her hands in the air and then slapped them against her sides. "Exactly as I thought." She spun on her heel and was gone before he could utter another syllable.

Suddenly, he didn't want to explain because he had nothing more to say to her. He didn't care if he never saw her again. He'd *prefer* it that way. Nick was so heated he didn't remember making his way to the buggy, and when Penny accelerated to a rapid canter on the way home, Nick derived no pleasure from the animal's agility or relief from the frigid air against his stinging cheeks.

By the next afternoon, Nick's anger had fizzled to a sullen numbness, and he went through the motions of waiting on customers and wishing them holiday cheer although the words rung hollow. His ire was briefly ignited again when Betty Knepp entered the store and inquired after his mother's whereabouts.

"She's staying put at the house today. *Grischtdaag* baking and all that," Nick's father told her as Nick dallied within earshot in the fasteners aisle. "You should call on her. She'd *wilkom* an opportunity to take a break and have a cup of tea with you."

Nick's stomach flipped; he could guess why Betty Knepp would wish to call on his mother. Two days ago he wouldn't have dreamed Lucy would squeal on him, but two days might as well have been another lifetime. Everything had changed since then. Or everything had stayed the same: Lucy Knepp was still the same stuck-up, finger-pointing Goody Two-shoes she'd been as a child. Nick had no doubt he was going to get an earful from his parents that evening.

Indeed, after Nick closed shop and returned home, his parents were waiting for him in the parlor. He'd barely removed his boots and taken a seat by the fire when his mother bluntly inquired whether he was romantically involved with an *Englischer*.

Until that moment, he'd been holding out hope Lucy hadn't done exactly what he feared she'd done. Even when his mother questioned him, he still couldn't quite believe his ears. "Who told you that?" he asked, knowing full well it was Lucy.

"That's not important," his mother replied. "What's important is if it's true."

Nick looked directly into his mother's eyes. "*Neh*, I absolutely am not romantically involved with an *Englischer*, and anyone who told you that is sorely mistaken," Nick asserted.

His mother's expression softened. "We believe you," she replied, and his father seconded her sentiment, nodding. "We know you've had a—er, a difficult time finding someone who was a *gut* match for you, but we doubted you'd ever court an *Englischer*. Especially while you were courting Lucy. The idea was unthinkable to us, but out of a sense of fairness, we wanted to confirm the truth with you before setting the wom—the person who started the rumor straight."

Nick couldn't let them do that. As immaturely as Lucy had behaved by tattling to her stepmother about him, Nick wasn't going to respond like a child himself by letting his parents defend him. This was something he had to handle directly. "Please don't do that, *Mamm* and *Daed*."

"Why not?" his mother protested. "I shouldn't have to hold my tongue when someone is spreading an unfounded rumor like that about my *suh*! I actually wish I would have trusted my intuition and said as much when I first heard it."

"If Nick doesn't want us to say anything, we shouldn't say anything," his father intervened. "He's a man now and I trust his judgment. Let's go to bed, dear."

Nick's mother furrowed her brow, but instead of arguing she stood, walked over to Nick and planted a kiss on his forehead before saying good-night. Nick shot his father a look of gratitude as he led Nick's mother from the room. After disappointing his parents so often during his *rumspringa*, Nick should have been more pleased to hear his father say he trusted Nick's judgment. But all Nick could think was, *Some gut judgment I have—I trusted Lucy more than I've ever trusted any woman, and look what happened.*

The more he seethed, the more impatient he became to tell Lucy exactly what he thought of her vengeful, juvenile behavior. The thought ate at him until he finally decided it wasn't too late to pay her a visit. He crept out of the house and made it to Lucy's as swiftly as Penny could carry him. It was after nine o'clock, but a light shone in the window, and a few moments after Nick knocked, Lucy opened the door.

She'd barely stepped outside before he hurled his accusation at her. "It's one thing if you're so inherently suspicious you'd make up stories about me and an *Englischer*, but it's another thing to be so vindictive that you'd tell my parents I was courting Jenny Nelson. I thought you were different, I really did."

Lucy's arms were folded like a shield across her chest. "What are you going on about?"

"Don't give me that wide-eyed innocent look. You're not fooling me. You told Betty I was dating Jenny Nelson—you *thought* I was dating Jenny

Nelson—knowing full well she'd run right over and blab about it to my *mamm*. If you wanted to ruin my *Grischtdaag*, you failed. You might not know me very well, but my parents do and they don't believe a word you said."

"I didn't tell *anyone* about you and Jenny Nelson, but I wish I had," Lucy exclaimed. "I wish someone would finally expose how irresponsible, immature and self-centered you are. You haven't changed a bit since you were Naughty Nick Burkholder. It wasn't cute when you were a *kind* and it isn't cute now."

"Talk about not changing! You're the same uptight, self-righteous tattletale you've always been!" Nick jeered. "Keep it up, Lucy, and a pretend courtship is all you'll ever have!"

Nick turned and jumped down the stairs two at a time. He worked Penny into such a hard run that when they came to a quick stop before turning onto a side road, the box containing the teacup he'd gotten Lucy slid out from beneath the seat. He stomped on it, repeatedly and hard, as if he were putting out a fire.

Then, his anger temporarily extinguished, Nick guided Penny wearily the rest of the way home.

Chapter Eleven

Lucy had no desire to get out of bed on Friday morning. The party at the soup kitchen—which Nick had completely ruined for her—was over. She'd delivered her donation to the organizer of the festival auction on Thursday morning. And her fake courtship with Nick had ended. Not even the thought of Bridget coming was enough to motivate Lucy to leave her cozy nest of quilts. Depleted of holiday gladness, Lucy wished she could skip Christmas altogether this year. Or she at least wished she could mark the occasion with individual prayer and Bible study instead of celebrating with anyone else, even her family members.

"What's wrong?" Katura asked, brushing her hair as she sat on the edge of Lucy's bed. "You're usually the first one up. I actually made breakfast this morning."

Despite Katura's recent change of attitude, Lucy didn't quite know if she could trust her enough to confide in her. But tears spilled down her cheeks, leaving her little choice.

"Nick and I..." she blubbered, unable to continue.

She'd been preparing to say they'd broken up ever since they began their phony courtship, but now that it had happened for real, she couldn't speak the words. "It's over."

"Oh, Lucy," Katura clucked empathetically. "Are you sure? Maybe it's just a disagreement. Maybe it will pass."

"*Neh*, there's no getting past this," Lucy said, sniffing. Then, putting on a facade of resilience, she added, "I'm okay. You should go now. You're going to be late for work."

Katura secured her *kapp* with a pin and stood up. "Why don't you *kumme* caroling with us tonight? *Grischtdaag* music always makes you happy, and there's a big party afterward at one of the *Englischers'* apartments."

"*Neh*, that wouldn't be fair. I didn't attend any of the rehearsals. I didn't participate in them, anyway."

"That's okay, you have such a pretty voice you don't need practice. You love caroling. Please *kumme*."

Lucy sighed, aware her stepsister hadn't changed her crafty ways overnight. Katura preferred to ride with Frederick, but she knew Betty wouldn't let Mildred go out on her own. Lucy couldn't blame Katura for wanting to spend time alone with her suitor, so, in the spirit of Christmas, she figured she could summon enough goodwill to help Katura enjoy an evening out with Frederick. What's more, Lucy was suddenly filled with a stubborn resolve not to allow her "breakup" with Nick to ruin any more of her pre-*Grischtdaag* festivities. "Okay, I'll go," she agreed.

But when Mildred told Betty their plans for the evening, Betty objected. "I don't like the idea of you going to a party at an *Englischer*'s home, Mildred. And Lucy probably wants to go out with Nick tonight, don't you, Lucy?"

"Nick's…working late tonight," Lucy guessed, glad Katura wasn't in the room to mention their breakup. "I really don't mind accompanying Mildred."

"Maybe not, but you're still as pale as can be. It doesn't seem wise for you to be traipsing around outdoors in this weather."

Seeing the disappointment in Mildred's eyes, Lucy countered, "The fresh air will put a little color in my cheeks."

"Please, *Mamm*," pleaded Mildred. "If we promise to be home by midnight, can we go?"

"Eleven o'clock," Betty compromised. She set down the dishcloth and pointed her finger at the girls. "Not a moment later. And I want the two of you to stick together, do you hear me?"

"Jah, Mamm," Mildred promised. To Lucy she said, "This is going to be a blast! *Denki* for going with me, Lucy."

But as they journeyed to the central meeting place, the parking lot behind the mercantile, Lucy regretted her decision. For one thing, Betty was right about the bitterly cold weather. For another, the first person she saw when she arrived was Dan, who gave her an enthusiastic wave, causing her to feel even worse. Nick had been partly right; she'd put on a big act, falling into Dan's arms on Wednesday night at the soup kitchen. It wasn't because she liked Dan; it was because she hoped her theatrics would make *Nick* realize other young men cared about her, too. She doubted Dan thought twice about it, but seeing him brought unpleasant associations of Nick to mind.

"Hi, Lucy. It's *gut* to have you join us," Dan said. He was standing on the periphery of the large group of singers milling about the parking lot. "Would you like to share my song sheets? I've marked which stanzas we'll be singing since I can't remember and I don't want to embarrass myself."

"Denki," she replied. Since this was the final night of caroling, the youth were visiting homes in the Amish section of Willow Creek before journeying over to the more industrialized side of town, where they'd sing to shoppers entering and leaving a small strip mall.

Shuffling her feet to circulate blood to her toes, Lucy scanned the crowd and inhaled sharply when she spotted a young hatless redhead. But when she realized it was an *Englischer*, she let her breath out again. Relieved Nick was nowhere in sight, Lucy relaxed enough to concentrate on the words of the carols, which announced the joy of Christ's birth. Her Christmas might not be turning out the way she had hoped it would, but she had the promise of God's love to sustain her. *Romance might be fleeting, but the love of the Lord endures forever*, she reminded herself.

Still, as the large group moved from house to house and then journeyed to the mall, Lucy kept thinking about the sweet, vulnerable look on Nick's face when he'd confided how much he disliked his singing voice. She'd gotten to know a side of him other people didn't know—or at least, they never mentioned—and a knot of nostalgia twisted deep within her heart. She was glad when the group ended its final carol.

The large three-story duplex where the party was held afterward was crowded with *Englisch* and Amish carolers, as well as dozens of other *Englisch* young people Lucy assumed were home from college for the holiday. Music blasted in every room, and the *Englischers* had pushed the furniture against the walls so they had space to dance in the living room. Others lounged on the stairway or gathered near the fireplace holding drinks Lucy assumed from the smell were alcoholic. As crammed in as they were, everyone was jubilant and friendly.

In fact, they were *too* friendly for Lucy's comfort; one of the *Englischers* tugged Mildred's hand and told her he had room next to him on the sofa if she didn't mind squeezing in real close. When her stepsister merely giggled in reply, Lucy understood why Betty had been so hesitant to allow her youngest daughter to attend this party. *Nick might think it's okay to be involved with an* Englischer, *but Betty's counting on me to keep Mildred from making a mistake like that,* she thought. She resigned herself to spending an hour sticking to Mildred like glue, but after that, they were both going home.

Since Kevin knew Nick had completed the cabin repairs and because he had nowhere else to go anyway, Nick remained at the hardware store long after their father left for the day. He even told Kevin he'd handle the shop on his own, but to his surprise, Kevin declined the offer.

"After all you've done for me, the least I can do is help out here on one of the busiest nights of the year," Kevin insisted. The brothers agreed to keep the store open extra late in order to accommodate the scores of panicked *Englisch* shoppers who needed to purchase last-minute hardware essentials for Christmas, including tree light bulb replacements, batteries for their children's toys and additional gifts for the men in their families.

As they were finally closing up, Kevin announced he was going to the after-caroling gathering on West Elm Street. Nick knew the place; an *Englisch* college student and his roommate lived there and they frequently hosted big, raucous parties. "You should *kumme*. You'll have a lot of *schpass* now that you don't have to pretend you're courting Lucy anymore. I've heard that *meed* from as far away as Shady Valley are going to be there."

"*Neh*. You go on by yourself." Nick said, advising, "Just don't get into any trouble."

"I won't. I've learned my lesson," Kevin promised. He seemed to hedge before asking, "Are you okay? You seem a little down."

"I'm just beat," Nick glumly replied.

On the way home he allowed Penny to trot at a fast clip, but the velocity didn't bring Nick the sense of excitement it usually did. Instead, he recalled how much Lucy enjoyed it when Penny galloped at top speed. *Dan might have a great singing voice, but Lucy isn't going to have nearly as much fun riding in his courting buggy as she did in mine.* Just thinking about Dan and Lucy embittered Nick and he suddenly decided, *Kevin's right. I should go to the party. It'll be a lot more* schpass *without having to hang around pious, priggish Lucy Knepp.*

He turned the buggy around and headed in the

direction of West Elm Street. Brian's house was so crowded Nick could barely squeeze through the door, but when he did, the first Amish person he crossed paths with was Melinda Schrock.

"Hi, Nick. I didn't recognize you without Lucy at your side. She's clear across the room." She took a sip of soda through a straw before adding, "But you better be careful, because your other girlfriend is here, too."

Nick fell right into her trap. "My *other* girlfriend?" he asked.

"*Jah.* Jenny Nelson," Melinda tittered. "Neither of them has probably seen you yet. There's still time to escape. I won't say a word, I promise."

Nick's mouth dropped open. He hadn't expected Lucy's false rumor to travel quite that fast, and he wondered if her stepsisters were responsible. "Who told you Jenny Nelson is my girlfriend?"

"I figured it out myself," Melinda bragged. "It was so obvious—although your *mamm* sure seemed surprised. I hope I didn't get you in any trouble." Melinda's voice dripped with complacence, not contrition.

As she turned to elbow her way back through the sea of people, Nick tried to collect his thoughts. He was so stunned to discover it was Melinda, not Lucy, who had started the rumor about him and Jenny that he might have collapsed to his knees if it weren't for the crush of people pressing in on all sides, forcing him to remain upright. It hit him like a lightning bolt: he'd wrongly accused Lucy just as she'd wrongly accused him. But his accusation was worse, because it was completely unfounded, whereas Nick had been at least partly to blame for Lucy suspecting he was interested in Jenny. After all, Nick wouldn't confirm he'd been completely honest with Lucy when she'd asked him to. And Lucy *had* seen Jenny hugging him the day he returned her key. Other than the fact Betty Knepp wanted to talk to Nick's mother, what reason did he have to assume Lucy had started a rumor about him and Jenny?

I have to get to her, he thought. *Even if she doesn't believe me about Jenny, I owe Lucy an apology.* Excusing himself as he knocked into people, Nick picked his way through the crowd. *Lucy's so tiny, I'll never see her*, he thought, raising himself on his toes to peer over the shoulders of the group of *Englischers* in front of him.

It took nearly fifteen minutes, but he finally located her chatting with Mildred, Eve and Dan. After greeting them he said, "Lucy, may I speak with you a moment?" He had no idea how or where he'd find a private place to talk, but the other three graciously turned their backs and began edging away.

"I have nothing to say to you," Lucy replied. She tried to walk away, but the room was so thick with people she didn't get very far.

"Could you at least listen to me?" Nick implored, trailing behind. The music was so loud he had to shout to be heard.

"Stop following me!" Lucy tried to continue weaving through the crowd, but a cluster of brawny *Englischers* wearing sweatshirts emblazoned with the name of a local college on the back stood shoulder to shoulder, forming an impenetrable wall in front of the door leading to the hall. Realizing there was no way around them, Lucy turned back and faced Nick, who encircled her wrists with his hands.

"Luce, please hear me out," he begged. Just then someone behind him wrapped her fingers around his bicep.

"Hey, Nick. Am I glad to see you!" It was Jenny Nelson.

Before he could stop Lucy, she tore from his grasp and ducked beneath the arms of one of the students as he lifted a drink to his mouth, tunneling past the young men.

"Hi, Jenny. Look, I, um, I've got to go—" he said, but it was too late. He'd lost sight of Lucy in the swell of partygoers.

Jenny laughed. "You can't go anywhere fast in this place. But I won't keep you long. I just wanted to tell you how great the cabin looks. My mother didn't have a clue anything ever happened, especially because we were dragging in so many boxes of decorations it was hard to tell if anything was amiss or not."

"I'm glad it all worked out," Nick said. *If only everything had worked out that well for me.*

After they wished each other a merry Christmas, Nick searched in vain for Lucy. Moving at a snail's pace from room to room without finding her, he finally decided he'd wait outside. She'd have to come out eventually. But it was Mildred, not Lucy, who emerged an hour later to unhitch their horse.

When Nick asked where Lucy was, Mildred said, "I assumed she'd left ages ago—with you. Now I'm going to have to go back in there and try to find her." She shivered. "Some of those guys give me the creeps. The way they bump into you when you're trying to get past them, it's like they're doing it on purpose."

Nick knew exactly what she meant and she was

probably right. "You go on," he said, motioning toward the Knepps' buggy. "I'll go get Lucy and bring her home."

Mildred brightened. "*Denki*, Nick. I'd really appreciate that."

The fact Mildred didn't argue proved she knew nothing about Nick and Lucy's breakup; otherwise, she would have waited for her stepsister instead of letting Nick take Lucy home. Feeling even guiltier that he had suspected Lucy of telling anyone about him and Jenny, Nick urgently jostled his way through the crowd, desperate to apologize.

What Lucy lacked in height or strength she made up for in fury, doggedly prodding her way past bony elbows, avoiding sloshed drinks and sidestepping embracing couples as she dug her way from room to room in search of Mildred, but her stepsister was nowhere to be found. Lucy knew the rule of thumb for being lost was to stay in one place, but she didn't want Nick to catch up to her. Especially not with Jenny Nelson in tow.

How can he keep denying what I can see with my own eyes? Maybe that was just it; maybe when he approached Lucy, Nick was going to come clean about his relationship with Jenny. Lucy didn't want to hear it. Not yet. She didn't want him to apologize because she wasn't ready to forgive him. Not for being dishonest about his relationship with Jenny and not for accusing Lucy of telling anyone about it.

So she kept searching for Mildred as best she could, growing increasingly frustrated. The house was thrumming with the pulse of what the *Englisch* considered music and on the basement level people were smoking, which caused Lucy to cough uncontrollably. Someone handed her a mug of something—peppermint schnapps, they called it—but after one vile sniff, she realized it was alcoholic and set it down without drinking it, coughing even harder. Finally, she cut a path to the balcony. She anticipated no one would be outside since it was so cold, but there were so many people huddled on the little rectangle of wood Lucy feared it would collapse, spilling them onto the concrete two stories below. But she couldn't reenter the smoky house until her lungs cleared.

Lucy peered down at the driveway. *Is that Dan leaving?* she wondered, since it was difficult to tell from above whose buggy was whose. She had to find Mildred and get out of there, but when she turned, she noticed an *Englisch* couple was kissing passionately right in front of the door, blocking anyone from leaving. Everyone else was engaged in chatter and didn't seem to give them any heed. Too modest to interrupt the couple's embrace, Lucy stayed where she was, wiggling her toes and hugging her cloak to her chest to warm herself. By the time the couple finally moved, Lucy felt as if her bones were icicles.

Poking her way through the room, she prayed in vain to find Mildred. Lucy stood in the threshold of the door leading to one of the bedrooms, which was surprisingly empty except for a lone man who appeared to be asleep next to a pile of coats on the bed. Lucy shivered and turned to find herself face-to-face—or actually face-to-chest—with an *Englischer.*

"Are you lost?" he asked, slurring his words.

"*Neh*, I was just looking for someone."

"Well, you found him," the young man said, extending his arms.

"Excuse me." Lucy tried to dodge around him.

The young man didn't budge. "You're awfully cute, but you should ditch these." Before Lucy could stop him, he reached down and removed her glasses. "There, just like I thought. You have beautiful eyes."

The room was a blur. "I'd like those back." Lucy tried to sound firm, but she heard the quaver in her own voice.

"How about a trade? You give me a kiss, I'll give you your glasses," the *Englischer* said. Lucy didn't know whether he was teasing or not, and her stomach churned with a sickening feeling.

"Please give them to me, now," she repeated in what she hoped was a demanding tone.

"Please give me a kiss, now," the *Englischer* said, mimicking her tone. Then he pointed upward. "We're under the mistletoe, see? You have to kiss me."

"No, she doesn't," a male declared adamantly. Lucy couldn't see him clearly but she recognized the voice. It was Nick. Just when she didn't think this evening could get any worse, *he* had to turn up again. *If he thinks I'm going to feel indebted toward him for* kumming *to my rescue, he couldn't be more deluded.*

"Sorry, it was just a joke," the *Englischer* said, handing Lucy her glasses. She put them on immediately and propelled herself past both of them.

"Wait," Nick called loud enough for her to hear above the music's hammering beat. "You can't leave—"

"That's what you think," Lucy retorted. She jabbed her way through the crowd to the kitchen door, and then ran down the steps and along the path leading to the driveway. She was so frazzled she must have forgotten where she'd hitched her horse because she didn't see it anywhere.

"Lucy!" Nick called again, a couple paces behind her. "Mildred took the buggy. I told her I'd bring you home."

She spun to face him and shouted, "You had no right to do that! Now leave me alone." She stormed across the lawn and scurried along the sidewalk, leaving Nick behind. She'd trekked several blocks when a horse came clopping along from behind and then flew by her. It was Penny and Nick. But instead of continuing down the main stretch of pavement, they stopped about an eighth of a mile up the road and Lucy realized Nick was climbing down and coming her way. She'd have to pass him in order to continue her journey home.

"Be reasonable, Lucy," he said. "You can't walk all the way home."

"Don't you dare tell me what I can do," she shouted. She was so fed up with everyone deciding what she was or wasn't capable of doing. She'd show him! When she passed his buggy without getting in, Nick climbed in and followed her as she made her way down the street. *Penny must hate walking so slowly.* But that was Nick's fault, not hers. She thought, *He can follow me all the way home if he wants, but he's* narrish *if he thinks I'm going to break down and accept a ride from him.*

She must have walked for over an hour before the cold air made it so difficult to breathe she struggled to take in enough air. A tear dribbled down her cheek and then another and another before her eyes released a flood. Defeated, she wiped her face with her sleeve before marching toward the buggy and boarding the carriage. "If you say so much as one word to me, I'm going to jump out," she warned in a raspy voice.

Nick honored her demand although two or three times when her coughing became especially ragged, she felt him studying her. She turned her face and angled her body so he couldn't see she was fighting not to cry.

"You can let me off here," she said, indicating the end of her lane, but Nick brought the buggy up to the turnaround by the back porch. They hadn't even come to a full stop when Betty darted outside, a cloak covering her nightclothes.

"Where in the world have you been?" she demanded to know. "You were supposed to make sure Mildred got home safely!"

Lucy was annoyed. Mildred and Katura had gotten away with missing their curfew on countless occasions, but the one and only time it appeared Lucy didn't follow instructions, her stepmother worked herself into a tizzy. It wasn't fair.

"Mildred *did* get home safely, didn't she?" Lucy asked sarcastically.

Betty balked. "Young lady, you wouldn't be assuming that tone if your *daed* were still awake. I'd hate to think how worried he'd be. I told you to be home by eleven and it's after midnight!"

Lucy resented being scolded in front of Nick. Mildred was the one who had left without Lucy, not the other way around. *Why should I get all the blame, just because I'm older and more responsible?* But she did realize Mildred wasn't to blame for Lucy missing their curfew; if Lucy hadn't been so adamant about not accepting a ride from Nick, she probably would have arrived home a few minutes after Mildred did.

"It wasn't Lucy's fault," he piped up. "It was mine. I told Mildred go to ahead home. I'm the reason Lucy was so late. I'm very sorry."

First Nick had played the role of her hero in front of the boorish *Englischer* and now he was being chivalrous in front of Betty. If Lucy hadn't known how deceiving Nick's appearance could be, she might have been grateful to him. But nothing he did now could change Lucy's perception of what kind of man he was. Besides, technically he was right: he *had* told Mildred to go home, which ultimately caused Lucy to miss her curfew.

Betty apparently wasn't taken in by his apology, either. "You *will* be sorry if it ever happens again!"

"It won't," Lucy said emphatically before she followed Betty inside and quietly shut the door behind them.

Betty apparently wasn't done with her tirade. "I should have known it was a bad idea for Nick to court you. He's completely unreliable. I expected this kind of behavior from him, but I thought you'd have a *gut* influence on him. I never imagined he'd influence *you*."

Lucy felt a stitch of culpability, knowing she would have been home earlier if she had accepted his ride the first time. "It wasn't entirely his fault," she said weakly.

"There's no need to defend him, Lucy," Betty said. "I won't tell your *daed* about this, but I expect you to exercise better judgment in the future. You're not so desperate to keep a suitor that you'd abandon your common sense. This incident almost makes me sorry I invited the Burkholders over for dessert after the festival tomorrow night!"

"You did?" Lucy gulped. She had no idea.

"*Jah.* I wanted to surprise you. You've been such a *gut* sport about attending all of the social events for my side of the family over the years I thought it was time we had some of *your* friends over. Nick's mother agreed it was a lovely idea. Her sons have to close the shop first, but they'll join us here after we return from Piney Hill."

"It *is* a lovely idea. *Denki*, Betty," Lucy said, her eyes brimming with tears. As touched as she was by Betty's gesture, she couldn't fathom how she'd explain to her stepmother why Nick wouldn't actually show up. But maybe she wouldn't have to; maybe he'd be a gentleman and make an excuse for his absence. After all, excuses were his specialty.

Too tired to worry about the situation now, Lucy said good-night and slogged upstairs, but despite her exhaustion it took a long time for her to drift off. Her lack of sleep combined with her apprehension about the Burkholders' visit put Lucy in a foul mood the next day. The festival should have been cause for celebration, not dread, but Lucy wished the event were already over. Since Frederick had picked up Katura, Mildred and Lucy had plenty of room to themselves in the back seat of the buggy. On the way to Piney Hill, Lucy's father, Betty and Mildred sang a medley of carols while Lucy bit her tongue and tried not to cry. She could hardly taste the Philly cheesesteak sandwiches they bought from one of the vendors as they

strolled the festival grounds. Even when the auction-
eer announced the highest bid for her tablecloth-and-
napkin set was $1200, Lucy felt the knot tightening
in her stomach.

They were heading back to their buggy when their
paths intersected with Dan and Eve's. Was Lucy imagining things or did they just quickly drop hands? When
Eve gave her a wink, confirming what she thought she
saw, Lucy smiled in spite of herself. She couldn't envi-
sion a better couple, even if Eve had to return to Ohio
soon. *Maybe long-distance relationships are the best
kind*, she thought wryly.

"Lucy, it's great your contribution raised so much
money!" Dan exclaimed heartily.

"Denki," Lucy said, and wished them both a merry
Christmas. She was quiet the rest of the way back to
the buggy, wondering how she was going to tell everyone she and Nick were no longer courting. She knew
she should get it over with now, to spare everyone the
awkwardness when the rest of the Burkholders arrived without Nick.

"Daed, Betty, there's something I need to tell you,"
she began, but she was interrupted by a shout across
the field.

"Lucy!" She glimpsed a flash of red hair. Nick?

But no, it was Kevin. "I'm glad I found you. Nick
wants to give you a ride home," he said, pointing toward a parking lot on the opposite side of the grounds.

Lucy hesitated. The last thing she wanted was to
talk to Nick, but maybe he'd worked out an excuse for
the evening. She'd do anything not to have to admit
their breakup in front of their entire families tonight.

"You go ahead and ride with Nick," Betty insisted.

With levity in her tone indicating all was forgiven, she added, "Just don't *kumme* home too late."

"I won't," Lucy promised, following Kevin.

When they were out of earshot of the others, he stopped and said, "Listen, Lucy, I know you probably don't want to see Nick, but you've got him all wrong—"

Lucy butted in, fuming, "Whatever Nick has told you, you don't know half of the story."

"He hasn't told me anything, but I have eyes. I have ears. And unfortunately, some of our peers have big mouths. So I know enough to tell you you've got him all wrong."

Lucy began to contradict him again, but Kevin spoke over her, saying, "He isn't interested in Jenny Nelson and he never was. He wasn't using you to see her and he wasn't fixing her cabin because of some affection he holds for her. He was fixing it because I started a fire in it and he didn't want our parents to find out because my *daed*'s been under a lot of stress. Nick didn't want me to get into trouble, so he couldn't tell anyone about it, not even you."

Lucy had the sensation the earth was shifting beneath her feet. "Oh, *neh*," was all she could say again and again as Kevin's words sunk in. No, Nick hadn't been entirely honest with Lucy about the cause of the cabin fire, but that was because he was trying to help Kevin, not hurt her. He was protecting his brother, just as he'd tried to protect Lucy the night before when he told Betty it was his fault she was out so late. Lucy had called him immature and self-centered, but she was the one who had behaved like a spoiled brat.

"Where did he park his buggy?" she asked Kevin.

"Uh, about that…" Kevin faltered. "When I said he wanted to give you a ride home, I was making a guess. I mean, I think he will want to give you a ride, but—"

"Just tell me where he is," Lucy interrupted.

"He's still at the store," Kevin admitted. "If we leave now, we can make it there before he closes up and leaves."

"Let's run!" Lucy called, and she took off so quickly toward the parking lot Kevin could hardly keep up with her.

Nick was removing Penny's blanket when Kevin's buggy turned into the special hitching lot for horses behind the mercantile. Nick had grown increasingly nauseated ever since that morning when his mother told him she'd accepted a family invitation to the Knepps' house. *So* that *was why Betty Knepp wanted to talk to* Mamm *on Thursday,* he realized. All day he'd brooded about how he was going to avoid attending the gathering, but as it turned out, his stomach-ache gave him a legitimate excuse. He'd insisted his brother leave the store early, so he was surprised to see Kevin's buggy returning.

But it was Lucy, not Kevin, who got down and came toward him. As much as Nick had wanted to speak to Lucy at the party the evening before, he wanted to avoid speaking to her tonight. His stomach was in knots, he heart was wrung out and he felt like he was on the brink of either crying or throwing up. Quickly he adjusted Penny's harness straps and climbed into the carriage.

"Nick, can I talk to you?" Lucy implored, standing at the side of the buggy.

"Not now. I don't feel good and I was just leaving," he replied, looking straight ahead.

"Please don't," she said, but he picked up the reins. Lucy was suddenly in front of the buggy holding her palms toward him. "Stop," she commanded Penny.

"Lucy, get out of the way," Nick shouted. "You're going to get hurt."

"I don't care," she shouted back. "I'd rather get hurt physically than to let you to feel hurt emotionally from all of the things I said. The accusations I made. Please, Nick. Please let me talk to you."

Nick reset the parking brake and jumped down. Penny was agitated, so he stroked her neck, avoiding Lucy's eyes. "I'm listening," he said.

"Kevin told me you weren't interested in Jenny. He told me he started the fire, too. But he shouldn't have had to. I should have known— I *did* know, deep down—I was wrong about you. I called you immature and irresponsible and self-centered, but those words describe me, not you. You were right, I have such a self-righteous attitude. But I'm no better than anyone—in fact, I'm worse." Lucy was gasping, her words tumbling over each other.

"Slow down," he said, dropping Penny's rein and moving closer to Lucy's side. "You need to catch your breath."

She was really gasping now so he put his hand on her shoulder, the way he'd calm his horse. "Whoa," he said. "Breathe in and out, Luce. In and out."

When her breathing steadied, she said, "I'm so sorry for saying such *baremlich* things to you. I was just so incredulous that you would have genuinely liked me that I jumped to conclusions to prove that it was all a sham. It wasn't because I doubted you. It was because I doubted... I doubted anything so *gut* could be true."

Nick searched her face, which was contorted into a grimace. "I can see why you'd think I was interested in Jenny. I wasn't totally honest with you from the beginning. I'm so sorry about that and I'm so sorry about accusing you of helping spread false rumors about Jenny and me. I know now you didn't do that. But, just like you said, I should have known all along. That's not the kind of person you are. You're...you're not like any woman I know."

Lucy half coughed, half sobbed. "*Jah*, I'm sickly and dull."

"What?" Nick nearly hollered in bewilderment. "I didn't mean that at all. You may have health challenges, but I haven't seen them stop you from doing whatever you want to do. In fact, you work harder than most *meed* I know. And you're the most interesting woman I've ever met. I mean, you're quiet sometimes, but I like how thoughtful you are. You can also be really surprising, so being with you is an adventure. But more than anything, I feel like I can completely be myself when I'm with you." Then he emphasized, "I feel like I can be *better* than myself when I'm with you."

"There's no need for you to be better than yourself. You're *wunderbaar* just as you are," Lucy immediately responded, gazing earnestly at him. "You're so popular and outgoing sometimes I can't believe you're having as much *schpass* with me as I'm having whenever I'm with you. But you're not *just* fun to be around. You're also caring and hardworking and dedicated to the people you love."

Lucy lowered her eyes shyly, and Nick's chest

swelled as he allowed her words to settle over him. She paused before lamenting, "I would do anything to take back the awful things I said this past week."

"So would I. But since we can't, how about if we start completely anew right now, this minute?" Nick asked. "Complete honesty?"

Lucy nodded. "I can say with complete honesty that even though our relationship began as a fake courtship, it's become the most real thing I've ever experienced."

"I can say that it's the most real thing I've ever experienced, too. The only thing fake about it was that it was fake."

Lucy giggled and rubbed her arms. "I'm getting cold. Will you take me home?"

"I'd be happy to, after I do this." Nick bent down and kissed her. Then he straightened and said, "In the interest of being completely honest, I have to confess I just lied. I don't want to take you home. I want to keep kissing you."

"I appreciate your honesty," Lucy said. She stood on tiptoe and wrapped her arms around his neck, and they kissed several more times. Funny, but Nick's stomachache had vanished completely.

Lucy never knew a Christmas like this one. When she returned home, she was surprised to find Bridget had arrived a day early—she wasn't expected until late Sunday afternoon—and Lucy threw her arms around her cousin before tugging her into the hall.

"Listen, I was going to tell you this in private, but you're going to find out shortly anyway. Nick Burkholder is courting me. He's not like he used to be. I mean, not like when he was courting you and started walking out with Naomi Renno before you'd even broken up."

Bridget scrunched her forehead a moment before her eyes lit up. "Oh, *jah*, I remember that now. I'd forgotten all about it."

"You forgot Nick was seeing someone else behind your back? But you were devastated!" Lucy didn't want to bring up unhappy memories, but she couldn't believe Bridget was being so blasé about it.

Bridget waved her hand. "I'm sure I felt crushed at the time, but hearts mend. He wasn't the right one for me. Besides, I found out a long time ago he wasn't really walking out with Naomi. It was just a rumor, a complete falsehood, and I jumped to conclusions. That wasn't fair. I'm glad you're not as judgmental as I was."

"Oh, I'm not so sure about that!" Lucy said, laughing.

After Nick's parents departed and Lucy's went to bed, the young people continued playing board games until almost midnight. When it was time for Nick to leave, Lucy zipped upstairs and returned with something in her hand. They stepped onto the porch while the others said their goodbyes.

"Did you notice Kevin and Mildred seem to be enjoying each other's company?" Lucy asked.

"*Jah.* We'll have to keep an eye on them if they wind up courting."

"To be *gut* examples?"

Nick chuckled. "*Neh*, to be sure they don't make the same mistakes we did." He wrapped his arms around Lucy as they observed the stars. They stood in si lence and then Lucy gave him the flat little packet she was holding. "It's a sort of *Grischtdaag* gift I made a while ago."

"Aw," Nick moaned, recalling how he'd destroyed the gift he'd bought for her. "Yours will be a little late."

"Your forgiveness is the best gift I could receive. Besides, this is a silly little thing. *Kumme* into the light so you can see it."

Nick moved to the part of the porch where light streamed from the window and he carefully unwrapped the package. It was a handkerchief, and embroidered in the corner was a coppery, galloping horse, his mane flying back, his hooves lifted in speed.

"I know it's a strange gift, but I thought you could use it since you didn't have one to offer me that night I was crying."

"Denki," he murmured. "But I hope nothing makes you tearful when you're with me anymore."

She grinned up at him. "Only the wind against my face," she said. Smiling, Nick bent to kiss her, but she pulled back. "Not in the light—someone will see us."

"Gut," Nick replied. "I hope they do."

Epilogue

In the spring both Nick and Kevin were baptized along with several other Willow Creek young people, and afterward their church hosted a traditional potluck dinner.

"I'm proud you made the choice to commit to following Christ and the Amish church," Nick's mother said to him.

"There was never a question of if I'd commit. It was only a question of when," he replied. "I should have done it long ago, but I'm glad I did it today."

"So am I," his *daed* said.

"Me, too," Lucy added as Nick's parents left to tell Kevin they were grateful he was baptized, too.

"Now that I'm officially considered an adult in the eyes of the church, you know what this means, right?"

"*Jah*. It means you can't let Penny gallop so fast," Lucy joked. "It's not responsible."

"Hardly!" Nick uttered. "My running around days may have *kumme* to an end, but Penny's running doesn't have to. *Neh*, I was going to say now that I'm baptized, there's nothing to keep me from marrying an Amish *maedel*."

Lucy blushed, teasing, "Well, I can think of one thing. You have to find a *maedel* worth marrying, first."

"I already have," Nick said. He didn't kiss her, since that would have been inappropriate for the occasion, but he did lean over and whisper, "I love you, Lucy."

"I love you, too, Nick." She surreptitiously squeezed his arm and gazed into his eyes. It was the first time they'd spoken those words aloud, but it was no rumor they were true.

* * * * *

WE HOPE YOU ENJOYED
THIS BOOK FROM

LOVE INSPIRED

INSPIRATIONAL ROMANCE

Uplifting stories of faith, forgiveness and hope.

Fall in love with stories where faith helps
guide you through life's challenges, and discover
the promise of a new beginning.

6 NEW BOOKS AVAILABLE EVERY MONTH!

"You don't ever complain. You take care of someone else's *kinder* without hesitation, and you're giving them a home they haven't had in who knows how long."

"Trust me. There was plenty of hesitation on my part."

"I do trust you."

Beth Ann's breath caught at the undercurrent of emotion in his simple answer. "I'm glad to hear that. I got a message from their social worker this afternoon. She was supposed to come tomorrow, which is why I stayed home today to make sure everything was as perfect as possible before her visit."

"I wondered why you didn't come to the project house today."

"That's why, but now her visit is going to be the day after tomorrow. What if she decides to take the children and place them in other homes? What if they can't be together?"

Robert paused and faced her. "Why are you looking for trouble? God brought you to the *kinder*. He knows what lies before them and before you. Trust *Him*."

"I try to." She gave him a wry grin. "It's just…just…"

"They've become important to you?"

She nodded, not trusting her voice to speak. The idea of the three youngsters being separated in the foster care system frightened her, because she wasn't sure what they might do to get back together.

"Don't forget," Robert murmured, "as important as they are to you, they're even more important to God." His smile returned. "How about getting some Christmas pie before we have to fish three *kinder* out of the brook?"

With a yelp, she rushed forward to keep Crystal from hoisting Tommy to see over the rail. Robert was right. She needed to enjoy the children while she could.

Don't miss
An Amish Holiday Family *by Jo Ann Brown,*
available November 2020 wherever
Love Inspired books and ebooks are sold.

LoveInspired.com